AT HOME
IN
COVINGTON

ALSO BY JOAN·MEDLICOTT

The Ladies of Covington Send Their Love
The Gardens of Covington
From the Heart of Covington
The Spirit of Covington

AT HOME
IN
COVINGTON

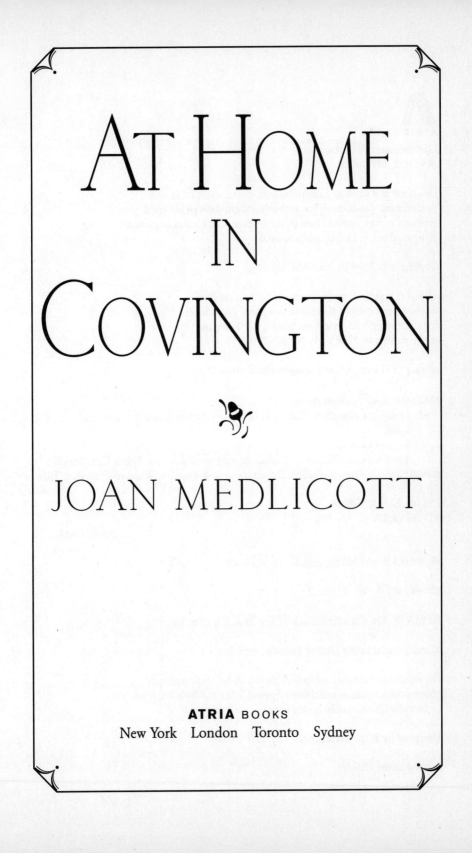

JOAN MEDLICOTT

ATRIA BOOKS
New York   London   Toronto   Sydney

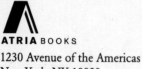

ATRIA BOOKS

1230 Avenue of the Americas
New York, NY 10020

Library of Congress Cataloging-in-Publication Data

Medlicott, Joan A. (Joan Avna)
    At home in Covington / Joan Medlicott. – 1st Atria Books hardcover ed.
       p. cm.
    ISBN 0-7434-7039-7
    1. Aged women–Fiction. 2. Female friendship–Fiction. 3. North Carolina–Fic-
tion. 4. Retired women–Fiction. 5. Farmhouses–Fiction. 6. Widows–Fiction. I. Title.

PS3563.E246A95 2004
813'.54–dc22

                                                                    2004043687

First Atria Books hardcover edition July 2004

10 9 8 7 6 5 4 3 2 1

ATRIA BOOKS is a trademark of Simon & Schuster, Inc.

Manufactured in the United States of America

For information regarding special discounts for bulk purchases,
please contact Simon & Schuster Special Sales at 1-800-456-6798
or business@simonandschuster.com

Designed by Rhea Braunstein

Printed in the U.S.A.

To my Virgin Island cousins
Marcia and Albert Paiewonsky

ACKNOWLEDGMENTS

Ann Morrison of Glendora, California, and her husband, Bob, by their love of dancing and jazz led me to the chapter "The Jazz Festival." I thank them very much for sharing information and editing the material.

I am grateful to Celia Miles, my friend and fellow author, for her ongoing interest in my work and for her excellent and generous editing skills.

"The Only Man for Her" chapter was greatly enhanced by the probing insights offered by my friend Sydelle Golub.

My sincere appreciation to Valerie Chipman of Maine for her careful scrutiny and helpful suggestions for the chapter "Maine Delights."

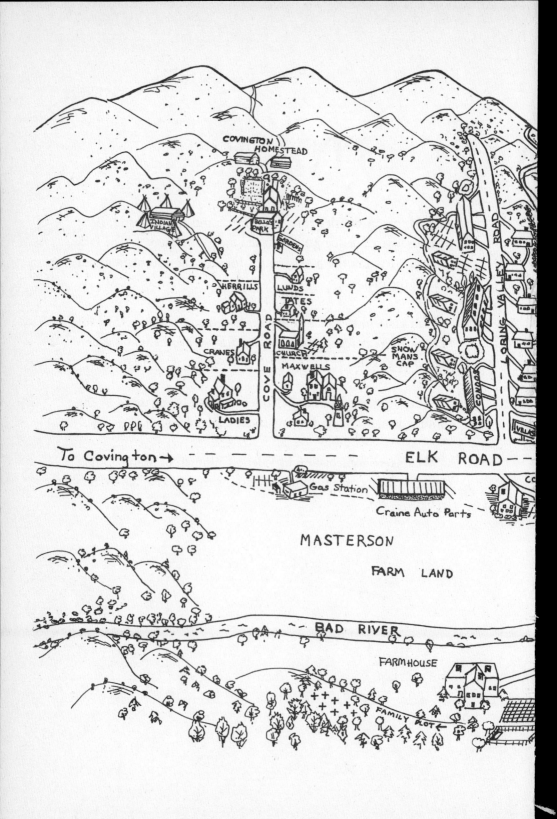

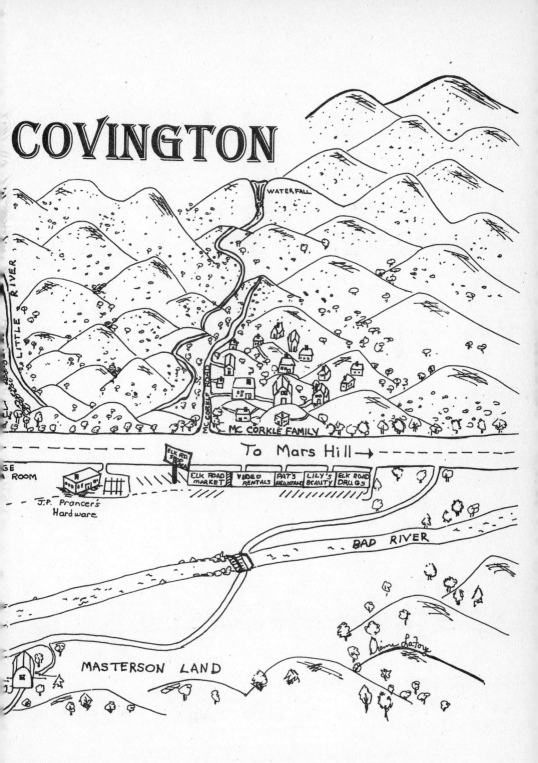

1

DUST THOU ART

The wind moaned as it skirted the white clapboard wall of Cove Road Church and snaked between the headstones in the small cemetery, tweaking women's coats and burrowing with stealthy fingers between men's gloves and wrists.

December, with its biting wind and gray, dreary days, is the most depressing time for a funeral, Amelia Declose thought, as she hugged her ankle-length coat more tightly about her slender body. Without the cashmere coat and the wool scarf draped about her head and wound about her neck, she could not have stood here under this cheerless sky as old Pastor Johnson droned on.

Finally she heard the words "Dust thou art and unto dust thou shalt return." Fitting that he would use those words, since Charles, as he'd wished, had been cremated, and a small marble urn had been consigned to the earth.

Amelia felt Grace slip her arm through hers, felt her friend's body shiver through the thickness of their coats. Grace was crying, and why not? Grace had loved Charles, her son Roger's longtime companion. Charles had been kind and generous, sensitive and caring of Grace. Amelia looked across the grave at Roger. Tall and somber, eyes shaded by dark glasses, Roger's handsome face was pained, his lips compressed.

Standing slightly apart from Roger, their housemate, Hannah Parrish, stoic as ever, stared into the distance. At seventy-five, the salt in her salt-and-pepper hair had superceded the pepper, resulting not in the white of freshly fallen snow, like Amelia's hair, but the time-worn white much like the patches of week-old snow that clung to the hillside beyond.

It was over now. The small party of mourners moved silently, slowly across the road and toward the ladies' farmhouse. Most of their friends and neighbors had not known Charles but had come out of respect for Grace.

Grace tucked one arm into that of her companion, Bob Richardson, and the other into Roger's. She could feel the heaviness, the sadness deep within her son, could feel his loss. Her legs, columns of ice, resisted her will to reach the farmhouse before the others, to remove covers from the platters of food she had prepared with the help of Laura, Hannah's pregnant daughter. Laura hadn't asked if she were needed. She had simply walked into the farmhouse kitchen, studied Grace for a moment, and rolled up her sleeves. Grace was grateful, and she looked with affection at the young woman who strode ahead of the others, pressing close to her husband, Hank Brinkley. Grace stopped trying to force herself to move faster. Laura and Hank could handle everything.

On a steamy August night more than a year ago, the ladies' farmhouse and two other homes on the east side of Cove Road had burned to the ground. This disaster had ultimately proved to be a blessing, for in rebuilding the ladies gained a new, modern kitchen, an additional bedroom, and two bathrooms, which left the living room and dining room smaller but, as Amelia said, "cozier." On this day, as the mourners crowded into the living room, Laura, Amelia, and Hank passed platters of food and cups of spiced cider.

Grace sat quietly on the couch next to Roger, who seemed uncomfortable among the crush of people, accepting condolences. Grace was tired, bone tired, from the last few weeks of supporting Roger and from the pain of watching Charles fade and die. She craved privacy and wished she could sneak upstairs to lie down and rest, but she couldn't leave her son. Instead, she smiled politely for what seemed like hours, and joined Roger in thanking the neighbors for coming.

Hannah separated herself from a group and walked over to Grace. "You all right?" she asked. "You look exhausted. Shall I shoo everyone off?"

"No. Thanks. It wouldn't be right. The Herrills and Craines didn't even know Roger and Charles, and they were kind enough to come."

* * *

Three weeks ago Roger, devastated and sobbing, had phoned her with the news of Charles's rapidly deteriorating condition. Grace placed her life on hold. With her heart in her mouth, for she had sworn never to fly again, she flew to Branston, Pennsylvania, to take her place beside the hospice team involved in Charles's care. Her contribution had been emotional support, and she had given Charles every ounce of love and energy she possessed.

When she had arrived and appeared in the doorway of his room, he smiled and his eyes lit with pleasure. "Mother Singleton, bless you for coming."

Tears had streamed down her cheeks as she moved toward him and took the chair alongside his bed.

Grace closed her eyes for a moment, remembering how she had held Charles's hand and listened to his regrets and the guilt he felt for the one infidelity that had brought AIDS into his life. As ever, his concern was for Roger.

"What will Roger do when I'm gone? He's really much softer than he lets on, Mother Singleton," Charles said in a barely audible voice.

"I know, Charles, dear, I know." But did she really? There were times when she felt she hardly knew her son. She leaned closer to Charles and recognized the look and smell of death. It had been like this with her husband, Ted. "We'll all be there for Roger."

"I know you will. We bought that condo in Covington when I began to get sick. We used to say we'd retire there." His clenched fist hit the bedcovers. "I was daft to think I could beat this horrible disease."

He lifted an arm so thin and frail she refrained from holding him for fear of hurting him. She took his hand, all bone and blue and black with contusions from the needles in the hospital. "We all make mistakes. We do the best we can."

"I'm not afraid of dying now that the pain's under control," he said. "I can't help wondering if I'll see a light. I remember when I read *War and Peace*— Did you read it?"

Grace nodded.

"When Prince Andre died, he saw light and felt peace, remember?"

"Yes, I do."

"I couldn't finish the novel after Prince Andre died," Charles said.

"Didn't much care what happened to the rest of them. Will I see the light, or angels, or my granny, do you think? Will Granny be there waiting for me?"

"I think she will be."

"You really think so?"

"I do," Grace replied.

His face grew calmer. "I do, too." He slept then.

The following day, when they were alone, Charles had asked, "Do you forgive me?"

"Forgive you? There's nothing to forgive. Life is life," Grace said. "We have our share of joys and sorrows. I love you, Charles. You're like a son to me. I'll miss you more than you can imagine."

"You've been more a mum to me than my own mum."

He closed his lids over sunken eyes. Under hollow cheeks, a wisp of a smile hovered about his lips. His body was shutting down. His shoulders and elbows were all bone, his chest concave. He was eating less each day. No one, she thought, should suffer as he had suffered before hospice took charge and medicated him to keep the pain at bay.

Bob, who had assumed the role of host, tapped her shoulder, pulling her from her memories. "Grace, the Herrills are leaving. Come say good-bye."

Grace rose to her feet. Bob offered his arm, and they walked with Charlie and Velma Herrill to the door. "We're here if you need us, Grace," Velma said.

"Thank you so very much for coming. It was a great comfort," Grace replied.

She meant it. She and Hannah and Amelia had not always been welcome in this rural area of the world, until the fire that had destroyed their home and those of the Herrills and the Craines had linked them all.

Bob shut the door behind their guests.

"I haven't even offered anyone a drink," Grace said, passing her hand across her forehead.

"Laura and Hank handled it all splendidly," Bob said.

"I'm so sorry to have burdened Laura. She's six months into her pregnancy."

"Molly, Brenda, Amelia, Tyler—they all pitched in."

"I feel as if I haven't slept in weeks," Grace said. When she did sleep, she dreamed of Charles, his eyes huge in the sockets of his pale, sunken face. She would awaken feeling the grip of his fingers, stripped of flesh, on her arm. "No more dreams like this," she prayed. "I want to remember Charles as the smiling, optimistic man he was."

Long ago, when Roger had first told her that he was gay, confirming long-held, unspoken suspicions, and when he had brought Charles home to meet her and his father, how upset and grieved she had been—upset because of what people might think and grieved because Roger was her only child and she would have no grandchildren. But Charles was a fine man, and she had come to love him dearly. Now he was gone. Grace shook her head, shook away the memory of his dying, and heard again the chatter of voices in the living room.

"Bob," she said, turning to look up at him.

Never far from her side today, Bob leaned forward, his lips brushing her cheek, his hands gently resting on her shoulders. "I'm here, Grace. I'm right here."

She reached up to touch his large, gentle hands. Her fingers played with the hair on his knuckles. It was one of the first things she had noticed about him, his gentle hands, and his eyes, brown as chestnuts and kind.

Bob's son Russell moved toward them with his son, Tyler, tagging along beside him. Tyler was almost fourteen and still fighting that ornery cowlick that topped his red hair. Grace leaned forward, clasped him to her, and held him hard until he murmured in her ear, "I can't breathe, Granny Grace."

She laughed then and released him. In loving Bob she had gained a whole new surrogate family and a grandson.

"You look like you feel icky, Granny Grace," Tyler said.

"I'm hot, but it will pass. Everyone will be gone soon, and I'll take a nice, cool shower."

"I could get you a cold cloth for your head," Tyler said.

The Craines—Alma, Frank, and one of their sons, Timmie—strode toward them. "Thanks for the eatin's. You take care now. Anything we can do, y'all just call us," Alma said.

Alma, the Cove Road gossip, the one who had most snubbed them, was eager now to be friends.

"Thank you all for coming," Grace said, clasping Alma's outstretched hand.

2

THE DIARY

George Maxwell—or Max, as he was called—had impressed Hannah deeply when he used the funds inherited from his wife, Bella's, estate to purchase a large tract of land at the end of Cove Road and created Bella's Park. In so doing he had saved the land from commercial development. Hannah had been flattered and accepted his request that she become director of gardens at the park. She and Max worked well together, with an ease to their relationship as if they were an old, comfortably married couple, which they assuredly were not—not yet, anyway.

Two weeks after the funeral, the weather, always unpredictable in the mountains, had warmed to a delightful 59 degrees. Hannah went into the Canal Garden, one of the four gardens already completed, and found one of the gardeners trimming a tree. Unable to merely sit and watch him whittle away at the small dogwood, Hannah took the clippers from him and sent him on his way. Pruning a tree did not require crouching or kneeling, which the orthopedist had said she must avoid. After working for a time, she rested on a bench in the sunshine close to the canal. Periodically, sprays of water tickled her face as they shot into the air above the handwrought copper fish that leaped perpetually above the water.

As she sat, Mary Ann, the attractive, blond receptionist at the park, walked through the archway that connected this garden with the Cottage Garden. In her hand was a small package.

"Ah, there you are, Hannah," Mary Ann said. "This just came for you, special delivery." She held the book-size brown package out toward Hannah.

"Thank you, Mary Ann. By the way, where's Max?"

Mary Ann made a small fist and knocked at her temple lightly. "Oh, yes. He asked me to tell you he had to go into Mars Hill to the hardware store." She waited a moment, as if expecting a reply, then said, "Well, I guess I'd better get back to the front desk." With sprightly steps she took her leave through the arbor, back to the main building, where they all had their offices.

For a time Hannah ignored the package on her lap. She ran her fingers through her hair, then lifted the thick strands off her neckline, where they clumped, damp with sweat. A jet of water soared above the fish, spread into an umbrella shape, then cascaded down to form ripples before relaxing into the shallow water. Behind the long trough of the canal, empty tubs made Hannah long for the banana trees they would hold in the spring. On days like this one, she could visualize their thick juicy stems and the broad leathery leaves that would glut the half-barrel wooden tubs as summer progressed.

Hannah squeezed a finger beneath the folds of the thick brown wrapping paper, worked it open, tore it away, and lifted the lid of the box inside. A sealed envelope with unfamiliar, slanted handwriting lay atop a small leather book. Something inside Hannah tightened. Her throat constricted, and for a moment she looked about her with misgiving, as if she feared being apprehended and berated by the book's owner. Then, overcoming her presentiment of trouble, she extracted a letter from the envelope and unfolded it.

Hannah Parrish,
My name is Alice Britton Millet. I am the granddaughter of Dan and Marion Britton. I am forwarding this diary, which belonged to my grandmother. I believe that you are the Hannah Parrish referred to inside. If not, I apologize for sending this and ask you to please dispose of this diary and my letter.

A chill traveled up Hannah's arms. Alice Britton Millet. Her mind raced and collided with the gray stone wall that surrounded the garden. Dan's granddaughter? Hannah dropped the letter and stared at a patch of sunshine that warmed her toes through her brown work shoes. Dan, the man she had loved so dearly, had brought a photo once of a curly-haired grandchild whom he adored. The little girl in the picture sat on a swing, waiting for someone to push her. Could that have been Alice?

The cover of the diary was soft to her touch, fine leather bearing a few tiny cracks. *Do not open this book—dump it!* Hannah's whole being urged. The past was just that, and Hannah was not one to revisit it. She returned to the letter.

I feel I must tell you how I came upon this diary, and why I sent it. My grandfather was killed in a boating accident many years ago. If you are the Hannah referred to in its pages, you will know this. My grandmother remained in their home. She never remarried, and a year ago she passed away. It fell to my sister, Jane, and me to help our mother go through the house in preparation for selling it.

Whisked into the past, Hannah was once again in her car, which lacked air-conditioning. Stifling air poured through open windows before she turned from the four-lane road and drove slowly along the tree-lined street—his street, an oasis that offered shade and a gentle cooling. Hannah raised her fingers to her cheek as she remembered the tentative breeze that had touched her cheek just before she identified his home, a lovely Queen Anne Victorian behind a white picket fence. On the wide front porch, a woman sat in a rocking chair holding a little girl, probably her granddaughter, snuggled on her lap. Dan's wife's head was lowered over the child as if she were listening, and Hannah could not see her face. Desolate and trembling, her heart empty, Hannah had stepped on the gas and turned the corner, nearly blinded by tears.

Now she turned from memories to study the little book that rested indifferently in its box on her lap, and then at the letter in her hand.

This diary was found in my grandmother's dresser drawer. My mother knew nothing about you. She was shocked and cried for days. When she threw the diary in the trash, I retrieved it and set about trying to locate Hannah Parrish, to whom I thought its contents might be meaningful. My husband is a private detective, and based on information in the diary, his investigation led me to you. And so, with trepidation, and against the wishes of my sister, I am sending it, wildly, unreasoningly, as one would send a note in a bottle.

Alice Britton Millet

The idea of being investigated, of having her private life scrutinized by a stranger, angered Hannah. She lifted the diary from its nest in the box as one would lift an injured bird, gingerly, and held it between the palms of her hands. She had loved Dan Britton too much and for too long. His death had been a misery, sundering her heart into a million pieces, and now the memory tore at the mended places. Uneasily, she opened the cover. The first entry read:

Dan is in love, but not with me. I know, because I asked him point-blank and he confessed. Her name is Hannah Parrish, such an old-fashioned name, and Dan wants a divorce. The Church won't let him do it. He says he's going to ask the Pope for a dispensation. I laugh at him. Our children and grandchildren belie a plea of non-consummation of our marriage, though for years we've slept in separate rooms. I would never agree to a divorce. I prefer to live without sex, without love, rather than suffer humiliation in front of the community, my friends, my family.

Dan had told his wife about her, had asked for a divorce. It had been Hannah's impossible dream. Her heart leaped in her chest, and the next moment her stomach tightened and grew queasy. The next entry in the dairy was dated many days later.

I saw that woman today. She works for a chiropractor. She's tall, not nearly as pretty as I am. She's quite angular, really. What can he possibly see in her? I'm still beautiful, people say, and I've kept my figure. Men still look at me when I walk into a room. Dan says I flirt, and why not? I get little enough attention at home.

The diary slipped from Hannah's grasp onto the flagstone walk. She covered her hot cheeks with her hands. Dan's wife had seen her, knew who she was. Had Marion seen Hannah in the street, at the bank? Had she come into the office? Hannah felt violated. One nudge with the toe of her shoe would send the little brown book tumbling into the water, its writing doomed to blur, its pages to dissolve among the curry-colored koi and the matted roots of lilies in the canal. She extended her foot, then hesitated. The diary had provided an answer to the old tormenting question of whether Dan had really loved her. He had. He had wanted a divorce, would have fought for a divorce. Why hadn't he told her? She thought she knew. He was a cautious, thoughtful man who made no promises to her that he could not keep.

The pain of loss reasserted itself and speared her heart. She thought of Max, his kindness, his reliability, his availability. "Oh, God, no," she muttered. "I hardened my heart back then. I can't bear to love anyone that way again." Hannah bent and retrieved the diary. Placing it in the box, she secured the wrappings and rose from the bench as she tucked it under her arm. Then she strode through the archway. She wanted to get home to show the diary to Grace.

3

THE AFTERMATH

Amelia loved warm winter days. They teased her to resume photography treks in the woods, through open pastures and along streams. On days like this, Mike could be persuaded to close his photo shop and join her. Their friendship had grown over the years, and since he had no permanent gentleman partner, he gladly served as her escort to gallery openings, dinners, programs put on by the Madison County Arts Council in Mars Hill, and the theater in Asheville.

She sat now in her rocking chair, admiring the intricate fretwork of spindles and decorative half suns that framed the porch, proud that she had been most adamant about rebuilding the farmhouse after fire had destroyed their home.

Amelia set aside the impulse to rush inside, grab her camera, and head for the hills. For now it was enough to just be in this unsolicited moment of tranquility. Life of late had been shattering, starting with the events of September 11. The grief that deluged them all after the horrifying events in New York, Washington D.C., and Pennsylvania had spilled into Charles's illness and death. Winter had raged, periodically flinging fifty-mile-an-hour winds against the farmhouse, tumbling rockers, rattling windowpanes, and uprooting the newly planted apple trees in the orchard behind the house.

The fragility and preciousness of life and of those one loved demanded to be recorded in her photographs somehow, although she was unsure what would adequately demonstrate the resumption of ordinary, nurturing life and hope after the horrendous terrorist attacks of September 11th. Amelia mulled over possibilities and waited for inspiration.

Everyone seemed preoccupied: Hannah avoided setting a date for her marriage to Max, and though she hated shopping, busied herself in Asheville shopping for baby furniture and a layette. Laura's baby, a boy, was due in the spring.

People made decisions and reversed them. Who said you couldn't rebuild a bridge you had burned behind you? Bob, who had moved in with Max, was about to move back to his own condo on the hillside in Loring Valley.

"I need privacy, our privacy," he had told Grace, and she welcomed the diversion of helping him pack and move.

Emily, Russell's wife, was hunting a location for her own law office. "I just don't want to go on working on cases someone assigns to me," she had explained at their quiet Christmas dinner. She and Russell were selling their home and planned to buy closer to Covington. Tyler, Russell's son and Emily's stepson, relished the idea of going to the middle school that all of his friends from elementary school attended. The tragedy of September 11th seemed to have had that effect on people, prodding a return to home and family.

Last week in the shower, Amelia had said aloud to herself, "What we need is a vacation, someplace beautiful and warm. A Caribbean cruise." Once the idea came, it persisted. Amelia had visited J P Travel in Weaverville yesterday, and stashed in her room upstairs were a half dozen brochures she had spent several hours last night reading again and again. When she made her presentation to Grace and Hannah, it must be irresistible. But first she needed to clarify in her own mind how she felt about going away from home with the Homeland Security chief constantly issuing alerts to be on the lookout for terrorism. The whole business of staying alert was unclear. What was she, or anyone, to look for? She was turning into a fatalist—what would be would be—and numbed to his warnings. She rarely watched the news these days, filled as it was with talk about security for the upcoming Olympics. What worried her was the overall cost to the nation of all this security and weapons buildup. The terrorists could bankrupt America with their scare tactics while sitting in a cave in some godforsaken place.

*   *   *

That night, over a simple dinner of zucchini soup and salad, Amelia broached the subject to Grace and Hannah. "What do you think of a trip to someplace warm and colorful, maybe the tropics?"

Grace sat back in her chair, crossed her arms, and ran her palms up her arms to her shoulders, then down to her elbows, and up again.

"You cold, Grace?" Hannah asked. "Want me to build a fire in the fireplace?"

"No. It'll turn the kitchen into an inferno." She looked at Amelia. "Where do you propose that we go, to Florida?"

"No, on a cruise to the Caribbean."

"On a cruise ship," Hannah said. "A perfect target for terrorists, don't you think?"

"No, I trust they're being extra careful, screening those ships and everyone on them," Amelia replied. She hadn't considered cruise ships as targets until this minute. What will be will be, she reminded herself. "If we live in fear, they win, don't they?"

Grace leaned forward. "You're right about that, Amelia. But how do we live . . . so much has changed. Life's not as simple . . ."

"Life," Hannah declared, "was never simple. Something is always happening to rock the boat, to keep you up at night. Change is a given. Okay, let's hear the cruise ship pitch, Amelia."

Amelia brightened. "I'll run up and get the brochures. We can find a ship we all like."

"It might be fun, a cruise," Grace said. "No cooking. No responsibilities. Warm, sunny days."

"We'd have to go soon. Laura's baby's due in March," Hannah said.

With Amelia gone, Grace turned to Hannah. "I have never seen you so thrilled about anything as you are about this baby."

"I wasn't much of a mother to my two girls, and not much of a grandmother to Miranda's sons. Somehow this baby feels special, as if I get another chance at being a grandmother he'll remember with love. And his birth seems doubly important now, as if by giving birth we honor the memory of those innocent people killed in September," Hannah replied. After a quick glance at the doorway, she grasped Grace's hand. "Something unbelievable happened today. I got a package with, of all things, an old diary from Dan Britton's granddaughter. It belonged to her grandmother. She writes about Dan and me."

"After all these years, his granddaughter sends you a diary? Why, I wonder?"

"I can't stop even to wonder about that at this point. It's so shocking, I can hardly think straight."

"I'd be totally overwhelmed if I got a diary like that out of the blue," Grace said.

"Overwhelmed about what?" Amelia asked from the doorway.

Hannah did not trust Amelia the way she did Grace. In her opinion, Amelia lacked good judgment. Not in everything, of course, but certainly in matters where men were involved. There had been that incident early on when Grace first knew Bob and Amelia had flirted with him. But that was years ago, and she knew that Grace had long since forgiven Amelia. Then came the fiasco with Lance. Amelia had behaved like a silly schoolgirl. She had literally abandoned her friends and her work for that awful man. Hannah could see he was a no-good bounder right from the start, and, of course, she'd been proven right. But now, with Amelia standing in the doorway, there was no way Hannah could be silent without offending her.

"A package came today from the granddaughter of an old lover."

"You had a lover? When? Where?" Amelia asked.

"It was long ago, over twenty years. When I worked for the chiropractor." Hannah tried to be flip, but couldn't manage it. "Anyway, this diary was written by the girl's grandmother, Dan's wife. She's dead now, and her family found it in a drawer."

"I can't believe you had a lover," Amelia said.

Hannah bristled. "Can't you? Why not?"

Amelia dropped the glossy brochures on the table, then carried her dish from the table to the sink and returned.

"You hardly seem the type."

"What type am I?"

Grace intervened. "How did Dan's granddaughter find you?" She was eager to stop this conversation before it escalated into words they would both regret.

Hannah turned to Grace. "It came to the office, which I thought was odd. Dan's granddaughter's husband is a detective. Apparently he traced me, so she decided to take a chance and send it."

"What a romantic she must be," Amelia said, settling into her chair. "A detective found you, my goodness."

"I was appalled at the invasion of my privacy," Hannah said. She picked up the small brown book and read them the first two entries, then turned to the third.

Yesterday I followed them to a hotel—the best in town, not some cheap joint for that woman. Wasting our money, money that our daughters could use, on that bitch. I detest her, and I detest Dan.

The tone of the next entry was even harder, and Hannah's voice reflected it.

I've cleaned out our savings account, and I've demanded a new car. He'll give me anything not to ruin that woman's reputation, not to drive her out of town. I'll just play along for a while, then I'll show them.

"She must have made Dan's life a living hell," Hannah said. "I never felt guilty back then. Reading this, thinking what it must have been like for him, I do."

Hannah turned the pages, reading silently. The entries went on page after page: neat, tight writing in places, and wide, looping script as the woman wallowed in self-pity one moment, then raved in anger and made plans for revenge. "Listen to this one," Hannah said.

I knew Dan had plans to meet her tonight, so I invited his parents over for dinner. He hardly ate and kept looking at the clock. She was waiting somewhere, probably. I got the better of him, of them. I stretched the evening out. Each of the grandkids did a little skit for their grandparents. I thought he was going to hit me after they left, he was so furious. But Dan never hit anyone, not even our girls when they needed punishing. He stormed out of the house, but it was one a.m. and within ten minutes he was back. Guess she got tired waiting. Isn't that too, too bad?

"That woman definitely didn't love him. She's sounds so awful, so hard and cold. No wonder he . . ." Amelia broke off and looked away.

"You can say it. No wonder he turned to me."

"I didn't mean that." Amelia's voice softened. "How did you meet him?"

Hannah sighed. No reason to be secretive about an event that was over twenty years old. "He was a patient at the chiropractor's office where I worked. The doctor said his problems were stress related. I'm sure they were. It wasn't a happy marriage, long before we met."

They were silent for a time. Then Amelia's chair scraped the wood floor as she rose to run the faucet for a glass of water. "Want some water, Hannah?"

"No, thanks. I still have coffee." She lifted her cup and sipped.

The pipes in the sink gurgled even after Amelia returned to the table. "Problem there. I must remember to call the plumber." In the stillness that followed the large hand of the clock over the refrigerator clicked as it landed on the half hour.

Hannah picked up the diary and began to read again. Grace leaned forward while Amelia sat back, one hand fingering the brochures that sat on the table.

What's my life been all these years? I married too young, a man my father liked. I bore his children, nursed them through all their childhood diseases. What did Dan do? Slept through it all. When did he ever get up at night and help me with the kids? I don't love him. I think he knew it was a mistake right from the start, but well, we're Catholic. So why do I care if he's having an affair? I do care. What if people find out? I'd be the laughingstock at the club, with my bridge club."

There were many more pages along the same lines—fear of the affair becoming public knowledge, her anger at Dan, fights with Dan. And then an entry made after Dan's untimely death, when a young man in a speedboat smashed into his boat on the lake and killed him.

It was a beautiful service, flowers everywhere. Everyone in church was so solicitous. Our daughters couldn't stop crying. It was a shock, his dying like that. Why didn't I feel devastated, like you're supposed to when you lose a husband? Lord, it was stifling in that church. Father Tucker went on and on about Dan's virtues. I sat there thinking, I'm free. Hannah may be miserable, but I am free. She wasn't there. I would have recognized her. To hell with her. I'm free, and very rich.

"I hate her," Hannah said. "I loved Dan so much. Reading this stuff brings it all back."

"She's a mean, cold woman." Grace stood and rested her hands on Hannah's shoulders. "It was a long time ago. You have a good life now. You have us, and work that you love, and Max."

Hannah's fist came down hard on the diary, denting the leather. "I don't want Max. I don't want any man, not ever again."

"You don't have to want him," Amelia said. "You don't have to live with him or sleep with him. All he wants is to marry you so he can leave you his property without your having to pay taxes on it when he dies."

"Is that a reason to marry someone? Not to have to pay taxes? It sounds so ridiculous, his even asking me."

"Max knows that," Grace said. "His only son's married an East Indian woman. You heard Zachary tell Max that he's going to go into her father's business in India and wants no part of anything his father has—not the land, or the dairy, or anything but one of his mother's paintings. Max knows you'll take care of his land. He knows that you'll never let developers get their hands on it. Besides, I think he really cares for you, Hannah."

"I don't want to hear that, Grace. I don't want to care about anyone. It's so ridiculous when you think about it. I could die before he does," Hannah said.

"If you die first, Hannah, he can change his will," Amelia said. "It's a loving thing he's doing. He's asking nothing from you, nothing, and giving you everything."

"A loving thing? Well, I don't want his love. Especially not his love. I never, ever want to love anyone and lose them again."

"He hasn't asked you to love him, has he?" Amelia asked. She shuffled the brochures. "Far as I can tell, he respects your independence and treasures your friendship. The way you two work together at Bella's Park is pretty wonderful, I think. You function like partners."

"That's a blessing, working at something I love with someone I respect and admire." A quirky little smile edged Hannah's lips. "What am I making all this fuss about? Something like this"—she shoved the diary away from her—"arrives out of the blue and throws me off-kilter, but not for long."

"What will you do with it?" Amelia asked.

Hannah shrugged.

"Will you acknowledge receiving it?" Grace asked.

"No," Hannah replied. "There's a return address in Santa Fe, New Mexico." She shook her head vehemently. "No, I won't contact his granddaughter, Alice. Enough of this! The diary will be out of my mind in a few days." She reached for one of the travel catalogs that featured a gorgeous beach on its cover. "So what have we here, Amelia?"

Amelia spread the brochures out fanlike, and Hannah picked up one after the other. "This from Disney. Bunch of children running around. Not for me." She tossed it back onto the table. "Don't they offer a more adult, more focused cruise?"

"What's a focused cruise?" Grace asked, picking up a brochure. "Gorgeous beach on this one."

"A focused cruise is one where they offer lectures or classes on, say, investing, or music, or art," Amelia said.

"I would like that," Grace said. "Here's one about a ship that cruises the Red Sea and offers classes in the archaeology of the area, or deep-sea diving, which they say is marvelous in the Red Sea. Wouldn't that be fun?"

Hannah said, "Almost anything would be fun, except a typical 'fun ship' cruise with a lot of younger people partying."

"Look at this one." Amelia held open a catalog. "On this cruise a historian lectures on the history of the Virgin Islands." She set it down and selected another. "Here's a cruise that features the music of the big-band era, old movies, and lectures on the lives of Benny Goodman, Harry James, Glenn Miller, and the like."

"I'd prefer a trip to Alaska," Hannah said.

"Not this time of year," Grace said. "Think about it, Hannah: The Caribbean might be perfect. It's warm and, from these photos, very beautiful."

Exhaustion, like a bulldozer, plowed into Hannah's body. Never, in all the hours of work in her own garden or those at Bella's Park, had she experienced such extreme mental and physical weariness. She could rationalize: The tragedies of September 11 had devastated her, broken her heart for people she did not know. Charles's death had rubbed fresh grief into the wound. But most of all, the vitriolic writings of a woman scorned had disinterred Hannah's guilt and the excruciatingly painful memories of the loss of Dan. A cruise seemed almost sacrilegious. But when Hannah, responding to Grace's enthusiasm, closed her eyes and imagined the warmth of a summer sun and endless blue ocean, it suddenly seemed appealing. Perhaps it was that she needed, after all: a surcease of responsibility, a time apart to reclaim her equilibrium. Hannah shoved the brochures toward Amelia. "You pick one— just not one of those party ships, please."

Satisfied, Amelia shoved the brochures into a pile. "We could take a suite with a balcony for privacy when we want to sit outside."

"That sounds nice, doesn't it, Hannah?"

Too weary to argue, Hannah nodded.

"We need to make reservations soon, I imagine," Grace said.

"We have to go in February," Hannah said. "Laura's baby's due in March, and I have to be here for that."

The pleasure Grace experienced when she thought of a new baby in her extended, surrogate family welled inside of her. Melissa Grace, Tyler's little sister and a child she adored, would be two years old in the spring, and Emily had stated emphatically that she would not have another child. So Grace was almost as thrilled about Laura's baby as Hannah was.

Amelia pushed back her chair. *"Fantastique!* I'll take care of it tomorrow." A Cheshire cat grin spread across her face as she walked from the room clutching the brochures. Pride throbbed in her breast. For the second time since the fire, her will had prevailed over Hannah's and Grace's. They would have settled for a smaller house, but she had refused to compromise and insisted that they rebuild the farmhouse. Now everyone was pleased with the changes they had incorporated: another bathroom upstairs, another bedroom, and a full bath downstairs. It had worked out wonderfully well, and so would this cruise. She would select a cruise that stopped at St. Thomas and St. John in the Virgin Islands. As she climbed the stairs, Amelia could feel the ocean breeze on her face, smell the salt air, taste it on her lips. Her excitement grew as she anticipated photographing in the islands.

4

ASK ME NO QUESTIONS

"Something's wrong, isn't it, Hannah?" Max said.

Sitting behind the desk in her spacious, bright office at Bella's Park, Hannah shook her head no.

"I know you well enough to know you're stewing about something," Max said. Sprawled on the love seat on the far wall of the room, he drank deeply from the beer he had taken from the under-the-counter refrigerator nearby. He smacked his lips, leaned forward, and set the beer on the coffee table beneath which his long legs had vanished.

"Nothing's wrong," she replied, looking away. "I'm tired. Look at all that's happened. After almost a year, we finally move into our new house. We aren't even settled when planes slam into the Twin Towers in New York. Then Charles gets desperately ill and Grace dashes up to Pennsylvania, where he dies practically in her arms." She bit her lower lip and lifted her hands in a gesture of frustration. "Christmas wasn't the same. It lacked vitality, don't you think?"

"Considering it came so close to the funeral, I thought Christmas was fine. It was quiet, but that seemed appropriate."

"Maybe it was because we had the holiday at Emily and Russell's place instead of ours. And now Old Man doesn't look well. He's pale and more stooped than ever, and Lurina's called Grace several times in the last few weeks to drive them to the doctor. Old Man refused to go, of course."

"How old is he, ninety-three?"

"Something like that," Hannah said.

"Imagine getting married when you're in your eighties, as Lurina was, or nineties, like Old Man." Max shook his head. "Just amazing."

Outside, a shadow moved past her window and Hannah swung her chair around. Whoever it was, one of the workmen or her foreman, Tom, had disappeared. "I need to talk to Tom about the Rose Garden. Bare-root roses I ordered will arrive in March. The ground has to be prepared, dug down several feet, then compost and other amendments added."

"What did you decide about the location?" Max asked.

"It came to me last night." At four a.m, when she couldn't sleep. "I decided on low, easy-to-climb, wide steps leading up from the slope beyond the herb garden to the woods. It faces south. We'll lay out the rose beds on either side of the steps, but the steps have to be built first."

"Just tell Tom what you want. That's what a foreman's for." Max drew his legs back and sat up straight. "I worry about you. You work too hard. This was to be a fun job, remember?"

"Even when I love my work, and I surely love being director of gardens at Bella's Park, I take it seriously." She grinned at Max. "I'm not an old goof-off like you are."

"Yeah," he said, and returned her grin. He stood, downed the remainder of the beer, crushed the can in his hand, and tossed it into a wastebasket. "Life's too short at our age to not goof off. You should do more if it. I'm happy to be able to turn most of the work of the dairy over to José. I'd close the place, sell off the herd, but José's a good man, and he's taken the dairy business to heart. He can run it without me." He approached her desk and leaned on it, his long, muscular arms taut. "Which brings me to . . . when are we going to get married, Hannah, so I can change the deed into both our names and you can start bossing José around?"

Hannah looked away. His physical presence this close disturbed her, and she resented her body's response to him. Theirs was a platonic relationship, nothing else.

Hannah understood that Max wanted to take care of legal matters. He was a man of action: Once a thing was decided, he acted on it, and she had been stalling, unwilling to set a wedding date. He insisted that his offer of marriage held no motive other than to make certain that his property would come to her tax-free. It must be painful, she thought, that Zachary had so matter-of-factly—at the dinner table, with others present—rejected all that his father held dear. The younger man had simply informed his father, as one might remark about tomorrow's weather report, that he intended to make his life in India, so very far away.

Max had assured Hannah that he expected nothing of her: no conjugal duties, no taking up residence in his house, no wifely responsibilities in running his home. Anna, José's wife, handled his home and the cooking with ease. He professed no interest in her as a woman, and for a long time Hannah had laughed at his proposal and ignored it. Max had persisted, and finally Hannah agreed to marry him. She had not, however, set a date, and she could not do so now with Marion Britton's dairy in her dresser drawer and Dan Britton haunting her dreams, her days, her work. The Caribbean cruise that Amelia had proposed became increasingly appealing.

"When I come back," she said, forgetting that he had no idea she was going anywhere.

Max's eyes widened; his eyebrows raised.

"Oh. Amelia proposed we take a Caribbean cruise, get away from things, sit in the sun."

He stood straight and said not a word—merely looked at her.

Hannah saw the muscles tighten about his mouth, saw his eyes cloud, felt his hurt. She could hear the words he did not speak: *A trip, a vacation, and you never said a word?*

"When do you leave?" he asked.

"I haven't the slightest idea. Amelia's taking care of it."

"We'll miss you here," he said, then turned and walked from the room.

Hannah opened a file drawer on the lower left section of her desk and closed it. She opened the top drawer of the desk, rummaged, selected nothing, and closed it. Never before had she found it impossible to concentrate on her work. Her mind felt jumbled. So much had happened in the last two years. Two years ago her younger daughter, Laura, had been conveyed to Asheville by hospital plane from the Caribbean, and then to Covington by ambulance, her leg in an ankle-to-thigh cast, her face a mess of stitches and bruises, the result of a hurricane that had killed her companion, Captain Marvin, and destroyed their ketch, their home.

Hannah closed her eyes. The emotions of that day were still raw, just below the surface—from the racing of her heart at the whine of the siren as the ambulance turned into their driveway to the fear she felt as youthful medics rolled a heavily sedated Laura into the house and shifted her from the gurney to the bed. No matter how estranged she had been from Laura, seeing her daughter suffer had ripped her heart wide open.

Hannah swung her chair around to face the window, then back again to face the wall, where two framed black-and-white photographs hung above the love seat. One was of a grizzled Appalachian man fishing, the other, a serene mountain woman quilting. Both were gifts from Amelia when Hannah moved into the office. It seemed so long ago now, but it wasn't, really. Laura had been on the way to recovery. Hannah knew that she was often a bit short-tempered with Amelia, especially since the Lance episode, and she ought not to be. Amelia had been wonderful to Laura: kind, thoughtful, encouraging, understanding Laura's pain and grief in ways that she and Grace had not. And now Amelia had proposed this cruise. They could use a holiday after such a long, worrisome period.

It occurred to Hannah then that perhaps she ought to have discussed her cruise with Max. After all, they worked together, were good friends, and even planned to be married. But no, it was more than that. A sense of obligation hunkered in the back of her mind, as if she owed him something and was failing to perform as expected. As who expected? Her mother?

"You take good care of your man," her mother had said, "and he'll take good care of you." She would sit there sewing, turning Hannah's father's collars. "It's never fifty-fifty in marriage. A woman ends up giving eighty percent if she wants a happy life."

None of these clichés had been true of Hannah's life with Bill Parrish. Had she given 100 percent, it would not have made Bill less abusive or less of an alcoholic. Hannah shoved the sense of obligation from her mind. She owed Max absolutely nothing and she liked it that way.

The annoyance Hannah felt toward Max resurfaced on Friday night, when he, Bob, and Mike routinely had dinner at the farmhouse. Tonight Grace experimented with a rich new recipe, Royal Chicken

Divan, layers of chicken and broccoli smothered in a creamy sauce flavored with curry. After dinner, when they had filled the dishwasher, Mike and Amelia left for his workshop in Weaverville.

"We've so much film to develop," Mike said. "They're clamoring for more of Amelia's photographs in the New York gallery."

"Slave driver," Amelia chided, as they wrapped cashmere scarves about their necks and hastened out to Mike's car.

Content to be with one another, Bob and Grace snuggled down in the love seat in the living room, while Hannah and Max settled into armchairs across from one another near the fireplace.

"So," Bob said to Max. "The ladies are leaving us, going off to the Caribbean."

"Sounds like a trip we could all use," Max said.

Hannah's heart sank. She didn't want either of them along. She intended to wallow one last time in the diary before flinging it overboard. That done, Hannah anticipated having fun—plain old fun, with no obligations. After carefully reading the brochure, she could imagine long tables of marvelously delicious food. She would shop in St. Thomas, buy something she did not need. On board the ship, she would have her hair and nails done in the Salon de Marie. She would eat her fill at late-night buffets and enjoy the Las Vegas–type shows the brochure promised. She might even try her hand at poker. She'd been a good player, way back when. But most of all Hannah anticipated sitting on their private deck alone at night, listening to the deep, dark ocean roar with shock and outrage at encountering the strong, steel casing of their ship. There she would read through the diary one last time and then consign it to the depths.

Bob's deep laugh pulled her back to their living room. "I think it's great for the girls to get away. They'll have a wonderful time. I vacationed on Saint John once, long ago. From the pictures in the brochure I wouldn't know Cruz Bay. Now there are shops and stores where there was only sand and palm trees. I stayed at Caneel Bay, Rockerfeller's resort. What a view, lying on the beach looking at Saint Thomas, twenty miles across the water. Great sunsets." He turned to Grace. "Bring me back a jelly coconut." He patted his stomach. "There's nothing like a young nut right off the tree. They cut a hole at one end, and after you drink the coconut milk, they crack the nut in half and you scoop out the jelly, before it gets hard. Delicious."

Bob licked his lips. "Be sure you have someone cut you a jelly co-conut, Grace, honey."

From his chair by the fireplace, Max said, "Hannah. Please, tell me what's bothering you."

Hannah's body stiffened. For a moment she glared at him. "Ask me no questions."

Max lifted both palms toward her. "Okay. Okay. No more ques-tions."

Her eyes softened. "Max, I'm sorry. It's not anything I want to talk about right now. Perhaps later."

Several minutes later, he yawned, then pulled his solid frame from the chair. "Guess I'll be going home now—long day tomorrow."

"What's tomorrow? Isn't it Saturday?" Hannah asked, rising to walk him to the door.

"Yes. I thought I told you. José and I are taking two truckloads of beef cattle down to Greenville. We leave at the crack of dawn and won't get back until after dark."

He had told her his plans, and they had passed right through her head. She had not given his schedule another thought. "Of course you told me." They were at the front door. Hannah placed her hand lightly on his shoulder. "I'm sorry. Max. I'm a sour pickle these days."

He kissed her cheek. "You have a lot on your mind. Wish you'd share it with me."

"I do, yes. One day, maybe—just not now." She stepped back.

He took his cue and departed.

Hannah watched Max stride down their driveway and cross the road. In his yard he stopped for a moment to touch the bark of a dogwood, pulling a branch down close to his face, perhaps inspecting it in the light of the streetlamp for those darling buds of May that Shakespeare wrote of—only it was January and not May. Max loved spring and spring flowers, especially white dogwoods.

Some things, Hannah thought as she watched him, are too private to speak of. Was it because of Dan that she had memorized every line of Max's face, the shape of his lips, the color of his hair and eyes? She would recognize his walk—long strides, feet planted solidly and with confidence—anywhere. Had Dan's hair been blond or a light sandy brown? How had he walked? What had his voice sounded like? How could she have loved Dan so deeply and not remember all those things about him? *Fool,* she told herself. *Without a picture you ex-pect to remember after so many years?*

One foot poised before the other, Hannah nearly stumbled as she headed back to the living room. "No," she said aloud.

"No what?" Grace asked from the living room.

Hannah pretended not to hear. "I'm going upstairs. Have some things to do. Night to you both."

"So early?" Grace called, her voice plaintive, but Hannah knew that Bob and Grace enjoyed sitting alone, talking, if he intended to go home to his apartment or necking like teenagers before going up to her bedroom.

5

CLAY FEET

The cruise they chose offered fantastically low rates for a suite: twin beds plus a convertible couch and a private balcony. The ship boasted a game and shopping arcade, indoor and outdoor swimming pools, a casino, Las Vegas–type nightclubs, a historian speaking on the American Virgin Islands, and more. In their price range, the suite shown in the brochure looked like a pleasant motel room—not elegant, but quite comfortable. Pictures of the ship's public rooms and lounges enticed with their elegance. Glass elevators rose the height of the four-story atrium that glittered with faux-gold columns, glass walls, and Persian carpets. Well-appointed dining rooms promised sumptuous meals in a relaxed atmosphere.

Grace took the brochure to her room to plan her wardrobe for the trip. She puttered about her room checking her closet and drawers for summer clothing, wishing that she had packed things away in a more orderly fashion last fall after moving back to the farmhouse.

In a bottom dresser drawer she found lightweight slacks rolled up and shoved in there in haste. They needed ironing, which she hated doing, and she couldn't for the life of her find her short-sleeved summer blouses. Where were that nice plaid and the solid blue? They had to be somewhere.

A car door slammed in the yard below. Grace paid no attention to the front door closing and the steps that followed up the stairs, and was unprepared for Tyler when he strode into her room, walked over to her, and kissed her cheek.

"Granny Grace, Dad said I should talk to you."

"Why, Tyler, dear? Why should you talk to me?" She closed her dresser drawer.

"Dad says you're the only one I'll listen to."

"Talk about what, Tyler?"

At thirteen and a half, he stood tall—taller than her five feet two inches. Taking her hand, he led her to her rocking chair by the window. "You sit down," he said.

She sat. "It sounds serious."

Tyler flopped on the edge of her bed. His face clouded, and he clasped and unclasped his hands, and shuffled his feet back and forth against the carpet. "It's about Melissa."

Grace adored Melissa, and it showed. She guessed that Tyler, young as he was, would measure his words.

"You know that Emily's opening her own law office in Mars Hill, and we're hunting for a house closer to Covington, right?"

"Right."

"Well. It's taking more of her time than Emily expected, and she and Dad want me to babysit Melissa every day after school and sometimes on Saturdays. Why should I have to do that? Melissa's in day care when I'm in school, then I'm out of school and I'm supposed to come home and watch her?" His face flushed, and tears welled in the corners of his eyes. "I have a life: basketball, friends, homework. You can't concentrate on homework with a little kid pestering you. So . . ." He squared his shoulders and stopped shuffling his feet. ". . . I won't do it."

His eyes pleaded for her approval, her understanding. "Dad and Emily had a big fight over this. She cried. Anyhow, Dad says I have a responsibility to my little sister, and I have to do it. Why should I do it? I didn't ask him to marry Emily or have a baby. It's not my job."

Grace reached for his hand, and he let her draw him to her and place her arm about his waist.

"What am I gonna do, Granny Grace?"

"We're going to start by going down to the kitchen and having a nice cup of hot cocoa and some cookies. Putting something warm in your stomach helps a person think better." As they crossed the room, Grace closed her closet doors. Had she given those blouses to Goodwill by mistake?

With Tyler lagging a trifle behind her, Grace proceeded down the stairs to the kitchen. Tyler sat at the kitchen table and watched her perform the familiar ritual of making cocoa and filling a plate of cookies from the big round tin with the flowers on it. Under the spell of familiar satisfactions, his hands relaxed; his feet grew still. When Grace turned to pour the cocoa into cups, he automatically reached for a cookie. He sipped his cocoa. "I love your sugar cookies 'cause they're thin and crispy and they're not coated with sugar. I hate those fat sugared ones they sell in stores." He munched a cookie for a while, then mumbled, "So, what am I gonna do?"

"Sounds like your whole family's struggling with changing circumstances. Seems to me there's a need for understanding and compromise here."

"Granny Grace, I really like it that you don't talk down to me. I appreciate that, I really do."

"Why should I talk down to you? You're growing into a fine young man, and I'm proud of you." She smiled. "Now, this is what I'm thinking. You might want to sit down with Emily and your father and tell them that you understand the situation is in flux with Emily's change of job and finding a new house and everything, and tell them how much homework you have and what your after-school commitments are. You have basketball practice, don't you?"

Tyler nodded, his mouth full of cocoa.

"You could prepare a schedule for them to consider: days you can take care of Melissa, days you have basketball practice. And you might round up some friends from school—get their phone numbers—who might like to babysit for a few hours several times a week. That way, you help yourself and your folks."

He considered her proposal. Dad was right; Granny Grace was the one to talk to. "I could do that," he said. "You think they'll listen to me?"

"I don't see why not. Emily's a lawyer. She's used to hearing different sides of an argument. I imagine she's done her fair share of compromising."

"Dad's the one who's bullheaded."

Grace clasped her hands on the table. "The thing about parents, Tyler, love, is that when we're young, we put them on a pedestal. They can do no wrong. Then, as we get older, we see their flaws, and we get angry at them."

He reached for another cookie. "So?"

"So the best thing for you to do from here on is to realize that no one—not you, or your dad, or Emily, or anyone—is perfect. Some of us are stubborn, or self-centered, or talk too much or too little, or are never on time, or are obsessively punctual—you know what I mean."

"Okay, I get the point. So what?"

"You have to learn to accept the good and the bad about your dad, and work with it. Now your father tends to like things as they are, so he's not in a hurry to say yes. When you present him with something new, you have to give him time to consider it. I tend to step back, to hesitate, so I understand how your father reacts. But I believe Russell's a reasonable man who can be persuaded."

"Like you can be?"

"Yes, you could say that." She smiled.

"Emily can get anything she wants out of him, and I bet it's gonna be like that with Melissa, too. Little as she is, when she starts screaming, everyone hops to."

"Do I detect a tinge of jealousy?" Grace's voice revealed no hint of disapproval.

He bit his lower lip and looked away. "I guess so. A little. A detective I once watched on TV in some old black-and-white show said, 'Just the facts, ma'am.' You remind me of that detective, Granny Grace." He giggled. "Just the facts, ma'am."

"Where have I heard that?" she asked.

"Sergeant Friday, maybe. Not sure, but on TV. You reminded me of him." Tyler giggled, lowered his voice, and scowled. "Just the facts, ma'am." Then his eyes grew worried. "I didn't mean to insult you, Granny Grace. I appreciate the fact . . ." He covered his mouth with his hand and his shoulders shook with laughter. ". . . that you're so matter-of-fact about things." He punched the air with a loosely clenched fist. "You tell it like it is."

She laughed with him. "I try to. What do you think about my proposal?"

"Cool," Tyler replied. "Thanks." He leaned out of his chair to take three or four cookies.

Grace pushed the plate closer to him, then watched him hurry to the phone and call his father.

"Dad, Granny Grace and me have had our talk. Come get me, okay?"

Granny Grace and I. She wanted to correct his language, but decided this was not the time. Grace's stomach growled. Lord, how her mouth watered for some of those cookies. Her hand slipped closer to the plate. With determination, she pulled it back. She had to remember her diabetes, that cursed disease that had come upon her out of the blue, the disease she had chosen to ignore for a year, until her toes began to sting and burn at night, even at the touch of the lightest sheet. "Neuropathy," the doctor said it was, from the diabetes. That her body had betrayed her this way angered her, but adding sugar to her system couldn't make it better. Grace rose and returned the remaining cookies to the big tin box and shoved the box into the cupboard.

She and Tyler put their coats on and moved outside, where the sun warmed a corner of the porch. They didn't talk much, and as she rocked, Grace ruminated that she could have offered to keep Melissa after school. But much as she loved the little girl, she didn't have the energy to run after an active child five afternoons a week. One day a week, perhaps, but not every afternoon.

Grace began to feel guilty for not babysitting Melissa and not relieving Tyler of this burden. What if Roger had not been gay and he had married and Melissa were his child, her own flesh and blood—would she feel differently? *No.* She would have loved a child of Roger's as much as she did Melissa, but she would still not spend her afternoons wearing herself out with an active toddler. What if she had never left Dentry? Back then she hadn't been good at saying no. She probably would have denied her own needs and said yes. Bless Hannah and Amelia. They had taught her to value herself, to take care of herself, and to put her own needs on a par with the needs of others.

She glanced over at Tyler, rocking Amelia's chair at three times the speed with which she rocked. Youth. All that frenetic energy. Bless him. He was right about Melissa being spoiled. That adorable little face was something to be reckoned with—big blue eyes, dimples when she smiled. Who could blame Tyler for being jealous?

Grace stopped her chair, leaned over, and patted Tyler's shoulder. "You're a dear young man, Tyler, and I love you. You know that, don't you?"

His grin warmed her heart. "Sure do, Granny Grace. And I love you, too."

6

MEMORIES

That night Grace and Bob, Hannah and Max, and Mike and Amelia drove to Mars Hill for a sold-out musical performance billed as *Down Memory Lane*, presented by the Madison County Arts Council. The Mars Hill College auditorium filled rapidly, mainly with folks their age, a representation of baby boomers, and some college students. People dressed casually. Grace searched the crowd for familiar faces and saw several—their neighbor Brenda Tate had her daughter, Molly Lund, and Brenda's housemate, Ellie Lerner. They stopped to chat.

"You getting used to country noises? Crickets, frogs, and things?" Amelia asked Ellie.

"I bought a white-noise machine," Ellie said. "It's helped a lot. But not living alone has made all the difference. Brenda and I get on quite well together. I hear you ladies are going on a Caribbean cruise."

"News spreads fast, but yes, the first week of February. I'm so excited I can hardly sleep," Grace said.

They continued moving toward the doors of the auditorium. They were hardly inside when a hush replaced the shuffling of feet as people quickly settled into their seats. Moments later, the conductor lifted his arms and the music began. At first low and lilting, it increased in volume and tempo, then descended to slow and mournful, and concluded on a lively upbeat. The curtains parted. The male singer, a tall, dark-haired man with a well-trimmed beard, stepped from the darkness onto a pool of light and stood center stage. He lifted a hand microphone to his lips. Everyone clapped.

"The Fantasticks is the longest running musical," he said. "Here's one of its many memorable songs."

Grace sat up straighter. *The Fantasticks* was the first musical she had ever seen, put on by the Dentry High School music and theater department. As good as off-Broadway, the local paper reported the following day. How she had dreamed of going to New York, to Broadway and the theater . . . but she never had. Now, especially since September 11th, the dream had all but faded.

" 'Try to remember the kind of September . . . '" the singer crooned. Grace's heart caught in her throat. So much to remember, if one took the time: a naive eighteen-year-old saying I do, certain of love and happiness, visualizing children's footsteps on the stairs, their laughter filling the house. Innocence that ended with the loss of two babies, and their father's seeming indifference.

"We'll just have to try again," Ted had said both times.

She'd needed so much more from him. After all, she had carried the babies under her heart, and had borne the pain of childbirth. His stoicism, his inability to discuss the loss of their infants, hurt her immeasurably. Now she heard snatches of words. " 'When grass was green and grain was yellow . . .' "

Memories of the bandstand in the park in Dentry came: old Mrs. Windsor from the bakery, Dr. Turner with his black bag, the Tolson family with their towheaded boys, five in a row, like steps. Friends, neighbors, families strolling, chatting, picnicking. Children running and playing out of sight of their parents. A safe time, when a stranger abducting a child was inconceivable.

Think of something else, something mundane like beating cookie batter, Grace told herself, or you are going to cry and embarrass yourself. Once, long ago, someone had said to her, "Don't think of polar bears." Of course that was all she could think of, and she had zero interest in polar bears. She wished the song would end and something lively would follow. It did, a rollicking folk song, and Grace focused her attention on the tale of an old woman and her tricky ways and how the children teased and loved her. By the time it was over, Grace had regained control.

Overall, the program was primarily doleful tunes of lost love and rueful songs of leaving one's home, with a smattering of patriotic songs thrown in. The audience around her seemed to love it. Had she known the content of the program and how melancholy it would make her, Grace would never have come.

"I enjoyed tonight's performance," Bob said on the drive home. "Nice to hear old songs."

"I needed an *Annie Get Your Gun* kind of show," Grace said. "Loud and brash and it all turns out happy."

"Plaintive is what I'd call it," Hannah said. "Not sure that's what people need these days."

"The place was full." Max slid his arm across Hannah's shoulder. "Well, whether you liked it or not, it was fun to get out a bit, and easier than driving all the way into Asheville."

Hannah stiffened, and Max withdrew his arm.

Grace promised herself that she would never go to a performance again without calling the box office and grilling whomever she could until she extracted the tone and content of the event. "Is it a sad or a happy show?" she would ask. "Will I laugh? Will it make me cry, do you think? Did it make you cry?"

Talk turned to the ladies' cruise.

"It's a huge ship and quite upscale," Amelia said.

"I'm going to gamble," Hannah declared. "Fifty dollars. When that's lost, I'm done with it."

"And if you win?" Mike asked.

"Fifty is all," Hannah replied.

"'You got to know when to hold 'em, know when to fold 'em . . .'" Mike sang from Kenny Rogers's "Gambler" song. They all laughed.

"Tell you what," Bob said. "I think we've got enough talent between us to put on a show for our friends and neighbors on Cove Road. Emily's got a sweet singing voice, and Russell can tell a good joke."

"Now that just might be a fun thing to do," Hannah said. "We could close a portion of Cove Road for one night, I guess."

"Only happy or funny songs, please," Grace said.

Max joined in. "Maybe we could use our lobby at Bella's Park. We could shove the reception desk to the side and set up a small stage."

"Place would hold—what?—twenty-five chairs plus the stage?" Hannah asked.

"Who'd come but the neighbors and a few of our friends?" Amelia asked.

Back in high school, Hannah had played bit parts, mainly offbeat characters, in school theatricals. She'd bent double with nerves before the curtain rose, but when it did, Hannah remembered, a feeling of exhilaration, the sense of being fully alive came over her. There'd been no time for theatricals once she had married Bill Parrish, however. It was hard staying one step ahead of him, walking on eggshells to avoid his temper, waiting for bruises to heal before going out of the house. After she'd fled with the girls, keeping food on their table had consumed all of her time and energy. Now she had time, but would she be able to do it? Heck, she thought, give it a try. "Might be a hoot," she said.

Amelia giggled. "I could dance with seven veils."

"Sure," Mike said. "You do that. I'll photograph you."

"Seriously, I like the idea," Grace said. "I can't act, sing, or dance, but I'm a great gofer."

In this lighthearted mood they arrived at Cove Road and turned into the ladies' driveway. "Want to come in for tea or coffee?" Grace asked.

"Whose car is that? Someone's on our porch," Amelia said. "It's a tall man."

"Good Lord, it's Roger." Grace's voice rose in surprise.

"Did he say he was coming back down here this soon?" Hannah asked.

"Hurry, Bob." Grace pushed Bob's shoulder, urging him from the car.

Sitting alongside Mike in the backseat, Amelia noted his controlled excitement. She remembered the planned meeting that Mike and Roger did not have in New York, but now, with Charles gone, perhaps . . . *None of my business.* But, yes, it was her business. After all, she was the one most attached to Mike. He was her photography teacher, her friend, and her escort to social events. What if Mike and Roger . . . ? *Oh, stop it.* As she slid from the seat of the car, she grasped Mike's arm to steady herself, and felt the tightness of his muscles, saw the set of his jaw.

On the porch, Roger rose to greet them. Grace hugged him, her head resting briefly against the shoulder of her son's tweed jacket. It felt scratchy against her cheek.

He grinned. "Hi, everyone."

The men shook hands.

"Welcome back, Roger, my boy," Bob said. "Come to stay a while?"

"Come to stay, period," Roger replied in his firm baritone voice.

Mike tightened his hold on Amelia's arm.

They moved inside, removed their coats and hats, and hung them on the coat stand in the foyer. Grace asked, "Can I get anyone tea, coffee, anything?"

They shook their heads and headed for the living room.

Roger explained, "With Charles gone, life in Branston is totally flat and empty. One morning as I was shaving, I could swear I heard Charles say, 'What the hell are you doing here, Roger?'"

He crossed his legs and looked at Hannah. "It occurred to me then to sell our share of the business to Miranda and her family. Philip, especially, loves the business." He wiggled and shifted in his chair. "Besides, I like it down here." Briefly, Roger's eyes sought Mike's. "Charles and I never talked about it, but we knew what was coming. That's why we bought the apartment in Loring Valley." Roger turned his attention to his mother. "Charles loved Covington, loved each and every one of you, especially you, Mother."

Grace nodded.

Charles's voice rang in her mind. "How could I be so daft as to think I could beat this thing?" he had asked that final morning. Then he whispered, "I love you, Mother Singleton. You've been the mother I never had. Bless you." They were his last words. A lump settled in Grace's throat. Knowing she would never see him again hurt her heart.

Bob rose from the arm of Grace's chair and turned the knob that lowered the heat in the gas fireplace, then returned and slipped his arm about her shoulders. "You look hot. Should cool off in here in a minute," he said.

"I loved Charles," Grace managed.

"I didn't mean to make you cry, Mother," Roger said. He did not go to her or reach to take her hand.

Had Roger been as unemotional and unaffectionate with Charles as he had always been with her? Grace wondered. Had Charles known the bitter disappointment and frustration with Roger that she had experienced with both Ted and his son? She had not coped well with either of them. With Ted she had nagged and demanded more affection. But when Ted slipped his arm around her in response to her insisting, it held the weight of a heavy boulder, and when he hugged her it was too tight, too perfunctory, and without tenderness. After a time, she had simply stopped asking. With Roger she had hoped for if not closeness, then respect and consideration at least, but she had gotten little or none of those things from him. Charles, on the other hand, had respected her, had been openly warm toward her, and always welcoming. He had taught her about expectations.

"In time I gave up my expectations of Roger," he'd said. "Expectations lead to frustration, unhappiness, and often bitterness."

Before coming to Covington, Grace had discovered what Charles meant. Accepting people as they were and dropping her expectations had freed her from stress and pain, and made life easier. With Roger it had been harder to apply this new way of thinking. Yet, she had never lost hope that something in his own life—some loss, perhaps the loss of Charles, now—would soften him. She studied her son. Like a little boy's, Roger's blond hair fell over his forehead into his eyes in long strands. Essentially, he was a decent man. He had loved Charles and taken care of him. Her musing was interrupted by Max's voice.

"So what are your plans now, Roger?" Max asked.

"I'm thinking of opening a party-planning business in Asheville." Roger's eyes strayed to Mike's.

A flicker of hope was followed by steely resolve before Mike looked away.

Be careful, Mike, Grace thought. Roger rejected you, hurt you. Remember how angry and depressed you were when you came home from New York last year, after that fiasco when he said he would meet you? You waited and he never showed up. Remember how hurt you were.

Sitting close to Amelia, Mike seemed to be deliberately ignoring Roger now.

Roger, Grace knew, was egocentric. What would it be like with him living permanently in Covington, without Charles to smooth the edges? How would his being here, his behavior, impact her life, or Mike's or Amelia's? Why had he come now, causing her to worry just when she was about to leave for a supposedly stress-free cruise?

Grace felt Hannah's palm on her arm, felt a gentle pressure of understanding, as if Hannah were saying, *It's going to be all right, Grace.* If only she believed that. Then guilt swept over her. Roger was her son, her only child. She wanted him to be happy—but not at her expense, and not, she hoped, at Mike's expense. Then there was Amelia, who counted on Mike for so many things. Amelia's eyes, wide and worried, glistened in the light cast by the fireplace. Damn Roger for appearing out of the blue like this, giving them no notice, no time for any of them to prepare for the changes that would inevitably accompany him.

While he shopped for furniture for his apartment, Roger stayed in the ladies' new downstairs guest room.

"You're the first to sleep here," Grace said. "I hope you find the bed comfortable."

Roger looked at the wallpaper and smiled. "You must have picked this paper, Mother. It reminds me of the wallpaper in our guest room in the house in Dentry—all those tiny flowers."

Was he making fun of her? It was hard for her to read him. "Is that good or bad?"

"Neither. It's quite charming, actually."

Roger was polite and unobtrusive. By eight thirty each morning, he took his leave, returning late in the day to shower before departing for dinner or a movie, usually with Mike, thus avoiding, Grace thought, any possibility of having to sit and talk with her.

"Let it be," Hannah said. "Don't ask questions. Let matters unfold."

It was easier to follow that advice now that they were all a-dither with packing, unpacking, hauling suitcases downstairs, reopening them to insert a hairbrush, a pair of shoes, slippers, a bag of cosmetics, an extra blouse.

"I'm forgetting something important, I just know it." Amelia paced the foyer, then circled her two new green leather suitcases.

"Stop fussing. There are shops on board. Anything you forget you can replace," Hannah said.

Amelia tossed her head. "Goodness, no! I don't want to spend money on things I have at home."

"So take your suitcases back upstairs, unpack, and start again," Hannah said.

Amelia clasped her head in her hands. "Tomorrow," she said. "I'll ask Mike to help me."

"Roger can help carry them up when he gets back," Grace offered.

Amelia shook her head. "I'll ask Mike."

Grace understood. She raised her hands. "Okay, wait for Mike."

The night before Bob drove them to the airport, Roger sought out his mother in the kitchen. "I think I've found a space in Weaverville for the new business. I can't believe how expensive space is in Asheville." He sat and propped his feet up on one of the chairs. Grace ignored his posture.

"Is that a good location?" she asked.

"I think so. Customers only come to the showroom one time usually, and it's ten minutes from Asheville. After the initial visit, we work with them in their homes and on the phone."

"Who is we?" Grace drained potatoes, dumped them into a bowl, poured in milk, a huge spoonful of mayonnaise, chunks of butter, and set the mixer whirring. "Your favorite, mashed potatoes."

"Thanks," Roger muttered absentmindedly. He drummed his fingers on the table. "Now I have to find someone to go in with me. You interested?"

She laughed. "When Bob and I had the Tea Room, I learned that you don't own your own business, it owns you."

"You have to love it, or maybe you have to have spent years working for some autocrat of a boss who takes his problems out on you," Roger replied. A scowl crossed his face.

He's still handsome, Grace thought. Always was handsome. Girls would kill for his looks. "How old are you now, Roger?"

He laughed. "You ought to know."

"I never quite remember. You're what, forty-one, forty-two? I was thirty when you were born, and I'm seventy-one now."

"You're seventy-one? Hard to believe. You look about fifty-five, sixty. There's not a line on your face."

She held out her hands. "Read the spots and wrinkles. They say it all."

"Mother, you're an inspiration to me, to anyone, reinventing your life after so many years." He hesitated, lifted his feet off of the chair and turned to face her.

The mixer stopped whirring. Grace transferred the mashed potatoes to a glass bowl and secured a plastic cover over it. Her eyes fell
on a coffee mug from Tyler that read GRANDMA'S KITCHEN. On it, a
fat little woman sat rocking. Thinking of Tyler warmed her heart.

"You know, Mother, I used to think of you as sort of, well, weak
and mindless."

Her hands went to her hips. "Mindless?"

"I mean when I was a kid. Dad said jump, and you flew into the air."

Grace sat down across from him. "I guess I did, didn't I? But not
mindless, I hope. I read a lot, tried to educate myself."

"I remember really weird stuff about Egypt, astrology, ancient
times."

"Those were my interests. But I read the classics, too. Arlene Gree-
ley, the librarian, suggested Dickens, Stevenson, Hardy, Thackeray,
Alcott, James, Tolstoy, Twain, Thomas Wolfe, and heaven knows
whom else. I read them all."

"That's right. When you weren't doing something for Dad or for
me, you had your nose in some book."

"How, then, could I have been mindless?"

"Well, not mindless," Roger amended.

Grace continued, "I did what I thought I had to do for you and
your father." She realized how defensive that sounded. "But that's
long ago. It's time to drop the old images and see me as I am today.
In the last four years I've become a person in my own right, and
made important decisions about my life. Such as not marrying Bob."

He reached for a toothpick in a little plastic stand on the table.
"Yeah, I've wondered about that. Why haven't you?" He chewed the
toothpick.

"Do you really care?" She leveled her gaze at him. She would not
let him intimidate her, not anymore.

"Sure I care. Why don't you marry Bob?"

Grace crossed her arms over her chest and leaned against the
kitchen counter. "I've had enough of taking care of a man, reporting
my goings and comings, watching the clock to be sure dinner's ready
on time even when I didn't feel like eating. I want to be totally free
to live my life as I see fit, to set my own schedule, express myself in
whatever way I choose."

"What?" His eyebrows shot up.

"That's right. Your father never wanted me to express myself or have much freedom. It might change things, and he did not like change of any kind. Besides, I enjoy living with Hannah and Amelia. I value the cooperation and companionship they offer. I like going and coming as I please. I don't want to do anyone else's laundry, including yours, by the way."

Roger removed the toothpick from his mouth and laughed. "I admire your spunk. Who would have guessed?"

Grace's hands slid to her lap. "You're right. Who would have guessed? Certainly no one in Dentry. But Hannah and Amelia saw past the frightened ninny I was. They prodded me into driving Hannah's huge old car down here. I was terrified. Know how fast I went on the highways?"

He shook his head.

"Forty miles per hour on the interstate, and I was scared stiff." Her expression was grim. "I clutched that wheel and tried to ignore all the cars passing and the people giving me dirty looks." She raised her chin. "But I did it. It was like climbing a mountain. And who encouraged me? Hannah and Amelia. By the time we drove back to Branston, I was moving along at sixty miles an hour, which was a huge step for me."

He let out a deep breath. "You've come a long way, baby. Charles knew who you really were. He saw the depths of people."

She nodded. "And he loved you very much."

"He knew what a son of a gun I am, selfish and arrogant. Know what he said before he died?"

"No. What did he say?"

"He said, 'Roger, life isn't going to give you another me, so you'd better take a good, hard look at yourself and lighten up on people. For starters, get to know your mother. She's a great woman and she loves you, even though you're a bastard. Don't denigrate or reject a love like that.'"

Grace wiped her eyes with her apron. "You're making me cry. I loved Charles."

His voice was low and husky. "I was jealous."

Her heart melted. He seemed four years old, and she wanted to comfort him. She reached across and covered Roger's hands with hers. "You never needed to be. I love you very much."

Roger flushed and gently slipped his hands from beneath hers. He smiled. "You may not always like what I do, but, well, I love you, too, and it's good to know you love me."

Would his words change things between them? Grace doubted it. A car door slammed. "Bob's coming for dinner." Grace dried the last traces of tears. "I don't feel like answering a lot of questions. You run along now."

He stood.

"Roger," she said as he left the kitchen. "You'll find the right partner. Just give it a little time."

Grace heard him greet Bob. The men chatted in the foyer for a few minutes, then the front door closed. From the kitchen window she saw Roger take the steps two at a time, then stuff his hands in his pockets and whistle as he opened the door of his car. *You'll find the right partner,* she had said to him. That could be taken two different ways: that she was wishing him a partner in business or that he would find a life partner. What had she actually meant? Both, really, and she hoped that life partner would not be Mike. Hannah's sage advice came back to her. "You're the worrier in this household. If there's nothing to worry about, you'll find something. Stop doing that."

Grace thought she'd heeded that advice. At least she'd tried, but obviously not hard enough, for here she was stewing over her own words to her son and worrying that they would be misinterpreted.

She thought of Charles's admonitions to Roger to change, to lighten up on people. Roger's car turned from their driveway onto Cove Road and headed for Elk Road. Grace sighed. Change was hard, and even with the best of intentions it did not happen overnight. How many lives would Roger turn upside down, run roughshod over, before he found what he wanted?

7

CRUISING

At the Atlanta airport, a bulky, unsmiling woman patted down Grace and the others with the backs of her hands. Hannah remained her usual stoic self, while Amelia fussed and fumed at the procedure. Grace, like Hannah and many others, took a "rather safe than sorry" attitude and tolerated the long lines, the searching of her suitcases, the indignity of standing with her legs apart and arms outstretched. And then their plane was late. When they finally boarded, Grace scrutinized the incoming passengers for odd behavior or foreign looks. Would she have the nerve to point a finger at anyone she thought looked or acted suspicious? She had, after all, no guidelines to go by. But all seemed normal.

Grace clutched the arms of the seat and assured herself that everything was fine—that the pilot was highly competent, that the flight attendants seemed cool-headed and in control. Surely they would have spotted a dangerous passenger if one were on the plane.

When they touched down at Ft. Lauderdale, the ladies were met by a uniformed escort, Manny, who flashed his badge, validating his authority with the cruise line. Manny escorted them to a bus, where they waited for another late-arriving plane. It brought a group of enthusiastic couples, who filled the bus and joked and yelled at one another across the aisle.

As they stood on the dock, the ship towered over them. Grace tried to count the layers of portholes, but Hannah took her arm and swept her toward the gangplank and up onto one of the decks of the ship, where they were greeted and welcomed by staff. Grace gasped as she looked about her. Above them stretched walls that rose several stories high. Grace marveled at the tall fluted columns, the plush carpeted staircase, the mirrored walls, and the enormous glittering chandeliers.

"Ladies, may I show you to your suite?" a young staff member in uniform asked.

"You two go ahead. I'll find the suite later. I want to stop at the purser's office," Amelia said. "I'm going to establish a credit card account before there's a line a mile long."

"Should we each be doing that?" Grace asked.

Amelia had moved away and was lost to sight among the milling passengers.

"You can establish an account with the purser at any time," the young man said.

"Let's see our suite first, Grace," Hannah said.

"Right this way, please." The young man, who introduced himself as Sidney, led them to a bank of elevators at the far end of the deck. When they exited the elevator, they moved down a corridor to a room on the left. Sidney entered with them, showed them where the air-conditioning was and how it operated, and explained that a schedule of activities would be slipped under their door every morning.

"Before we leave port, there'll be a fire drill." He showed them where the life jackets were stored on a shelf in one of the closets. "Bring yours along with you, but don't put it on before you get up on deck." He pointed to the inside of the door. "You'll find other information you need posted here."

Posted on the door was a diagram of the ship and information such as one would find on a hotel door. Hannah tipped Sidney. He smiled and departed.

Hannah and Grace laid their carry-on bags and purses on their beds, and walked through the suite to the balcony. Below, in the hustle-bustle of the dock, cabs and limousines continued to discharge luggage and passengers. Luggage was whisked away by porters, as theirs had been, while passengers lined up to board the ship.

"This is exciting," Grace replied. "I'm going to stay right here until we leave shore."

Grace remained on the balcony until she tired of the confusion below and joined Hannah inside. Their luggage had been delivered and they began to unpack.

"Let's go up on deck when we're done, have a drink, and watch Fort Lauderdale grow smaller and smaller as we get farther and farther out to sea," Hannah said.

As the Florida shoreline faded from view, Hannah glanced at her watch. It was almost 6:30 p.m. "We're signed up for the late seating for dinner. Eight o'clock. That gives us time to rest before we dress."

By seven thirty, however, Grace was exhausted from the long day's travel. She showered, but could not summon the energy to get ready for dinner. "I don't think I can swing my legs off this bed," she said.

"Want me to pull you up?" Hannah asked.

"What I want is to stay right here in our suite. Do you think they have room service?"

"I'm sure they do," Hannah replied. Moving around the corner, she sat on the couch that would convert to Amelia's bed and called the steward. "They'll deliver a tray. What do you want?" she asked Grace.

"Something light. Scrambled eggs. No, an omelet with mushrooms and cheese, and hot tea and toast with butter."

Amelia emerged from the bathroom looking stunning in a black dinner gown. Pearl earrings hung gracefully above the milky cream-colored silk scarf draped stylishly about her neck.

"You do amazing things with scarves, Amelia," Grace said.

Amelia smiled. "I could show you how it's done."

"One day, perhaps," Grace replied.

Amelia pirouetted in front of the full-length mirror.

"You look absolutely beautiful," Grace said. "If I tried to wear my hair pulled back from my face the way you do, I'd look like a peasant. On you it's so elegant."

"Not bad for a woman of seventy." Amelia regarded herself in the mirror. "I don't feel seventy. I feel forty."

"So do I usually, but not tonight," Grace replied.

"It's been a very long day. I'm tired, too," Hannah said. "I'll go up for dinner and come right back. You rest, Grace." She turned to check herself in the mirror. No looker, like Amelia, but not half bad with some makeup and her new beige pantsuit with the touch of velvet at the wrists and collar.

"You look terrific, Hannah," Grace said.

"I'm glad we came," Hannah said.

"Me too. I'm so excited," Amelia said. "Something wonderful is going to happen. I feel it."

Taking Amelia's arm, Hannah steered her to the door into the hallway. "Let's go to dinner, Amelia."

Amelia took one last look at herself in the mirror, smiled, and sang, " 'Oh, they should see me now.' "

"Get going, you two," Grace said. "It's almost eight. When you come back, I want a full report about our tablemates. What are we, a table of eight?"

"A table of eight," Hannah confirmed. "Out. Out." She hustled Amelia out the door. Grace could hear Amelia singing in the hall.

Grace propped two pillows under her head and studied her surroundings. Painted a soft blue, the suite was larger than she had anticipated. There was ample room on either side of the twin beds for tables with four drawers and good reading lamps. In the L of the suite, a couch and two barrel chairs covered in a flowered print gave the room a soft and cozy look. To Grace's right, sliding glass doors opened to their balcony. She must have dozed because a soft knock on the door brought her wide awake.

After signing the check and tipping the waiter, Grace carried the dinner tray onto the balcony. Securely bolted to the deck, an aluminum table and three chairs filled the space, eliminating the opportunity to put one's feet up and relax. Grace wondered if one of the chairs and the table could be removed and replaced with a lounge chair. Stretching out under the dome of heaven would be perfection, with a star-studded sky her ceiling. Grace's eyes swept the vast expanse of ocean to the horizon, which still bore a tint of sunset. Slowly, as she ate her dinner, she began to relax.

Hannah and Amelia followed the maître d' past gilt-framed reproductions of Italian masters hung on the lemon-yellow walls of the elegant dining room. In keeping with the tone of the room, conversations were low, as was the chamber music of the trio in the far corner. As they moved across the room, their heels sank into the lush midnight-blue carpet. The maître d' seated them near a window, where they joined two couples Hannah judged to be in their early fifties and one woman closer to their ages. Five pairs of eyes regarded them with interest and curiosity.

Accustomed to meeting and mingling with strangers from years of traveling the world with her husband, Thomas, a Red Cross executive, Amelia responded to their tablemates with enthusiasm. Amelia's ability to charm total strangers with lighthearted banter always amazed Hannah, who found it difficult to talk to those she did not feel comfortable with unless they were interested in gardens and plants.

As they took their seats, Amelia's eyes swept the table, acknowledging each person.

"*Bonsoir, madame,*" the husband of one of the couples said.

"*Bonsoir,*" Amelia replied.

"*Vous parlez français?*" the man asked.

Amelia used her thumb and first finger to indicate a little. "*Un petit peu.*"

He introduced himself and his wife. "*Je m'appelle Andre Mallenaux.*" He switched to English. "And my wife, Barbara."

Barbara grunted. The corners of her mouth turned down and her eyes flashed Amelia a decidedly unfriendly look.

Amelia chatted with everyone except Barbara, who avoided looking at her. As the meal wound down, the chamber music ceased and was replaced by a small orchestra scheduled to play big-band music. The strains of "Sentimental Journey" filled the room.

"Grace should have come with us to dinner. She'd have loved this music," Hannah said.

Once again, Andre spoke to Amelia in French. Amelia murmured, "*Oui,*" and set her napkin on the table. Andre rose, circled the table to pull back Amelia's chair, and she floated away on his arm to the dance floor. The band played "On the Sunny Side of the Street."

"Your friend is quite affected, pretending to speak French," Barbara said to Hannah.

When they had first met, Hannah had considered Amelia affected, but no longer, and she defended her. "Amelia does speak French. She lived overseas for years." Aware that she sounded edgy, Hannah softened her tone. "Amelia's enthusiastic. She means no harm. She's quite a serious person, a photographer whose work is sold in a New York gallery."

"I don't give a hoot who she is or what she does," Barbara said. "I might have expected this from Andre if Amelia were thirty, but my God, she's our age."

"She's quite vivacious," the other wife, who had introduced herself as Angela, said.

An uncomfortable silence followed. Barbara pushed back her chair. "Andre can be such a fool. You can tell him that I'm in the bar."

Hannah remembered seeing several bars. "Which one?" she asked.

Barbara glared at her. "He'll just have to try them all, won't he?" Her long taffeta skirt swished as she made her way stiffly between the tables.

The single woman, Norma Greene, smiled at Hannah. "Inauspicious way to begin a journey, wouldn't you say? My astrologer told me there would be trouble."

"Amelia's just excited with everything tonight." She waved her hand. "It's all so glamorous. We live in the country."

"Maybe you could talk to her, get her to tone it down a bit," Angela said.

Hannah's irritation increased. What was this, anyhow—some kind of silly high school charade? "Wait a minute," she said. "I'm not Amelia's keeper."

"No, of course you aren't." Angela flushed and turned to talk softly with her husband.

"Don't dump all the blame on Amelia," her husband, Richard, said. "Andre asked her to dance."

Angela gave him a sharp look.

"And speaking of dancing, would you like to dance, my dear?" Richard extended his hand.

Angela smiled, her eyebrows arched. "Indeed I would." They rose and made their way to the dance floor, where Amelia and Andre were now dancing to "Smoke Gets in Your Eyes."

Norma changed her seat, moving closer to Hannah. "Do you think they allow you to change tables?" She was small, with sensitive brown eyes and ash-colored hair cropped close to her face. Her clothes were simple and discreet, a gray suit whose sole adornment was a large silver and turquoise pin of a leaping deer on the lapel.

"I don't know. You mean just you? Does Amelia bother you?"

"I find her charming. I thought Barbara behaved imprudently."

"Yes," Hannah replied. "She embarrassed herself and everyone else."

"Enough of Barbara." Norma changed the subject. "Where are you ladies from?"

"North Carolina," Hannah said. "Covington, a small community in the mountains. Amelia and I share a home with Grace. You'll meet her tomorrow. She was worn out by the plane trip." She directed the conversation from herself. "And you—where do you live?"

A moment later a waiter appeared. "Coffee, tea, ladies?"

"Coffee, please," Norma said. Hannah shook her head.

"My home is in Forest Hills on Long Island now, but my husband worked for Mobil Oil, two, three years here, there, all over America. I would have liked living overseas, but he preferred to stay in the United States." Her voice dropped. "Malcom passed away nearly a year ago. My sons insisted on this trip; they handled everything—my first foray into the world without Malcom. We were married forty-three years." Her eyes filmed with tears. "It's difficult being alone, traveling alone."

"I've been alone a long time," Hannah said. "But I can imagine how it must be when you're accustomed to a companion."

"He was my best friend," Norma said.

Flushed and laughing, Amelia and Andre returned to the table. "My wife?" Andre asked.

"Gone to a bar," Hannah said.

"But which one—there are so many bars?"

"I imagine you'll have to look for her," Norma said. The corners of her lips twitched, and she brought her napkin to them as if to stifle a laugh.

Andre lifted Amelia's hand to his lips and kissed it. *"Merci, madame."* Then, with a long sigh, he departed.

"You upset his wife," Hannah said.

Amelia tossed her head. "Is it my fault if Andre wanted to dance with me?" She straightened the scarf about her neck and laughed. Her earrings swung merrily.

"You're quite a striking woman," Norma Greene said. "I'd be jealous if my Malcom preferred to dance with you rather than with me."

"His wife hates to dance, he told me. Except to dance, what would I want with her husband? He's much too young for me. Silly for her to get upset," Amelia said.

"Let's drop it," Hannah said. "I'm going to play the slot machines. Coming?"

"I'm going to dance," Amelia said. She looked up as a tall man with thick, graying hair approached the table.

"George Herrick," he said, shaking hands with everyone, but his eyes were focused on Amelia. "Would you care to dance?"

Amelia rose, accepted his arm, and strolled away to the dance floor.

"They hire good-looking men to dance with us ladies without escorts," Norma said.

"Amelia's on a high tonight," Hannah said.

After a moment Norma asked, "Mind if I join you at the slot machines?"

"Not at all."

Out on the balcony, the splash of ocean, the roar of wind resounded in Grace's ears. A crescent moon floated in an ebony sky. Grace leaned against the sturdy railing. No soft and fluttery wind tonight—it prickled her face and licked her cheeks with its salty tongue. Wind teased her hair, driving it in wild tendrils about her face.

A line from a poem learned in high school came to mind: "Roll on, thou deep and dark blue Ocean,—roll!" Names were hard to remember these days, and numbers; she reversed numbers. And yet from the depths of memory had come a line of a poem by Lord Byron. Another line of the poem came, and she spoke it aloud: " 'Time writes no wrinkles on thine azure brow.' " And yet another: " 'Calm or convulsed,—in breeze, or gale, or storm.' " The words rose and fell on the wind as she gazed into the dark water below.

And then, inexplicably, everything changed. Grace experienced something undefined and mysterious. An invisible force, a silent explosion, shattered her consciousness. She no longer felt the rail beneath her hands, the deck beneath her feet. She drifted on the wind, became the wind, floated high, dipped low, swirled, roared, and whispered. Her senses mingled with the sea, and she knew its ebb and flow, its power and its tranquility. Events flashed before her and throbbed with meaning, no small or large thing wasted—not her stillborn babies, not the lonely years with Ted, not Olive Pruitt's dreary boardinghouse in Pennsylvania, nor the recent diagnosis of diabetes.

Tears streamed down her cheeks. A near orgasmic joy swept over her as she experienced the unity of all things and the mystery of life in all its aspects.

Then, as suddenly as it came, the inexplicable, exquisite connection to that immanent presence that infuses and pervades all that we see, feel, taste, hear, and smell faded and disappeared. For immeasurable moments she stood there, her mind wordless, weeping, the same and yet changed.

Grace finally turned from the railing to one of the chairs. In an effort to ground herself, she pressed her feet hard onto the deck while she sat. Her fingers wrapped around the cold metal of the chair. The wind dried her tears, and her heart settled into its normal rhythm. Her encounter with the cosmos had been mysterious and magical, a special and most sacred experience. All she could think was that in some ways it had been like taking off layers of clothing and standing naked and unashamed before God.

Later, through books she turned to, she would learn that there were many ways to the numinous, including through meditation and communing with nature, as was her own experience. She would also come to know that what had occurred this night was a gift to be treasured, for many people meditated and followed a spiritual path all their lives without ever reaching a state of transcendence.

Shoes in hand, Amelia breezed into the suite singing. Spotting Grace on the balcony, she tossed her shoes on a chair and headed for the sliding glass door. "What's happening?" she asked. "Hey, you look different. What is it? And what's the wind done to your hair? It's wild."

Grace nodded.

Without waiting for an answer, Amelia leaned against the rail, looked out at the sea, then turned to Grace. "I had the most glorious evening. I danced and danced. First, there was this French gentleman, and then . . ."

From somewhere outside of herself, Grace heard Amelia babble on and on about the music, the dining room, the ease and sophistication of the men she had danced with, how charming, gracious, and what excellent dancers they had been, and how young and carefree she felt.

Grace forced her attention to Amelia. "Who did you dance with?"

"Andre, one of the husbands at our table—we're seated with two couples and one other woman—and two of the escorts they hire to dance with women. One of those escorts, Melvin—Mel"—Amelia rolled her eyes—"ooh-la-la, but he's so handsome and young. Dances like Gene Kelly." She tossed her head. "We were the stars of the dance floor."

"I'm glad you had such a good time."

For a moment, Amelia looked at Grace intently. "What's happened to you? You've got this kind of beatific look on your face."

"The wind." It was hardly an explanation, but Amelia seemed not to notice. "Where's Hannah?" Grace asked.

Amelia shrugged. "Can you get this zipper down for me?" She turned so Grace could release the snagged zipper. The dress slid from Amelia's shoulders, clung to her hips for a second, then puddled at her feet. She stood in her slip and bra and hugged her naked arms. "Chilly out here." Collecting the dress, she waltzed into the suite and returned a few minutes later in pajamas, robe, and slippers. "I'm stuffed," she said. "I have never seen so much food, and the desserts: *mousse au chocolat, crème brûlée,* and *profiterole.*" To Grace's puzzled look she explained, *"Profiterole*—that's a miniature cream puff with a savory filling. I thought of you. You would love it."

"Where's Hannah?" Grace asked again.

"I left her and Nora, or Norma something, at the table. Maybe she went to a movie."

They heard the door open and close and Hannah joined them. "You two still up? Great, you can congratulate me." She dropped her winnings onto her bed. "Gambling loot."

"From the slots, or poker?" Amelia asked. "How much did you win?" She reached for the bills and began to count them.

"One hundred and thirty dollars from the slot machine," Hannah said.

"Trouble ahead." Grace laughed. "I can see that I'll be alone most of this cruise, with one of you gambling and the other dancing."

"I'll share it with you, Grace. We can both gamble until it's gone."

"It's so big, this ship," Grace said. "Where do you gamble?"

"The casino. Two floors up," Hannah said.

"The ship's a floating palace. You can get lost easily, but anything you could want is available somewhere on board," Amelia said. "There are so many mirrored walls, I actually got tired of looking at myself. We'll show you how to find the dining room, and you can use it as a point of reference."

For a moment Grace, the least traveled among them, felt intimidated, but then she remembered her experience on the balcony and knew that she was so much more than what she seemed to be, that all was as it should be. "I'll take my time and learn my way about," she replied.

Hannah asked, "What's different about you, Grace? Something's different."

"I'll tell you tomorrow," Grace said. She intended to share it with them, but what words could she use to express the immensity of what had taken place? Not tonight. Tonight she would lie in bed and let the wonder of remembered bliss and the hum of the ship lull her to sleep.

8

TOURING ST. THOMAS

It seemed to Grace that Amelia was the only one of the three of them who had brought proper cruise attire. Each day and each night she appeared to wear a new outfit. Watching her, Grace realized that Amelia's skill lay in selection. Amelia transformed a simple black evening gown into four elegant outfits by adding different tops: a delicate, silver lamé shawl, a long jacket with velvet trim, a black-and-white overblouse with a mandarin collar. For daytime Amelia's smart, well-cut skirts, casual jackets, and broad-brimmed hats (worn to protect her fair complexion from sun and wind) reminded Grace of a traveler and suspect in Agatha Christie's *Murder on the Nile*.

Afraid that she might be cold, Grace had stuffed one of her two suitcases with a bulky sweater and sweatpants and a matching top. It was February, after all. The suitcase remained unopened. Clothes never hung right on her, with her full bosom and short legs, and she had long ago resigned herself to belted shirtwaist dresses in summer, and jackets or long-sleeved shirts over slacks or skirts in winter. Having given up on style, Grace attempted to gain a dressier effect with solid colors, and for a dressed-up feel she had brought a strand of pearls—a gift from Bob last Christmas. The pearls made her feel classy.

Hannah's classic Ralph Lauren–style clothes seemed stuffy by day and overly casual at night. In her long silk blouse under an even longer jacket and black slacks, Hannah reminded Grace of Dorothy Zbornak in the sitcom *The Golden Girls*. What people wore and how they looked never interested or fazed Hannah, but Grace often felt out of place among the passengers who paraded the decks in their new cruise wardrobes. Grace noted that the younger they were, the scantier the clothing. Some of the bathing suits—especially the thong, shocked her.

Grace postponed sharing her experience of that first night with Hannah and Amelia. It had been so unexpected, so strange and inexplicable, that as the days passed a sense of unreality set in. Had she dreamed it? Also, they were rarely together other than at meals with others.

A shipboard pattern developed. After late nights dancing, Amelia slept in, while Grace and Hannah availed themselves of the lectures on the Virgin Islands. These were held in a large, conference room with plush, theater-style seats and thick carpets. The speaker, Dr. Paul Nolan, a university professor, proved to be charming, articulate, and concise, and his talks brimmed with anecdotes as well as historical details that fascinated Grace.

"The Virgin Islands," he began, after greeting his audience, "were named by Sir Francis Drake for Saint Ursula and her Thousand Virgins. The islands had been the home to Carib Indians, Frenchmen, and Spaniards. The Danish government acquired Saint Thomas in 1672, Saint John in 1718, and in 1734 they purchased the plantation island of Saint Croix from France. The Danes governed what would become the American Virgin Islands until the United States purchased them in 1917.

"During those nearly three hundred years, while wars raged in Europe, Denmark remained neutral. So Saint Thomas, with its naturally protected harbor, provided safe anchorage, a place to refurbish, and a trading port for ships of all nations. Saint Croix, on the other hand, with its fertile plains and valleys, became a leading sugar island. Thus, in contrast to the port-based culture of Saint Thomas, a slave culture developed on Saint Croix and on the island of Saint John.

"Immigrants from Europe, North America, and the Dutch, French, and English Islands farther to the east and south flocked to the Danish Virgin Islands, and this polyglot of planters, merchants, adventurers, and entrepreneurs of many faiths and customs mixed and blended in an atmosphere marked by religious and ethnic tolerance that characterized island society almost to the present day."

The room grew chilly, and Grace regretted not bringing a sweater. Several seats down the aisle from her, a woman struggled into a blue blazer and held it snug across her chest. Then she sat forward on her seat and raised her hand. "Will you discuss the Rockefeller purchase of Saint John? It's the only pristine island of the three."

"And the smallest and most hilly," Dr. Nolan said. "I hope you will all take advantage of its exquisite beaches. In the 1950s, the Rockefellers bought eighty percent of the land and donated it to the U.S. government. It is now administered by the National Park Service."

"My husband and I used to come to the islands. We hated the changes on Saint Thomas," the woman said. "At least Saint John won't go the way of overdevelopment." She sat back in her seat, flushed but seemingly satisfied. "Can you tell us about the slave rebellion on Saint John?"

"Of course. The slave uprising took place on Saint John in 1733. Absentee landlords, lax discipline on the plantations, drought over several years, followed by hurricanes and a plague of insects, set the stage for the tragedy.

"On a Monday morning in November of 1733, a group of slaves carried bundles of supplies into the fort at Coral Bay. Once inside, they drew knives and cutlasses from their bundles and massacred all but one soldier, who hid beneath a bed. Later he made it to Saint Thomas bearing the terrifying news.

"The slaves on Saint John robbed and burned approximately half of the plantations on the island, sparing a few whites but killing many. It took six months and French soldiers from the island of Martinique, trained in jungle warfare, to bring the rebellion to an end in May of the following year.

"When Saint Croix became part of the Danish West Indies, most of the planters transferred their holdings and slaves to that more viable plantation island, and the economic life of Saint John slipped into decline."

During the next talk he gave them, Dr. Nolan spoke of the growth of St. Thomas as a port. "Saint Thomas had a thriving slave market before the abolition of slavery by the Danes in 1848. The old marketplace at the end of Main Street was the site of the slave market. St. Thomas became a major trading port, and remained so until ships shifted from sail to coal to steam. The island was no longer needed as a refueling port for transatlantic shipping and trade declined. The island languished for years, even after the United States bought the islands from Denmark in 1917."

Someone behind Grace raised his hand. A deep voice asked, "Wasn't there an effort made to buy the islands way back in 1867 when Secretary of State Seward bought Alaska?"

"Indeed there was, but fate intervened. A fierce hurricane struck the islands, followed by a tidal wave. Huge battleships in the harbors of Saint Croix and Saint Thomas were washed onto the land. Negotiations ended. It was not until 1917 that the United States bought the Virgin Islands."

"Why'd we do that, anyway?" asked a tall man in the row in front of Grace and Hannah.

Grace wished they'd all just be still and listen to Dr. Nolan.

"We feared that Germany had an interest in acquiring the islands. We bought them to defend the approaches to the Panama Canal and the mainland of the U.S," Dr. Nolan replied.

"So did we get the island economy going?" the same man asked.

"Sadly, no. The U.S. more or less ignored the islands for a long while. In 1931, President Herbert Hoover visited the islands. He is remembered for having called them . . ."—he wrote on the board as he talked—"the 'poor house of the United States.' It was not until the 1950s, when tourism became the stock in trade, that the island's economy began to flourish again."

Dr. Nolan shuffled his papers and removed his glasses. "One last thing. Tomorrow you'll be going ashore on Saint Thomas. Suggestions of places to visit is really the job of the cruise director's staff, but as an historian, I urge you take time to see several of the fine old buildings that date back to the mid-1800s. The Synagogue is the second oldest synagogue in the Western Hemisphere. The Dutch Reformed Church, just around the corner from the Synagogue, was constructed in 1844 in classical revival style. And don't miss a tour of Fort Christian. The Danes constructed the fort in the late 1600s to protect the harbor, and at least one of the original cannon is still on the roof. You might find it interesting to tour the museum, and to go down into one of the prison cells." He gathered up his notes. "Enjoy your stay on Saint Thomas. The island is amazingly beautiful."

* * *

At 6:00 A.M. an impatient Grace, her heart racing, stood beside Hannah on their balcony. Because of its size, the ship had dropped anchor outside the harbor of St. Thomas. "Look, Hannah, that's the Marriott Hotel that Dr. Nolan told us about. Up there on the right, on that peninsula. And over there, on the left, are the ruins of a fort dating back to the 1700s. What island did he say the fort is on, do you remember?"

"Hassell Island," Hannah said.

At breakfast Grace was so excited she could hardly eat.

"You must eat, Grace. It may be hours before lunch, and you could have a blood sugar drop," Hannah said.

Grace drank the juice and nibbled at her eggs. "I've asked the waiter for an apple and a piece of cheese to take with me," she said.

After breakfast, passengers lined up to board the launches that would carry them across the harbor to the town of Charlotte Amalie. It was nerve-racking for Grace to follow Hannah and Amelia down the steps lowered from the side of the great ship to a platform hovering just above the waterline. For a moment she considered retreating, but people crowded behind her. Grace squared her shoulders, accepted a sailor's hand, and stepped into the launch, a frail minnow beside the whale of a ship. She took the seat between Hannah and Amelia and looked down at floorboards, scuffed from the thousands of feet that had shuffled across them.

"It's perfectly safe, Grace," Hannah whispered. "These boats make the trip to and from the ship all day long and half the night."

The motor of the launch roared to life, and they started across the placid water toward the picture-perfect town. Lilliputian in the distance, the town's white houses and red roofs shimmered in the sunshine. Grace imagined Gulliver climbing the hillsides, one red roof at a time. In her mind she conjured up pirate ships with skulls and crossbones flying from their masts, and it amused her to think that today ships deposited tourists where pirates once drank and brawled and disposed of stolen treasure.

Green hills embraced the harbor on three sides. The tightness in Grace's shoulders began to lessen. She basked in the beauty of the landscape, lifted her head, and breathed into her soul the resplendence of undulating hills, the jeweled town, the blue-green Caribbean. *Stop the boat!* she wanted to cry out. *Be silent. Let me sit here.*

"We're here." Amelia nudged Grace. Grace looked up. They had pulled to the dock, the lines cast ashore. Amelia pushed her gently. "You're holding everyone up. Let's get off the boat."

Grace grasped a man's hand and stepped onto a wide concrete apron that topped the seawall. To her right, a steel band played loudly. Cars on the four-lane road alongside the dock honked at taxis that stopped to pick up passengers. She had somehow expected the island to be as quiet and pristine as the scenery suggested. Now, surrounded by the noise of music, cars, and people, Grace put her hands over her ears and stopped walking. Stepping between Grace and Amelia, Hannah took their arms and guided them toward the only visible stoplight so they could cross the street. As a backdrop to the cacophony of sound and color, the terra-cotta walls of old Fort Christian rose against an amazingly blue sky.

"I don't want to go in that direction," Grace said, pointing to the steel band and the cluster of tents from which hung shell jewelry, bright shirts, and other trinkets.

Amelia adjusted her camera bag on her shoulder. "Later I'd like to get some shots of that band. Their shirts are so colorful, and there's a woman playing with them."

"Later," Hannah said.

"We must go to the Synagogue and the Dutch Reformed Church Dr. Nolan told you about, but I'm coming back here." Amelia rummaged in her purse. "I picked up a street map. Let's find Main Street." She handed the map to Grace. "You direct us. How do we get to Main Street?"

One of the crew from the launch stood on the dock holding a loop of rope, ready to cast off. "How do we get to the Main Street?" Hannah asked.

The man turned to respond and nearly lost his footing as he jumped onto the boat. As the launch eased from shore, he called, "Take any side road toward the hills."

The crush of cars passing pinned them to the sidewalk.

"Sorry, Grace. Looks as if we'll have to go toward the steel band in order to get across this street," Hannah said. "There's only that one light."

They joined a cluster of people moving toward Fort Christian. When the light changed to green, they hastened across the road. Ahead they could see two-story terra-cotta walls and the wide, graceful arches of a large building just beyond a park, which was surrounded by a low blue stone wall.

Grace covered her ears with her hands. "Faster, let's go faster."

"Don't be a party pooper. Let yourself go with the music," Amelia said, as her hips and shoulders responded to the beat of the drums.

When they turned left at the post office, the music faded. The cruise director had told them that the solid old buildings on Main Street, now shops, had once been warehouses. Many of the buildings had second stories, and were formerly merchants' homes. Their balconies and wrought-iron railings were much like those in New Orleans.

Main Street proved to be two lanes wide and jammed with taxis hawking rides or discharging people. Exhaust fumes, confined by the buildings, contaminated the air. Air-conditioned shops offered respite. It was like stumbling into an oasis in a desert, Grace thought, as they stepped into a large jewelry store.

"Why do they allow all these taxis and cars on this street?" she muttered.

"Such pollution in a lovely place like this. Be pleasanter as a walking mall," Hannah said.

Amelia took out her camera, stood on the sidewalk, and began to photograph. In the store, Hannah and Grace waited. By noon they had visited, and Amelia had photographed, the Synagogue and the Dutch Reformed Church, and they had found a route to Fort Christian that bypassed the carnival confusion of Tent City.

Once inside the fort, they toured the museum. Photos lined one wall: photos of horse-drawn carriages on Main Street in 1898, photos of black women toting enormous straw baskets of coal up a narrow gangplank to ships docked at a wharf, and a photo of a man riding a donkey laden with goods for market. The man's bare feet dangled nearly to the dirt road. Another photo was of the original waterfront with its wooden piers. The piers extended out from shore, and sailing sloops were tied to them. On the closest pier stood a scale for weighing fish, which lay in a basket nearby, coconuts stacked in a pyramid, bundles of sugarcane, and more.

"Look, Amelia, Hannah," Grace called. "Here's a photo of a huge ship lying on its side on shore. This must be after that hurricane Dr. Nolan told us about." Grace cocked her head as she studied the framed photographs of the wreckage. "Seems fated, doesn't it, for the purchase of the islands by the U.S not to take place at that time."

"Things happen arbitrarily. Hurricanes don't send messages like 'Don't buy the islands,'" Hannah said. She eased Grace out into the courtyard with an eye to ascending narrow stairs.

From the roof of the old fort they looked down on the tents. Blasting steel band music shattered any sense of a time gone by. With a long lens Amelia photographed the steel band, then they returned to the courtyard below and turned their attention to the dungeon, where thick whitewashed walls enclosed a corridor that led below-ground to the arched cells.

"How damp it is," Grace said. "Must have been horrible being locked up down here. I bet there were rats."

"Just give me a minute, you guys. Now, both of you, pretend to be prisoners." Amelia waved Hannah and Grace into an open cell, then photographed them behind the flat bars of the iron doors. "Put your noses up to the openings. I can hardly see you behind those bars. I've never seen such wide bars in a jail."

"Been in many jails?" Hannah asked.

"Western movies, silly." Amelia raised the camera to her eye.

The veranda restaurant at Bluebeard's Castle that overlooked the harbor was furnished with wicker tables and large, comfortable chairs. Besides their ship, there were two smaller cruise ships anchored at sea, and two larger ones secured to the dock at one side of the harbor. A ring of high green hills formed a backdrop for the red roofs of the houses and stores, and for the launches that sped from dock to ships and back again, trailing ribbons of white wakes across the gleaming turquoise water.

Grace thumbed through the guidebook. "The tower we passed on our way to the veranda was never part of a real castle. It was used to store ammunition and supplies, as a lookout tower, and as a place for inhabitants to gather in case the island was attacked, which it never was."

"How unromantic," Amelia said. "But they do have honeymoon suites in the tower and, I hear, a heart-shaped bed." Her eyes twinkled. She set her elbows on the table and leaned her chin on her hands. "If I lived here, I'd use a hundred rolls of film each week just on the scenery."

The buffet lunch was excellent. Their waitress, a bright, cheerful young native woman, suggested they have papaya chunks for dessert. "Papaya settles the stomach good," she said.

After lunch they sat for a while, relaxing. Then Grace said, "Let's tour the island by car, then we can shop and still get back to the ship in time for dinner."

"Sounds good to me. My feet hurt," Hannah said.

Driving on the designated left side of the narrow two-lane road, their taxi rounded yet another curve. In the backseat, Amelia slid against the door and felt the press of Grace's shoulder against her. The view was breathtaking. The harbor seemed to widen and glinted clear turquoise in the sunshine. They crested the hill and the contour of the land changed, for the hill dropped off steeply on the passenger side, Amelia's side of the taxi. Her heart pounded. She leaned away from the door. Why didn't the driver move closer to the middle of the road? She imagined the scrunch of gravel, tires slipping, the taxi plunging over the cliff into the underbrush, and tumbling down, down, torn branches whipping past them, rocks flying. Horrible. Amelia whimpered, then grabbed Grace's hand. "This is awful, just awful, and he's driving on the wrong side of the road."

"Ouch. Ease up on the grip," Grace said.

"You don't see how steep it is. There was plenty to photograph in town. We should have stayed there." Amelia winced as an oncoming car whizzed past them.

"My heart's in my throat, too" Grace said. She closed her eyes.

"This is the correct side of the road here. Our driver's been on these roads a thousand times. He knows what he's doing," Hannah said from the front passenger seat.

A short while later the road seemed to flatten, and Grace, her eyes still squeezed shut, felt the surface of the road deteriorate and the car slow. Its tires shimmied as the taxi turned from a paved onto a rutted road and stopped.

"Grace, open your eyes," Hannah said. "You're missing the view you came to see."

They had joined other cars and their passengers at a lookout. Hannah offered her hand first to Amelia, then to Grace, assisting them from the cab. An astounding view unfolded. Below, nestled between the arms of hills flung wide in welcome, lay heart-shaped, mile-long Magens Bay, and beyond the beach, low hills, and beyond the hills an archipelago of verdant islands, small and large, cast by the hand of some divinity across a velvet, azure sea.

Grace's heart soared.

"De water on de beach so shallow, you could walk out a long time before you get water in your mouth," the driver said. "Look 'round there." He pointed across the road to a solid stone bench set in a cut in the hillside. "Dat's Drake's Seat. Go up and sit and get your picture take. Sir Frances Drake heself sat right there after he sail all up and down between the islands." He waved his arm toward the archipelago. "It called Drake's Passage."

Amelia shot several pictures of Grace and Hannah sitting on Drake's Seat, then Fred, their driver, took several of the three of them.

Fred's skin was cocoa brown, his eyes black chunks of coal, and when he smiled his teeth were white and even. He exuded friendliness. A veritable chamber of commerce, he raved about the trade winds that blew from the east and cooled the islands. He explained that the brilliant orange blossoms of the flamboyant trees that covered the island bloomed in July. "Same time as mangoes come ripe," he said. "Island people could live off of the land. We got bananas, papayas, and coconuts every day of the year, and we got fish, lobsters, and crabs from the sea."

His tour included a stop at Mountain Top for a banana daiquiri and a drive along a ridge overlooking steep, narrow, terraced slopes where the descendants of French Huguenot settlers still farmed.

When they returned to town, Fred suggested that they shop at the West Indies Company Dock on the eastern side of the harbor. "It won't be so jam up with people, like Main Street," he said. "They got places to eat there, too."

He deposited them at a dockside restaurant, not far from one of the cruise ships tethered to the dock with thick ropes. They ordered iced teas and watched tourists laden with bundles board the ship from ramps that stretched from the dock to an open door on one of the decks.

"Now that's easy," Grace said. "I'd like that a lot better than taking the launch."

It was not long before they separated to shop among the rows of narrow buildings that housed smaller versions of many of the Main Street shops. Unhurried and content, Grace strolled from store to store. Like a child in the proverbial candy shop, she bought soft dolls for Melissa, a book of island ghost tales and another of olden-day island tales for Tyler. A waterproof watch for Bob. A replica of a Waterbury china-cased shelf clock for Russell's collection. After the clerk had shown her tray after tray of jewelry, Grace chose sterling silver earrings for Laura, Molly, and Brenda. Then, feeling guilty for taking so much of the woman's time, she bought a large bottle of Joy perfume for Emily at a third less the price, the woman assured her, than it would cost in the States.

It was fun picking out T-shirts for everyone: yellow shirts with electric blue and green iguanas clinging to the branches of trees, neutral-colored shirts with black and red pirate ships, and a shirt with the wide sweep of Magens Bay emblazoned in bright blues and green on the front. Bob, she knew, would love the gray T-shirt she selected for him. In bold red letters on the back it read: "I SLEPT ON A VIRGIN"—and in tiny lowercase letters, the single word "island."

For Lurina Grace chose a shell-encrusted hand mirror and brush set, and for her little friend Lucy Grace decided on three silver bracelets. It was hard to find a gift for Old Man, but finally she found something she thought would make him laugh: a T-shirt based on a story about ghostly pigs from *Virgin Islands Tales of Ghosts, Haunting, and Jumbies,* one of Tyler's new books. On the T-shirt ghost pigs raced to overtake a bent, gnarled figure that reminded her of Old Man. She realized that she had forgotten Roger and Mike and rushed back into a shop specializing in Irish goods, where she purchased a herringbone wool scarf and a beer stein. When exhaustion stopped her in her tracks, Grace's shopping spree had added $779 to her credit card debt.

Back on the ship, it was show-and-tell as they pulled their gifts from bags and boxes. Hannah had purchased cashmere sweaters—deep blue for Max, red for Laura, tan for Hank, and a pale blue for herself—and red cashmere gloves for Mary Ann, the receptionist at Bella's Park. "I like to keep it simple," she said, as she rewrapped the sweaters and returned them to their box.

For Amelia, it was all photography: a Cannon macro lens and a new camera bag for herself. A Nikon digital camera for Mike. "He's been talking about buying this for weeks now." She opened the last box and took out two lightweight Cannon automatic cameras. "These are for Tyler and Lucy."

"You're going to teach Tyler and Lucy how to do photography?" Grace asked.

"Tyler asked me if I would. He said Lucy Banks would also like lessons." She held a camera in each hand. "Why not? It's good to start kids early."

"I see," Grace said, and looked away.

"Now let's see what you got for yourself, Grace."

Tissue wrappings crinkled as Grace sank onto her bed. T-shirts slid onto the floor, and she grabbed Russell's clock before it joined them on the carpet. "Nothing."

"Why not?" Amelia asked.

"I don't need anything."

"But it's your vacation. I'm going to buy something for you when we're in Saint John."

Grace flushed. She set the clock on the end table and bent to gather up the T-shirts. "I'd rather you didn't."

"Why? You're annoyed with me about teaching the kids, aren't you? They asked me to give them lessons, Grace."

"I'm not upset at all. You're making more of this than I am."

"The heck I am. I can read you like a book." Amelia sat on the bed beside Grace. Her voice softened. "I'm sure Tyler meant to tell you. He tells you everything."

Grace pushed up from the bed. "I'm delighted that you're going to give Tyler and Lucy lessons, and yes, I'm sure I'll hear all about it when we get back."

Amelia shrugged and consulted her watch. "I'm going to shower now. Remember Andre, the husband from our table that first night?" she asked Hannah.

"They changed tables. Don't think I'd recognize either one of them if I passed them on the deck," Hannah replied.

"I'm having a cocktail with him before dinner," Amelia said, then bustled off before Hannah could respond.

"Amelia's looking for trouble," she said to Grace. "That man's wife is one angry lady, and I doubt it started with her husband dancing with Amelia."

Grace covered her mouth with her palm and yawned. "I am so tired, Hannah. I think I'll stay in, have my dinner out on the balcony. We'll be setting off about the time the moon comes up."

"This isn't about Amelia and Tyler, is it?"

"Not at all. I am bone weary."

"Okay, but I'll miss you," Hannah said.

Grace smiled. "Sure you will. You and Norma will eat like starving hounds and race to the slot machines."

Hannah sat on the edge of her bed across from Grace, who had flopped down on hers again. "Funny about that. I haven't gambled in years. It's fun; maybe I'm getting addicted."

"That's silly," Grace replied. "If anyone got addicted to anything, it wouldn't be you."

But winning that first night had whetted her appetite. Hannah discovered that she enjoyed the rush that came each time she sat at a machine, each time she shoved that quarter into the slot and yanked down the handle. Eyes glued to the spinning numbers or letters or objects, she concentrated on a win, a hit, and anticipated, each time, the jingle of coins tumbling out in a rush to land with a clatter in the metal tray, and the cheers and applause of nearby players. That first night, it seemed as if she and the machine had conspired against the establishment. Norma must feel the same excitement, she thought, for she also played every night.

In the last few days, Hannah had made excuses to Grace or Amelia, lied about where and what she was doing, and sneaked away for an hour or two to gamble. Lied? Sneaked away? That sounded awful. She was on vacation, after all, and having fun experimenting with activities inconceivable at home, like swimming in one of the heated pools late at night and afterward, relaxed and confident, hastening to the casino to gamble. To date Hannah had lost $375.25 in quarters. Addicted? Ridiculous. She was merely challenged to win back her losses.

*   *   *

At Magens Bay the shifting shades of blue, azure, sapphire, teal, and turquoise had filled Grace's soul with immense quiet. Now, alone on the balcony of the ship, she stretched out on the lounge that they had exchanged for the table and a chair and was content. Puffy white clouds like stuffed-full pillows drifted across the Caribbean sky. Grace watched them change shape and take on the hues of sunset. As she relaxed, she remembered a Thanksgiving long ago, at her paternal grandma Annie's house.

They'd gotten up early, Granny and she, and she had carried in dry wood and helped Granny start a fire in the living room fireplace. They'd sorted the pinecones collected in November and made trees by attaching the cones to forms Granny made from thick paper. These they placed on wide gold and green ribbons on the table. They had decked the mantel with paper pumpkins, turkeys, and pilgrims, too. Then Grace had pitted prunes, mashed them, and helped Granny stir them and applesauce into the stuffing. Everyone loved Granny's special sweet stuffing. Granny had praised her efforts, and everyone, even her reserved, mostly unsmiling mother, had clapped.

The clouds shifted shape. Fluffy pillows became a dog, a camel, a lion's face. Memories shifted. In their first summer of love, she and Bob had taken a picnic to a wide and shallow river overhung by gnarled trees.

"Do you think these were planted by someone or did birds unwittingly drop seeds?" she'd asked Bob.

"I'd bet on the birds," he replied.

An ordinary, simple picnic. Bob had spread an old army blanket on the grass. She had brought two sandwiches for each of them—egg, and ham and cheese—and slices of cake. He had filled a small cooler with ice and tucked in beer for him and iced tea for her.

A rabbit ventured from beneath a bush, so close that they saw the moisture on its quivering nose and the alertness in its curious eyes before it vanished. Birds trilled and sang. The icing on the chocolate cake melted and smeared Grace's fingers. Slowly, Bob licked them clean. She remembered looking up at the gleam of sunshine trickling through leaves and giving thanks silently. *Thank you. Thank you for blessing me with this amazing day.*

Since her extraordinary experience on the balcony that first night out, Grace had taken to thanking the universe for all her blessings: for feeling well, for the willpower to stick to her diet for an entire day, for the pleasure of a hot tub, for a comfortable bed and pillows, for love and kindness whenever shown her. At Drake's Seat overlook, she had opened her soul to the radiance of the day and wordlessly expressed her gratitude for the privilege of sight and the gift of so much beauty. Now, with Hannah off gambling and Amelia off dancing, she would simply relax and just be, as the sky turned rose and scarlet, changed to mauve, then gray, before bidding the day farewell.

On the hillsides of Charlotte Amalie, lights twinkled. Effortlessly, the great ship slipped from the mouth of the harbor. It would be dark when they crossed the sea between St. Thomas and St. John. Dr. Nolan had said that the twenty-mile stretch of water was popularly referred to as The Graveyard, for here the titan Atlantic Ocean clashed with a placid Caribbean Sea. In days past, ships in sight of land had lost their battles with wind and sea, and released their spirits and those of the men who went down with them to a watery grave. Would it be rough when they crossed? Would she feel the roll and toss of waves in such a powerful ship?

9

BEACHES, BAY RUM, AND SEA EGGS

A grove of coconut palm trees met their eyes as the launch deposited its passengers on the pier in Cruz Bay, St. John. At the end of the pier, tour buses packed the narrow road. En masse, the passengers stepped from the small boat and hastened toward the buses, as if to miss a tour would be a disaster. Grace hung back, waiting for the hustle and bustle to end. Jane Exeter, who had raised so many questions at Dr. Nolan's lecture, and her husband passed Grace.

"Where are all the wooden houses?" Jane asked her husband, who merely shrugged. "There's no quaint little town left. It's all shops and big new buildings."

"At least the buildings are traditional island style, and not glass and wood like . . ." His words were lost as they vanished in the crush of tourists.

To Grace the buildings seemed quite charming. Two-story, painted blue or coral or yellow with white hurricane shutters, they echoed the style of the buildings on Main Street in St. Thomas. The shutters of doors and windows were secured against the exterior walls by large iron hooks and brackets.

Grace followed Amelia and Hannah along the length of the pier, and found herself climbing up into a small bus nearly filled with other tourists. Bright yellow fringes dangled from a blue canvas top. Amelia sat between Grace and Hannah on the narrow seat.

"I is Alex Joseph. Welcome to Saint John, the beautiful island," the driver said. "We going to Cinnamon Bay. Saint John has the most beautiful beaches in all the Caribbean. I show you them as we drive." He looked back at his passengers as he started down the road.

Amelia clutched both Hannah's and Grace's arms, certain they would end up in a ditch or over a cliff and wishing she had never climbed aboard.

Up and around one curve and another, below them glistened a beach with sand the color of bleached white linen. "Hawks Nest Bay," Alex Joseph said. "National Park." A pristine beach boasting a grove of coconut trees behind a strip of sugar-white sand came into view. "Trunk Bay. Very popular with divers. Dat island off the shore got an underwater trail around the coral reef."

They arrived at Cinnamon Bay. "Dis where the park service got its campsites. Busy beach." The driver's cell phone rang. "What you want, man? I comin' right back."

Hugging canvas bags from the ship, everyone except the ladies climbed down. Alex Joseph looked puzzled. "You ladies not going to swim? You going back to Cruz Bay?"

"I think we got in the wrong tour bus. Sorry. Yes, we'll go back to Cruz Bay," Hannah said.

"Where are you going from there?" Grace asked.

"They got a load for me to go to Coral Bay, dat way over to the other end of the island. A long trip."

"How long?" Amelia asked, though she was quite sure she did not want to take it.

"Hour an a half one way," he replied. "Long and hot. It's a good fare, otherwise I wouldn't go at all, at all. Why I don't take you ladies back to Cruz Bay? You can shop there. Buy some of our bay rum to take home for your family and friends."

"Bay rum?" Grace asked.

Alex Joseph laughed. "It's not rum." He slapped his cheeks. "It's aftershave. The ladies love it." He flashed a smile.

"Can we eat lunch at Caneel Bay?" Amelia asked

"Caneel Bay's a private resort. You can't just walk in for lunch. You got reservations?"

"No, we don't."

"Then I drop you off in Cruz Bay. It got places to eat there."

Minutes later, they were back in the small town of Cruz Bay. They tipped Alex Joseph, bade him good-bye, and watched a dozen enthusiastic young people with knapsacks and hiking boots climb into his vehicle. An empty launch reversed from the dock, while a hundred or more feet out in the bay, another waited to dock and discharge its full load of passengers.

"I need to eat," Grace said.

"Let's find a place, have lunch, shop, walk down by the beach," Hannah said. "Did you see those neat rowboats pulled up on shore?"

In an arcade of shops they found a pleasant restaurant with bamboo tables and chairs. A waiter, whose T-shirt advertised Cinnamon Bay, slipped between tables holding his tray high. At the far end of the long, narrow room stood a bar. A shaft of sunlight from a high open window fell across the counter. On the soft breeze came the sounds of the street: the patois of island voices, the blowing of shrill horns of the cars going by. Before long, they were sitting at a table eating sandwiches and drinking iced tea.

"After lunch I'm going to walk up to the Administrators' House on the point and take pictures. Then I'd like to wander about Cruz Bay and take a couple of rolls of film," Amelia said.

Grace held a pamphlet in her hand. "I picked this up at the counter when we came in. It shows where all the shops are. I'm going to the bookstore."

"I'll go with you," Hannah said. "I'd like to buy a book on the history of the islands."

Amelia ate rapidly, then sat jiggling her leg and tapping the table with her fingers.

"Why don't you just go on and take your pictures," Hannah said. "We'll get the check. Meet you back on the ship."

"Thanks. I'll do that." Amelia retrieved her camera bag from the empty chair, slung it across one shoulder, and headed for the entrance. The bag weighted her shoulder, pulling it down.

"She's so trim and neat, she even looks good lopsided," Grace said.

Amelia turned and waved. They waved back.

"She's a trifle too flip sometimes. She makes me nervous," Hannah said. "Haven't you noticed? She's been agitated from the moment Roger arrived in Covington."

Grace nodded. "I hoped the trip would relax her."

"Seems to have had the opposite effect. All that partying, dancing with any man who can stand upright."

Grace handed Hannah the pamphlet. "Take a look. Maybe there's something you want to get. Bay rum?"

"Bay rum aftershave might make a nice gift," Hannah replied.

"Grace," Hannah called.

Grace sat under an awning on the deck outside the bookstore reading a magazine. She looked up. Hannah stood in the doorway, her sensible oxfords speckled with dust kicked up by tires on their tour, a red cap with a wide brim covering her hair. She hugged a bookstore bag close to her chest and looked like a child who had hoodwinked her parents. Grace laughed.

Hannah ambled over and sank into a chair opposite her friend. "Where does time go? It's two hours since we came in here."

"Find what you wanted?" Grace asked. While she waited for Hannah, she had enjoyed the play of light and shadows cast by the broad leaves of banana trees, and the colorful leaves of potted crotons planted in a long trough on the deck. Tiny lizards scurrying along the railing near her hand had also captured her attention. Occasionally one stopped and seemed to be waiting for her to notice it before it scurried away.

"Several books on the islands." Hannah tugged a book from the bag and flipped through the pages. "Seems that the Moravians were the first Christians to establish a church on this island. In Saint Thomas and Saint Croix, Lutherans, Episcopalians, and other denominations were there first, and they looked down on the Moravians because the missionaries worked with their hands, just like the slaves. They taught the slaves to read and taught them trades. They didn't just convert them, they created a generation of skilled craftspeople, masons, sail makers, carpenters, blacksmiths to name a few, and the women learned to make baskets, straw hats, and mats for sale."

She slipped the book into the bag and pulled out another. "I found a book of superstitions. In the old times, when someone died they tied a string around the big toe to prevent the body from turning into a jumbie."

"What's a jumbie?" Grace remembered the word from the name of Tyler's book.

"A ghost, I think. Not good."

Hannah turned a page of the slim book with a red cover. "It says here that in olden days when a hurricane was coming, mothers would tie strips of white cloth around their children's heads, so if the kids were blown away, they could find them more easily."

Grace grimaced. "Imagine having your child blow away."

"And I've learned that in the thirties the industries on Saint John were burning wood for charcoal, which they sold in Saint Thomas, and making bay oil, also sent to Saint Thomas to be used in making bay rum." She rummaged in her deep bag and pulled out a bottle wrapped in decorative woven straw packaging. "This is bay rum." The bottle was about seven inches high and square. A small red ribbon tied in a bow decorated its neck where the straw wrapping stopped. "Here, smell my hand. The saleswoman rubbed some on."

The smell of bay rum was unfamiliar, tangy, and pleasant to Grace. "I'll get a bottle for Bob and one for Roger. Maybe I should go back and pick up a bottle for Amelia to give to Mike."

"Why? If she wants it she can get it herself," Hannah said.

"You're really annoyed with Amelia, aren't you?"

"Yes, I am. She's a fool. And we're living in too close quarters on that ship," Hannah said.

Grace considered that for a moment. "Maybe you're right. I'll get the bottle for Amelia, and if she doesn't want to give it to Mike, I'll give Bob two bottles."

That done, they strolled along the sandy shore to the tumble of rocks below the promontory on which the Administrator's House sat. Amelia was nowhere in sight. Three small island boys clambered barefoot over the rocks, stopping periodically to squat and examine something the ladies could not see. The children wore no shirts, and their dark backs glistened with perspiration in the sunshine.

"Heaven, but those rocks look jagged and mean. That plus the heat would cut and burn their feet," Grace said.

"Probably used to it. Hard as leather," Hannah said.

A boy looked up, grinned, and waved.

"What you looking for?" Grace called.

"Sea eggs," the child replied.

"What are sea eggs?" Grace asked.

A short, heavyset man with a fishing rod and bucket came up be-hind them. "A sea egg is a sea urchin." He pointed into the shallow, clear water. "That's a sea egg, or urchin. You step on one of them, it's hell to get the prickles out."

Somewhere in size between a baseball and a golf ball, the round, black creature was protected with ominous spines that swayed with the tide on the sandy bottom.

Hooting and yelling, the children joined the adults. The tallest boy carried a stick with a sharp point. They pointed to the sea egg and jabbered so fast that Grace could not understand a word they said. Moments later, the oldest boy stepped carefully into the water and stood immobile.

"He's waiting for the sand to settle," the fisherman said. "He has to be able to see the sea urchin. Once he strikes, he'll stir up the water. If he misses, he could step on it and get badly hurt."

"My granny does use hot candle wax to draw out de spines them," the smallest boy said.

Grace repressed the desire to pull out her handkerchief and wipe away the sweat that glistened on his sweet brown face, but the child squatted, swooped up handfuls of water, and doused his face and shoulders. His friend followed his lead, and soon the boys on shore were as wet as the one in the water.

Sitting on a large rock, the two women and the man watched the boy in the water. He stood absolutely still as he waited for the sand to settle. Then he raised the wooden spear and stabbed. Moments later he lifted the ugly black thing impaled on its tip high into the air. Black spines quivered and glistened in the sunshine. Screaming with pleasure, the boys on shore leaped from one rock to another and clapped their hands.

"What will they do with it?" Grace asked the fisherman.

The man gathered up his pail and fishing rod. He shrugged. "I don't know. I doubt they're edible."

"We does chop them up," the victorious killer of the sea egg said as he stepped from the sea onto a rock.

"Why?" Hannah asked.

"For fun, for fun." The smaller boys doubled over in laughter.

The fisherman spoke. "Tourists sometimes walk barefoot in the water along these rocks. They don't know about sea urchins, and they can get hurt. Every sea egg the kids kill makes it that much safer." He tipped his cap. "Got to be off now. Afternoon, ladies."

Hannah and Grace trudged back to the launch.

"It's so good to be off my feet," Grace said as she sat down.

Hannah wiped her brow. "I'm hot and tired."

Ten minutes later, their bags dangling at their sides, they climbed up the steps onto the ship, found the elevator, ascended to their deck, and plodded down the corridor to their suite.

Amelia had returned earlier and was stretched out on the couch that became her bed at night. Her eyes were closed, her hands clasped over her chest. Amelia opened her eyes, smiled, and stretched her arms over her head.

"You look smug. Did you find some man to walk about with and carry your camera bag?" Hannah asked before she disappeared into the bathroom. Immediately, they heard the sound of water running. Hannah hummed something without a melody.

"Why does she say things like that?" Amelia asked. "She drives me crazy. I was alone all the time."

"You needn't explain to me," Grace said.

"I shot ten rolls of film, some in color, some in black-and-white. Once you get behind those new buildings, there are dozens of charming little wooden houses, mostly white, but some painted blue or pink, all with hurricane shutters. People grow flowers in pots on their steps and porches, and one nice woman told me that the bushes in the yards are pigeon peas, and they have papaya, banana, and mango trees. I had to stop at a photo shop for a filter. The sun's so bright."

Hannah stepped from the bathroom, drying her face with a towel.

"So much time spent photographing on your holiday," Hannah said.

"Do I criticize your hours at those slot machines?" Amelia propped up on her elbows and eyed Hannah. "I had no idea you liked to gamble."

"And so what if I do?" Hannah said.

"Bet you're losing money," Amelia said.

"I'll break even by the time we get back to Florida."

"That's ridiculous. No one wins at those one-armed bandits," Amelia said.

"I did, the first night." Hannah looked at Amelia with annoyance.

"Stop it, you two," Grace said. "Stop snapping at one another. Maybe we're overtired, all of us, and we need some space. Hannah, you use our bedroom, and I'll go sit outside. Amelia, stay where you are. Read." Grace tossed Amelia her new magazine.

"*Style?* You bought *Style* magazine?"

"Why not? We could all improve in some area of our lives." Grace headed for the sliding glass door out to the balcony. "Now, you two, do not talk to one another."

Amelia snorted, rose, and went into the bathroom. The water splashed on the plastic floor of the shower stall.

Hannah threw herself on her bed.

Grace slipped onto the balcony, leaned against the rail, and was again amazed and awed by the beauty of her surroundings. In all directions, islands dotted the sea. *Oh, day, don't end!* she wanted to cry out. *I'll come back. I'll bring Bob.* Slowly the ship moved away from St. John and across The Graveyard, which, with the coming of evening, was smooth as glass.

Later, after dinner and after Amelia had flitted off for an evening of dancing, Grace and Hannah returned to the suite. Intending to slip into her pajamas and robe, Grace began to unbutton her blouse. She asked, "You going to the casino, Hannah?"

"Not tonight. Why don't you change into something comfortable, and we'll go up on deck and people-watch for a while."

"That sounds nice. I'd like that," Grace said. She rebuttoned her blouse. "I'm fine as I am."

"Bring a sweater," Hannah said. "It's windy out there, and it can get chilly."

The deck served as a promenade for people of all ages. Some strolled or ambled, some hurried along, while others paused at the rail to chat or observe the star-filled sky or stare into the ebony sea. Two women, chatting busily, moved past their lounge chairs.

Grace poked Hannah's arm. "Look. Doesn't that woman remind you of Olive Pruitt? The one in the long green skirt."

"My goodness, she certainly does."

"Gives me the willies just to think about Olive and those days and months living in her home in Branston," Grace said. "I remember how horribly depressed I was when I got there. I honestly thought I'd curl up in a ball and die after Roger deposited my suitcases and boxes in my room and drove away."

"When I first got there, before you and Amelia came, I thought Olive didn't like me," Hannah said. "I wanted to pack back up and leave." She shrugged. "And go where? It was close to my old plant store and Miranda. After you came, and then Amelia, it became obvious that Olive was the same with everyone."

"She didn't make any of us feel welcome," Grace replied. "I wonder if she hated having people living in her house? Maybe she did it for the money? Maybe that's how she was able to keep her home."

"I wonder how long the average boarder stayed with her. I feel sorry for the women who took our places, whoever they are. Remember how awful Olive's food was? She hated making salads," Hannah said.

"And you insisted on having a salad with nearly every meal."

"You were itching to cook, and she wouldn't let you into her kitchen except to eat her boring meals," Hannah said.

As the woman and her companion strolled back along the deck, the Olive look-alike returned their curious glances with a haughty stare.

"She must think we're so rude," Grace said.

"Grace, can you imagine what our lives would be like today if we were still at Olive's place?"

"It's too awful to think about, too depressing." Grace smiled. "We were courageous, weren't we, picking up like that, almost strangers, and moving to Covington?"

"Desperate circumstances call for desperate measures," Hannah said. "But yes, it was rather a risk. We knew each other, but not well. I didn't know Amelia. Did you think you knew her?"

"No. She was elegant and very private, never talked about her past."

"God bless genealogy and the computer. Without it, that relative of hers, Arthur Furrier, would never have found her and left her the farmhouse."

"Bless Cousin Arthur, and Amelia, too. She's really quite generous. After all, she didn't have to change the deed, add our names to it," Grace said.

"I feel like a cad snapping at her all the time, but she does annoy the devil out of me sometimes," Hannah said. "More so on this trip than at home."

"It's too-close quarters in the suite, I think," Grace said. "There's a kind of fey, whimsical quality to Amelia. Sometimes she's very present—you know, solid, sure, effective—and other times, well, she's unpredictable, and you're not sure she's hearing you or if you can depend on her." Grace's sigh was carried away by the wind. "I guess it's a matter of simply taking her as she is and not expecting her to be different."

"I have more trouble with that than you do, obviously," Hannah said. "And I, of all people, ought to be more generous of spirit. Amelia was wonderful to my Laura."

Grace's mind lingered on the past. "Remember when Amelia was in the hospital, and you and Olive insisted I go into her room and hunt for a letter or anything with the name of a relative or friend who we could contact if Amelia died? I felt like a criminal opening her bedroom door. I recall that when I stepped inside, I was thinking how pristine everything was, all white and lacy, Amelia's slippers under the bed, everything in place. Too refined and clean and perfect to touch."

"Arthur Furrier's letters to Amelia provided more information about her life than she ever did," Hannah said.

"I thought the earth would open and swallow me when I pried into her dresser drawers and found those letters, and then read them," said Grace.

"We had to do it. What if she had died?"

"That's what you and Olive said, but I thought we could have searched her things, well, afterward, if she died," Grace replied.

Hannah ran her hand along the smooth surface of the arm of the chair. "No harm was done. You confessed to Amelia. She forgave you. She even apologized for not telling us about herself," Hannah said.

The women fell silent. Grace pulled her sweater tighter across her chest. When she spoke, it was with a sense of wonder mixed with pride. "We've come so far, especially me, since we moved to Covington. I'd still be driving thirty-five miles an hour. I'd never have had the courage to date a man, much less say no to a marriage proposal. On the other hand, if a man had come along and pursued me back then, marriage probably would have seemed the way out of Olive's place." The wind picked up and seemed to harmonize with the hum of human voices and the ongoing rush and swish of ocean.

It's nice, Hannah thought, not having to talk, just sitting together, people-watching.

After a time, Grace spoke. "I'd never have gained so much self-confidence or met so many wonderful people, like Lurina, and Brenda, and Bob and his family. I would never have felt confident enough to do something like fight for Lucy. I could never have done any of it without you and Amelia, but especially you, Hannah."

"You were always a strong woman. It's just that your potential was waiting to sprout like a seed waits for water." Hannah laughed lightly.

They fell silent again, until Hannah said, "I've grown, too. I'm not as guarded as I used to be or as distrustful of people. You've taught me about honest friendship." She reached over and squeezed Grace's fingers. "I do cherish our friendship."

"So do I."

"You're the first real friend I ever had, did you know that?" Hannah asked.

"Why, goodness, no. I assumed you'd had many friends. You're so sure of yourself, and such a good friend to me."

"It's easy to be your friend, Grace."

A waiter came by. "Can I get you ladies anything?"

Grace smiled up at him. "Why, yes. I'd like a fruit punch."

"A sherry for me," Hannah said. The waiter departed, and she turned to Grace. "We'll toast ourselves and our accomplishments. Tomorrow, finally, I'll tackle that diary."

10

AN END TO IT

Hannah turned the pages of Marion's diary. Rising as if embossed onto the stark white paper, the letters of each word harked back to years of penmanship classes. There was no mistaking an *i* for an *e*, an *a* for an *o*. *T*'s were firmly crossed and *L*'s clearly looped. Line by line, word for word, Hannah reread the woman's innermost thoughts, for long after Dan was gone, Marion had continued to pen her rage.

I hate her, that awful woman. Her presence in my hometown is an affront to me and my children. Why didn't they both die? Then it would really be over for me. Not only is Dan gone, but she's a constant reminder of his infidelity and a threat that someone might find out. Everyone in this town thinks he was such a saint. A saint—that's a joke. I hate him.

In another entry, Marion wrote:

I must know someone who can talk to that chiropractor she works for, someone with influence who can put a bug in his bonnet, cause him to question her competence, anything that would lead to his firing that woman.

Some of the entries were dated, others not. Hannah noticed large gaps of time between many of them, especially toward the end:

I saw that Hannah woman yesterday. I drove to the dune, and there she was, sitting by the water, staring out at nothing, same as a year ago. Dan's been dead that long, and I still detest that woman. I wish she'd disappear so I could get on with my life and forget about her, about them. You never know. She could tell people. I'd deny it, of course, but there'd be the embarrassment. I just wish she would go away, far away, and soon.

Hannah's cheeks burned as if on fire. Her hands trembled as she turned the pages. That first long, hot summer when she had struggled to sleep, struggled to rise, struggled through each day; those gut-wrenchingly lonely summer evenings when she mourned Dan on the shore of the lake where he had been killed. Filled with venom, Marion had watched from her car on the bluff above. Had she known, Hannah would have packed her few belongings and given Dan's wife her wish. She would have fled the town. Why, Hannah wondered, had Alice sent the diary? Had she been so stunned, so appalled that, following in her grandmother's footsteps, she had decided to strike out, to punish an unknown woman?

Sitting on the balcony alone—Grace and Amelia were off exploring the Old City of San Juan in Puerto Rico—Hannah closed her eyes. Immediately, flashes of Dan's face appeared. It was his eyes she remembered most clearly, the way they brimmed with regret each time he had to part from her after a night, an afternoon, a stolen hour together at midday. They had not always made love. Often they talked or walked the shore of the lake or shared a picnic in a park in a nearby town. Theirs had been a true meeting of minds, shared humor, and common sympathies. They enjoyed local politics, foreign movies, and slow dancing, and he had become interested in her hobby, gardening. He comforted Hannah when she worried about Laura traipsing about the country, rarely in contact with her mother or even her sister, Miranda.

"She's sowing her oats," he had said. "If she's half the woman you are, sweetheart, she'll land on her feet. She'll be fine." He'd been right, of course.

When Dan held her close, she had felt safe. Marion did not exist.

Hannah forced the memories away and turned another page. She was nearly at the end of the diary, and the writing turned to issues of adjusting to life as a widow:

I thought I'd be more sought after, asked out, but maybe it's too soon. My mother tells me a year is considered appropriate. I did catch Judge Vinton looking at me in church over his prayer book last Sunday. Judge Vinton's not my type, and he's too old. Where will I meet someone? There are so few "right" men in this town. Mother says I'm too fussy, too judgmental. Why wouldn't I be? What does Mother know? She and Daddy always got on well, or did it only seem that way? My daughters think their father and I were the perfect couple. That's a joke! Still, I hate walking into the club without a man to escort me.

In another entry, Marion again bemoaned her situation:

It's creepy living alone in this big house. Louise suggested that I hire a live-in housekeeper. Someone to talk to, Louise said. As if I'd sit around and chat with a housekeeper. No one really understands me or how my life has changed.

"I don't need to be reading any of this," Hannah said aloud. She slammed the book shut, and as she did so, her eyes fell on her hands. Rivers of skin ran between mounded flesh, and a network of wrinkles crisscrossed the valleys between the mounds. Hannah squeezed her hand into a fist and bent her wrist until the skin across the top grew smooth and taut. "Like it used to be," she muttered. Then she unbent her wrist and spilled wrinkles. "Old," she said.

Last November, when Max had surprised her with a seventy-fifth birthday party, she had not felt old. She had good friends, a good life, and good health. Teaching children at Caster Elementary about gardening and the environment sparked her creativity. Her work at Bella's Park challenged and satisfied her, and she felt alive and vital. So much to do and no thought of age, until now. Old, she had always believed, was in the mind. But was it really? Who could deny sagging belly and breasts, a wrinkled neck and hands? Suddenly, a great weariness dropped over Hannah.

She closed her eyes. She could hear Dan's hearty laughter. She had shared a silly happening with him. She could not recall what it was, only that they had laughed until their sides ached before they collapsed against one another. They had held one another, and in time they had made love.

Enough! Hannah pushed up from her seat, took two long strides to the rail, lifted the diary high above her head, and with both hands pitched it into the wind. The brown leather journal flew open. It rode the wind for a moment before plummeting to the ocean, where it floated for a second before sinking. Relief, regret, and relief again swept over Hannah. Tears spilled down her cheeks, and for a change she let them come.

Weary but excited, Amelia and Grace returned from their day in Old San Juan, Puerto Rico. Hannah rested on her bed, watching reruns of *Hogan's Heroes* on TV. She had spent the afternoon watching back-to-back reruns of *All in the Family, The Beverly Hillbillies, M*A*S*H,* and *The Golden Girls*. They didn't look alike, but there was something about Dorothy on *The Golden Girls* that reminded her of herself—maybe Dorothy's height, or her sense of responsibility, or her inability to engage in casual relationships with men.

"I had a heyday," Amelia said as she flopped onto the foot of Grace's bed. "The buildings painted such wonderful colors—rust, gold, rose, yellow—and the life on the streets of the Old City, those marvelous Spanish faces."

"Amelia's amazing—what she can get people to do!" Grace said. "I was sure someone was going to clobber her or tear her camera away from her and stomp on it. She approached people, and next thing I knew they were posing for her, calling to their friends or kids to get into the picture. All this without speaking a word of Spanish."

Amelia's laugh was lighthearted. She waved her hands. "I use sign language. I act helpless. They take pity on me." She looked at Grace. "What about that nice taxi man, Antonio, who took us to the Fortress of San Cristóbal? He was helpful, wasn't he?"

Grace nodded. "The fortress was massive," she said to Hannah. "It sits on a point of land overlooking the harbor. The guidebook said that in its day the fort deterred pirates and ships of other colonial powers from entering the harbor. We watched a cruise ship pass. Passengers on the deck waved."

"In Old San Juan, we had lunch at hotel El Convento," Amelia said. "It had been a convent. You can tell. It's quite stark, really, but attractive. Terra-cotta walls and floors, and our driver, Antonio, was charming. He had the cutest accent. He took us past an exclusive club, Cascada Esposia. Only people of pure Spanish heritage can be members, sort of like the DAR, and we saw La Fortaleza, the governor's mansion. It's on a hill right in the city."

"It was so noisy in the Old City, I couldn't wait to leave it. Crowded streets, chaotic traffic." Grace removed her shoes, shirt, and skirt, and slipped into her robe and slippers. She sat on a chair and rubbed the soles of her feet and toes. "I'm pooped."

"I could have gone on and on," Amelia said. "Splendid city, a different world. Each island's so different and I love them all. I could become a beachcomber and spend a month taking pictures and, of course, lying on the beach. Antonio took us by one of the big resort hotels. We had drinks under an umbrella on the beach."

"You won't believe this, Hannah," Grace said, "but Amelia shot pictures of a fat man and fat woman bending over to pick up shells."

"Their rear ends looked so funny sticking up in the air like that."

Grace stretched her arms over her head. "I was afraid they'd see her and get really mad."

"Nonsense." Amelia flicked her hand at Grace. "They were so intent on whatever was in the sand, they hadn't a clue I was photographing them. It'll be a great picture, wait and see." Amelia laughed, picked up her camera bag, removed a dozen or so rolls of film, and stacked them on a dresser. "I'm going to take these to the photo store right this minute."

"Now?" Hannah asked

"*Oui.* That's what 'right now' means, *mon ami.*"

"Where do you get all that energy?" Hannah asked.

"From my grandmother. She had boundless energy, could shop all day and dance all night even when she was eighty-years-old." With a reach of her hand, Amelia swept the film into a plastic bag and departed.

"No wonder you're pooped trailing about after Amelia all day. She's so . . ." Hannah shrugged. "So flighty."

Grace looked at Hannah quizzically. "There's nothing flighty about Amelia when she works. She's purposeful, earnest, and dedicated to her work, and you better not interrupt her when she's doing it."

"Well, at least she's focused on something," Hannah said.

"Maybe that's why she's so good at it." Grace lay down on her bed and shoved two pillows under her feet. "I miss my own bed." She looked at Hannah. "So tell me, what have you done today?"

"I reread the diary. I cried. Then I flung it overboard. I hate reliving a past I thought I'd buried." Hannah rested a hand on her heart. "It still hurts, Grace. I can't go through anything like that again. I can't marry Max. Truth is, I've fought my attraction to him from the beginning. I keep things distant, impersonal, and light always. If I marry him, even if he says I'd have no 'conjugal responsibilities,' as he puts it, maybe I'd want to—and then it gets even more complicated." She looked away.

Hannah seriously in love, in lust, even, was a concept Grace was not prepared for. "You love Max, or did?"

"I don't love him, I just told you. I keep that place in my heart and head slammed shut. Especially now."

The sliding glass door stood slightly ajar, and the sea air flowed in fresh and cool. From the balcony adjoining theirs came a child's high-pitched scream and a woman's raised voice calling, "Peter. Peter. Get back from that railing." Then a child began to wail and a door closed hard.

Hannah grimaced and closed their glass door.

"Would it be so bad if you had sex with him? It's kind of nice at our age—slower, more relaxing. Nice," Grace said.

Hannah's shoulders stiffened. She shook her head. "No. I don't want to do that or to love any man ever again."

"So what do you want to do?"

"Not marry him. Go on as we are."

"Is Max okay with that, do you think?" Grace asked. She knew Hannah well enough not to argue with her or try to dissuade her from a course of action.

"Don't care what he thinks." Hannah's face was set, her eyes determined.

Grace raised both hands. "Okay. It's your life. You'll do what you want, no matter what I say."

"What do you mean?"

"I mean you're a stubborn old codger, and nothing I say will matter."

Hannah shoved the backs of her hands at Grace. "*Old* is right: See the wrinkles? I am old, and I won't pretend to be forty and coy or whatever. I can't be cutsie or flirtatious. I won't act like a silly fool the way Amelia did with Lance, the way she's behaving right now with the men on this ship."

"Who says you have to be anything but yourself? Am I cutsie with Bob?"

"Sometimes."

"What the devil is cutsie, anyhow?" Grace asked. She giggled.

Hannah stared at her. "Cutsie? It's a funny word isn't it? Cutsie, cutsie." They began to laugh, then, in the incoherent, silly way of teenagers.

When they regained their composure and wiped their eyes, Grace said, "I don't know what to tell you, Hannah. Do you think Dan would want you to remember your time together with such anguish? Yours was a special love, a marvelous experience that not every woman is privileged to have. Have you ever considered that you may be hanging on to guilt over an affair with a married man, and that the diary refueled those feelings, as well as the love and your loss?"

Hannah studied Grace, then turned and stared out the large glass door. Beyond, a heavy bank of gray clouds clumped above the railing. She said, "I hate it when you're right. I hadn't realized it, but maybe I do feel guilty. I used to, then, but Dan would reassure me. 'If there were anything between Marion and myself, I wouldn't be here,' he'd say."

"Why punish yourself, or Max, at this stage of your life?"

"So, you're telling me to marry Max?" Hannah wrapped her arms around her shoulders.

Grace's face was flat with exhaustion and very pale. "I'd never presume to do that. Besides, just as you worried I'd go off and live with Bob, I worry you'll move across the street." In the silence that followed, Grace considered telling Hannah about her experience that first night on the ship, but she found herself tongue-tied, unable to share her sense of having been connected to all things with her closest friend. How did one talk about the ineffable, approach a topic so important and yet so fragile?

The moment passed.

"Never. I am not moving from our home." Hannah's brow furrowed. She paced the suite, reopened the glass door a few inches, closed it, stooped and switched on a bedside light, then switched it off. "I'm a wreck," she said. "Don't need all this crap, not now, not ever."

"You certainly don't," Grace said. "Now that the diary's gone, try to relax and not think about it for the rest of this trip."

"Can I, I wonder? It's hard to shake my mind free of Dan since that whole period of my life's been forced open by that diary."

"Is that why you've been gambling?"

Hannah shrugged. "Maybe. I like it, but it's costly."

That night rain hammered their balcony. Darts of lightning sliced through the crease where the curtains met, and wind whipped and rattled the glass doors. A storm at sea. Hannah rose from bed and went to the curtain. She would have liked to step outside, to stand in her pajamas in the rain, to shout her anger at Alice for sending the diary, to weep. Thunder came, and jagged lightning tore across the sky. Quickly, Hannah stepped away from the doors. The great ship did not roll or toss. She returned to bed and lay awake for a long time. She must calm herself, must bury whatever feelings she might have had for Max.

11

THE TROUBLES OF
LUCY BANKS

Home seemed a treasure. Welcoming lights gleamed from the front porch, the kitchen, and the living room when their cab from the airport pulled into the driveway of the farmhouse on Cove Road. Fog grounded them for hours in Atlanta, and Grace had phoned Bob.

"We haven't a clue when we'll leave Atlanta. Don't come to the Asheville airport. We'll take a cab home."

"You sure? Max and I don't mind hanging around the airport."

"That's silly. It could be hours. Maybe we'll have to stay overnight in Atlanta."

"Well, okay. Can't wait to see you, honey," he'd replied.

Four hours later, she had phoned him prior to boarding the plane. "We're on our way. We'll get a cab from the airport—just you be home to greet us."

"We'll be here, and darn glad to see you."

Now, seeing the lights, Grace felt warm inside and happy and eager to see Bob. He's inside waiting for me, she thought, and smiled.

The front door opened. Bob, wearing no coat, dashed out, followed by the entire Richardson clan except Melissa—Emily, Russell, Tyler—and behind them Max, and moving at a slower pace, Mike and Roger. Grace had the oddest feeling that something was amiss: Was it the way Mike and Roger hung back?

Tyler raced toward her, a worried frown on his face, and flung himself at Grace, hugged her tightly, and hung on. She returned his hug and kissed his cheek.

"Tyler, Granny Grace must be very tired," Bob said, putting his hand on Tyler's shoulder. Tyler stepped back. "She's had a long trip." Bob enfolded Grace in his arms and kissed her. "I missed you, honey." His aftershave, warm and fruity, warmed her.

Amid the confusion of hugs and voices raised in welcome, suitcases emerged from the taxi's trunk and were carried into the house. The cabdriver waited impatiently to be paid. Max took care of that.

The short distance from cab to porch seemed interminable to Grace. Winter cold, happily forgotten during a week of warmth and sunshine, nipped at her nose and fingertips, slid along her neckline, and burrowed through her coat. Never far from her side, Tyler took Grace's hand when it dangled free. Was something wrong, she wondered? Had he failed an exam? Had he been hurt playing basketball?

Although it was after 9:30 P.M., Bob waved them all to the dining room to a festive table set with a variety of cold cuts and salads. Balloons rose above a cake in the center, and a banner suspended over the door between the dining room and kitchen read WELCOME HOME.

Amelia seated herself across from Mike and Roger. Usually she sat alongside Mike. Her heart sank. It was obvious to her that they were a couple now. She recognized the small gestures and intimate glances that passed between them. And why not? Charles was dead. Roger was free, and their mutual attraction was not new.

For a moment Amelia considered how her life would be affected by this turn of events. Loneliness and the sense of being abandoned punched her ego and settled into a pit in her stomach. Once again she had discovered that she could not depend on anything or anyone. Things changed. People changed. She forced small talk and smiled, but jealousy nagged at her, and underneath it all, the ache of loss.

Hannah would have preferred a quiet evening, a hot bath, and bed and time to think, but she smiled at Max when he pulled out a chair for her. "Thank you. This was so good of you all," she said.

The table was crowded, chairs pulled close, and Hannah, aware of the heat of Max's arm and shoulder alongside hers, moved slightly away so as not to touch him. When their arms did brush each other's, she felt her resolve not to marry him waver. Like a mantra, she said silently, *I will not allow myself to love anyone and be hurt ever again.* She had repeated this so often since receiving the diary that it was impossible now to relax with Max, and she avoided the slightest contact of their fingers or hands as they passed rolls, or butter, or platters of cold cuts. Tomorrow, when they were alone at work, she would talk to him, explain about Dan, about the diary. Now she needed to get through dinner and off to bed, for a good night's sleep. I'll be totally honest with him tomorrow, she thought.

When Grace stepped into the dining room, she clapped her hands. "What a grand welcome home. So thoughtful of you. Thank you."

Tyler rushed to sit beside her. "Granny Grace, I've gotta talk to you."

Grace nodded and patted his hand, but with everyone talking at once and passing bowls and platters, she overlooked the urgency in his voice.

"We're calling it Celebration," Roger said. He was focused on Amelia.

"Calling what 'celebration'?" Grace asked.

"Mike and I are planning to open an event-planning business here, Mother. We're going to call it Celebration. Like the name?"

Grace felt caught between the pain in Amelia's eyes and Roger's enthusiasm. "It's a fine name," she said.

"A marvelous name," Max said. "Where will you open your display rooms?"

"Looks like Weaverville," Mike said. "We only thought of the name this afternoon." He looked at Amelia across the table. "And we'd like you to work with us."

Amelia, caught in the act of feeling flustered and resentful, flushed. "You want me to work with you?" Her gaze fastened on Roger.

"You're one of the most creative people I've ever met. Yes, we want you, if you'll have us," Roger said.

Amelia's mind raced. *Roger knows how I feel. He's extending an olive branch. Take it.* Stalling for time, she set down her fork and knife, picked up her glass, and sipped her wine. *No,* the stubborn, injured part of her psyche said. *I'm a photographer, not a party planner. My work is serious, not frivolous.* Her eyes locked with Mike's. He had told her just before the cruise that his doctor suggested he find another way of making a living, that all the bending, kneeling, and twisting involved in his photography irritated his knees.

Mike had said, "The doctor says my kneecaps don't fit right, and I better not kneel, squat, walk too many steps, or down slopes. Not walk slopes, in a place like this where it's mostly slopes." He had pursed his lips. "They've darn well complicated my life. I never should have gone to that old doctor in the first place."

"You were in pain. You could hardly walk," Amelia had reminded him.

"Well, darn it anyhow," he'd pouted, and slammed a picture frame on his desk on its face.

Now, across the table, Mike's eyebrows raised slightly in a way she recognized as meaning that he was pleased and expected a positive outcome from a print being developed or a shot he had taken, or a fine dinner placed before him in a French restaurant. The prospect of her life devoid of Mike, her only friend outside of Grace, and, well, sometimes Hannah, hurt. Amelia's heart plummeted. Why? Why did things have to change, and so fast? She absolutely, positively hated change.

In the few seconds it took for Amelia to weigh the pros and cons, she concluded that rather than be left out she would give their invitation a try. She set down the wineglass. "I'd like to be a part of Celebration. Thank you for asking me."

"Terrific," Mike said, and Roger's face lit with a wide grin that Amelia interpreted as relief.

Mike probably feels guilty, she thought, making arrangements for a new business and moving in with Roger while I was gone, without giving me time to adjust to the change.

Sitting next to Grace, Tyler tapped her hand. "Granny Grace, I gotta talk to you. It's important, about Lucy."

"What about Lucy?" Grace asked, turning from Emily. They had been speaking about Melissa, who was asleep upstairs.

"I think she's in bad trouble."

Lucy in trouble? Grace gave him her full attention. "What do you mean? What kind of trouble?"

"Well, you know, at school they've got all the computers in our lab blocked."

"Blocked? What does that mean?" Grace asked.

"Certain things, like chat rooms and games, are blocked off so students can't use them. It's like that in all the schools. But there was this one computer that all the kids knew about, and the teacher didn't. Lucy used a lot of her study hall time on it."

Grace asked, "And how was that computer different from the others, Tyler?"

"Some kid, a computer nerd, typed in some kind of a Web site, I think, or maybe a password, so he could download whatever programs he wanted. Then he showed other kids how to do it."

"Isn't there supposed to be a teacher in the computer lab?" Bob asked.

Russell's voice was stern. "There ought to be someone there at all times when the kids are in the room."

"There is, but one day our regular teacher, Miss Tucker, was out sick, and we had a substitute. Only she left early, and that's when Travis broke into the computer system."

"And Lucy used it?" Grace asked.

"Travis showed her how. Lots of other kids used it, too, but she did it the most."

"I see," Grace said, feeling frustrated because she did not really see.

"You didn't get involved in that, did you, son?" Russell asked.

"No way, Dad."

"I'm sorry to be so ignorant, Tyler, but what exactly is a chat room?" Grace asked.

"You're not ignorant, Granny Grace. You just don't have a computer. A chat room's a site where people write to each other."

Add *site* to the computer language she did not know. Grace nodded, but she felt lost at not making the connections she needed.

"You sign on with a fake name," Tyler said. "Like, I might type, 'This is Slugger. Anyone out there like boxing?' Then people interested in boxing might write back, and we'd chat by mail about it."

"Well, what's wrong with that?" Grace asked.

Russell answered. "Chat rooms are absolutely forbidden on school computers, as are sites that carry pornography and certain violent or racial games. They're blocked out." He shook his head. "But if you get some computer-savvy kid, like this Travis fellow, and he figures a way around the blocks, he can get into the computer as Tyler says he has."

Everyone at the table was listening now.

"Wouldn't your teacher know this was happening?" Hannah asked.

"If Miss Tucker had walked around the room every day, and paid attention to what every kid was working on, she'd have known a lot sooner," Tyler replied.

"Isn't that part of her job?" Grace asked. "Doesn't she have to do that?"

"Yeh, and she's done it now. Miss Tucker caught Lucy in a chat room, and she took the brunt of the blame."

"Didn't anyone tell your teacher it was Travis who unblocked the computer?" Grace asked.

Tyler shook his head. "Travis is a nephew of the principal. I guess everyone was scared to say he'd done it."

"I'm not sure I understand," Amelia said. "Why are chat rooms bad things? I was under the impression many people communicate via chat rooms. There are support groups for just about everything, I hear."

"There are also sites where not-so-nice guys pretend to be just another kid with problems and prey on a girl's sympathy," said Bob. "Kids this age are going through all kinds of adolescent stuff, Amelia. They're fair game to predators."

Tyler nodded. "That's what's happened to Lucy."

Grace felt her chest tighten. "Are you saying Lucy's been writing to some awful person?"

"I think so. Only Lucy believes that he's a poor orphan, and she's hooked right into him," Tyler said.

Bob reached over and rested his hand on Grace's. For once his gesture of support did not comfort her.

"Before Miss Tucker caught her, Lucy was on that computer every day for two weeks with this guy, Ringo. That's the name he uses," Tyler said.

Mike leaned across the table. "This doesn't sound good, Grace. You've gotta talk to that girl. She could get herself into big trouble."

Computers were as alien to Grace as many of the characters in the movie *Star Wars* had been. Now she wished she had taken the time to learn how to use a computer. Her anxiety mounting, she unwittingly squeezed Tyler's hand.

"Ouch! You're hurting me, Granny Grace."

"I'm sorry, Tyler."

He leaned in close. "I'm sorry I upset you. Your face is getting red."

"Yes, I know." She touched her hot cheeks with her palms. "It'll be all right. What else should I know?"

"Not much. Just that Lucy is all gaga about Ringo. You could see it in her face, the way her eyes lit up when she was writing to him or reading his replies, or talking about him."

"She talks to you about him?" Grace asked.

"Not anymore. She thinks one of us in the classroom betrayed her to Miss Tucker. I didn't, that's for sure. Maybe someone else did, but not me."

"What did they do or say to Lucy when they found out she was using a chat room?" Hannah asked.

Tyler shook his head. "I dunno. This happened last Friday, and I haven't seen Lucy since."

"Wait a minute. What about the other kids who used that computer?" Bob asked.

"No one's admitting it and Lucy won't squeal on them. I told her she ought to, after the way they've treated her, but she won't, so . . ." He pulled on Grace's arm. "Granny Grace, you gotta talk to Lucy. You gotta help her, or something real bad could happen to her. If she'll listen to anyone, she'll listen to you."

Everyone at the table had stopped eating. Hannah looked stunned. Amelia seemed both shocked and annoyed. Melissa had awakened, and Emily had left the table to go upstairs. Grace hoped she would not bring the child down. Melissa would insist on sitting on Grace's lap and would cling to her, and Grace's mind was far way. Her feelings kept shifting.

Primary was the awareness, and the fear it brought, that Lucy had been exposed to grave danger. Waves of anger swept over Grace: anger at Lucy for not coming to her—until she remembered she had been away—anger at that boy, Travis. He had interfered with the computer, broken the rules. Why wasn't he in big trouble? Or was he? Had Tyler said so? She couldn't remember. And there was the substitute. How dare that woman walk out of that classroom and leave those children unsupervised? Mingled with all of this was sheer confusion caused by a lack of understanding. Amelia's voice brought her back to the table and to those around her.

"Schools are getting to be scary places to send your kids, with all the shootings. Imagine, parents having to also worry about a computer at a school being dangerous," Amelia said.

"Grace will talk to Lucy," Hannah said. "She'll find out whatever's been going on, get her to stop this nonsense."

Tyler shook his head. "I sure hope so. She's real stuck on Ringo. She's in really big trouble with Miss Randall, the principal, now, but she's been in trouble at school since last year."

Grace's heart skipped a beat. "What kind of trouble has Lucy been in at school?"

"Kids tease, laugh at her. Her one friend, Mary Jean Holmes, is a creep," Tyler said.

"A creep?" Grace asked.

"Yeh. She's got pimples and her hair's stringy. No one likes her. She's a loner, like Lucy."

"No one likes Mary Jean because she's got acne and her hair's not styled?" Hannah asked.

"But you like Lucy, don't you, Tyler?" Grace asked.

Tyler flushed. "Well, sure I like her, but, well, we don't hang out together much."

His eyes are bright, Grace thought. He looks nearly feverish with the excitement he must surely feel at being the center of everyone's attention. He must like Lucy a lot to be so worried about her. Grace had recently watched half of a PBS television program about children in schools being shunned, teased, harassed, and even physically hurt by bullies. Appalled, she had switched to another channel. Now she wished she had not turned it off, that she was more savvy on the topic. Why hadn't Lucy said something about being bullied? Was she miserable? Is that why she had turned to a chat room and this Ringo? "Why do kids tease and laugh at Lucy?" Grace asked.

"For one thing, Lucy doesn't wear the right clothes," Tyler said.

"What are the right clothes?" Hannah asked.

He shrugged, then listed brands. "Buckle, Abercrombie and Fitch, American Eagle jeans. They cost, like, fifty or sixty dollars a pair. Her clothes come from Wal-Mart or Target. The other girls make fun of her."

"Why didn't she come to me? I would have bought her what she needed." Grace set her crumpled and knotted napkin on the table.

"And Lucy always rides the bus," Tyler continued.

"Don't most kids?" Hannah asked.

"It's one thing if you and your pals choose to ride the bus, another if you *have* to, and Lucy *has* to. Also, she doesn't bring her lunch—she eats yucky cafeteria food with Mary Jean. The girls tease her, and she gets furious. One time she threw a roll across the table at a girl and hit her near her eye."

"Oh, my goodness. That's terrible. Was the girl hurt?" Amelia asked.

"She screamed like she was, but her eye didn't swell or turn black and blue or anything. Lucy had detention for three weeks."

"I'm so upset," Grace said. "She didn't say one word to me or to any of us. Why?"

Max's voice hit the air like a hammer. "What matters here is this chat-room stuff. It's serious business. Once a girl gets taken in, the guy suggests they meet, and the girl often disappears."

"Disappears? What do you mean, disappears?" Grace had not carried the matter to its grave conclusion.

"You're so innocent, Grace," Hannah said. "Don't you listen to the news?"

"I do, but less and less, and when I do, I try not to think about it afterward."

"I don't watch the news at all anymore," Amelia said.

Grace fought back her tears and turned to Tyler. "I'll talk to Lucy, of course, but at the school who shall I speak to?"

"Probably talk to Miss Tucker first," Tyler said. "She's a lot nicer than Miss Randall."

"When's a good time for that?"

"She's always free at ten o'clock, and she's usually alone in the computer lab, room twelve on the first floor, near the gym."

"I'll call for an appointment and try to go see her tomorrow," Grace said.

* * *

Worry banishes sleep, and Grace spent endless hours creating scenarios for her talks first with Miss Tucker and then with Lucy. She hoped Lucy had not been suspended. She would explain to Lucy the dangers of what she was doing. Grace slapped her head lightly. That was stupid; Lucy would insist her situation was different, not at all like anything you read about in the newspapers or hear on television. Grace could demand that Lucy tell the police about Ringo. Would Lucy listen to her? If not, what then? What would work with a determined fourteen-year-old, who looked sixteen or seventeen? Under her covers, Grace shivered as a horrendous thought struck her. What if tomorrow, when she got to the middle school, Lucy had been suspended, and what if this tipped the scale and Lucy took off with Ringo? Oh, God, no.

Grace's heart pounded in her ears, a frightening physical phenomenon. She must get control of herself. Being this upset would surely affect her blood pressure and blood sugar. Grace lay on her back, legs slightly apart, arms wide at her sides, and breathed deeply. "Relax," she repeated again and again, to no avail.

Exhausted from a mere three hours' sleep, Grace staggered to the bathroom the next morning and into the shower. "Got to wash these cobwebs out of my brain," she muttered as she shivered beneath prickles of chilly water. Once dressed, she wandered downstairs, forgot the milk and nibbled at a bowl of dry cereal, then dumped most of it in the trash, grabbed her coat, and drove to Lucy's home.

The small clapboard house was devoid of activity, its faded gray walls dull in the early morning light. The old car Mrs. Banks drove was not in the makeshift metal carport. Annoyed at herself for not phoning immediately on rising, Grace turned around and drove to Pace Middle School. It was only nine o'clock. An hour to wait.

Grace entered the school unchallenged and wondered why there was no guard to stop and question her. Since Columbine, didn't all schools have guards at the doors and metal detectors? No one seemed to notice her as she wandered along the first-floor corridor. Grace moved past the entrance to the gym, heard the bounce of a basketball and cheers, then the sharp whistle of the coach, followed by low voices. When she found classroom 12, a glass window in the metal door allowed a glimpse into the room: four rows of computers, eight to a row. Boys and girls bent to their work over every keyboard. A young dark-haired woman moved slowly up and down each row.

A hard wooden bench in the hallway offered the only seating, and Grace sank down onto it to wait. After what seemed like hours, a jarring bell brought students pouring from the computer lab and the gym. They moved in clusters like sheep huddling together for the familiarity and safety of the group: four girls here, three boys there, book bags weighing down their shoulders, laughing, jabbing at one another's arms. A girl with much too much makeup and huge hoop earrings passed close to Grace, kicked Grace's foot, and kept going. No "I'm sorry"—nothing. Grace tucked her legs as far under the low bench as possible.

This wild display of haste and unconcern for others differed from the behavior of children at Caster Elementary, where she tutored third-graders. Was this typical of adolescents? Was it a lack of discipline at this school? A group of girls, jostling one another and giggling, hastened past her. Boys followed, pointing at the girls, laughing and teasing. One of the girls, a pretty brunette, turned and made a face at the boys. Grace wanted to give each boy and girl a good shaking. She wanted to say, "Walk, don't run. Be polite. Be kind."

Finally, when the rush seemed to be over, Lucy appeared in the hallway, unsmiling, her head downcast, her gait shuffling. "Lucy," Grace called.

The girl's head snapped up, and she looked around. She seemed dazed, as if her eyes weren't focusing, but when they lighted on Grace, she smiled, and her anxious look changed to happy. "Mrs. Grace. Oh, Mrs. Grace. You got home."

Grace stood and held out her arms. Lucy ran toward her. A tall, heavyset boy raced by, slamming into Lucy, sending her books, and almost sending Lucy, to the floor.

"Hey, you, come back here." Grace shook her fist, but the boy had turned the corner.

Grace bent to help Lucy retrieve her books. A photo slipped from a notebook. The face of the young man that filled the picture was movie-star handsome. In fact, Grace thought the picture came right out of some star-studded magazine. "Who's this?" she asked, handing it to Lucy.

Lucy reached for the picture and stuck it back into the pages of her notebook. "No one," she said.

"No one doesn't get tucked into a girl's notebook and guarded so well."

Lucy laughed a high-pitched, self-conscious laugh. "It's this guy I met. He's very nice." She looked away.

A large boy in shorts with thickly muscled, hairy legs, his gym bags slung over his shoulders, sauntered by, his arm about the shoulder of a blond girl with heavy makeup and a tank top so short that Grace could see the smooth young skin stretching from beneath her breasts to her waist. Tyler was right. Lucy, in her simple, plain blouse tucked into worn jeans, her face devoid of makeup, did not fit the mold of these students.

"I need to see you, Lucy—soon," Grace said. "What are you doing at noon? Can you leave the school grounds?"

Lucy shook her head vigorously. "Can't leave. Listen, Mrs. Grace. I gotta go now. I have a class. Talk to you later."

"Wait, Lucy . . ." But Lucy was gone.

Just then, a young woman with short curly hair and a high, wide brow opened the door of the computer lab and moved toward Grace. "Mrs. Singleton?"

Grace stood. "Yes, are you Miss Tucker?"

"I am. I got your message this morning. The computer room's empty now—let's talk in there, shall we?"

They stepped into the quiet room. Miss Tucker pulled out a chair at one of the computer tables and motioned Grace to another.

"You've come to talk about Lucy Banks. She tells me you're a surrogate grandmother to her?"

"Yes, I am, and yes, I have come to talk about her. Thank you for seeing me."

"You must find her quite a handful. Lucy's quite incorrigible."

"Incorrigible? Lucy? She's a sweet, dear girl."

"Well, not here—not with me, or her other teachers, or Miss Randall, our principal. Lucy's been in trouble of one kind or another since school started last fall."

Grace felt her throat tighten. "What kind of trouble, if I may ask?"

"Fights with other girls, rudeness to me and several of her teachers, general lack of cooperation. She came into middle school with good grades, but it's been a steady decline from Bs to Cs and Ds and now Fs. We've sent notes home, but her mother's never even called the school."

"You notified Mrs. Banks by sending notes home with Lucy?" Grace asked.

"That is the usual way. We send home a note with the child."

Grace straightened her shoulders and her eyes narrowed. "And the students give their parents these notes?"

Now it was Miss Tucker's turn to stiffen. "Miss Randall believes that students must assume responsibility for their behavior, and that starts with delivering these notes to their parents or guardians."

"It's rather a foolish assumption," Grace said, thinking that Lucy had probably never given her mother any of those notes.

"Foolish or not," Miss Tucker replied, "that's our school's policy."

Grace's mind raced as the anger inside her built steadily. Showing it would not help Lucy. "So what happens to Lucy now?"

"Her case will come up for review next week. Maybe she'll be suspended, maybe expelled." Miss Tucker shrugged.

"What would be your recommendation?" Grace had the wit to ask.

"It will hardly matter. The final decision rests with Miss Randall." Miss Tucker stood and looked at her watch. "I must be going. Thank you for coming in. If you'd like, I will let you know what decision is made."

Grace, summarily dismissed, left the school feeling bewildered at Miss Tucker's apparent lack of concern about one of her students, and the seeming hard-heartedness of the principal. Lucy was not by nature unruly or undisciplined. What had happened, and why hadn't Lucy come to her about any of this?

Grace started for home, then turned her car around and headed for Caster Elementary and the office of her friend and the principal, Brenda Tate.

"This is all hard to believe about that child," Brenda said when Grace had told her the story. "I'll call Francine Randall and talk to her about this."

"Would you, Brenda? I'd be so grateful. Lucy's a good girl, and I'm scared to death she's going to get into trouble with this Ringo."

Grace sat there twisting a ring on her finger. Finally, she asked,

"Isn't that principal responsible for the substitute who left that class-room unattended?"

"Yes, she is. But we don't know why the substitute left. I'll try to find out. This computer business is serious." Brenda punched a button on her phone, picked up the receiver, and dialed the middle school principal's office. Then she covered the receiver with her hand and turned to Grace. "Go on home, Grace. Try to relax. I'll see if I can get Francine before she leaves school this afternoon. I'll stop over on my way home and let you know whatever I find out."

"Bless you, Brenda," Grace said.

As Grace opened the door to leave, Brenda whispered, "Francine Randall's a stubborn and uncompromising woman."

At six o' clock, Brenda's car turned into the ladies' driveway.

Brenda slammed her purse onto a chair. "At best, I find Francine a difficult woman. But today she was absolutely maddening. First of all, she blames Lucy, said that Lucy's the one who used the Web site to break into the computer."

"It was some boy, a computer-savvy nerd, according to Tyler. He says Lucy wouldn't name names—but they ought to know, if she's failing school, that she hasn't the skills to break into a computer."

Brenda paced. "I don't know. You'd think it would warrant further investigation. I just know that Francine Randall's hell-bent on expelling Lucy." She turned on her heel and faced Grace. "And what's the matter with Lucy, having all that trouble at school and never coming to you or anyone? If she'd been honest and open with some adult, all this never would have happened."

"Not even the chat-room thing?"

"I don't know about that, but at least Lucy wouldn't be facing a principal who thinks she's incorrigible."

"I'll go and see Miss Randall," Grace said. "I'll tell her about Lucy."

"The woman's a tiger. She'll tear you to pieces."

"Goodness, Brenda. I've never seen you so upset."

Brenda heaved a sigh and flopped into the chair, crushing her purse, which she then retrieved from under her. "God knows when I've been this angry."

"What can Miss Randall do to me? I'm going to make an appointment and go talk to her. Lucy shouldn't have used the chat room, but I don't want to see Lucy expelled."

"Good luck, Grace." Abruptly, Brenda stood. "I have to go home, take a hot bath, and calm down. Let's talk later."

Grace walked her to the door and down the porch steps to her car, then waved as Brenda drove away. She stood there watching until Brenda's car turned into her driveway, then she went inside, heavy-hearted. And her head ached, too.

Brenda's warning proved correct. Francine Randall, with her close-cropped dark hair, had towered over Grace when they greeted each other. Now she sat unsmiling behind her desk, a huge piece of walnut furniture. Her tailored business suit added to her severe, masculine, uncompromising appearance.

Misss Randall waved her arm, and Grace sank into a stiff-backed, armless chair and stared at the woman across the expanse of wood. Francine Randall set two files to the side and ran her palms across her desk calendar, as if she were brushing away crumbs at a dinner table. She squeezed her hands together, and looked coldly at Grace. "We have thirteen hundred children in this school, Mrs. Singleton. I cannot be expected to be continually annoyed by a child who has been nothing but trouble since September last year."

Grace felt immediately angered and yet intimidated. "I realize you are a very busy woman . . ."

"What is it you want, Mrs. Singleton?"

Grace felt unnerved. "I wonder if you are aware that the computer was tampered with by a boy named Travis?"

Francine leaned forward. She fixed cold eyes on Grace. "Just what is your relationship to Lucy?"

"Friend. Mentor. I tutored Lucy in elementary school, and I've been involved with the family from before her father's death a few years ago."

"Then why don't you know that Lucy Banks has been in trouble since day one?"

"You see, our home burned down last year and, well, I haven't spent as much time with Lucy this school year as I would have liked." This admission embarrassed Grace. Here she sat facing a female Torquemada, and she could hardly collect her thoughts.

Down the hall, a door slammed. Outside the office, footsteps hurried along the corridor. The principal's eyes turned to the door. Her lips tightened. Grace had the idea that if she were not in the room, Miss Randall would be out in the hall shouting for silence. She looked from the door to Grace. "Lucy Banks is a peculiar child."

"What do you mean, peculiar?" Grace asked.

"God knows what's going on in that home." Miss Randall made a noise rather like a snort. "These people without means who breed like rabbits—their children are often the most troubled."

The hair rose on the back of Grace's neck and she looked Francine Randall in the eye. This was no time to shrink away. She must stand up to this woman. "I don't agree with you. Children from wealthy, supposedly 'fine' homes can be quite troubled as well. Lucy's mother is a good woman. She loves her children, and she tries hard." Why were they talking about the lack of merit of Lucy's family rather than the computer?

"I've been told that Lucy Banks was molested by a relative some time ago," Francine said.

Grace's voice turned cold. "No, she was not molested. She had the good sense to run away. She came to me."

"Did her mother send her away because the girl was unmanageable?"

"Mrs. Banks sent all her daughters to her relatives down near Marion for a time. After the father died, the woman couldn't manage financially. When this thing happened with Lucy, she brought all the girls home."

Eyebrows arched in the disinterested, almost belligerently hostile face across the desk. "You're certain of that? Lucy, her teachers tell me, is quite well developed for a girl of thirteen."

"She's fourteen." Suddenly, Grace understood. "My God, what is this? You're trying to blame Lucy, her family, anyone but the fact that she, and heaven knows which other children, have been using a computer in your school to chat with some man, probably a pervert. You're responsible for the computer that was used as a conduit for possible disaster, and you want to blame the potential victim."

Francine's face reddened. Her eyes grew even colder and her lips tightened. "I will not suffer such ridiculous accusations. I am convinced that Lucy Banks opened that computer herself. If she used it to contact some man, probably she's been doing so at home or on some other computer outside this school." She stopped. "You have no authority to speak for the Banks family. This conversation is at an end, Mrs. Singleton."

They were silent a moment. The sun must have come out from behind a cloud, for the light emanating from the window behind Miss Randall framed her, softening her edges. Francine Randall no longer seemed a formidable adversary, a brick building against which Grace could batter and bruise herself. For an instant, Grace knew that the woman was filled with fears, and for that instant she felt those fears and pitied her.

Then Miss Randall stood, and the light paled, and she reminded Grace of a lion poised to attack. The sound of the school bell shattered the silence, shattered Grace's thoughts and any empathy she might have felt. Francine Randall strode past Grace and flung open her office door. "I have another meeting."

Grace left feeling defeated and blaming herself for not having been more tactful. She had let the woman throw her off balance.

Back in Brenda's office, shaken by her experience with the middle school principal, Grace wept.

"I should have gone with you. The woman's a tyrant," Brenda said. "Lucy must say who the boy was who hacked into the computer and showed her how to access that chat room. Otherwise it's going to go against Lucy."

"Why is such an awful woman a principal?"

"Tenure, political connections. Francine Randall's father was a well-known and powerful politician in these parts. People were—how shall I say—leery of him."

"And that secures her position?"

"Now her brother's in politics, and the family's power and connections are intact. He's a partner in Randall, Pike, and Waller law firm. A most influential law firm." Brenda leaned forward. "Let me tell you a story. Did you know, Grace, that the Randalls are related to the McCorkles over in McCorkle's Creek? There was a murder over there about twelve years ago."

"A murder in Covington?"

"An eighty-five-year-old woman, Hilda McCorkle, was found strangled, the house ransacked, her mattress shredded. Gossip had it that she'd stashed thousands of dollars under her mattress and owned valuable jewelry. Jerry McCorkle, a young relative of hers, no more than fifteen years old, was suspected.

"Randall had one of his top lawyers defend Jerry." Brenda shook her head. "One young fellow, a friend of Jerry's whose testimony might have convicted Jerry, disappeared from the area. They've never located him." She gave a skeptical snort. "I doubt they even looked. Anyway, the case was dismissed for insufficient evidence. No investigation was ever resumed, even when bits and pieces of Hilda's jewelry turned up at pawnshops in Asheville and Hendersonville. To this day, folks believe Randall's people shipped Jerry's friend out of town." She crossed her arms about her chest. "People have a certain . . . discomfort–"

"Sounds like fear of that family," Grace said.

"Correct." Brenda shook her head and slapped the desk with her palms. "Why in the name of heaven am I even telling you this?"

"I don't know, and I don't care who she is or what family she's from. That woman's attitude is unconscionable. She's not fit to be a principal."

Brenda handed Grace a tissue.

Grace stuffed it into her purse. "No. I'm not going to cry." She sniffled. "I'm too mad. I'm going to talk to Emily about this. She's a lawyer. She'll know what can be done."

"I'm so sorry about all of this. But I caution you, as a friend, don't be too upset if you find Francine Randall's too powerful to fight."

"I have to try, Brenda."

Later that day, Grace had shared her experiences with Amelia. Amelia had felt a strange excitement at hearing the Jerry McCorkle story. She'd read so much about family feuds, and Madison County was, half seriously, still referred to as Bloody Madison County. Now Covington, seemingly a bland, bucolic bit of countryside, took on an aura of mystery. In all these years of taking photographs, Amelia had never ventured into McCorkle Creek. It had seemed somehow forbidding: the narrow valley, the steep mountains, the single dirt roads crisscrossing the crowded flat plain on which, house hugging house, the McCorkles lived. People in the area always spoke in a denigrating way about the McCorkles.

Amelia remembered that shortly after they had arrived in Covington, one of the Craine boys had sported a gun at a local craft show and carnival they had attended with Brenda and Harold Tate. Harold (now deceased) had told him to "lose that gun, fast." He had, and Harold had remarked, "He handled that shotgun just like he was a McCorkle."

Locals, Brenda had said, could identify McCorkle women by their skinny, peaked look and the way they avoided eye contact. "They act like scared rabbits, and they breed like 'em, too."

"Do the men mistreat the women? Why can't they look you in the eye?" Amelia had asked.

"It's an old, well-rooted patriarchy with the women subservient to the men. Most times, I forget McCorkle Creek even exists."

So Amelia had assiduously avoided McCorkle Creek. But now, since Grace's story of murder, she drove past it slowly, scanning the bushes along the roadway for she knew not what.

12

HANNAH'S MALAISE

"Well, now that you're back a while, are you ready to set our date?" Max asked.

The day was exceptionally warm. Hannah and Max stood alongside the area being prepared for the Rose Garden, watching two men, immigrants from south of the border, dig and turn the earth. The men wore faded jeans above their creased and muddy boots. Another worker shoved a wheelbarrow filled with compost up the slope; his sunburned neck glistened with sweat.

Hannah had found it hard to communicate with these men with their limited English. To remedy that, she had hired a teacher and set up a class to teach them English, especially words and phrases having to do with plants and planting. The class met for an hour each workday on company time with full pay, and communicating had gotten a bit easier.

"The men did a fine job on the steps, don't you think?" Max asked.

"They certainly did. And they laid out the rose beds just as I showed them." Hannah inhaled the sweet smell of freshly turned earth. Perspiration beaded her forehead even though she wore a wide-brimmed straw hat. The sun vanished behind a gray cloud, and it immediately grew chilly. Hannah tugged the front of her cardigan sweater closer, buttoned it, and glanced up at the sky.

"It's the unpredictability of weather this time of year that gets to me." She pointed to the west. "We could use rain. That cloud may be gray, but it's too high. Doesn't look promising."

"I asked you a question, Hannah," Max said. He stepped away slightly and looked into her eyes.

A breeze stirred between them, creating an invisible wall. Hannah lowered her eyes.

"Okay," he said. "I'm not stupid. What's the matter?"

She couldn't blurt out that she would never marry him—not here, not with workmen in earshot. "I'm not ready," she said in a low voice.

"You'll never be ready." His voice was low but firm, and she detected the hurt and annoyance. Having said that, Max turned and walked rapidly away.

Hannah's heart screamed his name. She wanted to tell him that twenty years ago she had loved a man, and that his death still haunted her and prevented her from opening her heart to Max. Had he glanced back, had he turned and beckoned her, or even merely smiled at her, or waved—anything—she would have run to him, tucked her arm through his, and opened her heart. But Max did not look back.

Overhead, the sun pushed aside the cloud that hid its brightness and warmed the landscape. Hannah unbuttoned the cardigan, but in her heart all was gray and gloomy, and the woods beyond the rose beds, usually so welcoming, seemed cold and austere. Suddenly she didn't want to plant this garden, or any garden.

"*Señora* Hannah. You *quiere,* ah, want me to plant this rosebush here?" one of the workmen asked.

She forced her attention to the hole over which he stood, holding one of the bare-root rosebushes from Jackson & Perkins. She nodded. "*Sí.* Yes, and all the roses soaking in water. They all need to be planted today."

"You told Max what?" Grace asked Hannah later that afternoon. They were in the kitchen, where Grace leaned against the counter and chopped vegetables for a stew.

"That I'm not ready to get married."

Amelia stood in the doorway. "It's my opinion that you'll never be ready, no matter how kind and generous Maxwell is." She sauntered into the kitchen.

Hannah flinched. "That's what Max said. I'll never be ready."

Amelia pulled out a chair at the table where Hannah sat nursing a cup of coffee. "For goodness' sake, Hannah, what's your problem? Not that stupid old diary? I could strangle that girl for sending it to you. You don't have to love Max, or even live with him. All you have to do is marry him, and you'll inherit his land, his house, his money. Why is this such a problem? It makes good sense to me. I'd jump at the opportunity."

"You would." Hannah's voice dripped sarcasm.

Grace set down the knife, scooped the vegetables into a pot, and joined them at the table. "Why do you have to decide today, Hannah? Give it time. The diary was a terrible shock, I know that—"

Amelia's voice cut in. "Is it worth penalizing your life, and Max's, for something that happened twenty years ago?"

Hannah's eyes narrowed. Her mouth set in a firm line.

Grace glared across the table at Amelia.

Amelia shrugged, slipped from her chair, and left the kitchen.

Starting the next morning, when Hannah and Max met at work, they exchanged brief nods and went their separate ways. From that day on, Max did not join her in her office for lunch, nor did he step in for a beer or a Coke, or to talk about his plans or hers. Hannah began to feel like an employee rather than Max's partner, as she had considered herself to be and he had said she was from the beginning.

Many an afternoon, an edgy and tense Hannah looked out of her window for long periods of time hoping for a glimpse of Max. Somehow he managed to elude her. Her peevishness spilled over at home, especially toward Amelia. Small incidents irritated Hannah: a cup Amelia left unwashed in the sink, her front door key forgotten, even Amelia's voice raised in greeting Mike. Her sarcasm grew increasingly blatant until one morning, when Amelia came downstairs and found Hannah in the kitchen, Amelia fled the house and breakfasted alone at the new diner at Elk Road Plaza.

Shortly afterward, Grace came into the kitchen. Hannah stood at the sink, her shoulders slumped, her eyes clouded. "What is it? Talk to me, Hannah," Grace pleaded.

In the long silence that followed, Hannah did not move. When she finally turned, her face was drawn and sadder than Grace had ever seen it. Without a word, Hannah walked from the room. Grace, already burdened with anxiety over Lucy, felt her heart sink, and added Hannah to the list of people whom she worried about and felt powerless to help.

Crises, misunderstandings, and resentments occur in all relationships, Grace knew. But she believed that speaking about them deepened understanding, affection, and acceptance, and helped to forge truly meaningful relationships. After four years of house sharing, four years of living through trivial annoyances and individual personality quirks, after surviving the stresses of the fire that had destroyed their home, how could there be this rigid silence between herself and Hannah? Hannah's abrupt withdrawal, her sullen behavior, shocked Grace into further silence. This was a Hannah she did not know and had never imagined existed.

That night Amelia appeared in Grace's bedroom doorway. "Hannah's unbearable and impossible. She was nasty to me on the ship, and since we're back it's worse, much worse."

"It's probably this decision about Max worrying her to distraction. Give her some time. Want to come in and sit?"

"No. I don't want to sit. How much time do you suggest I give her?" Amelia stood with her hands on her hips. "I can't take much more of her crap."

Grace had just showered and was propped up in bed with a book. She set the book beside her and gave Amelia her full attention. The silence that followed began to feel odd and uncomfortable to Grace.

"I'm ill at ease in my own home," Amelia finally blurted. "I come in and dash upstairs way before I want to go to bed. I eat out as often as possible, mostly by myself, since Mike's hardly ever available anymore without Roger." The edge in Amelia's voice tightened. "Frankly, Grace, I'm thinking of moving out."

Grace's hands flew to cover her lips. "No. How can you even think that, Amelia? This is your farmhouse, your land. None of us would be here had it not been for your cousin. You were so generous to include us on the deed, but it was yours to start with."

"I changed the deed because I wanted to." She lifted one shoulder, turned her head away from Grace, and raised her chin with a proud, indifferent air. "Things have changed. If I leave . . ." She hesitated. "I wouldn't normally suggest this, but I've lost money in the stock market, so if you and Hannah could buy me out—over time, of course—it would help."

"This is ridiculous, all of it. There's got to be some way to clear the air between you two. Hannah was never snippy like this. Please, Amelia, I don't want you to even consider such a thing."

"Well, I'm going to go away for a while." Amelia walked into the room and plopped onto the foot of Grace's bed. "When I come back, I'll decide. I just know that I can't go on like this."

Grace moved her feet. Lately her toes felt tingly, and even the lightest sheet on them caused burning, aching sensations. Diabetic neuropathy, her doctor said was irreversible. "Get the weight off, and maybe it won't get any worse," he had suggested.

It was that important, and yet she couldn't lose the weight and keep it off. It was a vicious circle. When she checked her blood sugar, if it registered in the normal range for several days, Grace gave herself license to sneak a cookie, a spoon of ice cream, or extra potatoes. She turned her attention from her feet and her diabetes back to Amelia.

"In one of my photography magazines, they advertise a ten-day workshop in Maine. I've never been to Maine," Amelia was saying. "I've always wanted to go. I called and reserved a place. If Hannah hasn't settled her problems by the time I get back, I'll find someplace else to live."

"Maine, this time of year? Isn't it too cold?"

"It's essentially an indoor workshop." The catalog had read: "There will be some outdoor work, so bring warm clothes," but Amelia decided not to mention that to anyone so they wouldn't try to dissuade her. "I have to get out of here, away from that witch."

"I'm so sorry. I don't know what's going on with Hannah, but we've got to find out. I'll talk to Max."

"You find out. I don't give a damn anymore." Amelia stood and stomped from Grace's room.

Grace felt cold. A lump formed in her throat. What was happening to them? Hannah and Amelia had never been bosom buddies, but now they were at each other's throats and making no effort to disguise their animosity. Grace looked about her. She loved her room, loved the house, the land, Covington. What would she do if Amelia carried out her threat? She had no money, other than Ted's pension and social security. She doubted if Hannah did, either.

Amelia had always been in the stock market, but how deeply, how much invested or lost Grace did not know. Amelia had never spoken of this until tonight.

Grace phoned Bob.

"Bob Richardson here," he answered in his usual manner.

She told him first about Hannah's attitude toward Amelia, her overall tenseness and irritability toward everyone. "Amelia's considering moving out. We can't let that happen. I never anticipated anything like this could happen, that one of us would want to leave. In the past, we've been able to work out our differences."

"Sounds like something's really eating Hannah. Maybe she and Max had a fight. Want me to talk to Max?"

"No. She'd be furious with me for telling you."

"Just let me know what you want me to do, honey."

She could picture that funny little puckering of lines between his eyes when he was worried. It was comforting talking to Bob. She should have told him about the diary and the friction between Amelia and Hannah on the ship, but so many things had happened since they came home.

Grace told Bob about her meeting with Francine Randall. "Do you think Emily will help me?"

"I can't speak for Emily, but she's got a soft spot for the underdog. Talk to her. I agree with Brenda—it's not going to be easy going up against that family with so little hard proof."

"There are witnesses, all those other children."

"Whose parents might not want them to get involved, or might be afraid of coming up against the Randall family."

Frustration and the sense of being hemmed into a box came over her. "Bob, what are you saying?"

"I'm being practical and realistic, honey. I don't want you to get your hopes too high on this one."

"Well, I'm going to try."

"Fine. I support your efforts." There was silence a moment, then Bob said, "I missed you, honey. Be nice to watch TV with you, snuggle a bit; what say I come over there?"

"I love you, Bob, and I missed you, too. I wished you were with me in all those romantic places we visited on our cruise. But frankly, right now, I'm pooped. I'd be no good to either of us. I'll watch some mindless show on television and go to sleep. How about dinner tomorrow, and I'll stay over at your place?"

"Sounds great, honey. You have a good rest."

As Grace set down the receiver, she noted that her window was open several inches and the lace curtains flickered in a light breeze. The room had grown chillier. Sliding back her covers, Grace moved to the window. The moon, its belly full and golden, rose above the hill, and as Grace watched, a band of steel-gray cloud pinched its middle, giving the yellow orb the appearance of an hourglass. Time is running out, especially for Lucy, Grace thought. She may feel the need to act, to meet this Ringo. It can't wait. I can't wait.

Wearily, Grace dressed, went downstairs, bundled into her coat and hat, and opened the front door. Icy air, burdened with winter, burned her nostrils. The occasional car passing on Cove Road sent brief beams of brightness across their lawn. Max's house was dark, his porch light out. Had it burned out, she wondered, or been deliberately turned off? Above the treetops, the clouds had drifted on, and the moon had regained its rotund form. Grace turned on the engine of her car and checked the time. Nine P.M. It got dark so early this time of year that she lost track of time in the evenings.

"Dear God, help me convince Lucy not to pursue this thing with Ringo," she prayed.

Red and blue lights bounced off the exterior walls of the Banks's home. It took several moments for Grace to realize that those lights came from a police car parked in the driveway. She drove onto the grass alongside the police vehicle. Then, her heart racing, she hastened up the drive and onto the porch. She knocked.

A tall policeman stepped out and barred her entrance. "Sorry, ma'am, you can't come in."

"Are you a family member?" asked a second policeman, an Officer Hicks.

Before Grace could respond, Lucy pushed her way past the policeman. "She's my granny." Lucy looked defiantly up at him, took Grace's arm, and urged her into the house.

The policeman reached out as if to stop them, then apparently reconsidered and allowed them entry.

Inside, chaos reigned. Lucy's four younger sisters, huddled together in a chair in the living section of the room, were crying loudly. Lucy's mother stood against a wall as if frozen, her eyes wide and frightened.

"You told them, didn't you?" Lucy said to Grace. Her nostrils flared; her eyes filled with anger. "Who told you? Tyler, the shithead? And then you told *them?* How could you? All our letters, Ringo's and mine, are on that computer." Her shoulders caved about her chest, and she buried her face in her hands. Deep, heaving sobs filled the room.

"There's too much at stake here. I did talk to someone at the police station. I had no choice, Lucy, my love."

Lucy pulled back sharply. She lifted her head. The tears stopped. "Don't call me your love. You've ruined my life."

She hates me, Grace thought.

The shorter policeman, a Sergeant Ledford, was unsuccessfully attempting to gather information from Mrs. Banks. Grace walked over to them. "I'm Grace Singleton, a very close family friend. Is there any way I can be of help?"

Mrs. Banks wrapped her skinny arms around Grace's neck and began to cry. When she could speak, she said, "I dunno what Lucy's done. Has she stole something, Mrs. Grace?"

The sparsely furnished front room served as kitchen, dining, and living room, yet it was a great improvement over the shabby, derelict mobile home the family had occupied when the father was alive. Grace led the distraught mother to a chair at the 1950s Formica-topped table. Immediately, the four younger sisters dislodged themselves from the single living-room chair and claimed seats around the table. Their crying stopped, and Grace handed each of them a tissue from her purse. Officer Hicks still barred the front door, but Grace knew there was an exit in the small laundry room behind the kitchen, and she worried that Lucy might try to bolt.

"Lucy, come sit with us. These policemen only want information. They aren't going to hurt any of you."

"I ain't got nothin' to say," Lucy replied.

"I haven't got anything to say," Grace corrected her. When she looked at Lucy, the hostility in her face hurt Grace.

Sergeant Ledford fished a small notebook and a pen from his pocket and stood by the table.

"Give the policeman a chair." Mrs. Banks pushed one of her daughters from the seat at the head of the table. The child sat on the floor beside her mother and hugged her mother's leg. Absentmindedly, Mrs. Banks ran one hand over the little girl's hair.

The sergeant sat. "I need to ask you a few questions." He looked at Grace. "Are you the Mrs. Singleton who reported this whole affair? You're the grandmother?"

"She ain't really Lucy's granny," Mrs. Banks said. "But she's been just like one."

"She's nothing to me," Lucy blurted.

"Mind your manners, Lucy," her mother said.

Grace straightened her shoulders. "I believe the law has to get involved in this since you're in contact with someone named Ringo. Don't you see, Lucy? Didn't it ever occur to you that you shouldn't trust anyone who wouldn't give you his real name, tell you where he lives? Who is this person? What does he want from you? Talk to me, Lucy, please."

"Ringo loves me, and I love him, and that's all I'm gonna say to anyone."

Grace turned to the sergeant. "I want you to know that Lucy was not the only one who used that computer, and she did not break into it—you know, with a password or whatever." The correct computer words that Grace had been so carefully rehearsing simply would not come.

"It would be better for everyone if you'd give us the guy's name, Lucy," the policeman said.

Lucy lips were firmly compressed. She stared past him.

He looked at Grace. "There was no computer with a chat room available on it when we checked the school."

Grace suddenly remembered that Lucy had said her correspondence with Ringo was on that computer. She avoided looking at Lucy. If the girl was angry at her before, she would hate her now. God, but this was so difficult. But Lucy's very life could be at stake. Grace swallowed hard before continuing.

"If Miss Randall would give you access to the computer she's removed from the lab, you could read Lucy's letters to and from Ringo, couldn't you?"

"Reckon we could," the sergeant replied.

Sergeant Ledford directed his attention to Lucy, who stood behind her mother's chair now. He smiled at her. "Lucy," he said, "I believe everything Mrs. Singleton says. You used it, but you didn't break into it. You're not in trouble. We just need to know a few things about this Ringo fellow."

Emboldened, Lucy tore around the table and stood facing the sergeant. "Ringo isn't a bad person, sir. He's an orphan—he lived in one foster home after the other. He's a sad, lonely person, and I'm his only friend." Tears filled her eyes. "And now he has no one, and I've lost my best friend." She gave Grace a stinging look.

"There are men out there, Lucy," the sergeant said, "who tell a sad tale of woe to young girls. They know that you and other girls have soft hearts and will want to help them, but their intentions are otherwise, and they could hurt you."

"No." Lucy stamped her foot. "Not Ringo. He's a good person."

"He may be a very good person, and that's what we aim to find out."

"I ain't telling you nothing." Lucy crossed her arms over her chest and glared at the sergeant.

"If Ringo isn't a good person, and I'm not saying he isn't, he might just do a disappearing act on us," the policeman said.

"Ringo's not going to disappear. We, he . . ." Lucy slammed her hand over her mouth. "Damn," she said. "What'd I say that for?"

Sergeant Ledford said, "He got a real name, like Fred, or Henry, or Jimmie, or maybe Jerry?"

At the mention of Jerry, Lucy's face reddened. She turned her eyes away from the man's face. "I'm not saying another word."

The hair rose on Grace's arms. Shivers slid across her back. Wasn't Jerry the name of Francine Randall's distant relative, the one suspected of Hilda McCorkle's murder? There were hundreds of men named Jerry. But what if it were he? If this Jerry was fifteen years old twelve years ago, he'd have to be—what?—twenty-seven now. Her instinct told her it was the same Jerry, rotten then, rotten now. She must get Lucy away from him. She would leave at once and take the girl somewhere, to Hannah's daughter Miranda in Pennsylvania, anywhere. *Calm yourself, Grace,* her rational mind urged. *Lucy isn't four years old. She could, and would, refuse to go with you.*

"There was a Jerry McCorkle who was suspected of murdering Hilda McCorkle about twelve years ago," Grace said.

Sergeant Ledford turned to her, his eyes curious. "Suspected is right, ma'am, but never convicted." He raised his eyebrows.

A look of shock and horror appeared on Lucy's face. "How can you even suggest a terrible thing like that?" she raged at Grace.

Sergeant Ledford checked his watch. "Gotta be going now. Thank you, ma'am, for your help. Sorry to intrude on you, Mrs. Banks, kids. Lucy, you stay put right here now, you hear?" Shortly afterward, the police car backed out of the drive and disappeared down the street.

"I got to warn Ringo," Lucy said, and this time she did run, out the front door and down the street, faster than Grace or her mother could possibly run.

"Where's your phone?" Grace asked.

"They shut it off 'cause we was late payin' the bill."

Graces snatched up her purse and coat and dashed from the house to her car. Her mind was not clear. Where should she go? Home was thirty minutes away. The central police station in Asheville was closer than Covington. Grace headed for the center of the city.

Back at the house, Amelia packed for her trip to Maine.

"You'll freeze up there this time of year." Mike sat on the edge of her bed and shook his head. "Shouldn't you wait until it gets warmer?"

"Living with Hannah's like living at the North Pole. Besides, I'm going to a major workshop center. One of the classes is on lighting. It's indoors."

"And the other?"

She lied. "They have models, and there'll be some still-life photography. It'll be fine. I don't want to argue with Grace or encounter Hannah. Can I stay at your place tonight?"

"Sure." Mike nodded.

A few minutes later, he carried Amelia's bags down to his van. Early the following morning, he and Roger drove Amelia to the airport.

13

LUCY

It was nearly ten the following morning when Bob drove his Cherokee around the corner of Elk Road and into Cove Road. The front door of the farmhouse was unlocked, and he stepped inside. "Grace," he called. When he got no reply, he raced up the stairs. Grace's bedroom was empty, her bed unmade. Bob checked both bathrooms. In one of them, damp towels hung on the rack. Beads of wet filmed the shower door. Bob took the stairs down two at a time. He found Grace in a bathrobe sitting at the kitchen table, staring into space, a teacup grasped between both hands.

"Grace, didn't you hear me calling you?"

The look she gave him was vacant. "Hello, Bob. Sorry. I was having a cup of tea and thinking."

He took the cup from her. It was cold. "Your tea's not even warm. How long have you been sitting here?"

She shrugged. "Amelia's gone."

"Gone where?"

"To Maine."

"Maine? In winter?"

Grace nodded. "She didn't say good-bye. She didn't even sleep here last night. She stayed with Roger and Mike at the apartment. Mike called this morning." Grace looked up at the clock on the wall. "My goodness, it's after ten. Time got away from me."

"I've got news. Good news," Bob said.

"About Lucy?"

He nodded.

"Tell me quickly, what is it?"

"Emily called early. She said that last night the cops waited around the corner from the Banks's place because they thought Lucy might run. They followed her to a motel in town where Ringo was waiting. Seems it was a prearranged meeting. God knows what might have happened if the cops hadn't come when they did." He took her other hand in his. "You saved her, Grace. You intervened just in time."

"Thank Tyler, not me. He could have decided to keep his mouth shut, not to interfere."

"Tyler's a great kid. I'm proud of him," Bob said.

"Who is Ringo? Tell me. Did they identify him?" Grace asked.

Bob rose, poured himself a cup of coffee, and returned to the table. "They sure did. Some guy named Jerry McCorkle. They believe he killed an old lady in McCorkle's Creek years ago. I hope they hang him for that, as well as for preying on little girls on the Net. It turned out Lucy wasn't the only one. He had his adventure going with three other girls."

"Does Lucy know this? Where is she? Is she all right?"

"I think so. Upset, of course, but unhurt. And more news: Emily's decided if she can get some cooperation from some of the other kids in that class, she'll bring suit against Miss Randall charging criminal negligence."

Grace's eyes narrowed. "Good."

"Come on, get dressed. You're probably the only one that Lucy'll talk to now."

"Where is she?"

"Lucy's mother was at work, so Lucy's with Emily at home."

Once upstairs, Grace flopped into her chair by the window and made no move to dress. Bob opened her closet, selected a familiar-looking pair of brown corduroy slacks and a sweater, and brought them to her. "Get dressed."

Grace stood. She steadied herself on the back of the chair for a moment, then let her robe fall to the floor and stepped out of her pajamas. She turned and pulled out her dresser drawer, selected underwear, and unself-consciously began to dress. "Sorry to be so slow," she muttered. "I'm so relieved, but all my energy's gone right out of me."

"That's understandable. Take your time," Bob said. He wanted to take her in his arms, but he would only become aroused. With Grace's state of mind, they had not slept together the night Grace returned or anytime since then, and though he wanted her, he had not pressed her. Now that Lucy was okay, things would return to normal.

Finally dressed, Grace smiled at Bob and reached for him. Bob's arms circled her and held her close. "I love you, honey."

"I love you, too." For the first time since she heard about Lucy and the computer, Grace felt a stir of longing for him. Comforted, she rested her head on his chest. Why hadn't she turned to Bob for support sooner?

He released her. "Come on, now. Let's get going."

Bundled in a plaid wool throw, Lucy lay on Emily and Russell's blue denim sofa in their den. The moment she saw Grace, tears rose and spilled from her eyes. "I was awful rude and mean to you, Mrs. Grace. Can you ever forgive me?"

Two-year-old Melissa climbed into Grace's lap and pushed her little face up close, demanding Grace's attention. Their noses touched. "Granny," Melissa said. "Granny."

"I love you, precious." Grace kissed the child. "Granny has to talk to Lucy now."

Melissa clung to Grace.

"Please take her, Russell." Grace handed her to her father.

"I want Granny," Melissa yelled as Russell carried her from the den.

Lucy edged over, making room for Grace on the couch. Grace's arms circled the girl's shoulders, and she pulled her close. "There's nothing to forgive, Lucy. I'm only happy that they caught Ringo and that you're safe and sound. Now don't cry." Pulling out the bandana tucked into her belt, Grace gently wiped Lucy's cheeks. "Don't cry, honey. It's going to be all right."

"He didn't look nothing like that picture he sent me. He was old, and he had a scar across his cheek." Lucy lowered her eyes. Her cheeks were red, as well as her nose. "He was mean. He would have hurt me if the cops hadn't broke the door down and got me." Lucy's head dropped low on her chest. "You saved me. I'll love you forever for saving me."

"The policemen saved you."

"You tried to stop me from going."

"But you were so caught up in the passion of it all, no one could stop you."

"It's lucky they followed me."

"Lucky indeed." Grace remained silent then, allowing Lucy time to collect herself. Lucy began to cry again, and Grace held her.

Finally, Lucy said, "I didn't mean no harm. I hate that school. I hate the other girls." Her chin quivered. "No, I don't really hate them, but they're so mean to me, just 'cause I don't dress or act like them. We ain't—I mean, we don't have the money for clothes like most of them wear, or jewelry, or having my hair colored, or my ears pierced, or for rings in my nose or belly button."

That was a new one to Grace. "They wear rings in their belly buttons?"

"On their eyebrows, too," Lucy said. "Do I have to go back to that school, Mrs. Grace? Do I?"

"I don't really know, Lucy, dear. I'm not sure of anything right now."

Lucy covered her head and face with her hands, "Oh, my God. They're all gonna hate me worse than they did. My life'll be even more of a hell there."

"Now don't you worry. I'll see that nothing bad happens to you."

The worry and fear in Lucy's eyes gave way to trust. "You always have, Mrs. Grace, from the first I met you back in elementary school. You came out to see my pa before he passed, and you been lookin' out for me and my folks since then." She snuggled against Grace and closed her eyes.

Grace held her close. This girl was precious to her. She loved Lucy with all the hopes and dreams she would have if Lucy were her own child.

14

MAINE DELIGHTS

Lectures, assignments, and critiques were held in large heated buildings in Maine, but most of the work was out-of-doors. The damp cold assailed Amelia in ways she had forgotten, and made her miserable. Her toes ached and her hands were stiff, making it hard to use her camera. She'd traveled a little way down the coast to L.L.Bean in Freeport in a rented car and purchased silk long underwear, lightweight warm slacks, cotton-lined wool shirts, and a lightweight, ultrawarm jacket and gloves. Thankfully, she had brought her cashmere scarf and hat.

Now, on the third day of the workshop, Amelia stood on a cliff, one arm clutching her camera, the other hugging the rough bark of a slender, wind-blasted pine tree. Bitterly cold wind slammed the angry ocean against the jagged gray rocks below, and grasping fingers of foam reached high into the air. Amelia propped her back firmly against the tree and lifted the camera to her eye. White foam filled the frame. She followed the foam, watched it fall back and fold like whipped cream into the dark Atlantic brew. This fierce ocean and hard, unfriendly shoreline was as unfamiliar to her as death itself, and she found it frightening. I don't like Maine, she thought.

Her photography assignment had brought her to this cliff. "Emotional impact in nature" was the assignment, the shot she must capture. Amelia studied the line of trees braced precariously along the edge of the cliff. As if in dread or pain, their branches and barks recoiled from the sea and leaned away, making fine subjects for the amateur. But for Amelia, photographing them would be too trite, too easy.

Fifty feet below, her working partner perched on a huge boulder that was continuously smitten by wind and water. The woman, a stranger in her mid-twenties named Sarah, was shooting straight down into the whirlpools that formed at the jagged base where stone met sea.

"Sarah," Amelia called. She wanted to tell the young woman that she was heading back to the car, but the wind gusted past, dispersing her words in the woods behind her. "So, you're stuck here," Amelia said to herself. "You better concentrate on the assignment: 'emotional impact in nature.'"

Amelia could wring tears from viewers with her photographs of people, especially a child or an older man or woman. This assignment precluded people, and this location, with its never-ending, wailing wind and harsh gray sea, gave her the willies. "Quiet yourself," she whispered. "Don't feel, think." But she could not still her agitation. "What I need is a miracle," she muttered.

Suddenly the wind died down. Out of nowhere, it seemed, a large bird soared into view and settled onto a branch of a tree thirty feet from where she stood. It bent its head into a nest she had not noticed. Magically, four small bald heads with sharp, grasping beaks poked above the edge of the nest. Amelia lifted the camera and clicked off shot after shot, zooming in at the propitious moment, just as the parent bird lifted its head and looked directly at her. At the same instant, one of the babies leaped above the edge of the nest, snatched a remnant of food from its parent's beak, then disappeared among its siblings. She had her shot. Satisfied, Amelia sank into the hard, cold, pine needle cushion at the base of the tree. Ever since she had been lost in Pisgah Forest off the Blue Ridge Parkway and nearly died of hypothermia, forests held no appeal to her. With unabashed dismay, Amelia looked about her as she waited for Sarah to finish her work.

The woods were thick with evergreens, and the earth, deprived of sunshine, lay smothered beneath accumulated pine needles. There was little undergrowth. Filtered light added to the green aura created by the moss-covered tree trunks. She remembered a book she had read ages ago about archaeologists who wandered into a crevice in a hillside and were trapped in a green world: green sky and water, green flowers and fauna. Their adventures in that bizarre environment had frightened and appalled her. Amelia shivered, and turned her gaze to the silver sheen of sun on water, the slick surfaces of dark wet rocks below, and was glad for the sight of Sarah's red hair.

Sarah raised her head and waved. She placed her camera into her camera bag and slowly, carefully eased herself up from the rock and started toward Amelia. Seeming as surefooted as a mountain goat, Sarah ascended, her camera bag swinging from her shoulder. Then, suddenly, the young woman missed a step and slipped. Amelia gasped as Sarah crumbled to her knees. Amelia saw her fingers grasp, lose their hold, grasp again, and find a crevice. Then she was on her feet, and moments later reached the top of the bank and collapsed alongside Amelia.

Amelia sat pressed against the tree, both hands over her heart, which was racing. "I was frightened for you," she said.

"Exciting. Scary there for a minute, but I made it. That's what matters."

What if you had tumbled off that rock face? Amelia remembered that the car was Sarah's and that Sarah had stuffed the keys into her jeans. Tomorrow, Amelia determined, she would use her own rental car, and would steer clear of forests and this rough-and-tumble coast.

There was, of course, so much more to Maine than the rugged stretch of shoreline. There were endless stretches of evergreen hillsides and mountains, and charming villages tucked into coves with gift shops and great seafood restaurants. Amelia wandered past bed-and-breakfasts tucked between homes on hillsides overlooking harbors where boats abounded and lobster traps were piled high against weatherworn buildings or on docks.

In the villages, Amelia photographed fishnets spread out to be mended, lobster boats on dry dock, sturdy fishing vessels, and small ferry boats that took tourists whale-watching, fishing, or sightseeing along the coast in summer. She spent an hour dealing with the shifting light as it played on the sea and on a bright yellow rowboat that stood out among the smaller boats moored close to shore.

As Amelia explored these small towns and villages in her rental car, her concept of her trip to Maine changed from strenuous workshop to relaxing holiday. The endurance test of struggling physically to keep up with the young Master of Fine Arts students on spring break was over.

When she photographed around Covington, or anywhere in Madison County, Amelia worked at her own pace. After first testing rocks for safe perches, she would ease her way down steep slopes and step gingerly across streams. At this workshop, she simply could not keep up with her fellow enrollees.

When the assignment for the class included a long hike to a waterfall, Amelia feigned a headache. When the instructor announced a trip to an offshore island and explained that they would climb a steep hill to a cliff devoid of trees, a cliff turned white from the accumulated, calcified droppings of birds, Amelia declined. "I'll pass on that," she said.

"You scared of birds?" Sarah asked.

"Hardly," Amelia retorted with a flip of her head.

"The birds are accustomed to humans," the instructor was saying. "They carry on with their lives. You can photograph to your heart's content. Prize-winning photos have been taken on that hilltop."

Instead, Amelia drove to a nearby harbor town. Blessed with sunshine and a warmer wind, she spent the day leisurely photographing the life of the harbor: fishermen in yellow oilskins repairing a lobster trap, young boys in brightly colored down vests racing along the shoreline, a man and a boy with ruddy cheeks and noses scraping barnacles from the bottom of a skiff that sat in dry dock. They had rolled up the sleeves of their plaid flannel shirts and worked with such concentration that they did not notice her photograph them.

Amelia roamed the narrow streets of the town, up hillsides dotted with gray and white clapboard homes and gardens waiting for spring tilling and planting. She turned a corner and photographed a small boy and girl in red sweaters playing tag under a long line of sheets hung to dry in the sunshine.

Amelia walked to the top of a rise, closed her eyes, and breathed the fresh salt air. Memories of a childhood of summers in Rhode Island assailed her: a hillside overlooking the sea, gray wooden steps descending to the beach, wild grasses waving in the strong sea breeze, her hair blowing, her hand in her father's, contentment, and her mother's voice drifting down to them, calling them for dinner from the porch of the house. Amelia wondered what memories of this glorious day the children in red sweaters might carry with them into adulthood.

By the end of the third day, Amelia could no longer tolerate the raucous late-night parties, the yelling in hallways, and the slamming of doors. She checked out of the workshop's dorm and moved into a comfortable bed-and-breakfast in one of the towns she had been exploring.

The Harbor View Bed and Breakfast was owned by a woman whose graying, wiry hair flowed to her shoulders and seemed always to be windblown. Margaret Smelter was widowed, a transplant from Canada, her children grown and gone, scattered across America. In early March, Amelia was the sole guest, and as the days passed, she grew increasingly comfortable with Mrs. Smelter.

"Call me Maggie, everyone does," Amelia's hostess said.

After the first day, they breakfasted each morning at a small round table in the large, pleasant kitchen at a bay window overlooking the harbor, and Amelia invited Maggie out for dinner several times during that week. Sometimes they made a salad and ate it in the dying light of sunset, and chatted about their lives.

"Well," Maggie said, summing up her philosophy of life one evening. "There's a time for everything. A time to be young and bold, a time to be married and settled down and bearing children, a time for caution as you watch your children grow, a time to let them go. If you lose your husband, as I did, it's a time to be alone to consider life's meaning and purpose, and to prove that even in the dying light and the end of days, you can still be productive and vital."

The end of days, Amelia mused. Not something she cared to dwell on.

Maggie had come to Maine from Canada for college, became a U.S. citizen, joined the Peace Corps, and spent several years in Africa before marrying.

"After seeing how little those people had, I stopped complaining about my own life and tried to make do with less, to conserve what I could of goods and the environment," she said. "Fred, my husband, would have liked more kids, but I limited our children to two. I had three, but lost a little girl, my Susan. I could never bear to replace her."

A bond born of loss drew the women close. Both had lost a child: Maggie's daughter to cancer, Amelia's daughter to a rare tropical disease. And both had lost husbands: Maggie's to the sea, Amelia's in a car crash. Violent deaths.

"Cancer," Maggie said. "God, that was the worse time of my life, and Susan's, too, of course. Some days even now, when I'm making a bed or preparing breakfast for guests, or washing the dishes, I think of my Susan and I cry." Tears welled in her eyes. She brushed them away with the ball of her fist. "After all these years, I still cry."

Amelia understood. "Sometimes I dream of Caroline. It's always a shock to wake up and find it's only a dream. That's when I cry," Amelia said.

They were silent for a long time as sunset flame paled and faded to gray. "The shadows of evening," Amelia said. "I so long for summer and long evenings."

"Summer here is short, but I relish every moment of it," Maggie replied. "More coffee?"

Amelia nodded, and Maggie poured them each a cup.

"You're not lonely living alone, or find it too cold or bleak here on the coast of Maine?" Amelia thought of the blustery gray winter days, the bleak aspect of the saw-toothed rocky coastline, and the snowfalls that defined the limits of travel.

"Lonely?" Maggie replied. "Sometimes, yes, but there's life in that town down there, there's always work to be done preparing for the coming season, and on the darkest, coldest winter days, people gather at Joe's Pub. I like the sense of camaraderie. Everyone knows everyone; people help each other. Folks have been good to me since Fred passed away six years ago. I couldn't manage without their help in so many things: storm windows that must be put up every September and taken down in April or May, snow to shovel, a leaking roof, fencing down, or a shutter hanging on one hinge after a nor'easter." She shook her head. "Couldn't keep the place, couldn't make it without their help. Bless them."

For a moment, Amelia imagined moving to Maine, perhaps moving in with Maggie, but thinking of the weather—bitterly cold, gray, and blustery—she knew that this would never be.

One night, Amelia awoke from a dream of Grace and Hannah. In the dream they sat at a table with pictures of the farmhouse, the land, the orchard laid out before them, then cut the pictures of the house and land, even the big oak, into little pieces and divided the pieces: "One for me, one for you," like in a child's game. Moonlight lay like a silk scarf across her face, and she shifted away from the light and lay awake a long while thinking about her friends in Covington and about loneliness and friendship.

They were so different—she, Hannah, and Grace. Grace's small-town roots provided such solid values, while Hannah's lonely years as a single mother, her struggle to feed and clothe her girls, made her at times aloof and sure of her rightness, but calm and steady. Amelia knew she herself was by far the most sophisticated of the three, the most well-traveled, and yet she had been so dependent on her husband, Thomas.

She realized that like Maggie's appreciation of Joe's Pub and those who frequented it, she valued her home in Covington and the companionship and support of Grace and, yes, Hannah, and she loved and missed them. She also considered how barren of love Hannah's life had been except for her brief time with Dan Britton. Men had always flirted with Amelia. Thomas, with all his faults, had pampered and adored her. Even Lance, that no-good son of a gun, had, for a time, boosted her ego and reminded her that she was still a sensual woman. Compared to Hannah's life—married to an abusive bastard, having to flee from him—she and Grace had been lucky. When Hannah had fallen in love again, the man was married, and then he had died. Of course that awful diary would stir up old hurts and regrets.

Amelia's mind shifted to Max. Had he said "I love you" to Hannah? Amelia could see affection in his eyes when he looked at Hannah, but as far as she knew, he had merely offered her a business proposition. No wonder Hannah was on edge and irritable. Amelia promised herself that on her return home, she would be more sensitive to Hannah's situation.

15

A BABY BOY IS BORN

The house was very quiet. Although Hannah liked being alone in it at times, this Sunday she just felt lonely as she stood at the kitchen window and watched Max's truck back out of his driveway and head toward Elk Road. Her heart, already low, sank deeper in her chest. She missed Max terribly. He no longer came for dinner or dropped in to visit, and except for staff meetings at work, he avoided her.

At work it was difficult to keep her spirits up, and to make the effort to interpret the broken English of her workmen. As a result, holes lacked their proper depth and preparation, and some of the trees were not properly pruned. Rolled and rubber-banded, plans for the Shade Garden and the Woodland Garden sat ignored in the umbrella stand next to her desk. "I'm not ready to deal with them yet," she told Hank, the landscape architect at Bella's Park and her son-in-law. "I must finish the Rose Garden first." But the completion of the Rose Garden was hindered by her own sluggishness and indifference.

Preoccupied as he was with Laura and her pregnancy, Hank didn't push Hannah for decisions. With her swollen legs, her indigestion, and backaches, Laura was utterly miserable. When she managed to totter in to work, she held her back, eased into a chair, and required the help of others to regain a standing position. Hannah worried about her daughter, worried about her age and the apparent size of the baby.

Self-pity being an indulgence Hannah assiduously rejected, she now wiped her hands on a towel, collected weeding tools from the metal shelf in the mudroom behind the kitchen, and went down the steps into the yard. Weeding had always proven restorative for her. The day was cool but tolerable and Hannah sank down, sitting sideways to spare her knees as she spread fertilizer around each rosebush lining their driveway. As she worked, she composed sentences with which to tell Max about Dan, about the shock of the diary, and to explain her behavior. In her scenarios her words flowed easily, and he listened attentively with caring and understanding eyes.

Reality was another matter. Try as she could, in Max's presence, words failed. Why? Was she afraid? Ashamed? Of what? Of being laughed at for overreacting to reminders of a twenty-year-old event? Or was she afraid to admit to having deep and passionate emotions? Because she could not tell Max, she hated herself and directed her anger at others, like poor Amelia. She had abused Amelia verbally as surely as Bill had abused *her* physically, and just as Hannah had fled from Bill, Amelia justifiably had fled from her.

Hannah's fist closed around the stem of an oak seedling determined to establish itself under a rosebush a hundred feet from its parent tree. The pert green leaves rose five inches above the soil, but the taproot burrowed deep and resisted her tug. Using the trowel, Hannah poked around the small, tough seedling until she loosened the root. Satisfied, she yanked it from the earth and cast it onto a clear plastic trash bag, where it joined weeds destined for composting.

Brenda Tate drove by and waved. Ellie's car followed. Ellie honked at Hannah and waved. She waved back. An unlikely combination, those two, and yet Ellie, the city sophisticate, and Brenda, a mainstay of Covington, had become friends and now shared the former home of Brenda's daughter on Cove Road.

Hannah's thoughts drifted again to Laura. The baby was large. Laura was forty-two years old, and the dangers Hannah had heard or read about concerning older women giving birth flooded her mind: the onset of high blood pressure, incipient diabetes, a retarded child. Hannah's heart froze, and for a moment she stopped weeding and reminded herself that Laura had been free of such symptoms, and tests indicated the baby was not retarded. But there was still the delivery of a large baby. Though not one to pray, Hannah raised her eyes to the sky and whispered, "Please, God, let Laura be healthy and have a whole and healthy baby."

Still sitting, Hannah scooted over to the next rosebush and began to stir the earth beneath it. When a thorn stabbed her thumb, she dropped the trowel and sucked the bright red blood. The prick stung and burned, and the area around it started to swell. Tears welled in Hannah's eyes as they would in the eyes of a child who had been hurt. She wanted someone—no, not someone. She wanted Max to comfort her. Reaching into her pocket, Hannah extracted a handkerchief and wrapped it about her thumb. Blood seeped through the white cotton material. So much blood from a minute prick. At that moment she wished that, like Sleeping Beauty, she could fall asleep right here and be awakened by Max's kiss.

In the house the phone rang. Darn, she had left the portable inside. She'd never make it in time. Was the answering machine on or off? Sometimes Grace turned it off. Then she heard the crunch of tires on the gravel in their drive, heard the slam of the truck's door, and recognized Max's walk as he stomped toward her. Hannah jerked around and stared up at him.

Max sank down beside her and tucked his knees beneath him. "What's wrong?" he asked.

Hannah shook her head and held up her thumb.

He took her hand, unwound the handkerchief, and studied the round, swollen spot. "Stab yourself with a thorn?"

She wanted him to kiss it, to make it better. "Funny how much a little thorn can hurt," she replied.

"Not nearly as funny as how avoiding the truth can hurt," he said, releasing her hand.

Unwilling to let him see her cry, Hannah looked away.

"Don't look away, Hannah. I'm not moving from here until you level with me. If you dislike me, say so. If something else is bothering you—the way I walk, or talk, or handle people at work—whatever it is, tell me."

Hannah gathered her wits about her. "Max. It's none of those things, and it's nothing to do with you."

"Well, then, what is it? Something happen on that cruise? You meet another man?"

"Good God, no." Inside the phone began to ring again. "Let's go in. I must get that phone. I'm worried about Laura and the baby."

As Max helped her to her feet, Hannah felt a surge of pleasure at his touch. Max released her arm, bent and picked up her tools, and Hannah found herself longing for his hand in hers. She was relieved when he took her arm again and led her up the back stairs.

The answering machine was indeed turned off. The phone had stopped ringing again. Max reached for her hand and examined her thumb.

Silly woman. I actually want him to kiss it.

"Wash your hands," he instructed.

Hannah washed her hands, and Max smoothed on Neosporin ointment, then wrapped a Band-Aid around her thumb. The ache was nearly gone. Hannah poured two mugs of coffee, and they sat across from one another at the kitchen table.

"Laura's been fine, hasn't she?" Max asked.

They hadn't talked in nearly two weeks. "The baby's big. There're talking about a Cesarean," Hannah said.

He nodded, his eyes serious. "I'm sure it'll go well."

"I hope so."

An awkward pause followed.

"I can't stand what's happening to us," Max said.

"Neither can I," she replied. *Talk to him,* she told herself. *Be honest.* But the words formed a knot in her stomach, a knot so heavy she could not raise it to her throat and lips.

"Then what is it, Hannah? If you don't want to get married, fine. I won't bother you about that again."

His eyes were sad. Hannah thought of a stray dog her father had picked up somewhere and nursed to health, and the way that dog, Fritz, would sit close by her and mournfully look at her until she petted him. The dam in Hannah's heart burst.

She loved Max. She didn't want to love him, but she did. She had wallowed in a lost love, mourned the past, and had built a life avoiding love, an emotion too deeply associated with pain. Now she wanted Max—wanted to touch him, to run her hands along his back, his arms, to be held in those strong arms. Or was she too old for such things? Grace wasn't. Amelia wasn't. Even Lurina at age eighty-one wasn't, so why should she be? She didn't want to hide anything from Max any longer. Slowly, hesitantly Hannah began to speak.

"Like all girls in my day, I fantasized about a loving husband, a house in the suburbs, white picket fence, two kids, a dog. But Bill's drinking increased, as did his brutality, both verbal and physical. I had to get away from him, because either I would die from one of his beatings or I'd kill him. As it turned out, he died—his liver gave out—soon after the kids and I fled. If he hadn't, I am sure he would have come after us out of sheer meanness.

"I had no college education, no marketable skills. I cleaned people's houses and took a class in typing at night, then worked as a secretary, and eventually managed an office for a chiropractor. Years later, in my fifties, I met Dan Britton, a married man. After Bill I'd avoided men, especially married men, but I fell crazy in love with Dan." She stopped and squared her shoulders. "We had nine months, only nine months, and then Dan was killed in a boating accident." She spoke without emotion, as if telling him about someone else's life.

"I'm so sorry." Max said. His fingers touched hers.

Sunshine spilled through the window across the shiny new stove, across the kitchen floor, and cast a band of light across the table. The room seemed safe and cozy, a place where no harm could befall her. Hannah continued.

"Several weeks ago, out of the blue, I got a package from Dan's granddaughter: a diary she found while cleaning out her deceased grandmother's house. It was Marion, Dan's wife's, diary. Dan was Catholic, and certain that Marion would never give him a divorce. He was right. She never would have, but not for love of him or genuine religious reasons, but out of sheer spite. The diary was filled with vitriolic diatribes about Dan, about me. She knew about our relationship. How, I don't know. Reading it stirred up the whole sad affair, and left me as terrified of loving as I was before I met Dan." Her fingers reached out and touched his arm. "I couldn't let myself—well—care too much for you. You understand?" She raised her eyes and looked at him. "That's why I've been so horrid. I'm so sorry, Max."

Max took her hand in both of his, brought it to his lips, and kissed it. "It's all right, Hannah. We both have long years of history behind us. It takes a while to catch up. I'm glad you've told me." His eyes were soft and caring. "I've missed you, Hannah. I do care very much for you, and I'm sorry I've been so darn closemouthed about it. I'm sorry for all your pain. Bill was a monster, and then to lose Dan. I'll abide by whatever parameters you feel you need to set for our relationship."

Hannah flung her hands up. "I don't want to set any parameters. I care very much for you, too, Max."

They leaned across the table, the yellow-and-white checkered tablecloth puckering beneath the pressure of their arms. The band of sunshine linked them together. Their faces moved closer. They had never kissed. And then the ring of the phone jolted them apart.

Hannah jerked back, sprang up, and hastened to pick up the receiver. "When? Where are you?" she asked.

She covered the phone with her hand. "Laura's in labor."

Max was already on his feet.

Hannah said into the phone, "We're on our way. They'll both be fine, Hank." She hung up and moved toward Max. "Will it be all right? Hank said that by the time they got to the hospital, the baby's head was engaged, too far along for a Cesarean. Oh, God, Max." Hannah leaned against him. "Why didn't the doctor take that baby days ago? It's a big baby, big head—what if it can't come out naturally? Women and their babies used to die in situations like this." Hannah's body trembled.

"Not today, they don't." He hugged her for a moment, then gently eased her toward the door.

As many times as Hannah had traveled the roads from Covington to Asheville, never had the trip taken as long, never had traffic seemed so heavy or drivers so inconsiderate. The newly greening trees and shrubs, which would normally have delighted Hannah, whizzed by unnoticed. Max did not burden her with chatter but concentrated on driving.

When they reached Biltmore Avenue, cars were stalled bumper to bumper.

"Damn!" Max turned off at the first road he could, then detoured on backstreets until they arrived at the hospital, where he dropped her at the entrance door. "I'll park." In response to her worried look, he said, "I'll find you, don't worry."

At the front desk, a cheery volunteer directed Hannah to the elevator that would transport her to the delivery floor. An LPN directed her to a room at the end of a hallway. The hall, with its pale green walls, seemed a moss-covered tunnel, dim and endless. When she finally reached the waiting room, it was empty. Where was Hank? She remembered then that Hank would be with Laura. Ignoring the TV, which was set on CNN with the sound turned off and the ticker tape running below the picture, Hannah slipped into a tan leather chair near a wide window. When Max arrived a short time later, he found her staring unseeing at the range of mountains, turned lavender in the haze of the day.

"How is she?" he asked.

"I don't know. No one's come in here."

"I'll check with the nurse's station." Max hastened away and returned with no further news.

After what seemed an eternity, a haggard Hank, his eyes blurred with weariness, appeared in the doorway.

Hannah's stomach knotted. "My God. Something's gone wrong."

"It's a tough delivery." Hank shook his head. "They asked me to leave the delivery room. I guess I was asking too many questions, distracting the doctors." He began to cry, and buried his face in his hands. "It's my fault. I never should have let Laura talk me into having this baby. Of all people, I should know. My mother died having my sister. She was only forty-four."

This news stunned and frightened Hannah. She turned from him and brought her knuckles to her mouth. She wanted to scream, "Why did you, then?" But Hank looked so wretched, so helpless.

"They're putting her out," Hank said. "They're going to have to cut her cervix deep to get the baby out. It's a boy." He said it as if somehow the baby being a boy made it more crucial that it be whole and hardy.

Hannah bristled for a moment. She had two grown grandsons and would have loved it if the baby were a girl, but then, this was probably the only child the couple would have, and men wanted sons. The name thing. She recalled her husband Bill's face, uninterested when she had borne two daughters. Would Bill have been kinder had she given him sons? Looking up, she saw the tears in Hank's eyes and her annoyance melted.

Max laid a fatherly hand on Hank's shoulder. "It's not your fault. I'm sure Laura really wanted a baby. Medicine's changed a great deal since your mother died. They have new techniques."

The door opened and a nurse, all business, said, "Mr. Brinkley, you're wanted in the delivery room."

Hank staggered up, ran his fingers through his hair, and straightened his tie.

"Is the baby born? Is he all right? Is my daughter all right?" Hannah asked.

But the nurse turned and departed, and a dazed Hank followed.

Hannah sank into a chair. "Why won't they talk to me? I'm Laura's mother. Do they know that, Max? Did you tell them at the nurse's desk?"

"I told them. I think it's not their job to bring news. They have to wait for the doctor to okay it."

"I'm terrified, Max," Hannah said.

"We could go to the cafeteria and eat, or I could get us some coffee and doughnuts maybe?"

"I can't leave here. But yes, I could eat something," Hannah said.

Moments after Max left, two women entered: one older—a grandmother, Hannah thought—the other a woman of about fifty. Their eyes were red. The older woman's arm circled the shoulders of the younger one.

"How could Clara lose a baby? She's only twenty-two. I had two healthy babies when I was her age." The younger woman's voice was strained, close to tears.

"These things happen, Irene." The older woman sighed deeply, then nodded as they moved past Hannah to the couch at the far end of the room. After that, Hannah could hear only muffled words and see hand-holding and back-patting.

Frightened for Laura before, Hannah was now terrified, and Max was taking so long to get their coffee and doughnuts. *Hurry, Max. Hurry. I'm going crazy with worry.*

A short while later, the two women rose, the younger one leaning heavily on the older, walked slowly to the door, and departed. It seemed forever before Max returned with a cardboard tray bearing two mugs of coffee and doughnuts.

Hannah knew it was afternoon, because the sun hung in the sky and beat hot against the glass of the waiting room. She must have dozed, her head on Max's shoulder, and she awakened confused about where she was and why she was there. Suddenly Hank, all smiles, burst into the room. "It's over. Mother and baby are fine. A nine-pound baby boy."

"Oh, thank God." Hannah reached up from her chair and Hank bent to hug her.

His voice full of pride, Hank repeated, "A baby boy, and so big." He pulled up a chair. "They had to break his shoulder to get him out, but the doctor said that's not so unusual."

"Break the baby's shoulder?" Hannah whispered.

"Baby's bones are soft. He'll heal in no time with no adverse effects," Max said.

"Why didn't her doctor take that baby a week ago?" Hannah asked.

Hank did not reply to that. "The cord was wrapped around his neck. I thought I'd pass out waiting for him to breathe. But he's fine now."

"Laura saw that?" Hannah asked.

"No. She was out cold, still is. The baby's in the nursery. Want to see him?"

"Of course we do." Max helped Hannah to her feet. "Laura's all right?"

Hank nodded.

They followed Hank down a hall, turned, and walked down another hall until they came to a wall of glass through which they saw two dozen or so babies swathed in blankets in small cribs. Some were red-faced from crying; others slept benignly. Hank pointed to a crib three in from the glass. The infant's face was screwed into a grimace.

Hank pressed the ID bracelet he wore against the glass.

The nurse reached into the crib, took the baby in her arms, and brought him to the window. Not a strand of hair graced his head. His face glowed crimson. His eyes were squeezed shut, and tiny ears hugged his head. Hannah knew that babies did not focus this early, yet when he opened his eyes, he seemed to stare at her through the glass, and those eyes bore into her soul with so powerful a connection that she steadied herself against Max.

"What's his name?" Max asked.

"Andrew James, after my father," Hank said.

"Andy," Hannah whispered. "Little Andy."

"Not so little." Max squeezed Hannah's shoulder.

"When can I see Laura?" Hannah asked.

"They expect she'll sleep a while, and then they'll bring the baby to her. How about after dinner?" Hank asked.

"We'll come back then," Max said.

The nurse behind the glass wall departed, taking Andrew James away. Hannah wanted to reach through the hard surface separating them and grab him from her. Max tapped her arm. "Let's go." Hannah turned to Hank and hugged him. "Congratulations, Dad. I'm so glad it's over."

Laura and Hank had rented a house on the same block as Russell and Emily's new home, in a small cluster of redbrick houses recently constructed on knolls in a valley between Mars Hill and Covington. The development bore the peculiar name of Pickle Hill. Three days after Andy's birth, Hank brought Laura and baby home to Pickle Hill.

"His shoulder'll heal naturally, the doctors said," Hank told Hannah.

It seemed to Hannah that in those early days, every time she visited her daughter and new grandson, Emily was there giving advice, taking charge of things. Emily and Laura were, after all, women of the same age with young children. Wasn't this what Hannah had wanted, friendship between the two women? Emily had had an easy birth with Melissa, and Melissa had been a baby who within three months, after a 10:00 p.m. bottle, had slept through the night. Andy, on the other hand, fussed and cried, and Laura's recovery was slow. It hurt to sit and walk. Her nipples cracked, and Andy had to go on a bottle. Her swollen breasts hurt.

"I feel such a failure not being able to breast-feed Andy," Laura said to Hannah.

"He'll be just fine. I bottle-fed you," Hannah said. "Don't go on like this. Be glad Andy's healthy. You'll be on your feet again soon."

It was apparently not what Laura wanted to hear, and she turned from Hannah and cried.

"I'm as lousy a mother as I always was," Hannah told Max. "I can't even comfort my daughter now."

"You mean well. Laura will understand."

But when Hannah returned to apologize and assure her daughter of her love for her and her great passion for little Andy, there was Emily rocking Andy. It seemed Emily was always there rocking, and walking, and feeding, and changing the baby. Hannah hardly got to hold her grandson.

"Why doesn't Emily go to her office and leave my family alone?" Hannah muttered to herself. To Max she said, "Never in my life have I felt like such a disaster." They were sitting on his porch. They had grown closer, had kissed and held one another, but had gone no further. Why, she wasn't sure, but then she wasn't sure about anything these days.

"And what if Amelia decides to move out?"

"Now don't you start worrying about things that haven't happened. Amelia will return calm and peaceful, and she won't move out," Max assured her.

But Hannah's mind was full of concerns and would not be quieted. "Grace spends hours with Lucy. She gets her every day after school and takes her into Asheville to a counselor twice a week," Hannah said. "She asked if you and I would take Lurina and Old Man to his doctor. Seems he got dizzy and fell yesterday. They're squeezing him in at the office, or we could be there for ages." Hannah twisted her hands. "Grace is a great rescuer. Next thing she'll want Lucy to live with us."

"There you go again," Max said, "worrying in advance."

"I didn't used to do that," Hannah said.

"So don't start. And yes, I'll be happy to drive Old Man and Lurina to his doctor's office. You don't even have to come with us if you prefer not to."

"Of course I'll go. I don't like what's happening to us—Grace and me, that is. She's gone so much, and when she's free, there's Bob."

Max brought his rocker to a halt and rested his hands on her rocker, bringing it to a halt. "Okay, Hannah, out with it. What's really bothering you?"

Hannah hesitated. It was odd talking in an intimate manner to a man. Would he think her trivial? Lonely, and missing the companionship she had grown to depend on mainly from Grace, she finally confided in Max. "Amelia's on my mind a lot. She'll be coming back soon. Goodness knows what she's decided, or how I'm going to apologize to her." In the silence that followed, a brisk breeze stirred the stems of the wisteria vine twined about the fretwork of the porch.

"Amelia annoys me with her self-centeredness sometimes," Hannah said. "I knew this before we moved here. It's a question of acceptance; I know that, too. Yet I resist. I want her to change."

"Not very likely," Max said.

"She's a creative woman, and she can be very kind. Amelia was wonderful to Laura after that terrible accident. It was Amelia who got Laura to open up, helped her heal." She was silent for a time, then began to rock vigorously.

Max asked again, "What's really bothering you, Hannah?"

"Amelia was able to give Laura something Grace and I couldn't, as Emily can provide Laura and Andy with things I can't."

"Ah," he said. "Emily."

She looked at him. "I hate that I feel this way, Max. I resent Emily being there all the time. Don't laugh at me, but I want to hold Andy, and rock him, and coo at him."

"Ever consider telling Laura that?" Max said.

"You men." Hannah smiled at him. "You oversimplify things."

"And you ladies complicate things, worry them to death." Max rested his wide, callused, protective hand on hers.

For a moment Hannah felt totally at peace.

"Then there's Mike. He's moved in with Roger."

"What's wrong with that? They seem to get along well," Max said.

"Mike's been Amelia's friend and escort for years. She'll have to find someone else to drive her places at night, take her to the theater."

"She's a big girl, Hannah. Amelia can take care of herself."

But Hannah knew that Amelia could do impulsive and foolish things, and she worried.

"You'll talk to Laura?" he asked.

"I guess I'll have to, won't I?"

Max said, "There's a poem of William Blake's, I think. I recall only a bit of it:

> I was angry with my friend:
> I told my wrath, my wrath did end.
> I was angry with my foe:
> I told it not, my wrath did grow."

He stopped and scrunched his forehead. "I don't recall the rest of it—just the last two lines, where the foe ends up dead under an apple tree.

> *In the morning glad I see*
> *My foe outstretch'd beneath the tree."*

"That's a poignant poem, awful and realistic, isn't it?" Hannah said. "If you don't speak about a thing, it hovers like a huge winged vulture over relationships, as it did over you and me."

"So, you'll talk to Laura?"

Hannah nodded. Damn these life lessons, as Grace called such things, when situations demanded that you step outside of your comfortable box and engage in activities and behaviors completely out of character. It was darn hard to change.

But Hannah loathed being a whiner or a beggar. She knew that she must clear the air with her daughter if she were to have calm, quiet access to Andy, have a relaxed and happy relationship with Laura, and maintain good feelings about Emily.

16

WHO'S GONNA MIND
THE PIGS?

"Grace would know what to do. Grace always knows what to do," Lurina said from the back of Max's car. They were returning to Covington from the hospital in Asheville. "Not meaning to hurt your feelings, Hannah, but I'm used to Grace doing things for me. She's been like a daughter, if I'd a had one, since the early days you ladies come to Covington. She found my beautiful wedding dress and got me married off."

"She surely did." Hannah remembered what a time Grace had finding the right store, and arranging for the proprietor, Ellie Lerner, to bring three dresses to Lurina's house. Then there had been coping with the issue of which graveyard Lurina and Old Man would be buried in when the time came, the Mastersons' or the Reynoldses.' "

"Grace's been there to help me sort out things, especially since I married Joseph Elisha."

Hannah wondered what things Grace had helped Lurina sort through, but did not ask. "Grace is with Lucy today. She took her to a counselor in Asheville."

"That girl got money problems, so young?" Lurina asked.

"No. Not a money counselor, someone who works with psychological problems." Hannah turned around so she could see Lurina, and tapped her own head with a finger. "Worries, anxieties, things like that."

Lurina scrunched at one end of the big backseat. "What kind of worries anyone so young got?"

Hannah thought it would be easier not to tell the story now, since Lurina had obviously not heard it. "These young people today," she said.

With her gray hair and gray dress, Lurina seemed to melt into the gray leather of the backseat. "I knowed something was serious wrong with Joseph Elisha weeks past, the way he'd clutch a-hold of his back and have to stop whatever he was doing. What they say he's got, Hannah?"

"Kidney failure," Hannah said.

"Means his kidneys ain't so good no more? Come to think on it, he was having trouble peein'. Stubborn old man, bless his heart. I shoulda made him go to the doctor sooner."

"I'm sure you did all you could," Max said. "You were right on the mark, insisting he go to the doctor today."

"I ain't figured on him getting put in no hospital, though," Lurina said. "Joseph Elisha used to say, 'Keep me outta the hospital, Lurrie. Once a man gets in there, he ain't never coming out.' You think he's coming out, Hannah?"

"Medicine can do marvelous things today. I'm sure he'll get the best care."

"Ain't no care so good as care at home. I sure wish Grace was about." Lurina wrung her hands, sank even deeper into the seat, and fell silent.

Grace slept at Lurina's home that night. Without central heat or air, the Masterson farmhouse was damp and chilly, and smelled of mold. Grace hoped that the mysterious noises that startled her from sleep were no more than the scurrying of animal feet in the attic.

That afternoon, after dropping Lucy off at her home, Grace had returned to the farmhouse to find the phone ringing.

"Grace, Old Man's been hospitalized with kidney failure," Hannah said. "Max and I took him to the hospital. Lurina's been asking for you. Call her."

"Where are you?" Grace asked.

"At work."

"Okay, I'm going over there as soon as I change into something more comfortable."

Within fifteen minutes, Grace had driven across the one remaining bridge that spanned Bad River. Several years ago, the larger bridge closer to Lurina's house had been washed away in a terrible storm and was never rebuilt.

"This bridge's a piece closer to the shopping center," Old Man had said at the time. "We ain't got to be spending money to rebuild the other one. Leave it be."

Before she fell asleep, Grace listened for the shuffling of slippers that signaled the old woman's passage by her door. Then Grace heard one, two, and then a third lock being bolted. Lurina kept the front door barred and bolted, and the back door unlocked. It made no sense to Grace, but she'd always taken it in stride and written it off as another of Lurina's eccentricities.

Grace worried about sleeping in a house with an unlocked back door. As she lay awake in the too-soft bed in a room with water-stained, striped wallpaper, she berated herself for not insisting that Lurina stay with her until they had word of Old Man's condition. Grace decided that she would insist that Lurina pack a bag and come to their farmhouse tomorrow.

She must have dozed, for Grace started awake at the sound of a thud, followed by a scream that pierced the darkness. Her heart leaping in her chest, Grace bounded from bed, switched on a light, and tore open her bedroom door. There in the hall, lying in a pathetic little heap, was Lurina.

Grace kneeled beside her and cradled her head in her lap. As she looked down at the frail little woman, love filled Grace's heart.

She had pondered her encounter with the totality of the universe and puzzled over why it had happened to her. Through books, Grace learned that she was not alone in spontaneously and inexplicably experiencing an alternate reality. She had brooded about whether she ought to change her life in some way and how. Maybe her experience was a call for a more solitary, meditative life. Should she join a meditation group? Some were listed in the weekly *Mountain Xpress*.

Now, looking down at Lurina, it was all so clear and so very simple. Her work did not lie in meditation and solitude. Hers was a spirituality of action, as here, now, with Lurina.

"I love you, Lurina," she whispered, and softly touched the old woman's hair and face with her fingertips. "Lurina," Grace called several times. Finally, Lurina's eyelids fluttered and opened.

She looked bewildered at first, then seemed to collect her thoughts. "Grace, dear, what you doing here? Lordy me. I was going downstairs to check on Joseph Elisha. He's been doing poorly lately."

Old Man slept alone downstairs? Hadn't they converted the dining room to a bedroom for them so they wouldn't have to climb the stairs? But it was Old Man who had trouble with stairs, not Lurina. So they slept one up, one down. Thank God that Lurina hadn't made it to the stairs; she might have tumbled down them headfirst.

"I just checked on him," Grace lied. "He's sleeping. Come, let me help you back to bed." That done, an exhausted Grace sank into Lurina's mother's cane and mahogany rocker near the window in Lurina's bedroom. The light from the Elk Road Plaza sign lit a section of Elk Road and the roofs of several shops in the plaza. Grace checked the time on the bedside clock. Three a.m. Outside a rooster crowed once, twice, three times. Why was a rooster crowing in the dark of night?

Lurina's eyes flew wide open. "Cock crowing and it ain't daytime. Three times, it crowed. Bad news coming, my mother always said." Lurina closed her eyes again, leaving Grace to consider superstitions and trying to recall if she had ever heard a rooster crow at night.

Grace didn't leave Lurina's room until dawn, until the rooster crowed at the appropriate hour, until the lights from the sign at Elk Road Plaza were turned off and the cars of early risers moved along the road.

The first call from the hospital came at seven in the morning. After half a night spent sitting in a rocking chair, Grace's back, shoulders, and neck ached. She had showered, dressed, gone downstairs to make tea for herself, and set up a tray to take tea and toast to Lurina when the phone rang.

"Mrs. Reynolds?"

"No. This is Mrs. Singleton, a friend. Mrs. Reynolds can't come to the phone right now. Can I take a message?" How would the hospital know Lurina had kept her maiden name?

A long pause then indistinguishable whispered words, and the voice returned. "Ask her to phone Dr. Pyne at Saint Joseph Hospital, please." The voice gave a phone number and an extension number, which Grace jotted down. The line went dead.

A chill crept up Grace's arms. In the dark of night, the rooster had crowed three times. Bad news coming, Lurina had said. Surely if Old Man were ready to be released the voice would have been upbeat, not so somber or brusque. Had he taken a turn for the worse? Should she wake Lurina? Grace set down the tea things and phoned Hannah.

"My goodness," Hannah said, "is it daytime?"

"It is. Get up and open your shutters," Grace replied. "Listen, Hannah, the hospital just called about Old Man. They left a number. No, they wouldn't give me any information. I have this feeling it's not good news. He's either worse or maybe even . . ." She hesitated and swallowed hard. "Gone. Please, can you come over?"

"I'll be there as soon as I drag my body from this bed," Hannah said. She was by nature an early riser, and the days that she did not have to be at the office for a meeting she slept until at least eight thirty.

"I'm sorry to wake you. I didn't know if you were going to work."

"I took today off," Hannah said. "I'll be over soon as I can. Make a pot of coffee, will you?"

Hannah pushed away her covers. She lifted one leg as high as she could, lowered it, and repeated the procedure with the other leg. This she did six times. She intended to do ten leg lifts, but never seemed to get beyond six. She did the same with her arms: up and out, up and out. This, she believed, was healthy, got her blood circulating and helped shake the cobwebs from her brain. Certainly it made getting up easier. A hot shower followed by a cold rinse completed her routine. Twenty minutes later, she joined Grace in Lurina's chilly kitchen. Grace handed her a mug of coffee.

"I've been trying to decide whether to wake Lurina or wait for her to get up," Grace said.

"Let her sleep. Whatever it is, let it wait." Hannah nursed the warm coffee mug in her hands. "So, Old Man sleeps downstairs and she sleeps upstairs."

Grace shrugged. "People have all kinds of arrangements, I guess."

"What can you expect at their ages?"

Grace's brows puckered. "I don't think age has anything to do with it. Some people need the warmth of a body next to theirs, other people don't."

"You think some folks are having sex well into old age, don't you?" Hannah grinned.

Grace blushed. "Bob told me that at ninety his father was still chasing women. The nurses at the retirement home he lived in used to hurry to get away from him. Old Man and Lurina obviously didn't need to share a bed or a bedroom. Maybe they had sex and maybe not. Maybe they just enjoyed the companionship."

"To each his own," Hannah replied.

Grace shifted in her chair. "Imagine talking like this when Old Man could be dying."

"Or dead." Hannah rose and poured herself a second cup of coffee.

"Yes," Grace said.

"It's a tribute to them both that they married and had these few years together rather than living alone." Hannah raised her coffee mug as one would raise a wineglass. "To Lurina and Old Man."

"If Old Man dies . . ." Grace began.

"When he dies."

"Okay, when he dies. They've agreed that both of them will be buried up the mountain in the Reynolds's family cemetery. That's a long drive," Grace said.

"I imagine you'll be taking Lurina there every Sunday for a while to visit his grave." Hannah stopped, Lurina stood in the doorway.

"Whose grave you two visiting?"

"Just talking about where we'd be buried, so far from any of our homes," Hannah said.

"Make you a graveyard back of your house." Lurina limped toward them.

Grace hastened to pull out a chair for her. "Your foot's hurt? You took a fall last night, remember?"

"I don't rightly remember," Lurina said. "Just know this here ankle's giving me a fit this morning. I'll walk on it awhile. It'll work out." She stretched out her leg, rotated her ankle, and winced.

"Maybe you ought to stay off of it a few days," Hannah said.

Lurina gave a cackle. "Only sissys take to their beds over every little ache or pain."

Grace turned another chair to face Lurina, brought a pillow from the living room, and lifted the old woman's leg onto it. "You need to keep this elevated," she said. "I'll get you ice wrapped in a kitchen towel. Are you hungry? Want a cup of tea or coffee? Want me to scramble you some eggs?"

"Be mighty nice, a couple of eggs scrambled dry. And there's some bacon in the fridge. Fry me up three pieces, please," Lurina said.

Grace waited until Lurina had eaten before putting in the call to Dr. Pyne. When she did, the news was so bad that Lurina dropped the phone, clasped her hands over her ears, bent nearly double, and uttered animal moans. While Grace tended to Lurina, Hannah took the call.

"He passed away at three this morning," the crisp young voice reported.

So perfunctory, Hannah thought. But it's her job to make these calls. It can't be easy. One protects oneself the best one can.

"What funeral home do you want us to call to get the body?" the voice asked.

"His wife has about collapsed here," Hannah said. "Give us a half hour and I'll get back to you."

Hannah found a phone book and thumbed through the Yellow Pages. She read the list to Lurina, who chose one of the funeral homes. Hannah dialed the number, gave them the information, then relayed the name of the funeral home to the woman at the hospital.

Then Grace managed to help Lurina to the couch in the living room, where she lay on her side, moaning. Grace sat in a chair alongside her. Old Man dying and Lurina's anguish at her loss reopened old wounds for Grace. She felt again a rending emptiness and the gut-gripping fear of being alone that she had known the day Ted died. She wanted to cradle Lurina in her arms, to say "I know" or "I understand," but she realized that Lurina probably felt that she alone had ever felt such wrenching pain.

In the two days before they buried Old Man, Lurina stayed with the ladies. The phone rang off the hook as people called to offer condolences. The refrigerator brimmed with food. On the third day, those closest to Lurina and Old Man formed a caravan from the funeral home and followed the hearse to the church, located halfway up the mountain from the Reynolds's cemetery. Bob's Cherokee transported Grace, Lurina, Emily, and Russell. Max, Hannah, Brenda, and Ellie Lerner followed in Max's car. Amelia, who had returned from Maine the previous evening, accompanied Roger and Mike in Mike's van. Besides his favorite grandson, Wayne, several of Old Man's children and grandchildren had come from states to the south and west of North Carolina. Grace pressed the hands of the nieces from Tennessee, whom she had met before, as they stood on the steps of the small white church with the tall steeple.

"They been tolling the bell for a good half hour. They're gonna do ninety-three rings, like in the old times," Wayne said. "Old Man would sure like that." He hugged Lurina. She clung to him, her arms straining to circle his neck. A bright-eyed girl with short brown hair and a quick, friendly smile stood near Wayne. He introduced her to Grace and the others as Maureen Greenwood. The way they looked at one another, it was clear that they were more than casual acquaintances.

"We gather together this day to bid farewell to Joseph Elisha Reynolds, our beloved friend and neighbor," the preacher said. "He was a man who took great pride in work. Honesty was second nature to him. Shake his hand, and the deal was guaranteed. Joseph Elisha was a man who loved the land, preserved the land, and he sure did love those pigs of his." He related a touching anecdote about Old Man and a sick pig, which he placed in the front seat of his car and drove for two hours to an emergency room, only to be told that they did not treat pigs. The eulogy went on for what seemed to Grace to be an hour, but Bob later said it was twenty minutes.

Bob, Max, Wayne, one of old man's sons, another of his grandsons, and a cousin from Tennessee bore the casket from hearse to church and from church to hearse. They joined the procession of cars up the narrow mountain road until, finally, they descended into the valley where Old Man and Wayne had lived for so many years in twin mobile homes alongside the creek. Beyond, on a hillside knoll under a dark-green tarp, set among concrete angels and tall tombstones, a mound of fresh earth was clearly visible. Grace shivered at the sight.

At the gravesite, Lurina, shrouded in black, leaned on a cane and wept silently. Wayne stood on one side of her, Grace on the other. A prayer was said, and the casket lowered. Relatives dribbled handfuls of dirt into the grave. Then the assembled made their way slowly down the hillside to their cars. Those not returning to their homes in other states headed for the ladies' farmhouse, where Anna had prepared food and drink.

As they drove along, Grace could not help but notice that with the bout of warm weather they had been having, tiny leaves were beginning to unfurl on trees and bushes along the sides of the road. It startled her when Lurina bent close and whispered, "Who's gonna mind the pigs?"

Grace slipped an arm about the frail shoulders. "We'll figure it out. Don't worry."

Old and stooped, Pastor Johnson awaited them at the farmhouse along with their neighbors, the Herrills, the Craines, and the Lunds. Leaning heavily on Bob and Max, Lurina eased her way up the steps, across the porch, and entered the house. She greeted the pastor, who assisted her to a chair near the fireplace, where she sat like a queen.

Grace bustled about, directing Bob to get a chair for Lurina's leg. "Put your leg up on this chair," she said to Lurina.

"I ain't gonna sit here like no cripple with people coming," Lurina replied. She sat with her feet flat on the floor, her shoulders straight, her chin high, as one by one their neighbors offered their condolences.

"She's actually enjoying this," Amelia whispered to Grace.

"She's probably never had this much attention. I haven't had a chance to welcome you back properly, Amelia." Grace hugged Amelia. "I missed you. Did you have a great time?"

They moved into the kitchen, where Grace placed sugar cookies on a glass platter. Max's Anna took the platter to the living room.

"I did," Amelia replied.

When Anna returned with a tray of used glasses, Grace added them to the dishwasher.

"But not as I expected," Amelia continued. "It was incredibly cold, as you said it would be. I had to go to L.L.Bean and buy warmer clothes. The other students were all kids in their twenties." She held up her hand like a traffic cop. "I said to myself, Hold it now, Amelia.

This is too much, trying to keep up with all these energetic young people. So, I checked out of the workshop and into a bed-and-breakfast in a delightful little harbor town and spent the rest of the time moseying around, shooting film when and where I pleased."

"Sounds as if you did what was right for you." Grace studied Amelia's face. She looked rested and calm. "You're not going to leave us, are you?"

Amelia shook her head no.

"I'm glad. So very glad." Grace squeezed Amelia's hand.

"But I have to have a talk with Hannah, to get past the meanness we've both directed at one another," Amelia said.

"You cannot imagine how happy that makes me," Grace said.

"I hope Hannah feels the way I do."

"She does. I know she does." They pulled out chairs and sat at the kitchen table.

"Lord, but it's good to be home," Amelia said.

"I hope you don't mind, but I asked Lurina to stay with us for a few days. I spent a night at her place, in the most uncomfortable bed I have ever slept in," Grace said.

"You slept over there?" Amelia pinched her nose. "How could you stand the smell of the place—mothballs, mold, and God knows what else?"

"Lurina got up in the middle of the night and fell in the hallway. She hurt her ankle. I don't think she ought to be alone right now."

"I have no objection to her being here." Amelia's eyes narrowed in thought. "I'd love to photograph her in her widow's weeds."

Grace poked Amelia's shoulder. "Oh, you're so bad, Amelia."

"I am, aren't I?" She grinned.

It had been a long day. Grace sank into bed. Lying down was heaven. Normally she opened her window and fell asleep listening to the murmur of the stream, but not tonight. Instead, she lay there thinking about Hannah and Amelia, who had gone upstairs together earlier that evening to talk.

Grace had shooed Anna home when Max and Bob left, and had carried the few plates and glasses that remained to be washed out to the kitchen. After putting a final load in the dishwasher, Grace had wiped off the counters and helped Lurina settle down in the guest room.

"I sure would like a light in here," Lurina had said. She'd looked so tiny in the queen-size bed.

Grace had turned on a small lamp on the dresser and a light in the bathroom. She'd left the bathroom door slightly ajar. As she started to leave the room, Lurina had called to her. "Grace, come sit awhile."

Weary as she was, Grace had pulled a chair to Lurina's bedside.

"If I'da had a daughter, Grace, she couldna done no better by me than you done. I feel right bad I can't leave you my house and land."

"I love you, Lurina, and I don't need to inherit anything from you."

Lurina had shaken her head and uttered a sad little sigh. "I wish my father hadn't decided that when I was gone all the property should go to make a park." She sighed. "How'd he know there'd be a nice big park right over there on Cove Road?" She shook her head and seemed to lose her trend of thought. She folded her hands across her belly. "I couldn't a gone back to that house tonight, Grace, my girl."

"We wouldn't have wanted you to. You stay with us as long as you'd like." For a second, Grace had wondered if this could extend into weeks or even months, and how Amelia and Hannah would feel about that. She smiled down at Lurina. "As long as you want."

"Couple of days is all I'm gonna need." Lurina had closed her eyes. Grace could see her struggling to keep them open.

"When you get back home, when you're ready, I'll come over and help you clear out things or whatever you want done."

"I'm gonna move downstairs to Joseph Elisha's room. Steps is getting too much, like he always said."

"That's a good plan." Grace had bent and kissed Lurina's warm dry forehead. How frail she looks, Grace had thought, and yet how resilient she actually is.

Now, lying in her own bed upstairs, feeling the muscles in her legs, back, and arms relax, Grace gave thanks for the blessings of good friends, for Bob and his family, and for her comfortable life. She turned over and snuggled a pillow, but she couldn't still her mind. Old Man was gone. She had known him for only four years, yet it felt like the end of an era. Was Old Man a soul now, floating over them, looking down and blessing Lurina? She hoped so. It hit her that amazingly, she no longer feared death, only the act of dying, and then only if it were painful, long and drawn out like Charles's and Ted's last illnesses had been.

Until tonight, the idea of dying, of no longer being conscious of her own being, had been an absolutely frightening concept. She did not want to die for a good long while—not for another fifteen or even twenty years, if she got her diabetes under control. Her mind drifted from Old Man's death to her own health.

After the fire she had lost twelve pounds; all the stress and worry had taken away her appetite. Over time, she had regained six pounds and several more on the ship. Yesterday, when she checked her blood sugar, it had been almost three hundred. That scared her. Guilt at neglecting herself filled her, followed by anxiety. She must get a grip on this eating business or she'd be dead sooner rather than later. *But not quite yet, please, God.* At that moment, in the still, dark night, Grace resolved to change her eating habits. With that issue settled, within seconds she was fast asleep.

While Grace pondered dying, down the hall in Amelia's bedroom, Amelia and Hannah were deep in discussion. "I don't want us to be at each other's throats," Amelia said. "I'm sorry for anything and everything I've done to upset you."

Hannah swallowed. She wanted to hug Amelia, but as much as she told herself to reach over and do it, she couldn't lift her arms. "I haven't been the nicest housemate." How inadequate that sounded. Amelia had said she was sorry, and Hannah should respond in kind. "I'm. I'm . . ." she began and stopped.

"You're sorry, too?" Amelia looked hopeful.

Hannah nodded. "Yes. I'm sorry." Once said, it didn't seem so hard. "I've been intolerant, unkind, mean, rude, picky. Can you forgive me?"

"Heavens, yes. We all have difficult times in life."

Hannah paced the bedroom floor, then stopped at the end of Amelia's bed, where Amelia sat propped up with pillows. "I went a little crazy when I got that diary, thinking of what used to be, what could have been, how I was spied on, and all that evil intention Marion directed toward us, toward me." She walked to the window and stared out into the night for several long moments, then turned to face Amelia. "I was terrified. What if I let myself care—really care—for Max and I marry him and he dies? I couldn't bear that."

"You've had such an awful few weeks, and I didn't help. I wasn't sympathetic or thoughtful; I was flippant and silly, especially on the ship," Amelia said.

"I've been so crabby and judgmental. Why shouldn't you dance and have a good time?" Hannah heaved a deep sigh and sat in a nearby chair. "Well, all that said, can we still be friends? You won't move out, will you? This was your house. If you hadn't inherited it from your cousin, we wouldn't even be here."

"It's our home. And no, I won't move out." Amelia removed her shoes and rubbed her feet. "I met a woman in Maine. She'd lost a daughter and husband, as I have. Although she lives alone, she depends on people from her small town to help her. Otherwise she couldn't keep her business, a bed-and-breakfast, through the lean times and the cold of winters. Talking with her, I realized how much sharing a home with you and Grace means to me. I don't ever want any of us to leave."

"Good." Hannah stood. She'd had more than enough emotion for one day. "I'm glad you're back. I'm going to bed now."

"Thanks for talking. Sleep well tonight, Hannah."

"I'm sure I will. You do also. Good night, Amelia."

Hannah moved slowly down the hallway. This hall was wider, four feet wide rather than the three feet of their previous farmhouse. The tunnel effect produced by three feet of space was gone. Amelia had lined one wall with photographs, and Hannah stopped to really look at them. The glass was dusty. Hannah took out her handkerchief and wiped the light layer of dust away. All were nature scenes. One of the photos showed a half dozen cows descending a hillside, and above them, towering cumulous clouds built in the sky. In another, a young girl peeped from behind a tree trunk so thick she could not bring her arms to touch one another. The third showed fog-shrouded trees in a forest, and finally there was a photo of a rushing, tumbling creek careening over rocks, kicking up foam, probably taken just after a rainstorm.

It was the shadows and light in the pictures that made them so amazing. The woman does have talent, Hannah thought as she passed Grace's room. No light gleamed beneath the door. Hannah walked to the top of the stairs. A dim light downstairs lent warmth and friendliness to the darkness. In the stillness Hannah thought she could hear Lurina snoring. Deeply satisfied, she proceeded along the hall to her own room.

A few days later, from the kitchen window, Hannah noticed tiny heads of crocuses and pansies in her garden. They were gifts of spring. Her heart leaped. These small gems had sloughed off blankets of earth, and lifted violet and yellow faces to the sunshine. Hannah set her coffee cup in the sink and hastened outside.

Birds twittered from perches deep within the branches of the big oak. Soon there would be wide green leaves to provide the cover needed to build their nests. Summer tugged at her heart. Butterflies would arrive, bringing life and movement to the garden. Hannah loved butterflies, especially the monarchs, which she knew needed a temperature of 55 degrees before they could move their flying muscles. Instinct kept them south of the border, in Mexico and Equador, until the weather warmed. Then they began their long journey north, with a stopover in her garden. Hannah could sit for long spells of time watching butterflies flitter from plant to plant in graceful, complex aerial ballets. To welcome them, she planted flowers from which they drew life-sustaining nectar: monarda, red salvia, and the shrub known commonly as butterfly bush. Spring would bring the ubiquitous ladybugs, who would cling to exterior walls, cluster on ceilings, and ultimately fall to die as dried bits of shell on the floor.

Hannah lifted her head and sniffed the air. "Smells like rain," she said aloud. She bent and plucked a weed from the well-mulched flower bed alongside the front porch just as Wayne Reynolds's truck turned into the driveway.

"Hi, Miss Hannah." Wayne stepped from the cab. Hands jammed in the pockets of his jeans, he sauntered toward her. "I come to see Miss Lurina. How's she doing?"

"She's either still asleep or in the kitchen with Grace." Hannah brushed the hair from her forehead. "How you been, boy?" He wasn't a boy, except in Hannah's eyes. Wayne had worked in her greenhouse before it proved to be too much for her, and she had sold it to him. Last year, the fire had destroyed the greenhouse and left melted globs of glass and shattered clay pots scattered where it had stood. The insurance money made it possible for Wayne to go off to Haywood Community College near Waynesville to study horticulture.

"I'm just fine, Miss Hannah. Doing real good in my classes, mostly 'cause you taught me so much before I ever started at college."

Hannah sat on the steps of the porch and motioned for Wayne to join her. "Seemed like a nice young lady you had with you at your grandfather's funeral."

He grinned and rubbed his chin. "Met her in class." His eyes grew serious. "I wanna talk with you about her, Miss Hannah."

They stretched their long legs down across the steps. "What is it, Wayne?"

"I like her a lot, Miss Hannah, and I think she likes me a whole heap more, but she's city folk, and I been raised back beyond nowhere, up the mountain. Her folks went to fancy parties and drove fancy cars while Old Man and me milked cows, slaughtered pigs, and cured meat for winter." He looked sad and shook his head. "It ain't gonna work."

Probably not, Hannah waited for him to go on.

"I'm gonna break it off with her," he said. "Let her down gentle, like. I don't want to hurt her none."

"When a person breaks off with someone they've loved and who still loves them, someone does get hurt. It can't be helped. That's life. The rejected one is miserable for a while, but most people cope and go on."

Wayne nodded. "I been rejected myself and gone on." He sounded slightly encouraged.

"So, then, what next?" Hannah asked.

He clasped his hands in his lap. "I talked to them at the college. I'm gonna take just one class on campus this next semester and one class by correspondence, so's I can live with Miss Lurina for a time and take care of her and Old Man's pigs. If I run into any problems trying to take a class by mail, can I come to you, Miss Hannah?"

"Certainly, but remember, I'm not college trained."

He waved his hand as if to brush away her hesitation and grinned. "You know a heck of a lot more than some professors who ain't been out of their classrooms in years."

She heard the *ain't* clearly and thought of Maureen and her folks.

She thought about how she would have felt had one of her girls brought home an uneducated young man. She'd probably have rejected him out of hand. "Lurina know about your plans?"

"Not yet, she don't. That's why I come today, to tell her."

"Think she'll object?"

"Nah. Someone's got to tend Old Man's pigs. Besides, a woman her age oughten to be living alone."

"Better focus on the pigs. Don't tell her you think she needs you. She's a proud, stubborn old woman."

He nodded, and they sat comfortably in silence for a time.

"You're a good boy, Wayne. Lurina's frail, and it'll be a comfort to all of us to know there's someone in the house with her. But promise me you'll go back and finish college."

"I sure will, Miss Hannah—don't you worry none about that." He blushed. "Miss Hannah, Maureen and me, we been livin' together. She's gonna graduate the end of this semester, before I get back. So it could work out just natural, like."

They rose, and Wayne took the front steps three at a time and bounded across the porch, past empty flowerpots and rocking chairs pulled close to the wall, away from winter's weather.

Hannah sat back down on the porch steps for a while. How irresponsible and unreliable Wayne had been when she'd first met him. He'd certainly grown and changed for the better, which was evident by his desire to help Lurina. Hannah felt good, knowing she had had some small hand in his becoming the person he was today. She wanted to see him settled and happy, and she wondered, was he right about Maureen?

People from different backgrounds, races, and cultures met and married all the time. The world had changed; class lines weren't as strictly drawn as in the past. Or were they, when it boiled down to being accepted by in-laws?

All about Hannah, in the warm, sweet air, in the sticky new leaves, in the fat white clouds that drifted past, the world seemed as eager for spring as she was. High on Snowman's Cap, she could see that the snowcap had shrunk. As the snow melted, streams flowed full and fast, sometimes flooding. Even their small creek would fill to the top of its banks, though it rarely spilled over.

Hannah was pleased that Wayne would take Lurina home. Not

that she didn't like Lurina, but adding another person to their house-hold would, over time, disrupt their lives. Once Lurina was gone, their routines would resume. In the time that Lurina had been there, the TV downstairs was on all day long. Lurina loved her soap operas, her favorite being *Days of Our Lives*. Those characters were as real to Lurina as Hannah's staff and colleagues at the park were to her.

Hannah had grown accustomed to visiting with Grace in the evening, to share the day's events, to grouse about this or that, to ex-press concerns or go over plans. Grace now felt obliged to spend long evenings with Lurina, while Hannah waited impatiently to talk qui-etly and privately about Laura and Emily. She needed to do that be-fore stomping over to her daughter's home and messing things up by being too brusque or too importunate.

"I don't need nobody a-living with me. I can take care of Joseph El-isha's pigs right good myself," Lurina insisted when Wayne informed her that he was moving in with her.

"It's not forever, just a little while. And I'd feel much better and sleep better knowing that Wayne'll be with you for a time," Grace said.

Lurina's battle stance—legs wide, hands on hips—changed. Her eyes softened as she regarded Grace. "I'm a-doing it for you, then, girlie. I know you got a busy life and can't be running over to my place every two minutes." She shook Wayne's shoulder. "You can stay for a bit, but you mind your manners."

"Yes, ma'am," he said.

It was decided that Wayne would move his things into Lurina's place and move Lurina's bedroom downstairs. Then, on Sunday, he would come for dinner, after which he would take Lurina home.

That evening, long after Hannah and Amelia had gone upstairs, Grace sat with Lurina in her bedroom. The house, so dark and still, seemed to sleep deeply as Lurina talked on, and Grace lost all sense of time until Lurina began to speak about Old Man.

"It ain't that I don't miss Joseph Elisha. He was a good man," Lu-rina said. "We'd sit out on that there front porch come day's end and watch the cars go by on Elk Road. It's better, you know, if you can see lights at night. Not so lonely, especially when you get older. Makes you think people are near enough to give a holler to if you had to. I'll be missing that. Not much fun sitting out there alone."

Grace shifted in her chair and focused her attention on what Lurina was saying.

"Still, for certain, I ain't never gonna marry again." She waved Grace closer, and spoke in a conspiratorial manner. "No, ma'am. Never again." Lurina shook her head vigorously, dislodging a bobby pin, which landed on her shoulder, and slid down the covers to her lap. Lurina absentmindedly picked it up, running her thumb along the curve of its neck and down the metal prongs. "Before Joseph Elisha and me married up, I used to sit inside and look out the window. Guess I'll be doing that again." She slapped her leg with her palm. "I done forgot, Wayne's gonna be there. He can sit out with me come spring, till winter sends us running from the cold. Maybe that pretty gal he brought to the funeral will come visiting. What you think, Grace?"

"Maybe she will."

"Not going to marry again for the same reason I didn't marry sooner. Men want too much from you, take up too much of your time. It can be darnright harassing." Lurina looked at Grace. "Guess that's why you ain't married Bob."

Too tired to get into a long discussion of the merits or drawbacks of marriage, Grace merely nodded.

"That's what I been thinking. We think alike, Grace." Lurina fell silent for a time, then talked about her soaps. "One of them there characters been married four times. She's gonna marry again. She ain't learned a thing, the stupid woman."

"Not a thing." Grace yawned.

"I done kept you up real late. I'm sorry, Grace." She looked at Grace sheepishly. "Don't laugh when I tell you this, but Joseph Elisha's spirit is still here. He's been talking to me since he passed. I can hear him right good at night, and he says I'll hear him even better in his room than I can all the way up the stairs back in our place. So I'm gonna move downstairs and let the boy have the upstairs. That Wayne's a good boy."

17

ALL'S WELL THAT ENDS WELL

It had been a while since Grace and Hannah had a good heart-to-heart talk. Today, drawn outside by the glorious weather, Grace strode down Cove Road to Hannah's office, at Bella's Park.

Mary Ann greeted her with smiles. "Good to see you, Mrs. Single-ton. Hannah's in her office. Is she expecting you? Shall I ring her?"

"I'll just go down the hall and surprise her."

Moments later, Grace opened Hannah's office door and entered. "You've let this go way too long," she blurted. "You must talk to Laura. You need access to that baby and to your daughter."

"Look," Hannah said, as if Grace bursting into her office was the most natural event. "It's just not that important, really. I don't want to create problems for anyone."

"You want me to talk to Emily?"

"Good heavens, no. Please, Grace, don't do that. I'll do it in my own time."

Grace strode to the desk. It was a rare occasion when she could tower over Hannah, and she relished the sense of power it gave her. "You can't sit around and let this drag on as the situation with Max did. I hate to see you unhappy because you feel you can't go over there and pick up that baby, so it had better be soon, or I'll do some-thing." This was a role reversal for Grace; usually Hannah exhibited great confidence and directed others.

"I will, I promise."

"Soon, then." Grace sat on the chair alongside the desk, and the magic that derived from feeling tall and forceful faded.

"Want to see the new Rose Garden?" Hannah was eager to change the topic from her daughter and grandson.

"You bet I do," Grace replied.

They strolled through the Cottage Garden, where life in great abundance issued from the earth. The daffodils had finished blooming, and their leaves had been folded back and secured with rubber bands. "We don't cut the leaves. The plants need them to feed the bulbs that'll produce next year's crop of flowers," Hannah explained.

White and pink dogwoods flowered in great abundance. Tiny buds graced the tips of rose stems. Daisy, dianthus, and coneflower stems peeped from the mulch that covered the soil.

"Soon the annuals—salvia, petunias, geraniums, and in the shaded areas, impatience—will be planted," Hannah said.

"The work of a garden never ends, does it?"

"There's always the thrill of new beginnings." Hannah brushed away a bug that had settled on her arm. "Each year the garden's different, even with the same plants. A rosebush blooms more this year than last, or birds deposit seeds and new plants appear, some you never thought to bring into the garden. It's rather wonderful, and I love the smell of spring." Hannah stopped and inhaled deeply.

Grace did the same. "It smells good, so fresh and clean," she said.

They continued through the Canal Garden, with its leaping metal fish and drizzling water, and through the archway into the Children's Garden. "We're selecting plant material for this year," Hannah said. "The kids want a variety of tomatoes—long ones, yellow ones, early and late producers—and they want to plant watermelon, much as I tell them the vines will take over the garden. They insist they can train the vines up off the ground for much of their length. They'll learn by doing."

Leaving that garden, they made their way to the foot of the gentle slope leading to the woods. Buds, some no longer than a fingernail, others the size of a joint of one's finger, extended from the tips of the newly planted roses. "These will bloom a trifle later than the established plants we have at home," Hannah said. "I used Chrysler Imperial red roses again, for their fragrance. Do you like the way we flattened and widened the area every fifth step up to allow for a bench?"

"Yes, I do."

"We'll plant dogwood behind some of the benches for shade, for

whoever chooses to sit. We don't want shade on the rosebushes."
Hannah stopped abruptly and her eyes became unfocussed for a moment. "Andy is almost six weeks old."

"Six weeks already? All the more reason for you to get on over
there and do what you have to do."

They walked up the wide, deep steps until they stood in the
shadow of pine trees. "I'm planning a Shade Garden here. So many
things bloom in shade. I want to show visitors what they can do in
their own gardens in shaded areas."

Prodded and pushed by Max and Grace, Hannah finally gathered the
courage to phone Laura and request time alone with her to discuss "a
matter of importance." It had sounded so stuffy, the way she put it,
but it was the best she could do.

Now Hannah's legs wobbled and her heart thudded as she
mounted the front steps of the redbrick ranch house. This was a mistake. She knew it. She'd say or do something that would upset Laura
and make matters worse. Grace had reminded her that she and Laura
had bridged the gap between them, that they had enjoyed meaningful
talks about the past, about their lives. At work there was goodwill and
warmth between them. So why, then, did Hannah feel so agitated?

One foot on the top step, Hannah stopped. This wasn't important,
really. She'd get to know her grandson after a while.

The front door opened. "What are you doing, Mother?" Laura
stood there holding Andy. She was patting his back, and his head
bobbed against her shoulder.

"Coming to see you and the baby."

"You look as if you're about to turn and leave," Laura said. "Come
on in. I'm waiting for a burp."

Involuntarily, Hannah moved toward her. "May I burp him?"

"Sure." Laura closed the door behind them, slung a diaper over
Hannah's shoulder, and handed her the baby.

Hannah's eyes grew soft. She moved slowly, patting gently, whispering to the infant. The burp came loud and strong. "Can I hold
him awhile?"

Laura led them into the living room. A new rocking chair sat near
the fireplace. Laura motioned, and Hannah, with Andy in her arms,
took it. His dark eyes peered up at her. She would swear to Grace

later that he smiled at her. Deep within Hannah, a sweet, warm feeling spread.

"He's a dear baby," Laura said. "But I'm worn out, being up so many times during the night. Emily says I should add rice cereal to his ten o-clock feeding so he'll sleep until at least six in the morning. What do you think?" She ran her hand across her forehead.

Hannah noticed the tired eyes, and the hair grown too long and showing white at the roots. When had her daughter's hair turned gray? Why hadn't she noticed? "I hear doctors say you shouldn't do that. Why, I don't know. Ask your pediatrician."

Laura bit her lower lip. Her hands roamed back and forth along the arms of her chair. "Emily's here all the time. I know she thinks she's being helpful, but I want to handle things myself. He's my first, probably my only child. How am I going to get the hang of it if she's always telling me what to do? And most of it doesn't work anyway. Andy fusses a lot. "

"Emily's here a great deal," Hannah said.

"You've been wonderful, giving me space," Laura said.

The thrust of this conversation amazed and delighted Hannah. *Just listen,* she urged herself.

"What do you think I ought to do, Mother? How can I tell Emily I'd rather she didn't come here every day, give me instructions, and take charge of Andy? I don't want to hurt her. I like her. I want us to be friends."

Tell her to leave you alone. Thanks, but no thanks. Hannah said, "Let me think about it." Andy bore down, grunted, and grimaced. "Want me to change him, or would you rather do it yourself?"

"Do me a favor and change him, please," Laura replied.

Laura led her to Andy's room and pointed to a changing table. Everything Hannah needed was lined up on a shelf over the table. Her mouth fell open in amazement when she saw that someone had painted a veritable jungle on one of the walls: the cool blue greens and stunning yellow greens of tropical trees, monkeys climbing among branches, red and green and yellow parrots, and other birds flying or sitting on limbs.

"Hank did it," Laura said. "I thought that the smell of paint wouldn't be good for Andy, so Hank moved the crib into our room for a few nights. And you know what? Andy slept better in there.

Now we keep two cribs, one in here and one in our room. We move him where he seems happiest at the time."

"I had no idea Hank was such a fine artist."

"Hank is a remarkable man. He's got many talents. I love him so much, Mother. I never imagined it was possible to love anyone again the way I loved Marvin, but I do, and it's wonderful."

Hannah finished changing the baby and picked him up. "It makes me happy to see you happy. May I hold Andy a while longer?"

"Hold him for as long as you'd like."

They returned to the living room, and Hannah again took the rocking chair.

"I'm so glad you've come over, Mother. I thought maybe you didn't like babies. I asked Miranda, and she said you never paid much attention to her kids when they were little."

"You were asleep when I first saw this little boy," Hannah said. "The nurse brought him to the glass window, and silly as it sounds, he opened his eyes and looked at me. Oh, I know—you'll say babies can't see that soon—but it was as if he looked into my soul. He won my heart completely. I stayed away because I thought you wanted Emily here, and I'd only be in the way."

Laura shook her head. "I know. Every time you came, Emily was here. I didn't know how to handle it. I should have said something."

"It's all right. I'm here now, and I'm holding and rocking my little love."

Laura began to cry. "I'm sorry. I've been weepy like this since he was born." She wiped her eyes. "I'm so glad you love him. I want Andy to have family, a grandmother he can remember with love. Hank's folks are so far away; how often will he see them?"

"You and Hank should make the effort to assure that they know him. He's a special child."

"You think so?"

"Absolutely. I know so."

Once, in elementary school, so long ago that Hannah hardly remembered anything from that era, the class was told to finish the sentence "Happiness is . . ."

She had sat a long while staring out of the window, playing with her long braid, chewing the end of her pencil. "Happiness," she had finally written, "is feeling your heart fly."

"This is silly," the teacher had said after reading Hannah's work aloud to the class. "Silly."

Hannah had shrunk in her seat and wanted to die of shame.

Happiness is . . . , she thought, looking down at Andy. Happiness is this moment, this very moment, and yes, her heart was flying, soaring. The baby snuggled close against her. He smiled. She knew he smiled. And no one could convince her otherwise.

18

MIND OVER MATTER

Grace worried about Lucy. The girl sat listless and unsmiling when they drove to Asheville to the counselor's office twice a week, and was downright sullen when she left that office. Feeling decidedly less qualified than the counselor with whom Lucy had just spent almost an hour, Grace hesitated to probe, and a dark, heavy silence invariably prevailed on the return trip to Covington.

Private school was too expensive for Grace, and the other women felt they were already contributing all they could each month to the fund for the Banks family. If Lucy must return to Pace Middle School, Grace was determined that she would have clothes like everyone else. So Grace and Lucy shopped in the mall for jeans, T-shirts, shoes, and sweaters. Grace turned her back when Lucy's ears were pierced, and took her to the doctor when one ear became infected. When it healed, Lucy insisted on having it pierced again.

Grace expected Lucy to be communicative and revealing, as she had been as an eight-year-old when they had sat together at the library in Caster Elementary School. She was unprepared for and confused by the girl's sulky silence, her indifference, and seeming ingratitude.

Hurt by the change in Lucy, Grace turned to Brenda, visiting her again in her office.

"You're describing a typical teenager: secretive, moody, and uncooperative, plus with all that's happened, Lucy's probably depressed as well. At least Francine Randall didn't expel her; one call from Emily took care of that. So Lucy's back in school with a hostile principal, and she's probably embarrassed having to face teachers and fellow students every day. It's going to take a while for her to come to grips with what happened and to know that she's not damned for life because of it. It's hard enough for us grown-ups when we do something incredibly stupid and embarrass ourselves. Imagine what it's like for a kid."

Grace slapped the side of her head. "Of course Lucy's embarrassed and depressed. How could I not see that? How could I be so insensitive?"

"You are one of the most sensitive people I know. But you're human, and you have feelings. It's been traumatic for you, too." She patted Grace's hand. "Time. Give it time."

"Yes, of course. Time."

"What about the case? What's Emily going to do about Francine Randall?" Brenda asked.

"I don't know. I'm waiting to hear from her. Have you heard anything about Jerry McCorkle's case?" Grace asked.

"As a matter of fact, just today. Seems that friend of Jerry McCorkle's, the one who disappeared after Hilda's murder, had a religious conversion somewhere down in Alabama. He got saved, bless his heart. He says that God told him to come back here and tell the police all he knows about that murder. They're holding him as a material witness. Very little information is being released to the press."

"There's nothing about it in the papers," Grace said.

"Ah, but the grapevine is alive and thriving."

Grace pondered the information for a moment. "Is Ringo being tried for attempting to abduct a minor or for murder?"

"I'm sure it'll be murder. You ever been to a trial, Grace?"

"No."

"If you want to go, I'll go with you," Brenda said. "It's going to be an open-and-shut case. One look at that creep and anyone can see what a slime he is. If Harold were alive, he'd go to that trial. He'd want to be on that jury. They'd never take him, of course, if the defense knew how he felt. Harold was furious when Jerry got away with poor Hilda's murder. 'Real bad seed,' he'd say about Jerry."

Brenda's eyes clouded and she looked away. She rarely mentioned Harold these days. Grace thought of the nights, after Harold died, when Brenda had phoned her in tears to talk about how miserable she was, and lonely, and how desperately she missed Harold, and about her fears of living alone. After a while Brenda's grandsons began to spend the nights with her, and she stopped calling. Grace assumed that she had settled her issues and was moving on with her life. But clearly, speaking of Harold still devastated Brenda, and it was more than two years since his passing. Grace changed the subject back to Lucy.

"I just wish I knew what effect this whole dreadful business has had on Lucy."

"Isn't that what her counselor is for?" Brenda asked.

"I have no idea. I'm just the chauffeur."

"You're really hurt, aren't you? I'm so sorry, Grace. You've invested heavily in so many ways in that girl." For a time they stood side by side staring out Brenda's office window. A light drizzle had been falling all morning. "Was it raining on Cove Road when you left?" Brenda asked.

Grace shook her head.

"We need the rain."

Silence filled the room.

A woman without an umbrella ran from the entrance of the school to a parked car. "Amy Leeds." Brenda said, "Her husband took sick at work. They called from the hospital. Ruptured appendix. They're going to operate. I'll have to find a sub for her social studies class." Then Brenda seemed to shake off her school concerns and turned to Grace. "I have an idea. Why don't you make an appointment with Lucy's counselor for yourself? Tell her how you feel and ask how she thinks Lucy's doing."

"Can I do that?" Grace asked.

"Certainly. Get Mrs. Banks to give you a letter saying that you're her representative and for the counselor to feel free to talk to you in general terms about Lucy."

"Thanks, Brenda. I'll do that."

Grace felt better. She would make an appointment with the counselor. Having a plan improved her mood, and as she walked to her car she thought, Look at me, Grace Singleton, small-town girl. Ted Singleton's shy little wife. Cookie grandma to the neighborhood, and here I am involved with a girl who was nearly abducted. I've hired an attorney. Well, actually Emily is working pro bono, bless her. I'll go to court for the trial of that murderer. If he knew, Ted would turn over in his grave.

Yet she'd like him to see how far she had come, all the things she had done, her new friends, and Bob. Did Ted know? Was his spirit looking down on her? Grace blushed. She hoped he couldn't see Bob and her in bed. As she opened her car door, she thought how much she would like Ted to see her zipping along at sixty-five miles an hour on the highway.

Bob paced as he waited for Grace outside the Athens Restaurant in Weaverville. They never grew tired of the friendly atmosphere of the place, the welcome they received from the owners and the waitresses, and the good food.

It was early and few tables were taken. Grace finally arrived and they chose a booth in the front, settled in, and waited for Polly, the bright-eyed, good-natured waitress they liked so much, then ordered lamb shanks. Grace could hardly wait to tell Bob the news about Jerry McCorkle. "You'll come with me to the trial, won't you?"

"I guess so," he said. "Maybe we could all go, the seven of us."

"Seven, what seven?"

"You and I, Max and Hannah, Amelia, Mike and Roger."

Grace clasped a hand over her mouth and laughed. "I forget about my son living here." She sobered. "I hardly see him. Why should that surprise me? We were never close."

"Amelia going into the new business with them?" Bob asked.

"I think she plans to work with them, but not invest. I hope it doesn't mean she'll stop doing photography."

"People get sidetracked," Bob said. "It's as if the universe, God, whatever, demands that they reevaluate their lives periodically. Things happen that force them to reevaluate their choices. The key to all this, I think, is that by reexamining your life, you either confirm what you're doing or you make a change."

She set her elbow on the table and leaned her chin on her hand. "Are you doing what you love to do?"

He didn't answer for a long moment. "Well, yes, as a matter of fact, I am. But back when I finished twenty years in the army and took off my uniform, I felt like a nobody, as if I didn't exist anymore. Then there was the high school teaching, and a stint in sales. I never really fit into any of that. It was as if I were waiting to grow into my-self."

Polly brought their dinners. As she ate, Grace thought about his words "waiting to grow into myself." She hadn't grown into herself until she moved to Covington. If she had never left Dentry, would she have changed and grown? She set down her fork and drank some water.

"I never gave a thought to growing into myself. But when Ted died, I wasn't Mrs. Somebody anymore. I had no function. Widows often feel invisible, you know. Many of our couple friends stopped including me. It hurt, being left out by people I thought were my friends. Oh, there were some folk who were nice, and I was free to do what I wanted, but I never even considered maybe going to college, or into business, or even going to work outside my home. I had op-portunities when I was younger, but Ted didn't want his wife work-ing, so . . ." She raised her shoulders and lowered them. "I used to be so angry at Roger for insisting I move from Dentry to Branston, but to be totally honest, I didn't dig in my heels and refuse to go. Now I wonder if, secretly, I didn't want to leave Ohio. When I met Hannah and then Amelia, I began to open up bit by bit, and then we came to Covington and everything changed." She smiled at him, a wide happy smile, and her eyes sparkled. "For the first time in my life, I felt—and feel—like a real person."

"I drifted for years," Bob said. "It was Russell and Tyler needing me after Amy was killed in that awful car crash, and coming here, meeting you, that renewed my life."

"Funny," Grace said. "We used to talk like this when we first met, and we haven't for a long time. I like it. It makes me feel even closer to you."

"But not close enough to marry me." He sighed, a mock sigh.

"Maybe if we were married, we wouldn't talk at all when we ate out. You see so many couples sitting in silence." Grace raised her water glass. "To you, you dear, sweet man. I love you."

"To you, my love." He lifted his glass of iced tea.

After dinner, they shopped for dessert at the market, and took the "no sugar added" apple pie back with them to Bob's apartment, where Grace called Hannah to say she was staying the night.

19

ONE THING AFTER ANOTHER

Since returning from Maine, Amelia had felt disoriented. She forgot things. Once she drove for miles to a spot she planned to photograph only to discover that her camera and camera bag were empty of film. Then today, she had put on two different-colored socks with her tennis shoes: The round fuzzy pompom at the back of the left foot was blue, the one on the right, yellow.

"You have on two different pompom socks," Grace said.

Amelia hurried upstairs to change them before going to Asheville to the mall.

"I'd have been humiliated. Thanks, Grace," Amelia said when she came back down from her room.

Grace said, "If you noticed, you'd have just gone into a shoe store, bought a new pair, and changed them."

"Or I could have walked around all day with people snickering behind my back."

"Or maybe no one would have even noticed," Grace said.

"Will you two stop supposing?" Hannah said. "There is no 'what if' here. Grace noticed. Amelia changed her socks. Matter settled."

"So down to earth and practical. That's why we keep you, Hannah." Grace turned back to Amelia. "What are you going to the mall for?"

Amelia set her hands on her hips. "Not telling."

"So it's a secret." Hannah lifted her head from a plant catalog that had arrived in yesterday's mail. "I'm going to order dahlias. They're late blooming. I'll get some for Bella's gardens, also."

"Oh, all right." Amelia said. "Mike's birthday's coming up. I want to get him something nice."

"You didn't get him something on St. John, like bay rum?"

"No, I didn't shop in Cruz Bay."

"I got extra," Grace said. "Bob loves it. Think Mike would like a bottle?"

Amelia shrugged. "I have no idea."

You would have, before Roger moved here, Grace thought. You'd have had ideas and strong opinions regarding Mike. "I'd be glad to give you the extra bottle for Mike, if you'd like."

"Thanks, Grace, but I want to give him something really special, maybe something he can use in the new business," Amelia said.

"How are Mike and Roger doing, anyway?" Grace asked.

Amelia settled into one of the kitchen chairs, a puzzled look in her eyes. "I'm not sure. Mike's more independent than Charles was, I think."

"You're right," Grace said. "Roger will just have to adjust to that, won't he?"

"You sound peeved at him," Hannah asked.

"You bet I am," Grace said. "Something's always been wrong with my relationship with my son. Even when he was a child, we didn't really connect. Sure, he turned to me when he split his lip playing ball, and when he fell out of a tree and needed stitches in his arm, things like that. But otherwise he was a self-contained child, and then a self-contained man not given to sharing confidences."

"Maybe he was scared," Amelia said. "He must have known early on that he was, well, different, even if he didn't act on it or have a name for it."

Grace heaved a deep sigh. "I spent his childhood thinking how adorable he was, how handsome my future grandchildren would be. I certainly had no idea he was gay. I didn't know anyone who professed to be gay. If someone had referred to a gay person, I would have assumed that meant the person was happy. It was quite a shock and an education when Roger told me."

Hannah stood, walked to the sink, and leaned over it to better see out of the window. "Max is picking me up. We're going to Builder's Express in Weaverville to look at that new wood substitute for decking. You never have to paint it, they say." She stepped back from the sink. "Here he comes now. See you all later." With a girlish smile and a wave of her hand, she was gone.

Grace carried the remainder of the breakfast dishes to the sink. "Thank God that relationship's mended."

"Still, she hasn't set a date for the wedding. Anything could happen. Relationships change. That's how it is, isn't it?" Amelia said.

"What is?" Grace filled the sink with water and squeezed some liquid soap into it. A froth of suds rose almost to the top of the bowl.

"Not using the dishwasher?" Amelia asked.

"It's not working. I have to call the repair people."

"I was saying, relationships change, like things change and things break. You can often have something that's broken fixed, like a dishwasher. It's not always that way with people," Amelia said.

Grace turned to her. Soap suds trailed along her arms. She wiped them with a dish towel. "What are you talking about, Amelia?"

"The way relationships go up and down like a roller coaster."

"Goodness, not as high or as low or as swiftly as a roller coaster, I hope," Grace replied.

"Fast enough, though. Hasn't Lucy changed? And after you put yourself to so much trouble for her."

Grace wiped her hands again and came to stand beside Amelia's chair. "Who is it, besides Lucy you're disappointed with?"

A defeated look crossed Amelia's face. "You can see right through me, can't you? It's Mike, of course. And I met this woman, Mrs. Febbs, in the market with her kids—adorable triplets. She seemed thrilled when I asked if I could come out to her place and photograph them. I drove all the way out there, way up the mountain past Wolf Laurel, and found an irate husband on the porch with his arms folded across this massive chest yelling at his wife, how dare she let anyone take pictures of his kids. She looked like a scared rabbit, especially when I tried to persuade him, and he got more agitated and red-faced. He started inside, probably to get a gun, 'cause she ran after him, and I heard the word *gun* while they screamed and yelled at one another. I got out of there fast."

"What an awful experience. But you still see Mike, don't you, and didn't you go to the theater with him and Roger recently?"

Amelia pouted. "It's like being a fifth wheel, or like two women having lunch out with a man along. A man's presence dampens women's sense of freedom to say whatever they would have to one another, so they end up making small talk, or the man thinks he's a hot shot and never shuts up."

"What does Roger do?"

"Your son's a great, big, old wet blanket. He sits there and never says a word once he's ordered his dinner. And its the same between acts at the theater, or on the drive home. But he's there, so Mike and I can't really talk, not as we used to."

"That's the way Roger is, a huge, silent presence. He's like that with me. If not for Charles, who made me feel welcome, I hardly ever would have seen Roger."

"Really?"

"Where've you been, Amelia? I must have talked about this a hundred times." Then Grace asked, "You still thinking of working for them?"

"Probably not. Mike and I had a few moments in the lobby of the theater when Roger went off to the men's room. He urged me not to give up the photography. Maybe Mike's having second thoughts."

"You never know someone till you live with them," Grace said.

"You can say that again." Amelia's eyes clouded. "And even when you live with them and think you know them, they can change." She sighed. "What shall I do? So much of my work lies in what goes on in the darkroom. Mike did all the film developing and printing of the photos. He's a genius at shading and lightening. He can bring out the best in a photograph, the way Ansel Adams did. I hate darkroom work."

"I would imagine that there are technical people who can be hired to do this," Grace said.

"So I should get someone to replace Mike in the darkroom?"

"If Mike can't do it, yes. Let him find the person. And you go on taking your beautiful photos."

"Wow!" Amelia said. "I never heard you so forceful before."

"People change," Grace said, suddenly uncertain at being so decisive about Amelia's life.

She felt better when Amelia said, "Thanks, Grace. Your sage counsel is well taken." Amelia hugged her good-bye and left the house.

Hands to elbows in suds, Grace heard the tires of Amelia's car crunch the gravel on their driveway, heard the horn of an oncoming car warn of its approach. Heart in her throat, Grace used a towel to wipe the stream from the windowpane. A car whizzed by on Cove Road with Amelia's car positioned at the end of their driveway. Grace held the side of the sink and breathed a sigh of relief. After a few seconds, Amelia eased her car cautiously out onto Cove Road.

Old Man's rapid illness and death, Lucy and the chat room, the police and Ringo had forcefully brought home to Grace the fragility of their lives. She wished time could stop for a while, that everyone and everything could simply freeze and remain unchanged.

But it was not to be. That afternoon, Brenda Tate phoned Grace to say that Jerry McCorkle had escaped from jail.

"I wouldn't be surprised to find out someone bribed a guard or two," Brenda said.

Grace began to shiver. "I'm going over to the school and get Lucy." Within minutes, her heart pounding, she was driving through a narrow valley to the middle school.

"Miss Randall is out sick," the secretary said.

"Who's in charge, then?" Grace asked.

"Our assistant principal, Mr. Ulman."

"I must see him right away. This is an emergency."

The secretary hesitated.

Grace leaned over the desk. "This has to do with Lucy Banks."

"I'll call him right away." The flustered woman reached for the phone.

HENRY ULMAN, ASSISTANT PRINCIPAL read the plaque on his door. He listened attentively. Yes, he'd heard the news. The man bordered on obsequious in his effort to cooperate with Grace. "Do you really think McCorkle will come to the school? We have security."

"I walked right into this school the other day and again today. No one asked me who I was or what I wanted."

Mr. Ulman swallowed hard, then dialed the desk phone and instructed the secretary to locate Lucy. He held the phone to his ear and after a moment turned to Grace. "She's in Miss Pratt's math class. I'll be glad to take you down there, Mrs. Singleton."

Grace followed him along a hallway lined with metal lockers. Their footsteps echoed in the wide, empty corridor.

"Ah, here we are." He stopped. "I think perhaps it would be best if

I spoke to Miss Pratt first. Do you mind waiting out here? I won't be long."

Grace stood on tiptoe and peered through the glass panel in the door. Mr. Ulman was shorter by at least two inches than Miss Pratt. He gesticulated with both hands. The teacher listened with brisk nods and raised eyebrows. Then Miss Pratt walked over to Lucy's desk, bent, and said something. Lucy looked nervously about her, and began to gather her papers and books and jam them into her new backpack. She slung the pack over her shoulder and trailed Mr. Ulman to the door.

"What's going on?" Lucy looked from Grace to Mr. Ulman.

"There may be some trouble. Mrs. Singleton will tell you," he said.

Minutes later, a sulky Lucy sat in Grace's car as they headed to Covington. "This is just so humiliating. What will the other kids think? What's so important you had to get me out of school?"

Grace took a deep breath. "Ringo's escaped from jail."

Lucy clasped both hands over her mouth. Her eyes went wide and scared. "Really?"

"I'm afraid so. I was worried that he might go to your school."

Grace pulled into their driveway. Before unlocking the car doors, she looked in every direction. Then they hastened inside. Immediately Grace locked the three locks on the front door. They moved from room to room and from window to window on the ground floor. "I think the back door's locked, but let me check. Call Mr. Richardson for me, will you, Lucy? His number's right by the kitchen phone."

"What do you want me to tell him?"

"Ask him to come right over. Tell him it's important—oh, and tell him I'm fine."

Mumbling to herself, Lucy dialed. "There's no answer," she said. "He must have forgotten to turn on the answering machine."

Grace returned from checking the back door. "It was locked." She began to haul a chair toward the pantry. "I'm going to shove this chair under the door. Extra protection. What did you say?"

"There was no answer."

"Then call Hannah at work, and call my son Roger, please. Both numbers should be right under Mr. Richardson's. Same message, if you get them, or leave messages on their machines."

Lucy had just replaced the receiver when Grace, her face flushed, entered the kitchen. "Couldn't get Miss Hannah. I left a message on her machine. Your son's coming over."

Grace perched on the end of a kitchen chair, her hands on her knees, and leaned forward. "My goodness, I'm out of breath."

The phone rang. Grace pushed up from the chair and answered it.

"You all right Mother?" Roger asked.

Relief swept over Grace. "Harried and a trifle scared; it's just Lucy and me here."

"I'm on my way. I heard the news on the radio. Keep everything locked."

"We are locked up. Hurry, please."

But relief was short-lived. As she set the phone on its cradle, Grace heard the click of a lock from the hallway. She looked about her. Where was Lucy? "Lucy!" she called, and dashed into the foyer.

Lucy had the first lock opened and was struggling with the chain. "He'll look here first thing. I gotta go hide," she yelled over her shoulder at Grace.

"Lucy. No. Stay here. Roger's on his way."

The girl turned wild, unreasoning eyes to Grace. "Leave me alone! He'll find me! I have to get out of here and hide."

The chain slipped from its locked position. Unthinking, Grace hurled herself at Lucy and wrapped her arms about her.

Lucy shoved at Grace. Grace held on. The thud when they hit the carpet left Grace stunned, seeing stars. The room began to spin, but she did not loosen her grip on the girl's arm.

Lucy swung wildly. Unwittingly, her elbow slammed into Grace's cheek.

Grace cried out in pain, and she released Lucy and covered her face with her hands.

Lucy scrambled to her feet and bent over Grace, who lay on her side on the carpet, emitting soft moans.

"Oh, my God, Mrs. Grace! Talk to me. I'm so sorry! I musta went crazy. Oh, my God, I'm sorry. Tell me you're not hurt, Mrs. Grace!" She was kneeling alongside Grace, patting Grace's back. "Please, please look at me."

Grace's right cheek smarted. Her right eye stung, and she could tell it was swelling. The floor, even with the carpet, seemed made of con-

crete. She'd hit hard going down. Her back ached. The room continued to spin.

"Open the door." Roger's voice was urgent as he pounded on the
door.

Lucy unlocked the third lock to let him in.

"Mother." Roger rushed past Lucy to Grace. "Are you all right? Let
me help you up. There, just sit a bit, catch your breath. Take my
arm." After a time, he said, "There we go."

In slow motion, Grace sat, then carefully eased up from the
ground. She leaned heavily on her son.

"What happened here?" he asked Lucy. "Lock that door," he said
before she could reply. Lucy obeyed, then shrank against a wall and
broke into tears.

"The room's spinning," Grace said. "Please, Roger, I need something to eat—a piece of cheese and a slice of apple."

"Go get them," Roger told Lucy. He helped his mother to the
couch in the living room, unlaced and removed her shoes, and
arranged pillows behind her back. "Lie still. Don't move. I'm going
to get you a cold towel." He returned a few minutes later with ice
wrapped in a damp towel. "Here, put this over that right cheek and
eye." Roger looked up as Lucy entered the living room with a brick of
Swiss cheese, a cheese slicer, a knife, and an apple on a large plate.

She handed him the food. "I didn't mean to run away. I was so
scared Ringo'd come looking for me here. I'm so sorry. Musta been my
elbow done it. I'd never hurt Mrs. Grace; I love her. I *hate* myself. I just
hate myself!" She exploded into tears, and Roger turned away from her.

Ever so slowly, Grace raised her arm and beckoned. "Lucy," she
whispered.

Hesitantly, wary of Roger, who scowled each time he looked at her,
Lucy approached Grace.

"Sit here." Grace patted the edge of the couch. "Now slice me
some cheese."

"Let me do that," Roger said. He pointed to a chair on the other
side of the room. "You sit there, and don't try to leave this room,
much less this house."

Wide eyed and scared, Lucy nodded. "I won't leave. I didn't mean
to hurt Mrs. Grace." She lifted a hand to her head. "I was crazy
scared. I love Mrs. Grace. I didn't mean to . . ."

He interrupted. "I won't tolerate *anyone* hurting her in any way, you understand?"

"It's all right, Roger, dear. Lucy didn't mean to hurt me—it was an accident. I was holding on to her. She didn't intend to hit me." The pain in her cheek was worth it, for she had prevented Lucy leaving the house, and here was her son being concerned and solicitous for a change. "Thank you, Roger for coming over so quickly." Lord, but it hurt to talk. "I couldn't have gotten up off the floor without you. It's a comfort to me that you're here. Lucy is a good girl and she had no intention of hurting me. The real danger's out there, with Jerry McCorkle. He's the one we really have to be concerned about."

Roger extracted a handgun from a holster he wore under his jacket. "I brought this just in case the bastard shows his face here."

"Put it away, please," Grace said. "When did you learn to use a gun?"

"The oil company didn't send us to places like Saudi Arabia without some way to protect ourselves. I've never had to use it, thank goodness, but I shoot at a range regularly to keep up my skill. I'm a good shot."

From her place along the wall, Lucy stared from the gun to Roger and back at the gun, just as a knocking on the front door drew their attention.

"Who is it?" Roger called.

"Me, Hannah. Lucy phoned. Why is the chain lock on? Is something wrong? You all right, Grace?"

"Open for Hannah," Roger directed Lucy. "And don't do anything foolish."

"I won't," Lucy replied.

Once inside, Hannah locked the door back up and rushed to Grace's side. "I heard about McCorkle."

The cold cloth slipped from Grace's cheek as she turned to face Hannah. Hannah stepped back, alarmed. "Oh, my goodness! What happened to your eye, your face? It's all swollen, and your cheek's turning black and blue."

"I fell with Lucy. Her elbow gave me a good whack."

The room had stopped spinning. The pain in Grace's face stretched from her eye, across her cheek, and down into and through her jaw. She handed the towel to Hannah and managed, "More ice, please."

Roger reached for the towel. "I'll take care of that."

Hannah pulled up a chair and sat beside her. "My poor Grace. We must get you to a doctor right away."

Grace tried to shake her head, but pain stopped the movement.

"Shake your head, scream in protest, but you're going to the doctor," Hannah said. "The number's listed near the phone, on the chalkboard, Roger. Please, will you call?"

He nodded and left the room.

Lucy found her voice. "Mrs. Grace came for me at school. She told me to call Mr. Richardson, but there wasn't any answer. Only Mr. Roger was home."

"Covington's in an uproar about McCorkle breaking out of jail. The Herrill and the Craine men have joined a local posse. Bob, too, I think. They've all got guns. They're searching for McCorkle." Hannah reached for a magazine on a nearby table and fanned her face.

Grace tried to smile and winced. "Roger came right away."

Roger returned. "They'll work us in anytime we get there."

Grace reached for her son's hand and squeezed.

"Mother tried to stop Lucy from leaving. They skirmished and fell. Unfortunately, Mother got clobbered."

"It was an accident," Lucy said.

"Lucy didn't mean to . . ." Grace's speech was almost unintelligible now.

Hannah stood abruptly and moved with long strides until she towered above Lucy. "You tried to run away from Mrs. Grace? Are you crazy? Grace has done everything for you—helped your family, saved you from a bastard who would have hurt you in ways beyond your wildest imagination—and that's how you behave?"

Lucy's shoulders, her face, her whole being crumbled. She sobbed.

"Stop, Hannah. It was an accident." Grace struggled to raise herself from the couch and fell back.

"I'm raving angry, so don't any of you tell me what to feel or say or do." Hannah returned to her chair and resumed fanning her face, which was even more scarlet.

Lucy wiped away tears. "Please, Mrs. Grace. I think I know where Ringo is."

"You what?" Roger asked.

Grace beckoned to the girl, who looked first at Roger, then Hannah, before taking cautious steps toward Grace.

"Tell us whatever you know, Lucy," Roger said.

"He used to say he had a secret place where he hid from his foster father, who'd beat him. It's up McCorkle Creek, way up at the waterfall. He said it's hard to get there, and no one ever goes that far up the creek. There's a cave behind the waterfall."

"You wouldn't make this up, would you?" Roger asked.

"No. I swear it's so." She focused on Grace. "I'm not lying, please believe me. That's what he said."

"I think we have to pass this on, even if it turns out to be a bum lead," Roger said. "I'll call nine-one-one and let them know. How far up the creek is that confounded waterfall?"

"A long way," Hannah said. "Maybe one of the policemen will know."

"But right now, let's get you to your doctor, Mother. That eye's pretty swollen. Hannah, write down Mother's doctor's name and address and his phone number for me, will you? Can you get up?" he asked his mother.

"Go, Grace. That's a nasty blow. And don't worry. I'll call nine-one-one and stay here with Lucy," Hannah said. "We'll keep the radio on, and make a tuna salad. It'll be dinnertime when you two get back and Amelia gets home. Bob'll probably be over."

"If you see or hear from Bob, let him know what's happened," Roger said.

Grace's eyes thanked him.

Roger helped Grace to her feet, and she leaned on him as she walked from the living room. At least the walls were no longer spinning.

Hannah trailed them to the front door. "You keep that cold compress against your face, Grace." She closed the door and locked it, then went to the kitchen window and watched as Grace, leaning heavily against Roger, made it across the porch, down the steps, and to his car.

"You've got some sharp elbow, Lucy," she said. Then she turned all business. "Lucy, open that pantry over there and get me three cans of tuna. Get celery and a couple of apples from the fridge, and bring that chopping board over here to the sink. We'll put chunks of apple and chopped celery in the salad."

20

A GOOD
HEART-TO-HEART TALK

For a time, the kitchen bustled with activity. They peeled and cut the apples into small chunks and chopped celery into small pieces, then stirred them into the bowl of tuna. Mayonnaise followed. Lucy laid lettuce leaves around the edge of a large platter, then Hannah piled the center with tuna salad, covered the platter, and stored it in the refrigerator. They peeled and cut fruit—strawberries, melon, and bananas—and worked in silence until the fruit salad was stored in the fridge as well.

Finally, Hannah poured herself a cup of coffee, and with a deep sigh sank into a chair at the kitchen table. "It's always something," she said. "Get yourself a glass of milk, Lucy, and haul down that box of cookies from the top of the fridge."

"May I have a Coke instead of milk?"

Hannah shrugged.

Silence followed. Then *pop!* went the tab on the can. Lucy's eyes met Hannah's. "Please don't be angry with me, Miss Hannah. I didn't mean to hurt Mrs. Grace."

"I believe you, Lucy. I overreacted. No need to rehash that."

"He was horrible, that Ringo—so different from when we wrote to each other. I thought he was young, maybe seventeen."

"We may be advanced in our technology," Hannah said, "but it seems that every new technology requires laws to protect people from

some aspect of it. I hadn't realized how dangerous those chat rooms could be."

Lucy set down the Coke and pulled her chair closer to the table. "I sure didn't know. It started as a lark. After Travis fixed the computer, one of the girls in class dared me to go to a chat room. Lots of kids did it. At first it was just fun, nothing serious—a couple of girls talking about how their mothers didn't like the way they wore their hair, or objected to their having their ears pierced. One girl was into black—black pants, shirt, lipstick, eye shadow, everything black—and her parents wanted her to see a counselor. Then, one day, up comes this message from a really sad-sounding guy."

"Ringo?"

"Yeah, Ringo." Her mouth quivered. She set the Coke down hard on the table. "I fell for his lies. I hate myself for being so stupid."

Hannah knew Lucy had not been fully open with Grace. Should she stop Lucy, suggest they wait until Grace was home? But this was a "strike while the iron is hot" situation. Lucy wanted to talk, so Hannah decided to listen.

Lucy continued. "He said he was beat regularly by a drunken step-father, that he wanted to go to AB Tech to be a lab technician, but his stepfather wouldn't let him. He had no money. Work, work, work on the farm all day, until he'd fall on his face with exhaustion at night. The stepfather beat his mom, and she was so scared of him. You could understand, Miss Hannah, couldn't you, that my heart went out to him? How could I not be his friend? I was his only friend, all he had, he kept telling me." A perplexed look crossed her face. "Funny, I never wondered how he got to a computer to write to me in the middle of the day if he was working in the field. Stupid me."

"You can get so carried away sometimes that you don't think clearly," Hannah said, thinking of her attitude toward Emily.

Lucy nodded. She fell silent.

"What's life like for you these days at school and at home?" Hannah asked. That's what Grace would ask, and she was Grace's surrogate now.

Lucy's eyes grew sad. Her mouth turned down, and her shoulders slumped. "I feel awful bad at home. I don't know what to do. My little sisters act like they're scared of me. Ma acts like I done killed

someone. She keeps saying things like 'Thank God your pa's not here to witness this' and 'I wish Randy'd come home; he'd know what to do.' She wrote him about it. I wish she hadn't. I don't want Randy to hate me, too." Tears pooled in her eyes.

"Your brother's been out and about in the world. If anyone would understand what happened, he would. He wouldn't be mad at you, only at Ringo."

Lucy brightened. "You think so, Miss Hannah?"

"I certainly do."

Then the light faded from Lucy's face. "It won't help me none at school, Ringo escaping and all. Most of the kids walk to the other side of the hall when they pass me, and the ones who want to be friends with me are the kind you and Miss Grace wouldn't like at all. I don't like them."

"But you want to be accepted by somebody?"

Lucy nodded. "It's mighty lonely at school."

"Ever consider joining the garden club?" Hannah's coffee was cold, but she refrained from refilling her mug for fear of breaking the mood of the moment.

"I've heard of it, but I never gave it much thought," Lucy said.

"Why not come to our next meeting? We're just getting geared up to plant the Children's Garden at Bella's Park. Ever been to Bella's Park, Lucy?"

"I can't say I have, Miss Hannah."

"I invite you to come over and let me show you the gardens we've made. The Garden Club meets in room twenty-three after school on Wednesdays. Why not give it a try?"

"All them kids won't quit your club if I come?"

"I trust they will not," Hannah replied. "They're always a bit shy with a new member the first few meetings, but everyone settles down."

Lucy's hand went to her lips. "Oh, I forgot. I go to the counselor on Wednesdays."

"I'm sure that can be changed."

Lucy was silent for a time. "You really think it'll be all right if I come to your club?"

"It'll be just fine." Hannah would make sure of that; she'd have a little chat with the class before Lucy arrived. "Get me that calendar

from the wall, will you please, Lucy? Let me make sure I have the right week."

The calendar hung on the wall near the phone, and Lucy brought it to her. "Yes, we start next Wednesday, but this first session begins at three-thirty, not three. You come at three-thirty."

The small pixielike face lit up. "I'd sure like that. Thanks."

"Yesterday I started to weed that bed in front of the porch," Hannah said. "Want to come along and help me weed?"

"Yes." Lucy downed the last of the soda, stood when Hannah did, and deposited the can in the trash bag under the sink. At the door she stopped. "Miss Hannah, I can't go out there, Mrs. Grace said."

"My goodness, how could I forget? Of course, you're right. Well, let's sit and look through some garden magazines instead."

Minutes later, they sat side by side on the living room couch with magazines spread about them. "This here's a right pretty flower." Lucy pointed to a deep red flower on the lower half of the page. The name Ernest Markham was written under the flower.

"That's a clematis," Hannah said. "The photos on both pages are clematis."

"Even that one shaped like an upside-down pitcher?"

"That's right, Lucy. That's called *Clematis pitcheri*. It's native to the southern and central United States, Indiana to Mississippi. There are over three hundred different species of clematis. Different species, or types, grow well in different sections of the country. They're quite delicate vines with slender stems. Some of them are so light and airy that they are grown on a trellis along with climbing roses. The name comes from the Greek word *klema,* which means climbing or branching vine."

They continued turning the pages until they came to a page showing a field of white daisies and yellow coreopsis. "Those are pretty flowers," Lucy said.

"They're perennials. When winter comes you cut the stems back, but the roots live and send out shoots the next year. Know what a marigold is?"

Lucy nodded. "Ma gives the little kids a packet of seeds come June. The picture on the front says they're marigolds. They come up right pretty and all gold colored."

"They're annuals. Grow from seed every year. They bloom all summer and die in winter."

Lucy leaned back against the couch cushions and closed her eyes for a moment. When she opened them, she gazed at Hannah with a look of deep appreciation. "You know so much about plants. I learned a lot today." She smiled up at Hannah. "I feel better now than I've felt since the whole computer thing happened."

"Good," Hannah said. She wiped the perspiration from her upper lip.

Pain drilled into Grace's cheek. Talking with Roger, or even listening to him, was the last thing she wanted, yet he seemed unable to be quiet.

"I don't think this thing with Mike's going to work," he said as they drove along.

She asked why with her eyes.

"Mike and I don't make good companions."

"Hmm." If she didn't say much, maybe Roger would be quiet.

"Part of why I moved here was because I thought we had something, but he's, well, different from me, very different from Charles."

She did not reply.

"It's too soon. Maybe that's it. Yes, that's it. It's too soon after Charles died." Roger's hands gripped the wheel, and he hunched slightly forward.

Grace held the compress tighter against her cheek. It was taking so long to get into Asheville. This was ridiculous. She didn't need a doctor—what she needed was Tylenol, another cold compress, and bed.

"It's not that I don't fancy Mike. He's a very nice person, he's honest, a decent chap. So I ask myself, what's the problem? A while back there, I was thinking of leaving Charles for Mike." Roger fell silent a moment or two. "Yes, it's too soon. That should make Amelia happy. Damn, that woman annoys me. She's so possessive of Mike, as if she were—what?—his mother."

"Good friends," Grace muttered, and turned to look out of the window. The brief silence that followed was a balm to Grace.

"What is it about Mike that just doesn't feel right for me?" Roger persisted. He provided his own answer. "He's not sensitive as Charles was."

"Too independent?" she said.

"Why, yes, he is too independent. I guess I need someone to take care of, someone who needs me more than I need him. Charles was exceptionally well suited to me."

"Think you'll find a clone of him?" Lord, it hurt to open her jaw.

"Don't be facetious, Mother. I'm not so immature as to think that."

Why, oh, why, had she responded? *Drive faster, Roger,* she wanted to say. *Why are you crawling along at sixty miles an hour when you could go sixty-five?* But he was already edgy, and anything she might say would only agitate him.

After a time he said, "Well, what the heck—better someone than no one, eh?"

Grace cringed. No, it wasn't better to have someone you really didn't want. It wasn't fair to anyone concerned—in this case, Mike and Amelia. She knew no good would come of Roger moving to Covington.

"A nasty crack you got, Mrs. Singleton." The fresh-faced young doctor lifted the soggy cloth from her cheek.

Her own doctor was tied up at the hospital, the receptionist had informed her when she registered at the desk. Instead, Dr. Collins would see her.

Dr. Collins was, in Grace's opinion, too young to be a doctor. He looked twenty-two. He couldn't be, of course, with all the years it took to get through medical school. So he might be twenty-nine, but that was still too young.

"It'll be fine," Grace muttered, eager to be out of there.

"How did this happen?" Dr. Collins looked at Roger.

Look at me! Grace wanted to yell. *It happened to me; Roger wasn't even there.* She mumbled through her aching jaw, "I fell."

"Trying to stop a teenage girl from running away. The girl's elbow got my mother."

Dr. Collins's thin eyebrows shot up, but he did not ask why Grace had been trying to stop a girl from running away. He should have, Grace thought. It would have humanized him, indicated interest on his part.

Roger said, "My mother's a great rescuer. She was trying to save the girl from herself."

Dr. Collins made no comment, but gave his full attention to Grace's eye. He held it open, shined a too-bright light into it, directed her to look up, down to this side, and then the other. "Her eye isn't injured."

Grace bristled. He was talking to Roger again.

"In a couple of days it'll be fine. Till then, cold compresses are best."

"I told you," Grace said, giving her son an annoyed look.

"I'd like to have an X-ray of your cheek," the doctor said, this time to Grace.

"Why?" she asked.

"It may have a hairline fracture. Don't you want to know?" Dr. Collins looked puzzled and slightly irritated. He checked his watch.

"No," Grace replied. "When it stops hurting, I'll know."

The doctor wrote on a prescription pad. "For pain." He held the paper toward Roger.

If she didn't hurt so much, Grace would have snatched it from him and stalked out. Instead, she mumbled, "Thank you," and holding on to Roger, left the office. She would tell her own doctor when she saw him how she felt about Dr. Collins.

Once out of the office, Roger said, "You didn't have to be so snippy with the doctor, Mother."

"He annoyed me. He's too young to be treating senior citizens."

"That's ridiculous." Roger guided her across the parking lot to his car.

All the softness he had evinced when she was first hurt had vanished, and Roger was once again his usual blunt, undemonstrative self. His living in Covington was a constant reminder of the wall between them, which, although breached occasionally, was immediately rebuilt. Why was it this way? What would change it?

The pain pills knocked Grace out. She slept well that night, rested the next day, and nursed her cheek under cold compresses. Grace took the pills for three nights, until the worst of the pain eased. Then she flushed the remainder down the toilet.

Bob watched Grace comb her hair and dab on lipstick. He loved the fact that she was not vain, that her makeup consisted solely of pale pink lipstick, which vanished in an hour or two. The perfume she dabbed behind her ears was one they had selected together, a light, fruity scent that did not tickle his nose and cause him to sneeze.

Looking in the mirror, Grace tipped her head this way and that.

"Your eye's not swollen anymore, and the bruises are going away," Bob said.

She pointed with one finger. "See here? It's still not pretty across my cheek."

"All signs of the bruise will be gone soon." Bob handed her a brown envelope. "Look at this. It's a jazz festival down in Atlanta. I thought we could use a bit of a getaway and some fun."

She did not open the envelope. "Bob, how can I go anywhere now? Amelia and Hannah have been spelling me, taking Lucy to her counselor. Emily's working on the case against the middle school."

"I'm talking about a weekend event. Lucy doesn't see a counselor on the weekend, does she? And Emily doesn't need hand-holding, Grace. Lawyers take time collecting information, getting it just right before going to court. Then there's the waiting for a court date. It's going to take weeks, even months. As for Lucy, the times I've seen her lately, she seems quite bright-eyed, not at all depressed as she was. She probably doesn't even need a counselor anymore. The police finding Jerry McCorkle just where she said he would be, up back of that waterfall, must have relieved her mind and given her a sense of being less helpless."

Grace seemed not to be listening. She had casually thrown the envelope onto the seat of her rocking chair and was busy opening a small round jar. "Amelia gave me this." Grace pressed her finger against its contents, then applied it in sweeping motions to her cheek. The fading yellow and blue bruise disappeared. "Magic," she said. "It's foundation, and it certainly does work. How could I have lived this long and not known about makeup? Look."

"You can't see the discoloration at all now," Bob agreed. He nodded toward the envelope. "Look through it, Grace. Think about it. It's only for a weekend. We both like jazz, and we could use some time alone. Atlanta's close. If anything comes up, we can be home in four hours."

Grace picked up the envelope before sitting in her rocker by the window, but she did not open it. "Bob, have you noticed how much time Lucy spends with Hannah?"

"No. But then, I don't see either Hannah or Lucy very much."

"Hannah said when I was gone to the doctor's office, Lucy told her how lonely and depressing school was for her. Hannah suggested that Lucy join the Garden Club." She fingered the edge of the envelope. "Hannah gave her class a good pep talk about kindness and decency, but she really didn't have to. When Lucy arrived, they were thoroughly impressed by the fact that Lucy helped the police find Jerry McCorkle. Anyway, they welcomed Lucy, and it's given her a sense of belonging to something at that school. Hannah said that Lucy's a real asset to the Garden Club, and she plans to give her a job at Bella's Park this summer."

"And you feel how about this?"

"Honestly?"

He nodded.

Grace frowned. "I feel displaced in Lucy's affection."

"Simply put, jealous?"

Grace nodded and looked away. "Tyler's taking photo lessons from Amelia. Lucy's learning about plants and gardens from Hannah. And I'm just an ignorant old woman with nothing to teach them." She lowered her face into her hands.

Bob kneeled at her chair and pried her fingers away from her face. "Now you listen to me, Grace Singleton. You tutored both those kids, and more important, you gave them the love and concern they needed to bring them through terrible times in their lives. You helped Tyler cope with the loss of his mother, and where would Lucy or her family be without you? You inspired everyone to contribute to a fund that helps that family. Tyler and Lucy love you. They always will." She did not look at him, and he jiggled her knees. "Listen to me, Grace. If either of those kids felt that what they were doing was hurting you, they'd stop in a heartbeat."

Grace looked up. "I wouldn't want that. I want them to learn new things. I feel just awful, going on like this. It's so selfish of me."

"No, not selfish, honey. You're human. You feel left out, that's all. You don't garden or photograph, but that doesn't mean they love you any less. You're the conscience they come to when they need guidance."

"Lucy didn't come to me about Ringo. She fought me."

"She's a child, a teenager. Didn't Roger ever rebel?"

She frowned. "Only when I tried to force some girl on him, like for the school prom."

Bob sat back on his haunches. "Well, kids rebel at this age."

In a small, sad voice Grace said, "I know that."

"Think about it. Tyler and Lucy are doing the best thing they could do, learning something new. Maybe something they'll use for the rest of their lives. Be proud, honey. You've set an example for them of growth, and change, and learning. Let's *go* to the jazz festival, Grace. Let's have some fun, enjoy one another."

"Let me read through this, Bob."

"The festival's three weeks from now. Tell me soon, so I can call for reservations."

"How do people dress for this?" She remembered how inadequately attired she had felt on the cruise ship.

"The material they sent says casual dress by day, and you can see pictures of people in jeans and slacks, no jackets for men. It looks as if at night some younger folk dress up like 1920s and '30s flappers, but most of the people wear clothes like we'd wear to go into Asheville to the theater." He stood. "I'm off now. Got a golf date with Martin."

"Where's Ginger these days? Lord, I haven't seen Emily's mother in eons."

Bob kissed the top of her head. "I'm convinced she's got a lover somewhere, but Martin says she's just a Scrabble fanatic. Last I heard, Ginger was off to Bermuda for a ten-day Scrabble tournament."

"Thank God she's got an interest. She hates it here."

He shrugged. "And Martin loves it."

"Ginger's a strange woman," Grace said.

"All kinds of people in this world."

Once Bob had gone, Grace sat back in the rocking chair and closed her eyes. Without sight, sounds were magnified: the raucous warning of a bird defending its nest, the tinkle of the chimes Amelia had hung from a slender limb of a tree near the stream, the swish of water as it flowed past her window. Weariness was Grace's constant companion these days. She wasn't eating right again, not since returning from the cruise, and that was over two months ago. There had simply been too much stress.

Grace opened the envelope. The glossy lavender cover of the catalog, with its city skyline and banner of musical notes floating overhead, said *Jazz in Atlanta*. Once she got past the pages of advertising, it was all about music: jazz bands, big bands, feature performers from the old "Lawrence Welk Show," barbershop quartets, gospel groups, a banjo buddies series, a washboard concert. Classes were offered in ballroom dancing, swing, Latin jazz, and more.

The prospect overwhelmed her. It had been years since she had danced to swing or any kind of music. But Bob asked so little of her, and he wanted to go. She had read the eagerness in his eyes. The festival was still three weeks away; maybe they could take some dance lessons.

Grace set the catalog on her bed and went downstairs to find a phone book. There were fifteen instruction studios listed in and around Asheville, including one in Weaverville and one in the Mars Hill area. For a moment, excitement surged through her. They could take several lessons before they went, and the rest of the classes when they returned. But when she phoned them, Grace discovered that several of the studios had no dancing classes starting within the next three weeks, and others were in the middle of classes. "Call us back in the fall," was the routine answer.

Later that afternoon, Grace joined Hannah and Amelia on the porch for the first time since winter. They dragged their rocking chairs away from the wall of the house and moved them close to the railing. Hannah carried out a tray of tea and cookies, and Amelia, as usual, poured.

"My but it's a nice day! Can't wait until every day is like this," Amelia said.

Hannah leaned forward and poked around in one of the planters that hung along the railing. "Got to add soil to this," she said, then settled back in her rocker. "Look at the great oak. Pretty soon it'll be in full leaf, and Max's dogwoods over there are beginning to look as if fluffy white blankets have been thrown over them. Soon our roses will bloom."

Grace told them about the jazz festival. "Bob really wants to go. I'd hoped to sign us up for dance lessons before we went, but it didn't work out."

Amelia's eyes filled with excitement. "Now, a jazz festival is something I'd enjoy," she said. "Maybe Mike . . ." She stopped. Her voice turned cool. "Of course not. Mike's tied up with Roger."

"Perhaps not, or not for long." Grace recalled her conversation with her son on their trip to the doctor's office. "Mike might like a break from Roger," she said.

"Maybe," Amelia said with a questioning look.

"I hope you go to this jazz festival," Hannah said. "You and Bob need some time alone." She emphasized alone. "Grace, you'd be so proud of Lucy. She really has a green thumb."

It takes a village to raise a child. Where had Grace heard that? Hillary Clinton? They were all a part of Lucy's village: she, Hannah, and Amelia; Bob, Max, Mike; and Russell and Emily, too. In one way or another, at one time or another, each contributed to Lucy's well-being and to her future. "That is really great," she said.

"Tyler," Amelia said, "has the potential to be a good photographer, if he would just apply himself. He learns fast. Remember what a hard time I had learning to use my manual camera when I first got started? I wanted to dump it in a river. But Tyler—well, you know how smart he is, Grace." Grace did not reply, and Amelia said, "I want to talk to Mike about starting a photo class for young people, and at the end of the year, having a show for them. What do you ladies think?"

"Sounds great," Hannah said.

"I think it's a wonderful idea if you can get Mike to help," said Grace. "And yes, I know how smart Tyler is. I tutored him, remember?" Why had she said that? It was defensive and competitive. Grace had never considered herself competitive, but suddenly she was, and feeling bereft, too, as if someone had stolen her babies. She forced a smile. "Any hobbies the kids take up are good for them—they keep them busy and out of trouble."

21

THE JAZZ FESTIVAL

On the four-hour drive to Atlanta, the motion of the car lulled Grace into a doze, and she started awake when Bob suddenly slowed for traffic and changed lanes with a jerk. As they neared the city, traffic increased to fill the eight-lane highway. Grace preferred to keep her eyes closed to avoid the tension she felt when a driver switched lanes at seventy miles an hour or cars zoomed in from side lanes to join the flow. Finally they reached the bypass around the city and turned south, heading into Atlanta proper. The golden dome of the Capitol Building flashed brightly in the afternoon sun and stung Grace's eyes, especially the eye that had taken such a wallop.

The hotel where the jazz festival was held was more glamorous than any hotel Grace had ever stayed in, but then, she hadn't stayed in many. The lobby stretched the length of a large ballroom, with fireplaces at each end. Huge crystal chandeliers hung from high ceilings. Overstuffed chairs and settees framed thick Oriental carpets.

Their room on the eighth floor was no less grand: everything oversized, huge bed, enormous circular couch, floor-to-ceiling windows that spread across one wall of the room and offered a dizzying view of the city below. A railing at waist height inside made it possible for Grace to look down, though not for long. Cars looked like toys, people like ants.

"I'd suggest doing a bit of exploring the city, but I think we'd be better off just resting until dinner," Bob said. "I'm pooped from driving in that traffic."

Grace shuddered at the idea of exploring the city. Huge cities created a certain apprehension in her: fear of being mugged, fear of getting lost. "That's fine with me. I'm dying to try that Jacuzzi in the bathroom," she said.

"Mind if I join you?"

"Wait until I get in and soak a bit," Grace said. "I'll call you. Are you limping, Bob?"

"It's nothing. I'll take a couple of aspirin and it'll be fine. I must have twisted my ankle a bit when we got out of the car."

"We don't have to go dancing."

"I came to dance. A hot bath will help." He extracted a small bottle of pills from his pocket, poured a glass of water from a carafe on a table, and swallowed several pills.

Afterward, they lay propped up in the big bed and watched a movie on television, then ordered dinner in the room. Bob said his ankle was better, so Grace donned her black dress and Bob his blue suit, and they took the elevator down.

Grace had not anticipated that the Rose Room, situated along a hall on the third floor of the hotel, would be so huge. Chairs and instruments for the orchestra were positioned on a raised stage in front of an ocean-blue backdrop emblazoned with a white piano with large white musical notes floating above it. On either side of the stage were wooden dance floors. The remainder of the room was filled with chairs set up theater fashion.

"How does this work?" Grace asked.

"I think the orchestra plays, and people who want to dance get up from the audience and dance," Bob said. "I guess some folks come just to listen to the music."

"People sit here and watch the dancers?"

"Looks that way," he said.

"Imagine coming to watch other people dance. Your ankle okay now?"

"Feels fine." Bob led Grace forward to the second row of seats and they took the two on the end on the right. "We'll be able to see well here."

Grace kept turning her head as people entered. The clothes were amazing. Some women were dressed as flappers of the 1920s and early 1930s. There were young men in zoot suits, and young women in poodle skirts and bobby socks, as well as older ladies in evening gowns or ankle-length dresses. Many were more casually dressed, as she was, in simple black suitable for the theater.

The noise level rose as the room filled, and within fifteen minutes nearly every seat was taken. Then, dressed in black tuxedos, the members of the orchestra filed onto the stage. The orchestra leader, a saxophone in his hand, stepped forward and welcomed the audience. He turned from them, raised his arms, and moments later the deep, poignant strains of "Stardust" filled the room.

Grace closed her eyes. Music swirled about and through her, filled every pore of her skin, every nerve and muscle of her body. She finally relaxed. "Sentimental Journey" followed, and then a female singer, blond and pretty, rose from her seat and took center stage. Her voice was sweet and low as she sang "Bewitched, Bothered, and Bewildered," followed by "I Don't Want to Set the World on Fire" and "That Old Black Magic." Grace swayed to the music. The singer returned to her chair. The orchestra began to play "Do You Know What it Means to Miss New Orleans?" and Grace heard chairs being shoved aside, felt the brush of air as couples passed on their way to the dance floor. By then Grace's feet were tapping rhythm, and when the orchestra swung into "In the Mood," Bob took her hand and led her to the dance floor. She hadn't known what a great dancer Bob was, so at ease, so sure of himself. Never had she felt herself to be so light on her feet or so competent a dancer. Grace let herself go, moved to his touch, and smiled. "I feel young," she told him.

The pleasure of movement, of music buoyed her, and sheer exuberance overcame her inhibitions. As the musicians played one song after another, now a foxtrot, now a waltz, now swing, Grace found the old steps returning. "It's like riding a bicycle," she said. "It's all coming back."

The ballroom seemed to vibrate as with the beat of a thousand hummingbird wings. Those who had come just to listen to the music tapped their feet and swayed. They moved arms, hands, head, and shoulders to the beat of the music. Finally the orchestra swung into "Goodnight, Sweetheart."

"I think that's a wrap," Bob said.

* * *

Later, lying in the big bed, Grace snuggled against Bob and rested her head on his shoulder. "At the risk of using a cliché, I could have danced all night. At first, I didn't want to come, but I had the best time I've had in I can't remember when. Hey, there's a song about that. What is it?"

" 'Kiss me once, then kiss me twice, /then kiss me once again./ It's been a long, long time,' " Bob sang, stopping to kiss Grace several times.

"That's the song," she said. "I like it." She snuggled close. "So tell me, what are we going to do tomorrow?"

Bob reached over to switch on the table lamp, sat up, and reached for the catalog of events. "There are two barbershop quartets, one at ten in the morning and the other at two in the afternoon. Bands will be playing in one or another of the four ballrooms all through the day and evening." He turned a page. "We could be busy all day long, starting with the Jazz Parade at nine in the morning. Then there's a barbecue at noon at a local fire station. They have a band made up of firemen musicians. At two there's that barbershop quartet, and at four a Pianorama: 'Just ivory,' it says, 'no horns, drums, or other instruments.' "

"Let's do the barbershop quartet at two and the Pianorama at four." She kissed his neck. "Let's not rush in the morning. Let's sleep in, order breakfast in the room, and then I'd like to shop for a dress for tomorrow night. Something bright and cheery, more in keeping with the way I feel." Grace reached for the catalog and let it slide onto the floor, then turned to Bob and put her arms about his neck.

The following morning Grace found her dress, a paisley-print shirt-waist in clear spring colors: rose and green with touches of daffodil yellow. The material fell in soft folds beneath the belted waist almost to mid-calf. A pair of rose-colored pumps with inch-high heels and sheer stockings completed the outfit. After dropping off her packages in the room, Grace met Bob for lunch in one of the more casual restaurants in the hotel, where they shared a large chef's salad before taking the elevator to the third floor. Hand in hand, they drifted down the hall to the Rose Room, took seats near the front, and waited for the barbershop quartet to begin.

Dressed in blue-and-white pinstripe shirts, red bow ties, and straw hats, The Troubadours strode onto the stage. Grace wondered if their handlebar mustaches were real. After a few welcoming comments, they opened a cappella with "Let Me Call You Sweetheart." Their rich, full tones, the gleam of pleasure in their eyes, the lilt in their voices, and their enthusiasm proved infectious to the audience, who swayed in their seats, smiling and nodding. Lighthearted and merry, Grace felt swept up and part of a greater whole, that greater whole she had known ever so briefly at the railing of the cruise ship. Feeling splendid, Grace wanted to sing, wanted to stand up there on that stage and sing her heart out.

The Troubadours continued with "A Bicycle Built for Two," "The Sidewalks of New York," and many more, and when they ended their program with "In the Good Old Summertime," the audience rose to their feet clapping, and bravos could be heard throughout the room.

Bob wanted coffee, so they ambled downstairs to the snack bar, then back to the third floor to the smaller Lilac Room, where two baby grand pianos faced one another on the stage. First, the two performers played ragtime, then switched to the music of Chopin and Beethoven, pieces like "Moonlight Sonata" and others made familiar by television commercials and movies.

"What a marvelous afternoon," Grace said as they took the elevator back to the eighth floor and their room.

"Indeed it was."

"Thank you so much for suggesting we come," Grace said. "I didn't realize just how badly I needed a break." She hugged his arm. "I'm having such a good time."

"At home you get so involved with people—too involved," Bob said as he opened their door and ushered her inside.

"Only with people I love." Grace turned to Bob and slipped her arms about his neck. Music flooded her mind. She leaned against him, humming a bit of "I Can't Get Started."

"The heck you can't," he whispered, and led her toward the bed.

Later, when city lights below sparkled like stars and cars streaking past on the highway seemed as comets shooting through the night, they dressed for dinner.

"You look absolutely ravishing," Bob said.

"And you are utterly handsome," she replied.

Bob proffered his arm and she took it, and when they stepped into the elegant restaurant in the hotel, the rosy red light and deep mauve furnishings, with their suggestion of illicit romance, delighted her. Grace moved with unaccustomed fluidity and confidence, her head held high.

Duck, crisp and delicious under orange sauce, pleased her palate, and Bob said his filet mignon melted in his mouth. He insisted that she try the wine he ordered, but its dryness caused her mouth to pucker. For dessert they chose something unpronounceable, French, and delicious. The bill totaled $123.00.

"This is outrageous," Grace said under her breath. "I would never have let you bring me here had I known."

"Not at all. The ambiance is great, we both enjoyed our dinners, and we're worth every penny," he replied.

Out in the lobby, they studied the list of bands posted on a tall sign and chose one that the large black letters said hailed from "old Virginie."

"I feel so stiff. Think I can dance tonight?" she asked.

"You'll loosen up the minute we get going."

"I hope you're right."

They strolled to the Iris Room, which was smaller and more intimate than the Rose Room. Balls of light suspended from the ceiling circled unhurriedly, casting trails of silver light across the walls.

The room filled rapidly and the sense of anticipation grew. Then the curtain parted and an announcer stepped forward to greet the audience.

"Just imagine you're back in the early 1940s, dancing to the music of the great bands of Tommy Dorsey, Les Brown and his Band of Renown, or Benny Goodman." The announcer was tall, his arms long. He reached for his saxophone, lifted it to his lips, and played. The sound was plaintive yet sweet, and the orchestra picked up the beat and belted out the most delightful music.

On the dance floor, Bob pulled Grace close. They moved together, cheek to cheek, to "Don't Get Around Much Anymore," followed by "I'm Gettin' Sentimental Over You," and a song she did not remember, "Till Then." When the beat changed, they did a modified version of the jitterbug to "Little Brown Jug" and "Chattanooga Choo Choo." After an hour, the band took a break. Then and only then, feeling on top of the world, they rested and sat out a set.

"It's fun just to sit and watch," Grace said, then she whispered, "Look at that woman in green, how she wiggles her hips."

The woman in green stood out from others on the floor. She danced almost solo, as did her partner, while all about them everyone else danced close. Obviously relishing an audience, she looked out toward those seated, threw back her head, gyrated her hips under the smooth silk of her long skirt, and laughed.

"I'd call her Swizzle Hips," Bob said. He nudged Grace's shoulder. "See that couple in yellow? He's wearing a yellow jacket that matches her dress jacket. Yellow Jackets, that's what they are."

"Wonder what people say about us?" Grace said.

"They probably call us The Lovebirds." Bob grinned and squeezed Grace's hand.

"I'm having the best time," she said.

"Me too."

"Thank you so much for insisting we come."

"And the evening's not over, my lady. There's more to come." He looked at her suggestively, and Grace raised her lips to his.

22

THE POWERS THAT BE

Grace returned home at noon on Monday to find a message from Emily asking her to come to her office on Tuesday afternoon at 2:00 P.M. That evening, at dinner with her friends, she waxed ebullient about her adventure.

"It was the greatest time I've had in years." She stopped, remembering their cruise. "I mean with Bob. I had a terrific time on our cruise, of course."

"Yeah, yeah," Amelia said.

"All the old dance steps came back. I loved it. I find that when I master something I didn't think I could, I feel as if I can do anything—at least anything I want to do. How could it be that all these years I never felt the urge to dance? And the music, all the old favorites we knew when we were teenagers." She hummed a tune.

" 'September Song.' I absolutely adore that song," Amelia said. "I haven't heard it in a while."

"You'll all have to come with us next time," Grace said. "We'll have such fun."

"Max and Hannah can go. I haven't an escort any longer." Hurt and disappointment crossed Amelia's face.

"So what did you do this weekend, both of you?" Grace asked.

Hannah blurted, "A water main broke, or was cut, at the park. The plumbers worked for hours on Saturday, digging up part of the Herb Garden. Thank goodness it wasn't the Cottage Garden. Line seemed to have been cut. Can't tell if it was deliberate or an accident, one of the gardeners trying to dig a hole in the wrong place. The men all shake their heads and say they had nothing to do with it. We'll never know."

"It must have been an accident," Grace said. "Your men wouldn't deliberately cut a water main at the park."

"You're probably right," Hannah said. "Faulty pipe, maybe."

Irritation oozed from Amelia's voice as she said, "I had a call from New York, from the gallery that carries my photographs. They want more photos and fast, and Mike's time is consumed with Roger." She scrunched her nose. "Roger this, Roger that, or 'I can't make it to the darkroom today. Tomorrow, I promise.' Tomorrow never comes."

Unintentionally, they had rained on her parade. Well, problems took no holiday. "I'm sorry about the plumbing, and about Mike's being so occupied," Grace said.

"Deliberately unavailable," Amelia said. "You can't help it if a water pipe breaks, but people make choices about how they'll spend their time and with whom."

Hannah tapped on the kitchen table. "Listen to us, dumping our annoyances on Grace." She looked into Grace's eyes. "I'm very glad you and Bob had such a good time. Tell us more about it."

"Another time, when we have a quiet afternoon on the porch." But she knew she wouldn't speak of it again. Bob might, and that was fine, but for Grace the excitement had been reduced by the mundane events of ordinary living.

Emily's new office occupied the ground floor of a small two-story brick building in Mars Hill. Grace parked in a lot near the college and walked up the hill and around the corner to the office. Emily shared space with another attorney, a man who handled mainly divorce and family mediation.

"May I help you?" A slender young woman with bright, intelligent eyes sat at the front desk.

"I've come to see Emily—I mean, Mrs. Richardson"

"Certainly. Will you have a seat, please." She collected some files, rose, strode to the door on the far right, and disappeared inside.

Grace settled herself in a low chair. She selected a magazine, *Woman's Day*, and turned pages nonchalantly while her feet tapped to the beat of "Sentimental Journey," which kept playing in her mind.

When the door reopened, the woman Grace assumed was Emily's

secretary appeared, followed by Emily, who welcomed Grace with outstretched hands. Grace clasped them, perhaps too tightly from sheer nervousness.

"How are you, Grace? Did you have a wonderful time, you and Bob, in Atlanta?" She turned to the young woman. "Sandi, this is my mother-in-law."

Pleased and flattered by the introduction, Grace flushed. She wanted to explain to Sandi that although she and Bob were not married, they could be, and that she loved his family, considered Emily her daughter-in-law and Tyler and Melissa her grandchildren.

"Ah," Sandi said, her hand extended, "you must be Tyler's Granny Grace."

Grace nodded and shook Sandi's hand.

"Our secretary's ill. Sandi's my paralegal and she's filling in for Doreen," Emily said. "Hold my calls, will you, Sandi? Thanks." She ushered Grace into her office. "I don't know what I would do without Sandi helping out at that desk."

"She has the look of a smart young woman," Grace said.

"Now tell me." Emily took her chair behind the big desk. "How was your holiday? Did you and Bob dance a lot? How were the bands?"

Certain that Emily was merely being polite, Grace answered her questions briefly. The holiday was great fun. She and Bob danced a great deal, and yes, the bands were terrific.

Emily set her elbows on her desk and leaned her chin on her hands. "It's been years since I danced. Russell isn't one for dancing, you know."

"It comes back—the steps, I mean. Maybe you two could come with Bob and me. We loved it so much, we're sure to go to another jazz weekend."

"I'll suggest it to Russell. Perhaps his father can persuade him." She raised and lowered her shoulders. "You know men: stubborn. But we can't have it all, can we?"

Then, as if remembering why Grace was here, Emily sat back, adjusted the lapels of her tailored blue suit, slipped on her glasses, and opened a folder on her desk. "Well, let's get down to business, shall we?"

Grace sat straighter.

"Of course Miss Randall lays the blame totally with Lucy. Lucy, she claims, hacked into the computer. She denies all responsibility, even for the substitute teacher leaving that classroom."

"But the police caught Ringo. Doesn't that mean anything?"

"Miss Randall is claiming that Lucy must also have had access to a computer off of school grounds, as so many kids do today."

Grace sighed. "Ridiculous. Lucy can't afford a computer at home, and she has very few friends—I can testify to that."

Emily shook her head. "That's not going to help us. We need someone to stop covering up for that boy, Travis." She rummaged under papers. "Here's his full name. Travis." She broke off. "Grace, his name is Travis McCorkle."

"What does that mean?"

"That maybe Jerry put him up to this. Didn't Tyler say Travis encouraged the girls to use the chat room?"

"Yes, he did."

"So when I said Travis's name to Miss Randall, she probably knew exactly who I meant. Didn't you say the Randalls are related to the McCorkles?"

"You think she's protecting the boy?"

Emily sat back in her chair. "It hardly matters. It's the fact that she put a substitute in that room and the woman walked out. Who was this person? Is she still working there? And if so, why? A school is responsible for keeping its students away from chat rooms. It's their job to monitor all computers, and this chat room availability went on for a good two weeks. Someone was not doing their job, I'd say. It would also help if someone else would corroborate Lucy's story."

"What about Tyler?" Grace asked.

"Too close a relation to me."

"Other kids knew. Some of them used it, too."

Emily handed Grace a sheet of paper with lined columns. "Here's a list of the boys and girls who used that room at the same time Lucy did. The ones that she says either urged her to go online or went on themselves are starred, see?" She leaned over her desk and pointed. There were six names starred.

Grace nodded.

"If we could get these parents to allow their kids to give a statement, we'd have something to go on." She threw up her hands. "I've tried, with no luck. The Randalls must have gotten to them first. No one wants to get involved."

Clutching her purse to her chest, Grace said, "Why would they turn you down? Why wouldn't they want to help? Their girls used that computer. It could have been one of them as well as Lucy."

"My personal feeling is that they're scared. Someone's father may work for one of the Randall businesses—you never know."

"Brenda will help us," Grace said

"Why don't you take the list? See what you can do."

Driving home, Grace fumed, remembering Brenda's warning that Francine Randall was hard and mean. What had the woman, or one of her lackeys, said or done to those parents and their kids? Grace's sense of outrage grew. There were kids out there who knew that Lucy was telling the truth and no one wanted to help.

The parking lot at Caster Elementary School was empty. Grace checked her watch. It was after 5:00 p.m. Of course no one would be here; school was out, and everyone had gone home. She'd call Brenda tonight and see if her friend could help her.

When Grace turned into Cove Road, both Ellie's and Brenda's cars sat in the driveway of the house they shared. Driving past her own home, Grace pulled in behind Brenda's car, got out, and ran up the front steps. Ellie Lerner answered her ring.

"Grace, how good to see you. How was your holiday? Hannah told us you and Bob went to a jazz thing. How was it?"

"We had a great time. How are you, Ellie? Is Brenda here?"

"I'm fine, and yes, Brenda's here. Oh, here she is."

Brenda emerged from the back of the house. She wore an apron, and a smudge of flour decorated her face. "Molly's birthday is tomorrow. She didn't want a party, but at least I can bake her a cake. Come on back to the kitchen, Grace."

The three women moved down the short hall to the large wood-paneled kitchen. Whenever she came into this house, Grace wondered at the amount of paneling Molly and her husband had installed. Dark wood ran beneath the chair railing in the dining room. Dark wood paneling lined the wall of the staircase to the second floor. Perhaps it was an attempt at low maintenance; the Lunds had two little boys. Molly and her family now lived in the big, bright family farmhouse, while her mother and Ellie shared the Lunds' newer but darker house.

"One of these days, I am going to get a can of bright yellow paint and paint right over this wood paneling," Brenda was saying. Brenda had aged considerably since Harold died. Gray streaked her auburn hair, and her eyes lacked their former luster. Brenda and Ellie were both in their mid-fifties. Ellie's blue eyes retained their sparkle, and her hair, also auburn, remained as shiny as it had been when she arrived at Lurina's farmhouse several years ago, bearing three wedding gowns for the eighty-one-year-old bride to choose from.

"Sit, Grace, sit." Ellie pulled out a chair at their kitchen table and busied herself removing a bubbling casserole of macaroni and cheese from the oven. "Oven's all yours, Brenda," she said.

Grace hesitated. She switched her purse from her right hand to her left and back to her right hand. "I can come back. It's dinnertime, and you're busy."

"Nonsense," Brenda said. "I'd hate to think we stand on ceremony with one another." She poured batter from a large yellow ceramic bowl into two round baking tins and set the bowl in the sink. "There, I'm finished. Sit. I just need to pop these in the oven, wash my hands, get rid of this apron, and I'm all yours."

"I'll set the table. I make a mean macaroni and cheese, Grace. Have dinner with us," Ellie said.

Grace realized her stomach was growling. "I'd enjoy that. Thank you. If you're sure you have enough?"

"We have plenty," Ellie said.

"I'll need to phone home and tell Hannah and Amelia."

Grace and Brenda moved into the living room, where wood paneling framed the fireplace. "I'm going to get rid of that, too," Brenda said. "I thought all this wood was too dark and depressing when they built the house, but I figured, it's their house, not mine. Who'd have thought I'd end up living here?"

"At least it's fixable with a can of paint," Grace said, and wondered why the women hadn't made changes sooner. They'd been sharing the house for almost a year, if she remembered right.

"I need your help, Brenda," Grace said.

"Just ask."

"The families of the kids who used, and encouraged Lucy to use, that computer refuse to let their children give a statement to prove the computer ever existed in the school. Emily gave me a list of their names. She thought maybe I could talk to the families. I didn't want to do anything without talking to you. Do you know any of them?"

Brenda studied the list. "Sure, I know them. They all went to Caster Elementary. The Wellands live just past Covington in the Little Dove Creek area. The Wrights come to our church here most Sundays. I can talk to them."

"Oh, would you?"

"Certainly. I'll do it this week." She scrutinized the list again. "I wouldn't bother with the Henfords. The father's bullheaded, won't budge once he's made his mind up."

"If we could get three, even two, of the families to cooperate with Emily, it would be a great help, I imagine," Grace said.

Ellie called from the doorway, "Dinner's ready."

Grace's attempts to influence the remaining three families on Emily's list proved futile. People resisted letting her into their homes, and hung up when she called them. Lucy's close call with Ringo and the argument that it could have been their daughters was to no avail. The parents who did listen gave one another occasional furtive glances, and ended up saying no.

Brenda phoned to say that she, too, had been unable to convince anyone to cooperate. "I'm sorry. I thought I had Mr. Wright convinced, but in the end, his wife didn't want their daughter involved."

A disillusioned Grace reported back to Emily. "Neither Brenda nor I could budge any of the families."

"Let's wait and see what happens at Ringo's trial," Emily said. "I'm sorry, Grace, the law is slow moving. I know the Randalls. They live by their own law. Not that I think they're into criminal activity, but they throw their weight around in this county, and sometimes people get hurt. What went on at that school was inexcusable, but I'll do everything legally possible to bring Francine Randall and her school to justice."

The office windows were open. Grace breathed deeply of the fresh mountain air. Summer was almost here. Behind the building, across the street, a lone hill stood out against a pale blue sky. Suddenly Grace could not wait to get outside into the loveliness of this day. She stood. "Thank you for everything, Emily."

"I thank *you* for trying with those families, Grace. We'll not give up our efforts or our hope."

23

HANNAH SETS
A WEDDING DATE

That afternoon, as Grace drove slowly home from Mars Hill, Hannah rounded Max's house in search of him. The dairy barn had been freshly painted terra-cotta red, and his truck was pulled up to the side. Above the truck, the door to the loft stood open. Perched at the rear of his pickup, Max hefted large bales of hay from the truck bed up to José, who reached for them from the opening in the loft.

Hannah had often noted how strong and fit Max was, and now, as she watched the rippling of his muscles, she wondered if he found her at all appealing as a woman. Probably not. He had prefaced every proposal by saying that she would not be committed to conjugal duties. Was that his way of indicating that he had no interest in sleeping with her? When they were together and as they grew more intimate, she was certain he did, but then, like a whiff of wood smoke on a sporadic winter breeze, the sense of his wanting her would vanish. He seemed to rein himself in, and a wall fell between them as he changed the topic to some totally irrelevant matter, a bucket of cold water dashed on her emotions.

Hannah's hands settled on her neck. Wrinkles. Her most visible displays of age were these wrinkles and the brown spots on her arms and hands. She had always been muscular and firm—bless her heredity—but this neck of hers said it all. She was simply too old for passion. Still, as she watched him now, she recognized the reaction of her body for what it was: interest and desire. Stop this nonsense, she told herself, and mentally routed her own disconcerting sensuality.

Max lifted his head, saw her, and smiled. His eyes grew soft. José stuck his head through the door of the loft, waved to Hannah, then sat back on his haunches grinning, as if he knew there would be a wait before he received the next bale.

Max jumped from the truck and brushed his jeans free of bits of hay. A shiver raced through Hannah. There's not an ounce of fat on him, she thought as he took long strides toward her. "I didn't mean to interrupt you," she said.

"I needed a break." He turned and waved at José, who waved back, then moved from the opening and shut the door of the loft. "Come on around the house. Anna'll bring us out a tray of sandwiches and iced tea. It's nice and cool on the front porch. Not summer quite yet, even though I'm hot as Hades."

"That looks like hard work, pitching those bales of hay up to the loft."

"Been doing it so long, I hardly think of it as work until I stop and every muscle aches. That's the really hard thing about getting old—the loss of strength and vital powers."

Sexual powers, too? She blushed, thinking it.

"Get that pipe fixed?" he asked.

"It was cut right through, as if someone brought a sharp shovel down on it deliberately, but I can't imagine any of the workmen doing that. It's been replaced."

"Hopefully that's the end of it," he replied.

"You don't think it is?" she asked.

"Well." Max removed his cap and scratched his head. "One time a while back, we had an electrical problem here. The wire to the house was cut—not once, but four times. We staked out the place, and sure enough, it was kids about ten years old from McCorkle Creek playing at being linemen. One's father worked for the electric company, and the kid 'borrowed' some of his dad's tools. They found the main switch box and shut off the main fuse before they cut wires to the house, or they could have been electrocuted. They thought it was a lark until we caught them. I give the father credit; he gave his kid a good licking and grounded him for a month. Could be some smart aleck like that doing mischief. Let me know if it happens again."

"I sure will."

A screen door opened and slammed shut. Grace had said she was certain that Anna slammed doors to attract attention, and she succeeded. This time, however, Anna's hands were full: a platter of sandwiches in one, a pitcher of tea in the other. Max rose to take the pitcher. Anna handed Hannah the platter, and began to open drawers of the chartreuse-painted hutch that stood against the exterior wall of the house. She pulled out a blue tablecloth, and with a flip of her hands spread it over the table. Then she extracted plates, glasses, and utensils from the hutch. In two minutes, the platter and pitcher sat on the table and Anna waved them toward it.

"Eat and enjoy, Señora Hannah, Mr. Max." She smiled at them benignly. "When we gonna have a wedding, Señora Hannah?" she asked.

Without thinking, Hannah replied, "In the spring next year."

"You serious?" Max asked.

Hannah nodded.

Anna stood by the door, her hands on her hips. "*Bueno*. We make *una grande celebración*. I tell José." She beamed.

She had said it, picked a time. Hannah's heart raced. She felt a sense of being trapped mingled with relief, plus an indisputable longing for Max, and uncertainty about her future. How could she marry this man and carry on the same way she did now? From her bedroom window at night, she could see the lights in his room, see his silhouette move behind the drawn shade. Once they were married, how would she feel? And what would she owe him, having accepted his proposal to share his material assets and inherit them if she outlived him, God forbid?

"April, then?" Max's grin was that of a delighted little boy.

"April. When the leaves return to the trees."

"Can we celebrate afterward? Go somewhere together?" he asked.

The weakness she felt in the pit of her stomach caused Hannah to pull back. "Why would we do that?"

His smile vanished. "Thought it might be nice to take a road trip up north. New England is lovely in April, with all the daffodils and irises." He hastened to add, "We could take separate rooms."

Hannah's mouth went dry. As a teenager, having a beau had invariably resulted in her feeling at loose ends and out of control. That old reaction was back, and she did not like it. "Can we talk about this later? It's months away, almost a year."

"Certainly," he replied, the light fading from his eyes.

Feeling guilty, Hannah finished her sandwich in silence, bade him good-bye, and crossed the road to the farmhouse, while Max returned to José and the business of storing hay.

"You actually picked a month?" Grace asked when Hannah told her and Amelia the news later that day.

"As Anna would say, '*Sí, señoras.*'"

"How exciting! A spring wedding. Where will it be?" Amelia asked.

"At Max's house, I think, or maybe the courthouse in Marshall. Something very simple. Just family and a few friends."

"Why not this fall? Why wait that long?" Amelia asked.

Hannah shrugged. "We were having lunch on Max's porch. Anna asked when we were going to get married, and I blurted out, 'Next spring.' Don't ask me why."

"Max must be thrilled." Grace poured herself a cup of tea and sat back in her rocking chair. With winter over, she relished sitting on the porch with her friends. The wide green canopy of the great oak shaded half the yard. Its damaged side now sprouted vigorous new limbs and leaves, encouraged by Hannah's ministrations and Grace and Amelia's blessings. Red Chrysler Imperial roses lined their driveway, and the air was thick with their scent. Overall, Grace found that warmer weather had a salubrious effect: Bag boys in the market smiled more often, Buddy Herrill at the gas station proved more attentive, folks drove at a slower pace along Cove Road, and people you met in the stores at Elk Plaza stopped for longer periods of time to chat. Vegetable stands popped up along the road from Covington to Mars Hill, and just outside of Mars Hill, the Saturday morning Tailgate Market was in full swing. Fresh fruits and vegetables would be increasingly abundant. Hannah had decided against putting in a vegetable garden this year; it would be like taking coals to Newcastle.

"You'll be married in a long gown, won't you?" Amelia asked.

"Goodness, no," Hannah replied.

"A nice suit?" Grace asked.

"Pantsuit. Probably have something in my closet."

"Oh, Hannah. It's your wedding. At least a new suit," Grace said, and was seconded by Amelia.

"We'll go with you to pick it out," Amelia said.

Hannah almost said, "Like heck you will," but didn't. "Okay, you can come, but if you two harass me in the shop, out you go."

"A deal." Grace laughed.

"I can't believe you finally set a date," Amelia said.

Hannah's jaw tilted up. Amelia did have the knack of saying things that annoyed her, but she was determined not to allow small things to elicit a reaction that could be seen as hostile or mean-spirited. One of these days, she would have to sit down and figure out why Amelia's words so often irritated her. "Haven't set a date. Just said in the spring."

"In the spring. That seems like such a long time away," Amelia said. "Why so long? Why not this fall?"

"It just came out. And I like April. I'm thinking late April, but I don't want to commit to a day quite yet," Hannah said.

Amelia pursed her lips. "Once I decided, as you seem to have done at last, I'd do it and get it over with."

"I won't be rushed. Max had no problem with next April."

"Well, good luck." It was said by Amelia without enthusiasm.

Hannah ignored her and continued to rock for a while. Then she leaned forward and pushed her finger into the soil in a planter that hung on the rail near her chair. "Dry. Trouble with planters is they need so much water—more so here, since it faces west."

Grace folded the calendar back to May. "Have you told anyone? Have you told Laura?"

"Not yet."

"Miranda and the family will come down from Branston, of course," Amelia said. "Do you realize this is the first wedding among us?"

"Remember, it's a business transaction. I'm not moving out of this house." Hannah resumed rocking.

"Who'll give you away?" Amelia asked.

"Why should anyone give me away at my age?"

Amelia persisted. "What if Grace and I walk you down the aisle?"

"Hannah can decide all those kinds of things later," Grace said. She half expected Hannah to snap at Amelia and was glad when that did not happen.

"But half the fun's in the planning," Amelia said.

"Perhaps to you it is." Hannah rocked harder, leaned back, and closed her eyes. "It's something I don't want to deal with until maybe a week before it happens."

Amelia opened her mouth, but Grace's hand went to her arm, and Amelia remained silent.

Privately, Grace considered Amelia's idea a good one, and she would relay that to her later. She loved the thought of herself and Amelia walking down the aisle on either side of Hannah, and Max standing with Bob. Her fantasy crumbled. What if there was no aisle? Hannah might simply wake up one day, call Pastor Johnson, put on something casual, walk in the front door of Max's house, and marry him right there without inviting anyone. No, Hannah wouldn't go quite that far. There were too many people who cared: herself, Amelia, Hannah's daughters and her grandsons. At least she had picked a month, and April was a vibrant month luxuriant with color.

It was best, Hannah decided, to tell Laura herself about the date she had chosen for her marriage to Max. If she didn't, someone else was sure to, and Laura would be hurt. Early the next morning, Hannah drove directly to Hank and Laura's home. Hank's car was gone, but a frazzled Laura, her hair unkempt, her eyes red from crying or lack of sleep, opened the door. Without a word, Laura handed the screaming Andy to her mother and strode to the kitchen with Hannah and baby following.

The aroma of good strong coffee permeated the bright open kitchen. Laura poured herself a mug and plopped into a chair at the round maple table. "This was one awful mistake. What could I possibly have been thinking? I must have known that babies demand a lot of time and attention, but I didn't count on all these endless, sleepless nights. Sometimes I want to just shake Andy. Hank's a heavy sleeper, but I wonder at times if he's faking and too darn lazy to get up with Andy." She ran her fingers through her hair. "That's not fair. Hank can sleep through a hurricane. He would help me if I woke him up."

"But you won't, is that right?"

"I can't do that to him. He's at work all day."

"Asking for help's a sign of weakness? Don't make the same mistake I made, Laura. Ask for help when you need it."

"I don't mean to misrepresent Hank. He loves Andy, and he helps me after he gets home from work. But he gets away from it all, and I'm stuck here all day long with all the responsibility. I'm sure I'm not doing things right." Laura folded her arms on the table and lowered her forehead onto them.

Andy stirred restlessly on Hannah's chest and whined as if in pain. "Have you had this baby to the pediatrician? He seems to have gas; look at how he curls his legs up under him. Poor little tyke."

"My appointment is next week. I didn't want to seem like a hysterical or incompetent mother, taking him in sooner," came from beneath her daughter's mop of hair.

"Your doctor might have a simple solution to the problem, and you could get a good night's sleep," Hannah said.

"I haven't the energy," Laura mumbled. "You want to call him, you do it."

"Let me rock Andy a bit and rub his tummy. It might soothe him."

"Do whatever you want. Take him with you. If I don't see or hear him for a month, I'd be happy."

Hannah spoke gently, softly to the baby, then sat and began a rocking movement.

Laura lifted her head and stared at her mother. "How do women do it?"

"Do what?"

"Stay home and take care of babies."

"It's different for different women. Some women find it harder than others do. You have work you love. You're probably eager to get back to the office, so the time hangs heavy."

"God, I ache for my work, and a good night's sleep."

"You'll have both, Laura, dear, very soon. Andy will outgrow the cramps. He'll be fine. You never intended to stop working and stay home with him, did you?" Why hadn't they discussed this sooner? Why had she not paid more attention? Why had she let her daughter deteriorate into such a state?

"No one said it would be so boring and so hard, that I'd be on call twenty-four hours a day. I thought babies slept for hours on end."

"Some do."

"Not Andy. No sooner do I feed him than he's got gas, so I walk the floor, and by the time he's quieted down it's time for another bottle, and then he's got gas again, and on and on." She pinched her nose. "And all those stinky diapers! I'm switching to Pampers and putting an end to home delivery and cotton diapers. I don't *care* what Emily says."

"Would you consider leaving Andy with me some days, or part of some days, until you find good day care for him?" It wrenched Hannah's heart to think of her grandson in day care. "Bring him to work. We can keep a crib in both our offices." They could share in his care. Laura could have him in her office when she chose, and the rest of the time he'd be with Hannah, who absolutely adored him and found him irresistible. Andy had settled tightly against his grandmother's full, warm bosom now, and his little legs dangled relaxed.

Laura raised her head. She stared at the baby. "See? He hates me. I can't get him quiet like that." She began to cry.

"A baby doesn't hate anyone. If you're nervous or insecure handling him, he'll pick up on that and it could make it worse, that's all. You're exhausted, I can see that. Let me take him home with me right now, and you get a good rest. When you feel better, we can talk about a long-term plan. You come over when you're rested."

"Really? You don't mind? You'd do that for me?" Laura broke into tears again.

"I'd have done it sooner had I realized how worn out you were," Hannah said.

"Thank you, Mother. I keep thinking you don't like babies. Miranda said . . ."

"Whatever Miranda experienced with me does not apply to today, to now, to you, to this baby. Will you get that into your head? There is nothing, nothing in this world that I would not do for you or for him."

Andy whimpered, stretched, settled back against his grandmother, and burped, releasing the slightly sour, cheesy smell of milk. "Think about what I said. It might be the best solution for you, and Andy, and myself as well." She looked at the baby and her heart melted. I don't think I have ever loved anyone the way I love this child, she thought.

Without fanfare, Hannah transferred the car seat from her daughter's car to hers, gathered up the baby's diapers, formula, clothes, and departed. She drove slowly. Andy fell asleep immediately. Fifteen minutes later, she carried the sleeping child up the steps and into the farmhouse.

Grace opened the front door. "What have we here? Oh, he's so precious."

Hannah explained about Laura.

"I'm glad you brought the baby. I hadn't realized. We could have been helping her all along." In the bedroom downstairs, they fashioned a crib of pillows and lay Andy gently in the center of the bed. "He's so adorable," Grace said.

They tiptoed out of the bedroom. Grace made tea, which they took into the living room.

"I have a plan," Hannah said. "If Laura and Hank will go along with it, we could get two cribs, one for my office and one for Laura's, and Laura could come back to work and bring Andy to the office. I'd take care of him whenever she needed me to. People take babies to work all the time."

"What happens when Laura has to go to town or out in the country to take an oral history, or you have to be in the gardens?" Grace asked.

"I'll carry him in one of those newfangled slings I've seen in catalogs. I'm strong. I can do it."

Quiet hush fell over the room, as if both women were remembering their own babies, trying to recall how they had managed, how they had felt. Grace broke the silence. "Isn't this going to be a lot of work for you, Hannah?"

"It could be, I guess. But I want to do this for Laura, for Andy, for myself. You understand, don't you, Grace?"

They moved back into the bedroom to check on the baby.

"Of course I do."

"Melissa, you know, slept a great deal and started sleeping through the night very early. You and Bob babysat for them so that Emily and Russell could get out on weekends," Hannah said.

"And Emily hired a nanny after two months and went back to work," Grace said. "I'll help with Andy where I can. You'll let me know what I can do, won't you?"

"I will, when I know," Hannah replied.

"I'm home a lot," Grace said. "I don't mind watching him for a few hours now and then. He's a sweet baby. If you need to leave early and he's sleeping, I'll be glad to walk him down to you or his mother."

"This child could end up with two grandmothers, couldn't he?" Hannah said.

"No." Amelia's voice whispered from the doorway. "Three grandmothers. I'll do everything I can to help, too." Amelia's face was soft, her eyes clouded with affection and tears as she looked at Andy.

At that moment, Hannah loved Amelia. She went to the doorway and without hesitation, though totally out of character, she hugged Amelia. "Thank you, my friend, my sister." Hannah reached for Grace and included her in the hug. "My sisters."

After discussing the matter with her husband, a grateful Laura thanked her mother profusely and agreed to bring the baby to work. Two days later, a crib was delivered to the office, along with a changing table complete with all they would need for Andy's care. Hannah, Grace, and Amelia shopped in Asheville for the sling in which Hannah planned to carry Andy. Hannah bought one for Laura as well. She was certain that when Laura caught up on her sleep, and grew more accustomed to motherhood, things would be just fine.

24

ANDY CONQUERS ALL

A baby at the office, with its bouts of sleeping, fussing, or crying, can annoy some folks, elicit maternal or paternal feelings in others, or merely be treated with indifference by some. Mary Ann fussed over Andy and visited Hannah's office to coo at him, and bring rattles and stuffed animals. Hannah's foreman, Tom, ignored him, while Max treated Andy as if he were made of glass.

"Hold him," Hannah urged. "He won't break."

"It's been too long." Max held up his hands like a traffic cop and backed away. "I guess I didn't bother much with Zachary when he was a baby."

From day two, Andy seemed to understand that his life had changed decidedly for the better. He settled down to cooperate. Even the cramps he had suffered grew less by the day, and Hannah wondered if, like adults, babies could have cramps and even get ulcers from the stress of a distressed parent.

Andy spent most of the day in his grandmother's domain on the ground floor, and soon settled into his new life at Bella's Park. Doors opening and closing did not startle or awaken him, nor did the sound of voices jar him from sleep.

"This baby has an uncanny sense of what people want, especially his grandma. He adores her, young as he is," Mary Ann said to Max one morning.

"He's just a baby," Max said. "Don't you think you're exaggerating?"

But it was true, for when Laura brought Andy to Hannah's office and he saw his grandma, the baby smiled, his little eyes crinkled, and his legs plowed the air in excitement or pleasure.

At the farmhouse, additional cribs were purchased: One went into the extra bedroom upstairs, which became a nursery with blue walls, white-and-yellow-checkered curtains, a bright butterfly mobile dangling above the crib, and stuffed animals everywhere. Another crib was set up in the downstairs guest room. Every Friday night the ladies welcomed Andy, thus assuring his parents a good night's sleep, and Hannah insisted that the baby spend either Saturday or Sunday with her.

"You can see the difference in Laura," Hannah said to Grace one day as they sat on the porch. "She's like a flower opening. She needed rest so badly, and support. Now she has it, she's relaxing, finding it easier, pleasanter to be with her son. She's going to be all right, and so is Andy. This experience has me wondering how working women manage if they have no family nearby and no support system."

"My mother and mother-in-law lived in Dentry," Grace said. "One or another of them were there every day for weeks after Roger was born. Later, if I needed to get out, go to the grocery or to a movie with friends, one of them was invariably available. When Roger was sick, my mother came and stayed until he was back at school. At the time, I thought she was really neurotic and wished she'd go away, but looking back, I see how much help she was, bless her soul."

"I had no family around," Amelia said. "Thomas was great, but he was a man. When Caroline was seven months old, we hired an English nanny, and she traveled with us."

Hannah preferred not to rehash the horror of her life with Bill Parish. "I was alone with my girls most of the time," was all she said.

Hannah assumed some of her daughter's responsibilities. She phoned the pediatrician, made an appointment, and, accompanied by Grace and Amelia, carted Andy to the doctor's office. There the baby was poked, patted, weighed, and given shots, and drops were prescribed for the gas in his tummy.

"It's funny," Hannah said to her friends on the way home. "Andy hasn't had severe cramps in days."

"He knows he's safe with you, and his tummy doesn't have to curl into a knot. You've made life livable for this baby," Amelia said.

"With his mother so upset, he must have been a nervous wreck," Grace said.

Andy's presence changed each woman's life, awakening memories and maternal instincts long set aside. Amelia held and rocked Andy, cooed at him, kissed his tiny hands, and photographed him awake, asleep, eating, smiling, gurgling, crying. She spoke of her daughter Caroline as a baby and of herself as a mother.

"The best day of my life was the day Caroline was born. I adored her," she told the others one night in the kitchen. "Caroline was the best baby. Right from the start, we took her everywhere: It didn't matter if it was some ambassador's cocktail party. We took a folding crib; she could sleep through anything. As she got older, everywhere we went, people stopped to talk to her, to touch her. I hated their touching her. Some psychic I went to in Paris told me to take a piece of charcoal and mark an x on the sole of Caroline's shoes to protect her from the evil eye." Amelia blinked back tears. "She was such a beautiful child. She looked like an angel with blond curls, blue eyes, a smile that won your heart in an instant." Amelia heaved a deep sigh. "Maybe my Caroline was too sweet and too beautiful for this earth."

Grace walked around the house humming. She culled their books and carried several bags to the Weaverville library for its annual book sale, then filled the resultant empty shelf in their living room with children's books.

"Isn't it a bit soon for books?" Hannah asked.

"Never too soon for books." Many days, Grace sat alongside the sleeping Andy and read softly.

Soon Hannah made room in her office for books of nursery rhymes and did the same. Then she bought a CD player and tapes of children's poems and tales of bunny rabbits, and played them near Andy when she lay him down to sleep. He would turn his head toward the voice issuing from the tape player and smile until his eyes closed.

The baby responded with smiles to each of the women, and went to each with open arms. Hannah loved him too much to be jealous of her friends, or to resent their interest and his response. Love, sincerely offered, was always welcome and a blessing.

Hannah adjusted her schedule. She toted Andy on her morning rounds of the gardens. She avoided having him outside in the heat of the day, for with his fair skin and bald head, he sunburned easily. As he grew bigger and heavier, she switched to a stroller. Her workmen were happy to carry the baby for Hannah, or if he were in his stroller, to lift the stroller over bumps on the path and push it up and down inclines.

Hannah stopped the stroller often in the gardens to tell Andy the names of flowers, how they grew and where, and what they needed to grow well. When he was older, she would teach him about the medicinal value of certain plants, about soils and plant ecosystems. She pictured him at two years old, toddling behind her, asking "What this flower, Grandma?" And at five, while other children messed with clay, she imagined, Andy would be sitting at a table sized just for him and mixing ingredients: soil, Perlite, Vermiculite, sand. He would know the names of each ingredient, how much to use, and their purpose in the mix.

Mostly, Hannah loved those times when she was alone with the baby in her office. She would set aside her work, look at him, and wonder at his perfection. There were moments when she struggled to remember how she had been with her own children. Had she loved them this way? Had she been relaxed or as uptight as her daughter? Probably the latter, even though she had not worked outside the home. Having an alcoholic husband with a vicious tongue and a hard hand had hovered always in her consciousness, making it hard to think clearly or keep a cool head.

Unwittingly, memory carried her back to a time when her girls were little: Miranda at a year and a half throwing her bowl of cereal to the floor, the shattering of pottery, the slippery mess on the floor, Bill screaming that she was a lousy mother. She had believed him. It was her fault that Miranda acted like a small child rather than a perfect doll.

Reliving the panic she had felt, Hannah recalled a summer when Laura was almost three and could only be described as a terror on toddler's legs. They were at the beach. Miranda had tripped, fallen, and was screaming. In the time Hannah took to pick her up and brush her off, Laura raced pell-mell across the sand toward the water. Hannah ran—no, she flew. The child went headfirst into the water and under. Her head rose to the surface, went under, rose, and sank again before Hannah reached her.

Tears streaming down her face, Hannah relived carrying the limp body to shore, compressing the little chest again and again and praying. Water spewed from Laura's mouth. Coughing and crying, the child clung to Hannah. And then Bill's shadow fell across the sand. He had snatched the child from her arms.

In her office all these years later, Hannah covered her ears, remembering his voice screaming, "Bitch, lousy, stinking mother. I ought to kick you the hell out. You're unfit to take care of my children."

She had accepted his verbal abuse, relieved that it was not physical. My God, she thought, how could I have lived like that? Lived with that drunken oaf, believed his put-downs, and hated myself? Half the time he couldn't see his way from his truck to the house. All this, and pure love, were conjured up by the presence of one precious, sleeping baby boy.

Since Hannah had named a month for their wedding, Max could tolerate a baby in her office, even though it interfered with his customary visits with her. Usually he stopped by for a quick lunch or a beer, or to catch up on the day's happenings. But in those early days after Andy moved in, every time Max visited, he found Hannah distracted, unable to concentrate on business, and her eyes constantly wandering to the child, even if he were fast asleep.

Max collected brochures from restored and re-created historical villages around the country, and one day he handed Hannah a brochure from the Genesee Country Village and Museum in upstate New York. "Look at this incredible restoration."

She studied the glossy brochure, opened it wide, and noted its neatly presented streets and houses. "This goes on for streets and streets. They have a schoolhouse, churches, a post office, a drugstore, a park with a bandstand," Hannah said.

Max leaned over and tapped the brochure with his forefinger. "Look at the dates. They're even earlier than when the Covingtons settled this area. It's easy to forget that America was settled in stages, bit by bit, and by different economic classes of people. I don't mean we should try to emulate this restoration, just that, as time passed and more people settled here, they must have had a schoolhouse, churches, a meeting hall."

"Down in Marshall, yes, where merchants came through and folks settled along the river. There were taverns, whorehouses, and warehouses. But not here," Hannah replied.

"Then I think Laura should research Mars Hill and Marshall and find out when they were settled, when things were built, what they looked like back then. We have plenty of land. Why not create a Madison County living museum?"

"We're fifteen miles from Mars Hill and more from Marshall," Hannah pointed out.

"We're also the only museum of its kind in this county. We have an obligation to preserve the past," Max said.

All Hannah could think was that this would entail considerable work for Laura and more time out of the office. As it was now, the oral histories she must record, and the unending search for old farm instruments, photos, furniture, and clothing kept her on the go several days a week. "Laura will need an assistant. She can't oversee the homestead here and dash all over this county at the same time."

He waved his hand. "So get her an assistant."

"Your assistant, Molly, is who she needs—someone local who knows the county and has access to people."

"Oh, you are tricky. Molly Lund's the best help I ever had."

"Maybe Molly knows someone, then. You can't dump this on Laura without hiring someone very capable to help her. The work's just too much."

Max sank into a chair. "You're right. Let me think about this some more."

The baby stirred.

"Hush," Hannah said, "you'll wake up your soon-to-be grandson."

"Grandson, eh?" Max studied the baby with new eyes. He knew that he would probably rarely, if ever, see the children born to his son and his Indian wife, halfway around the world. His grandchildren would be raised in a foreign culture, speak a different language, and have no interest in a grizzled old dairy farmer like himself. But Andy—well, now, that was a different matter. The child had Hannah's genes and was already a big baby. He could teach this boy all he knew about his land and his cows, and when he died, Hannah would see to it that the land went to Andy–who, by then, would love every tree, and every meadow, and every darn cow on the place. "He's a cute little fellow, even if he has no hair," Max said. A wide grin spread across his face.

"What mischief are you thinking?" Hannah asked

"If he's to be my grandson, I'm gonna teach him everything I know and then some."

With those words Max sealed the love that Hannah carried for him in her heart.

25

THE GREEN-EYED MONSTER

Although she welcomed summer, the heat it brought caught Grace off guard. A walk down the driveway to the mailbox on Cove Road proved tedious in the blistering heat. The short walk down Cove Road to Bella's Park, taking Andy to his grandmother, left Grace with perspiration trickling down her sides and her blouse sticky and clinging to her back. Long-time residents vouched for the fact that summer had begun prematurely in May, and was hotter and more humid and muggy than they had ever known. Air conditioners, typically used intermittently during July and August, now ran day and night.

The animals felt it, too. Flank to flank, cows huddled under the trees in pastures. Old Man's pigs, Lurina reported, lay listless in their pens. On a global level, glaciers in Alaska and the North Pole were melting, and all about Grace in every direction, the mantle of haze, a combination of transpiration from forests and wind-borne pollution, screened the mountains from view. Tourists to the area, must be ever so disappointed with their inability to see through the haze to the mountains they had come to enjoy, Grace thought.

Last night on the evening news, a weatherman had stood in a parched field in South Carolina, and stooped and gathered a fistful of earth. The dry soil drifted from between his fingers. As he talked about the prolonged drought, the camera panned Lake Hartwell's bare clay banks, which sat well above the water level. The weather-man stood in a grove and pointed out the peaches, diminished in quantity and quality, and corn that should have been head high, now stunted and wasting above the dry earth. Years earlier, Grace had seen a book of photographs of families and land during the dust bowl era. She had never forgotten the haunted eyes of a young mother as she gathered her children about her on the slanting porch of a ramshackle house and the bleak landscape devoid of tree or crops. Even with the wells at Bella's Park, Hannah's gardens were watered only every other day, and for shorter periods of time.

As if making restitution for the drought and heat, nature compensated with magnificent sunsets. Grace sat enthralled, lit up by wonder as wave after wave of sulfur yellow, apricot, red, mauve, and crocus purple slashed their way across a pale blue sky. Often she watched these sunsets alone on the porch. Amelia preferred to photograph in the late afternoon, and Hannah and her gardeners chose to work in the diminished heat of early evening. Extended hours of daylight held Bob captive on the golf course. Grace did not mind. She had begun to keep a journal, and relished the privacy in which to think and to write.

The idea of keeping a journal came from an article she had read. Assigning your concerns to paper, the article said, could help you clarify your thinking, aid in making decisions, and assist you in gaining greater understanding of your motives. Grace's paramount distress centered around jealousy: jealousy about the hours Tyler spent learning to use the camera Amelia had purchased for him on St. Thomas; jealousy at Lucy's growing attachment to Hannah and her enthusiasm for the Garden Club. There were moments when Grace regretted having encouraged Hannah to volunteer and teach gardening at Caster Elementary, and Hannah had expanded her classes to the middle school. And now, there was baby Andy. Although she enjoyed him and loved the time spent alone with him, he belonged to Hannah.

The conflict within her was exacerbated by the fact that Grace loved Hannah. And now this thing, this ugly green-eyed creature, jealousy, traveled with Grace, joined them at dinner, on the porch, everywhere. And neither Amelia nor Hannah saw it, did not know. The strain of pretending exhausted her.

She reasoned that Lucy and Tyler were lucky to have people with skills and the interest to teach them, and that it was impossible for one person or family to provide everything another person needed.

Gardening and photography could become lifelong hobbies or even careers for Lucy or Tyler. Grace also reminded herself that love, like a rubber band, stretched to include many people, that the children loved her, that kids their age were wrapped up in themselves and disposed to neglect people and things beyond their immediate needs and wants. She assured herself that passion drove new interests and in time passion faded, and that later—months from now, perhaps— there would be time for her in their lives once more.

Compared to Amelia's and Hannah's skills, what could she offer them? Cookies? Food that could some day poison them, the way diabetes was poisoning her body? Along with jealousy, weight and food issues had begun to consume Grace's thinking. Having devoured *Dr. Atkins' New Diet Revolution* book and decided that at last she had found the answer to weight loss and diabetes control, she was desolate to discover that she could not bear the smell of eggs or anything else cooking in the morning. She craved her usual toast and cheese and a nice, big cup of tea with sugar. Artificial sweeteners tasted bitter and destroyed the pleasure of a cup of tea. And tea was not on Atkins' acceptable starting list, nor was bread. And there was to be no deviation, initially, from the program. Meat became an issue. She liked meat in small doses and did not like most fish. Planning and shopping for this eating plan became increasingly difficult, and indecision about what to eat and when to eat it drove her crazy and kept her awake at night.

So Grace had decided on a journal. Not a plain, lined notebook like children took to school, but a real journal. The shops had plenty of them, she discovered—expensive things with stiff bindings, decorative covers, and lined or unlined colored pages. Grace bought one with clusters of soft, rose-colored peonies on its cover, and she filled the first few pages with ramblings about her discomfort at writing in a journal at all.

Alone on the porch now, Grace turned to a blank page and began to write:

Dear Journal,
On every count, these days, I am a mess. Starting with my inability to convince any of the parents to allow their children to acknowledge their use of the chat rooms on that computer at school, or even their knowledge

of Lucy using the chat rooms. Emily says we don't have a case. I'm so frustrated and angry, I could weep.

I feel utterly sorry for myself. I don't know what to eat.

I hate that Hannah and Amelia are more helpful and interesting to Lucy and Tyler than I am.

Oh, stop it, Grace. You had a terrific time at the jazz festival, didn't you? Of course I did, but that was different. Different? Why different? It brought joy into your life and greater closeness to Bob. You had great sex, too. Bet you never imagined you would have such good sex after all those years with boring old Ted. Stop it. Ted was a good man.

Grace slammed the journal shut. She was turning into a grumpy old harridan. And yet the instructions for journaling said to relax and allow whatever came to come, not to argue with yourself or censor yourself, not to fight it. To simply let it flow. She opened the book again.

I hate the petty part of me. I see myself as noble, giving, helpful, tolerant. I have never been a jealous person. But I am now, and I hate it.

Jealousy. Resentment. Envy.

"The jealous are troublesome to others and a torment to themselves." Where did I read that?

Truly a torment to themselves.

Is fear related to jealousy, I wonder? If it is, what am I afraid of? That's easy. I'm afraid that Tyler will not love me as he did, will not come to me with his concerns. Why is it important that he come to me with his concerns? Because then I feel needed. It's important to me that I feel needed. Why? My head hurts. No more today.

Grace closed the journal. Her head did hurt. It was hard to analyze. No wonder people resisted going to therapists. Analyzing was not an easy thing to do.

Amelia's car pulled into the drive. Moments later, Hannah's old station wagon followed. Grace raised her bottom and slipped the journal beneath her. Smiling, she waved to them.

"The light was magnificent today," Amelia said as she set her camera bag on the floor beside her chair. "I think with this roll of film, I'll have what I need for a show in New York."

"What about another coffee table book? You still going to do one?" Grace asked.

"I can't deal with that now. I can't create photos on demand. I wish I could, but, well . . ."

"I certainly understand that," Grace said.

Hannah, a package from the market in her hands, had gone inside. Now she joined them, bearing a tray with three glasses of iced tea. "I think I am going to burst wide open from the heat. I feel as if I have a head of steam inside of me, like a train engine." She set the tray down and handed each of the others a glass. "I sugared it. Can you drink one glass with sugar, Grace?"

Grace nodded. Good for her or not, she would enjoy a glass of cold tea with sugar.

"Do either of you remember it being this hot any summer since we've been here?" Hannah asked.

"Our air-conditioning bill is going to be very high," Grace replied.

Each month they contributed to an account from which household bills were paid. Hannah kept the checkbook and paid the bills. At the end of the month she handed each one an accounting statement. Grace found them confusing and sometimes simply chucked them in the trash. Amelia gave the accounting a perfunctory glance, then stashed the sheets neatly in a shoe box. In February she presented the box, along with other items, to her accountant.

"Today the hummingbirds and butterflies were all over the gardens," Hannah said. "Even though it was full of seed, I watched three doves fight over space at the bird feeder outside the kitchen. There's room for all three at that feeder, and still they have to compete and fight."

"I hate it when the cardinals chase the smaller birds away," Amelia said.

"So bellicose and avaricious," Hannah said. She turned to Grace. "What'd you do today, Grace?"

"Not much. Picked up some magazines, made an appointment with my beautician."

"What's her name again?" Amelia asked.

"Totsy, at the JCPenney Salon in the mall. She's good, and she's very nice."

"Some days are fit for not much of anything," Amelia said. "I had to push myself, but I'm glad I did. Sometimes I pay no attention to road signs, and I'm not sure where North Carolina ends and Tennessee begins. I found this great wooden bridge across a rather wide shallow river. A man driving an old-fashioned hay wagon was crossing. There were kids on the hay, his grandkids maybe. Luckily, I had the camera ready. Some photo shoots are like that. Other times, there's no good subject and no inspiration, or I just miss the light."

"Are you still of a mind to do a book relating to September eleventh?" Grace shifted, and the edge of the journal poked into her thigh.

"I don't know. I'm not sure of the focus for a book like that, and with time passing, when I finally got it ready, it would be out of date."

"How could that tragedy ever be out of date?" Hannah asked. "They'll be publishing books and photographs about nine-eleven for years to come."

Amelia shrugged. "Maybe it's something I'm not really moved to do. My time's consumed with photos for the gallery in New York. Selling my photos there is a blessing and a curse. True, it's recognition, an affirmation of my ability, my work, but I hate the pressure. Maybe if I were younger, leaner and meaner, more driven, as they say. But I'm not. I don't even like to go to New York, and they're always badgering me to come. I won't fly. I'd have to go by train, and there are so many accidents with trains these days. I'm satisfied staying right here, and now we have a baby to be concerned with. How's the little fellow adjusting to life at Bella's Park, Hannah?"

"He's happy. Hardly fusses at all anymore. Loves it when I tote him about with me. Why wouldn't he? I'd like it if someone carried me about."

"I bet he walks early. He's a big boy," Grace said.

"Whenever is okay with me," Hannah replied. She rubbed her stomach. "I'm hungry. Did you cook, Grace, or should we eat out? We could grab something at the diner in Elk Road Plaza or go into Weaverville or Asheville."

"It's hard for me to eat out. I find spices give me a stomachache, and everything's so overly spiced these days. I wouldn't mind a good piece of broiled salmon. If we go into Asheville, I'd like to stop at Accent on Books, if it's still open. I want to pick up a book of Edna St. Vincent Millay's early poems," Grace said.

"I find her poems soppy," Hannah said.

Grace smiled. "I've loved her work since I was a teenager. I remember being transported by 'Renascence.' I still am. My copy of her work is dog-eared. Did either of you read 'Renascence'? I can still quote large chunks of it."

Hannah lifted a hand. "Don't, please."

"I'll make a few calls and find someplace for you to have salmon," Amelia said.

"Let's not dress up," Grace said. "I am not in the mood to get dressed up."

"I need to wash up a bit. My hands feel clammy," Hannah said.

"You two go ahead. I'm pretty much ready," Grace said. Once they were gone, Grace secreted the journal inside the front of her shirt-waist dress. Then she scooted upstairs to slip the little book into her dresser drawer, and in doing so, she thought of Marion Britton hiding her diary in the back of her dresser drawer, to be found so many years later by her grandchildren.

With Andy settled, Lucy seemingly happy, and Ringo in jail, life for Grace and the other ladies settled down to a pleasant and blessedly uneventful routine. Bob bought tickets for him and Grace to attend Big-Band Night at the Grove Park Inn.

"We'll make a night of it," he told Grace. "Have dinner at the inn, dance the night away."

"It sounds wonderful, Bob. Shall we ask Hannah and Max?"

"I'd rather it be just the two of us this time."

After a night of pounding rain, morning dawned trailing a wide-spread and pervasive haze that shrouded the mountains. The weatherman informed people with allergies, the ill, and the elderly that it would behoove them to stay indoors as much as possible. Russell, Bob's son, dropped by the farmhouse early in the afternoon with Tyler.

"I've got oodles to tell you, Granny Grace." Tyler launched into a recitation about making the winning shot in basketball camp. "We're playing a middle school from Candler. Please come see me play next Saturday night, will you? Look, I'll mark it on your calendar." Tyler drew a big red circle around the date on the kitchen calendar. "Please say you'll come. Grandpa will bring you."

"Of course I will. Did you tell your grandpa so he could mark his calendar also?"

"Not yet. You tell him, please. He doesn't like sitting on bleachers.

Says they hurt his behind. What about your behind?" Tyler walked around Grace. "Hum. Maybe you should *both* take pillows."

"You rascal." Grace hugged him. "How is photography coming?" She dreaded his reply, certain he would wax enthusiastic.

He sobered immediately. "That's another thing I want to talk to you about. Let's go get some milk and cookies." He took her hand and urged her toward the kitchen.

"Russell," Grace said. "Find a magazine and make yourself comfortable, or watch TV in the guest room."

"Will do." Russell looked at his watch. "You've got fifteen minutes, young man."

"Sure thing, Dad."

Settled at the kitchen table with milk and the tin of sugar cookies, which Tyler especially loved, Grace waited for him to begin. One cookie and then another disappeared, along with half a glass of milk. Then Tyler wiped his mouth on a paper napkin Grace handed him.

"About the photography," he said. "It sounded exciting to me, but it's really boring." He rolled his eyes. "You have to wait for the right subject, and that can take an hour, then you have to wait for the right light. I have too much to do, to hang around with Amelia out in the country somewhere. I dunno what to do. She bought that camera for me."

Relief and a perverse satisfaction swept through Grace. She hadn't lost her boy to Amelia after all. He didn't like photography, and he still came to her with his concerns. "You sure about this? Amelia says you have the makings of a good photographer."

Tyler shook his head. He lifted the milk to his lips and drank. "No way. Ever been in a darkroom, Granny Grace?" He set down the glass and pinched his nose. "It stinks."

Grace was glad to be able to say honestly, "It's good to try new things. You won't like them all, but it's important to try. Nothing's lost, after all."

"Lucy was smart never to begin. Amelia's insistent, you know that? She's set her mind on my being a photographer. How am I going to tell her I hate it?" He smiled at Grace, his eyes pleading. "You tell her? Please!"

"No, Tyler, I won't do that. You must tell Amelia yourself and in a very nice way, and thank her."

"What'll I say?"

"Tell her that you appreciate all the time she's spent with you, but that you have too many things going on at school: basketball, and your classes are hard this year, something like that." Grace pushed the cookie tin away from herself. "You can tell her that she's taught you well, and that you'll be your family's photographer. Tell her you'd like her to critique your pictures now and then. She'd like that, and you can start taking shots of Melissa and keeping an album of family events."

"I could do that. And have the drugstore develop the film."

Russell poked his head in the kitchen. "Ready, son?"

"Yep! Sure am, Dad. Granny Grace and I had our heart-to-heart." Tyler selected two of the largest, roundest, thinnest cookies from the tin. "One of these days you have to teach me how to make these, Granny Grace."

He wants to make cookies. He can be a chef someday—my little chef.

Hannah brought Andy home with her from Bella's Park on Saturday evening, just as Bob drove into the yard to pick up Grace.

"Do you need me to stay and help with Andy?" Grace asked.

"Heavens no. You and Bob run along and dance the soles off your shoes. Andy and I will be just fine, won't we Andy?"

The baby looked up at her from his stroller and smiled. He smiled all the time now.

"That child really responds to you," Grace said. "All working mothers should be as lucky as Laura. You're wonderful, Hannah."

Bob opened the car door for Grace. She stood for a moment looking up at the heavens. Stars hung like diamonds in the sky. "I love a night like this," Grace said. "I miss the stars when it's overcast." Bob looked handsome in a suit and tie. He didn't wear one often. "You look terrific," she said.

"So do you."

"It's fun sometimes to spiffy up and do the town," she said, and slid into the car.

Traffic on the highway was slowed by a wreck. By the time they crawled past the site of the accident, three cars had been pulled off the road and into the center median. Lights flashed from police cars, and an ambulance was positioned alongside the cars. "I hope no one was hurt," Grace said.

Soon they were on the bypass around Asheville, and in less than two minutes, Bob exited onto Charlotte Street. The parking lot at Fuddruckers Restaurant was crowded, as were the parking lots of the Jewish Community Center and the Unitarian Church.

"Busy night in town," Grace said.

"There's plenty going on in Asheville, especially on a Saturday night," Bob said. He turned right on Macon Street and started up the winding hill to the Grove Park Inn, then down into its driveway. The massive stone walls of the inn towered above them. Bob handed his car keys to a valet and escorted Grace into the hotel lobby.

Wood-paneled walls, a high ceiling, massive stone fireplaces at either end of the long room, and the Arts and Crafts–style furniture lent an air of rustic elegance to the lobby. They walked along a corridor, past elevators and potted trees, until they reached the dining room. A wall of glass windows offered a view that stretched across the city to the far mountains. Tonight the lights of homes and the city itself twinkled merrily.

The buffet specialized in prime rib, so they filled their plates and settled in for dinner.

"There's always so much food, and it all looks so delicious," Grace said. "I can never eat as much as I'd like at a buffet. I wish I had three stomachs."

"Don't overeat, now," Bob said. "We have a night of dancing ahead." He then proceeded to eat twice as much as Grace did.

They lingered over his coffee and her tea. Grace skipped dessert from the bountiful dessert bar. Bob had room for chocolate cake.

"Look who's eating a lot. You're going to fall over and roll around the dance floor," she said.

He patted his stomach. When she'd first met Bob, his stomach had been flat and tight. There was a bit of a paunch there now. "I won't. You'll see," he said.

They took the elevator several floors down to the Grand Ballroom, where the band sat on a stage set above a beautiful inlaid wooden dance floor. Grace learned how smooth it was when they joined other dancers and floated across it to the rhythm of Tommy Dorsey's music.

Small round tables for two lined the walls of the room, inviting dancers to sit one out and have a drink. Once a couple was seated, waiters appeared, offering champagne. Grace and Bob never sat; they danced, swept away by the music, until finally Grace said, "I can't go on another minute. It must be midnight."

He glanced at his watch. "Quarter to."

Grace slowed her pace and urged him from the floor. "Come on, Bob. You must be as tired as I am. It's been great fun, but it's time to go home."

He followed her from the dance floor, singing, " 'It's been great fun/but it was just one of those things.' "

While they waited for the valet to bring the car, Grace glanced up at the sky. Was it light pollution from city lights or a blanket of clouds that hid the stars? The air felt heavy and muggy. Grace's feet hurt. They were swollen, she knew, and would throb and sting when she got her shoes off and slipped into bed.

A hush hovered about the city. The Jewish Community Center, the Unitarian Church, and Fuddruckers were dark when they passed them on the way back up Charlotte Street. Ahead, they could see the bypass and the red taillights of a handful of cars.

As they drove past the exit to the Civic Center and turned right toward Weaverville, Grace said, "Bob, the weather's changed. There's a heaviness in the air. I don't like the feel of it."

"Maybe it's going to rain. We could use rain. Now, honey, don't you worry. We'll be home in no time, safe and sound," he replied.

At this hour, traffic was light on the highway. As they passed the Weaverville exit, ten minutes from Mars Hill, a wall of fog, dense and opaque as a theater curtain, cut off all visibility. In one astounding moment the rear lights of the car ahead of them vanished.

Grace gasped. "What's happening?"

Bob slowed to a crawl.

The lines that marked the shoulder of the roadway and those that separated the lanes dematerialized, obliterated as if by a giant eraser. Grace's sense of helplessness reminded her of a short story she had read, about a town isolated by a forest that grew thick overnight, sealing every road and every exit. Reading it, the sense of fear, isolation, and claustrophobia that swept through that fictitious town had cast its spell upon her. Those same feelings suffocated her now. Her throat tightened; she could feel the pounding of her heart in her ears.

"I can't see anything, Bob. I'm scared."

"I've seen fog before, but nothing like this," he replied. "I'd pull off, but where the hell are we? We could be on a bridge or near a ditch."

How far had they traveled since passing the exit? Grace tried to recall the precise topography of the roadside. Was there a ditch? Was it flat? Were they driving past fields or alongside the steep side of a hill? Somewhere along here, set back from the road, was an old gray barn. Was there a guardrail? She couldn't remember. The highway was being resurfaced. Anywhere there could be machinery pulled off to the side.

"We can't just stop in the middle of the highway," she said.

"I'll keep going slow. There ought to be a police car about in weather like this. Why isn't there a police car when we need it?"

Grace's hands were clasped, her jaw taut. "I'm really frightened."

"Just hold on, Grace, honey. These whiteouts come in patches. Couple more feet and we'll be out of it, I'm sure."

"I pray you're right."

The crash, with its rip of metal and screech of brakes, slammed Grace forward. Pain seared across her chest, shoulder, and neck as the seat belt tightened. The car spun wildly in a cocoon of amorphous white as thick as cotton batten, then hit what she assumed was a metal guardrail, for Grace heard the scrape of metal colliding with metal. Bob was slumped forward over the wheel.

"Bob!" she called, but there was no answer. "I love you," she whispered. "It was such a lovely evening." Then Grace lost consciousness.

Patches of light, fields of darkness, lights growing brighter, lasting longer. Grace opened her eyes. Hannah was bending over her, her eyes frightened.

"Grace, wake up. Grace, please, wake up."

"No."

"She said no. I heard her." Hannah backed away from the side of the bed, making room for the doctor who had just entered.

Someone pressed cool, firm fingers against Grace's wrist. Leave me alone, she thought. Let me sleep.

"Open your eyes." The voice was male and insistent.

Grace opened her eyes.

"That's better," the voice said.

Whoever he was, he was standing to the side. It wasn't Bob's voice, or Russell's, or even Max's. It was too much trouble to turn her head.

"How are you feeling?" he asked. His fingers tightened about her wrist.

"Go away," Grace muttered. "Let me sleep."

"We don't want you to sleep. Here, drink this."

A straw was pressed against her closed lips. "Open up, now—sip this."

They're not going to go away, Grace thought, unless I drink their stuff. She sipped the liquid. It was cool and refreshing, like Mountain Dew or ginger ale.

She pushed the straw out of her mouth. "Where am I?"

"In the hospital," Hannah said. "There was an accident."

In a flash, it all came back to her. "Fog—couldn't see. Bob—is he all right?"

"He's here, in the hospital," Hannah said.

"He all right?"

The male voice to the side answered. "We expect he will be."

Grace drifted away from them. She floated out of her body and peered down at it. There stood Hannah, looking frazzled and worried, and the doctor, young and good-looking, leaning over her, listening to her heart. He checked the intravenous drip and seemed satisfied.

"Vital signs are good," he said. "Keep an eye on her." His beeper went off. He checked it and walked from the room.

A woman in white, a nurse, stood by the bed. Hannah sank into a chair.

Grace followed the young doctor into the hall, lingered above him as he punched the elevator button, then decided on the stairs. Nurses, their faces intent and sometimes worried, bustled along the corridor, entered rooms and left rooms. Grace floated through a hospital window and down the street. Bright yellow flowers filled a flower bed at the corner. Traffic was brisk. A light turned red and brakes screeched. Grace retreated and found herself over the hospital bed, looking down at her body again. Moments later, she opened her eyes.

"There's a lot of traffic outside," she said.

"Always is this time of day," Hannah said.

"Pretty flowers on the corner," Grace said.

"How do you know that?"

"I saw them." Grace smiled. "I think I was out of my body."

"Sip some more of this," the nurse said.

Hannah patted her hand. "Of course," she said.

No one believed her. No one even asked questions. Perhaps this happened to so many people that it hardly mattered to the hospital staff. Every bookstore carried books relating experiences of leaving one's body during surgery, about dying and returning during surgery or accidents. So why wouldn't they ask her questions or be interested in her experience?

Grace was thirsty. She sipped the drink the nurse held for her until a sucking sound came from the end of the straw inside the plastic cup. "That was good. I feel better, except my shoulder and neck hurt, and my chest," Grace said.

"You got bumped on the head pretty bad," Hannah said.

"I don't remember much."

"The fog was some kind of weather anomaly. Stretched from Flat Creek to the Barnardsville exit. Five separate crashes; eight cars ended up off the road. Luckily there were only a couple of injuries, including you and Bob," Hannah said. "We hoped you'd hear the weather report on your car radio and stay in town."

"We never put on the radio," Grace whispered. "Bob?"

"He's had surgery on his shoulder and he's got several broken ribs. He took one nasty gash on his head. Hit the steering wheel, apparently."

A memory of Bob slumped across the wheel flashed into Grace's mind. "We couldn't see the road, the lines, anything at all," she said.

"Bob will be all right. Just take a while till he's swinging a golf club again," Hannah said.

"I want to see him."

"We'll ask the doctor. Maybe tomorrow," Hannah said.

"She should rest now," the nurse said.

"I'm going now, Grace. I'll be back later with Amelia."

Grace's eyes were already closed.

* * *

The next day when she awakened, Grace felt clearheaded and stronger. Her thoughts were fixed on Bob, and she nagged the doctor until he said that she could see him. An orderly brought a wheelchair and got her into it. They journeyed down a long hall, into an elevator, and then onto the surgical orthopedic floor. When she saw Bob, Grace began to cry.

His head was swathed in bandages, as was his chest. A cast mummified his right arm from his wrist almost to his shoulder. His eyes, mere slits and rheumy, peered at Grace from a face black, blue, and swollen.

Bob could barely talk. "Honey," he managed. "Sorry."

"It wasn't your fault," she said. "We're alive, thank heaven. You'll get well. You'll be fine." But would either of them ever really be fine again? Aside from the emotional trauma, Bob had been badly hurt, and she ached all over from the bruises sustained when the seat belt snapped her back from the dash. Grace knew from having seen her father deteriorate after a serious fall that a shock to the system and physical injuries took their toll, especially at their ages. Would she ever be able to lift Andy again without a tug or an ache in her shoulder? Would she ever feel safe driving at night? Would Bob play golf again? He loved the game, loved the exercise it afforded. Other than time spent with her, golf was his social life, his hobby, and his main source of exercise.

"They say I can go home today. I don't want to leave without you," Grace said.

"You'll rest and heal better at home," he said.

"I don't want to leave you here."

"I fuss and complain. They won't keep me long. Be home in a couple of days," Bob said. He reached with his left hand for Grace's hand, winced, and pulled back. "Sorry."

"Please, stop saying you're sorry. I love you. I just want you to get well. You'll come to our place when they discharge you."

He closed his eyes, and his lips twitched as if he were struggling against crying.

"I'll go and let you rest," she said.

The orderly wheeled Grace from the room. The hallway seemed interminably long. They passed a lounge where a man and woman sat on a couch talking earnestly with a young boy in a wheelchair.

One of his legs was extended and in a cast; his arm was also in a cast. The woman was crying.

"A lot of accidents," Grace said.

"That's Orthopedics. Sometimes it seems the whole world's breaking its bones," the orderly said.

"It must be hard, working in a hospital," Grace said.

"You can burn out real easy," the orderly replied.

Grace empathized. She'd never last a week working in this environment—she knew that.

The orderly reached her hospital room. Amelia and Hannah were fidgeting, waiting to take her home. "I can't go without seeing Bob again," she said. "I promised I'd be back later."

"Let's get you ready, and just before we check out, we'll stop by his room and have a quick visit," Amelia said.

"I hate leaving him."

"He's not alone," Hannah said. "Max ordered a private day nurse for him. That way he'll have someone with him all day, and you won't worry."

Grace looked perplexed. "Bob's insurance doesn't cover private nurses, I don't think."

"Max hired the nurse. It's a gift to Bob."

Grace's eyes brimmed with tears. "I thank him from the bottom of my heart. It relieves my mind to know Bob's not going to be alone in a hospital room, maybe needing something, ringing that buzzer and waiting, waiting."

Bob was sleeping when they stopped by his room. A stout young nurse met them at the door. She stepped outside. "I'm Susan Arondale," she said.

They introduced themselves.

"I'll see that Mr. Richardson gets everything he needs, and I'll tell him you were here when he wakes up."

"I'll phone him when I get home. If he's still asleep, please don't let it ring and wake him up," Grace said.

"I'll sit right beside the phone," Susan said. "I'll take good care of him. Please don't worry."

When they left, Susan closed the door quietly.

"Okay, that's settled. Let's get you out of here—now," Amelia said.

* * *

Their household had expanded to include a baby and now Bob, who, when he was released from the hospital several days later, took up residence in the downstairs bedroom.

"Wasn't I clever to insist on the extra bedroom downstairs and a full bathroom?" Amelia said. She had been adamant about that, and they had proven useful from the start.

With Bob settled and asleep in his room, the ladies gathered in the kitchen. A cradle on rockers stood alongside the kitchen table. Hannah kept it moving. Andy, sucking his pacifier, closed his eyes for a moment, then opened them as if afraid to miss anything.

"That baby is curious, isn't he?" Amelia said.

"He's so little and so smart," Hannah said. "He knows something's happening. He can sense we're all a-flutter with bringing Bob home and settling him into our guest room."

"All we need now is for Mike to move into our living room," Grace said. Instantly, she regretted her words.

Her face livened with interest, Amelia pounced on her words. "Why'd you say that? You know something, Grace. Fess up. What's going on?"

She had provoked this question; now she'd simply have to tell Amelia all she knew. "A while back, when he took me to the hospital that day after Lucy and I fell down, Roger mentioned that he and Mike *maybe* wouldn't make it as a couple, that's all. Roger hasn't mentioned it again, so I assume they've ironed out whatever the problem is or was."

Amelia's eyes grew calculating. She stood, then paced the kitchen from table to sink and back again. At the sink, she stopped to peer out of the window. "I knew it. Mike's been too quiet, too withdrawn, almost sullen lately. I had the sense things weren't right. He's also been available for lunch this last week. He used to watch the clock and dash off to have lunch with Roger. I figured things had changed, but I couldn't think how or why." She approached the table and leaned on it, facing Grace. "What else do you know, Grace? Tell me."

"Nothing. If you want me to, I'll ask Roger when I see him. Why don't you ask Mike?"

Amelia pushed away from the table. "I can't do that. I'd be prying, maybe alienate him." She shook her head. "I can't ask him."

"Well, I'll ask Roger."

"Soon? Please do it soon." Amelia smiled. "Mike would be free to go on photo shoots. I wouldn't have to go to New York alone. It would be like old times."

Not an hour later, Roger strode from his car and up the steps of the porch. Hannah had left for work, taking Andy with her, and Amelia was off on some errand. Grace, still aching in the hollow of her back, her left side, her elbow, and her collarbone, sat in her rocker on the porch. Roger lowered himself into Amelia's chair alongside his mother.

"How's Bob?" he asked.

"Not comfortable, but he'll be fine in time, thank God. He's sleeping. I left the living room windows open so I could hear if he calls."

"What a frightening experience you two had. How do you feel, Mother?"

"Somewhat better. I ache in odd places. The right side of my neck's really stiff right now. Hard to turn to that side." She tipped her head slightly, grimaced, and held it straight.

Although his sport shirt and slacks matched, his brown slip-on shoes were polished, and his nails manicured, Roger, who was usually impeccably groomed, seemed mussed. Grace realized that it was his hair, tousled and unkempt, as if he had run his fingers through it innumerable times.

"Where are the other ladies?" Roger asked.

"Amelia's shopping. Hannah's at work."

"Aren't you women too old for this, a baby to take care of and now Bob all banged up?"

"Andy's with Hannah all day, and Bob needs us. He can't be home alone now. There's strength in numbers, and good friends are a blessing." Grace kept her chair moving, and soon his rocked back and forth in unison with hers.

"I want to talk about Mike, Mother. Can I confide in you?"

"If it's about Mike, are you asking me not to say anything to Amelia?"

"You got it."

"I'm not sure I can promise that. She's got an idea that something's wrong."

"What the hell does that mean?" Roger asked.

"You needn't curse, Roger. You know Mike and Amelia have been close friends. She depended on him in many ways, in both her work and her social life. And she's got a sixth sense about things sometimes."

"She's got nothing to complain about. We took her with us to the theater a couple of times," Roger said.

Grace sighed. "Just say what you have to say. I'll decide then what I can keep secret and what I feel I can't. I won't lie to you."

"Mike and I are splitting up." His face showed no emotion. "I told you. I'm not ready for another relationship."

"You're the one who pursued it," Grace said.

Roger brought his chair to a halt and cocked his head toward her. She continued to rock. They were silent for a time. Grace focused not on her son, but on the creak of the floorboards beneath the blades of the rocker. His next words startled her.

"You don't like me much, do you, Mother?"

"I love you, Roger. You're my son." She took a breath. "Sometimes I don't like the things you do or the way you do them."

"What things?"

"Thoughtless things. You don't stop to consider how your actions could hurt others."

"I hung in there with Charles all those years he was sick."

Grace could feel the vibration of his rocker's blades against the floor, and was glad that he fell silent while she gathered her thoughts.

Finally, she said, "I would prefer to think that your years with Charles were years of love and commitment on both sides."

"Damn it, Mother, you know we were committed."

"I thought you were. But when you speak as you just have, I'm not sure."

Something cracked in his voice. "A house, any house, without Charles is utterly lonely. I couldn't handle being alone. I needed someone. Mike was there. He was interested. It was the course of least resistance, and I didn't think beyond the moment. I'm so sorry."

Grace slowed her rocker. When her son spoke again, she heard the tears in his voice, heard him struggle to gain control. Her heart wrenched, but she waited for him to go on.

"I loved Charles. I miss him so damned much. And I hate it that he was unfaithful one time and got AIDS. I hate him for that, for getting sick, for dying and leaving me." He lowered his head into his hands. "I couldn't stand it in Branston after he died. I can't stand it here, either. I don't know where to go or what to do. We were together so many years. I've never had another partner but Charles. I've no heart for work. I feel absolutely alone in the world."

She wanted to tell him that he was not alone, that if he would take the time, relax, allow the goodness inside of him to surface, he could be a part of a growing extended family—a surrogate family to be sure, but a wonderful, accepting one. She remained quiet, however, sensing that this was an inappropriate moment to speak to him of such things.

He was crying softly now. "I don't know what to do. I don't want to hurt Mike. He's a good man, a kind person, but we're not right for one another. I can't stop comparing him to Charles, wanting him to be like Charles, to enjoy the music Charles enjoyed. Mike prefers opera and doesn't like piano music. Charles loved jazz and classical piano. Charles and I could have a fight, then make up and go on as we were, no grudges held. When I fuss at him, Mike doesn't fight back; he pouts a bit, then he walks out of the apartment and he's gone for hours, sometimes days. I have no idea where he goes. I thought maybe here."

She shook her head. "No. Not here. Amelia doesn't know any of this—not about his leaving your apartment, nothing."

"I need help, Mother. Tell me what to do."

"What to do? I don't know. I do know that when we lose a loved one, we need time. It's unwise to jump into a new relationship. One needs to grieve. Why we're programmed that way, I don't know—but I've seen people stuff their grief away, and then one day, three years or five years later, something seemingly insignificant happens, and they explode in ways that don't seem warranted." Grace paused and looked out past him to the far hills. "It's one of the hardest things in the world, to lose someone you love, Roger. When the numbness wears off, you're left with pain that feels as if your heart is tearing into pieces. Then comes the anger at the lost one, at God, sometimes at yourself. A therapist might be helpful. Would you consider seeing one?"

He drew back. "I'm not going to a therapist to have my head messed with. I'm not crazy, Mother, just depressed and unhappy."

"Going to a counselor, a therapist, has nothing at all to do with being crazy, as you call it. It's someone to hold up a mirror to you, to help you explore your feelings, help you work through things that are troubling you."

"You ever been to one?"

"Well, no, but I know people who have." She thought of how angry she had been with Lucy's therapist, but the truth was, she'd resented the woman for usurping her place with Lucy. Lucy, she had to admit, had benefited from those visits. "All right, then, how about a good friend to talk to, someone who'll listen and be patient?" As she had done, those many nights when Brenda phoned and talked for hours after Harold died.

"You know Charles was my only confidant," Roger said.

"Sometimes writing in a journal helps," she said. "Or you could always go out somewhere alone and scream it all out."

"Go find someplace in the hills and scream my guts out?" he asked, aghast. "Is that what you're saying?"

She could feel her son glaring at her, imagined the anger in his eyes, but Grace maintained a steady rocking and kept her eyes on the hills. "It can help." She wished she could be more helpful to him, but on another level she wished he would just go away. Didn't she have enough on her hands right now?

"Don't keep making stupid suggestions," Roger said. "Just tell me what to do."

"I can't tell you what to do. You're a grown man."

"Damn it, I'm your son, and I need you to tell me what to do." Back and forth, back and forth, faster and faster his rocking chair moved. The cane on the seat rasped. The rocker blades grated against the porch floor.

Unwittingly, Grace's fingers closed over the arms of her rocker. She wanted this conversation to end, and she felt increasingly guilty, wishing that Roger would leave. "All right then. Do this. Go take a ride in the country, get out of the car, and cry and scream at Charles, God, me, your father, whomever."

His rocking ceased. All about them the air stirred with the heavy scent of jasmine wrapped around the posts at either end of the porch. Down Cove Road, Grace could see Hannah pushing the baby's stroller, then dawdling, stopping to peer over a fence, engrossed in a flower or a tree. Grace knew that Hannah had seen Roger and was allowing them time alone. Grace wanted to wave her on, to hurry her home. Across the road at Max's home, Anna stepped onto the front porch. She walked to the top of the steps, shaded her eyes, and scrutinized Cove Road. She saw Grace and waved. Grace returned the greeting.

"How can Max live in that rambling old house alone?" Roger said. "Mike says his wife's paintings are everywhere. That's creepy."

The change of subject came as a relief to Grace, and probably to Roger. After a moment she asked, "What did you do with Charles's things?"

"I packed them all up—his books, records, clothing, pictures, tools, everything—and gave them to the Salvation Army." He sniffled and blew his nose. "I'm a goddamned fool for doing that. Now I've got nothing of Charles. Not even a picture. Nothing. I feel so shitty, so guilty, like I've denied Charles's humanity, his very life. It's as if I slammed the door in his face."

"I have pictures of Charles and of you both. Charles always sent them. I'll give them to you," she said.

"Thanks. Mother, how am I going to pick up my life and go on?"

Grace took a deep breath. "Slowly. Very slowly. One step at a time. One day at a time." She looked at him. His misery was written all over his face and in the slump of his shoulders, the caving in of his chest. Her heart ached for him. "Roger," she said. "Take that ride in the country."

Hannah was closer now, almost to their driveway.

"Afterward, we'll talk again. Remember, you aren't alone. I'm here, and I love you."

Hannah turned the stroller into the driveway. She waved. Grace's heart lifted and she waved back.

Roger stood, nodded toward Hannah, and then, with long strides, went down the steps to his car.

26

ABOVE THE WORLD IS STRETCHED THE SKY

Hung with clouds pregnant with rain, the sky stretched gray and dim from mountain to mountain, mimicking the heavy, near-to-bursting feeling that weighted Roger's soul. His mother was right, of course, though he hated it. Grieving was a process. He didn't need her to tell him that. But life was for living, Charles was dead, and he must go on. So he had tried to bypass, or at least take a short cut around, grief. He had failed. What to do now?

All his life, Roger had been a pragmatist. He'd had to be. Being gay was completely anathema when he was a young man. In high school he had lived in shadows, had never "come out," worked hard to walk and talk like a regular guy. But he had never dated girls or attended dances and proms, and, they had guessed. He had endured the derision of his peers, their back-alley attacks directed at his belly, his legs, and back, leaving no visible scars. He had never reported the events to the school or his parents. He'd grown tough and distrustful, hardened his heart, worked out at the gym, and taken up boxing until he could give as good as he got. But that was long ago, and he must find a way now, today, to go on with his life.

Yet as he drove farther from the towns, higher into the hills on winding one-lane roads, he could not keep his mind on the present. He had sold the cottage, Charles's gift to him, bought with an inheritance from Charles's granny in England. He had had the good sense to pay off the mortgage on the Loring Valley apartment, and the poor judgment to invest the remainder in the stock market. Fifty percent of his formerly impressive assets were gone, lost, wiped out through no fault of his own. It was hard to comprehend.

Charles had been leery of the stock market. They hadn't a penny invested in it while he was alive. Roger pounded the wheel with his fist. "Charles, why the hell did you have to die? I hate you for dying and leaving me. We were a team, you and I, and I'm only half a person now." Blinded by his tears, Roger pulled the car off the road and under a tree. The gray sky vanished, hidden by the green of leaves, which soothed him. He felt limp and weary with the world, and sat there feeling numb and thinking about nothing.

He realized that the rain had begun when he heard its patter on the canopy of leaves above, followed by drops of water splattering his windshield. The splatter intensified to a drumroll on the roof of the car, loud and intense. Steam clouded the windows. When Roger cracked open both of the front windows, muggy heat filled the interior and rain splashed onto the seats. He turned the air-conditioning to its highest setting and the fan to its highest speed. Outside the car, the road quickly became an aqueduct bearing streams of water downhill. He felt trapped under this tree.

Furious, Roger struck the dashboard and steering wheel until his fists ached. At first he wept silently, but a burst of thunder weakened the dam that held his heart. A slash of lightning split the dam asunder. Great, gasping yelps of anguish spilled from his gut. After a time, Roger began to curse. He cursed the universe for his loss, cursed Charles for his infidelity, for falling ill and dying. Blood pounded in his ears. His face grew red and hot. His heart raced; his breath came fast and hard. Roger knew he must calm himself or burst.

The rain fell in a steady, slow pattern now. Desperate for air, Roger opened the car door, stepped outside, and lifted his face to the canopy of leaves. Water dripped onto his forehead and cheeks. He tore off his shirt and threw it into the car. Water trickled between tight chest and back muscles and down firm biceps. With clenched fists, he beat his chest and for a moment felt like Tarzan. When he was young he had longed to be Tarzan, to run away to the forests and away from people.

Roger threw back his head and uttered a Herculean, pain-filled bellow. He half-expected an elephant to come crashing through the underbrush, or a band of chattering monkeys to descend to his side from the tops of trees. To his left, the compact green leaves of a thicket of rhododendrons oozed steam. He moved toward them, touched the glossy, wet leaves. If he were Tarzan, he would know how to use plants for clothing, food, shelter. For a time he stood there, his arms outstretched as if to embrace all of nature. If he were Tarzan, he would be completely at home in the woods. He would be at peace.

Roger's arms fell to his sides. How helpless we all are in the modern world, he thought. September 11 had appalled and frightened him. Flight 93 had crashed in a field less than a hundred miles from Branston. The unpredictability of life terrified him. Illness, though unexpected, was at least predictable. People died. But airplanes used as rockets to kill human beings was so perverse, so devastating, that he had turned off the news for days after it happened.

He shut off the thoughts. No sense in revisiting that day now.

The silence around him was broken by the chatter of birds. Where were they? He looked and could not see them. Occasionally during Charles's illness, when he could still hope that Charles would go into remission, Roger had thought about finding a place off the beaten path. Someplace more remote than Covington, far from any large population center, where he and Charles could settle, perhaps live off the land.

Suddenly Roger knew that he did not want to open another party-planning business. That had been Charles's dream, and he had enjoyed doing it with Charles. But what could he do? He had become an engineer to please his father, and for years had worked as one before turning his back on that career. He had been in business and no longer wanted to do that.

What he did want to do right now was run away, far away from everyone he knew, and even that was scary. His mother would probably say that he would only be taking himself and all his problems with him. Before he could make a move again, he needed, as she said, to fully grieve for Charles. He must settle things in his soul, and develop a plan, and most of all, find a modicum of peace in his heart.

The rain had stopped. Beyond the shelter of trees, Roger could see slashes of bright blue sky. The hard, fierce rain had cleared the atmosphere of haze and dust. The mountains sparkled, vivid and enticing, in the summer sunlight. Roger heaved a deep sigh and felt a calmness he had not known for weeks. For the first time since Charles died, Roger felt his presence. He wrapped his arms about his own shoulders and smiled.

"I'm on track at last, eh, Charles?" he whispered.

Then he got back into the car, put on his shirt and wound slowly down the narrow mountain road.

27

AS DOMESTIC AS A PLATE

Bob recovered slowly. A bit too slowly, Grace thought, suspicious that he was enjoying living with them too much.

Ordinarily a man not given to washing dishes, or picking up newspapers from the living room floor, or wiping off the bathroom counter after shaving, Bob had become the model of cooperation and domesticity. With one hand, he managed to load and unload the washing machine, and load and unload the dishwasher. And complaining of being exhausted early in the evening, he disappeared into his room downstairs, allowing the women their accustomed privacy.

"That blow to his head certainly turned him into a gem, like alchemists' gold," Hannah said to Grace one evening when they were visiting in Grace's bedroom.

"But will it last?" Grace asked. "Can an old dog really learn new tricks? Men have a way of being totally attentive and cooperative when they're courting you, and he's courting all three of us, with an eye to taking up permanent residence."

Hannah drew back her head, slapped her thigh, and laughed. "Well, I'll be darned. You're probably right. We ought to fool him for a bit, give him some encouragement, then ask when he's leaving. That should keep him on his toes."

"Poor Bob," Grace said. "He's a good guy. He's been very good to me, to us all, but he just won't give up. He doesn't like living alone. If we hadn't met, I bet he'd be married to some eager woman long ago. After all those years in the service he's become a real homebody, a nester, and I've caused him to have to build a nest alone."

"You want him to live with us permanently?" Hannah asked.

"I don't know what I'm thinking. He's certainly been no trouble. He hasn't complained or asked for much help, considering he has one arm in a cast. Fact is, he's as domestic as a plate these days."

Hannah laughed. "Domestic as a plate. I've never heard that. It's funny. I wonder how Amelia would feel about Bob living here?"

Grace waved away the idea. "Well, it's just speculation. Not worth creating an issue over."

"Is that how you feel? That it would be an issue for Amelia?"

Grace shrugged. "I don't really know. Amelia's unpredictable."

"She's one happy gal, now that Mike's moved out of Roger's place," Hannah said. "She's spent days helping him locate a new place in Weaverville. I like her choice, Kyfields. It's a nice development, and he bought a villa with a view of the lake and hills. Very pleasant."

"Yes, it is," Grace agreed.

Hannah changed the subject. "So, Tyler stopped taking photo lessons with Amelia?"

"He said it was boring. He takes family snapshots." Did Hannah suspect how embarrassingly jealous and resentful she had been? Writing in her journal had certainly helped. Grace had never felt so free to express herself, could say whatever she chose without consequences. And slowly but surely, her jealousy of Hannah had evaporated like water in a lake during a long dry spell. Grace reached over to her dresser and handed Hannah a packet of photos. "Tyler took these. I have four albums' worth of pictures of Melissa."

Hannah shuffled through them: Melissa bent double, her little rear end in the air, Melissa sitting on the front steps smiling, Melissa banging away at the piano, Melissa squeezing the cat, and on and on. "Cute," she said before shoving the pictures back into the packet and returning them to Grace's dresser. "Anything new about Ringo's case?"

"Next year sometime. The trial will take place in the courthouse at Marshall. I hope you'll go with me."

"Wouldn't miss it," Hannah said.

28

THE ONLY MAN FOR HER

Ellie Lerner had entered their lives several years earlier, when Grace shopped for Lurina's wedding dress at Ellie's Bridal Shop in Asheville. Ellie had delivered several dresses for Lurina to choose from, and had met the ladies and been captivated by the idea of their sharing a home. When Molly Tate Lund and her family moved into Brenda's big farmhouse after her father's death, Ellie, who harbored a fantasy about county living, had rented Molly's house and moved to Covington. At about the time that ladies rebuilt their home after the fire, Ellie approached Hannah about moving in with them, but they had chosen to ignore her suggestion.

Then last year, Brenda, who found it inconvenient living with her daughter and family, moved into Molly's former home with Ellie. The two women were of the same age, in their mid-fifties, and seemed to be compatible housemates. Once a week, usually on the weekend, Brenda and Ellie drove off in one of their cars and returned quite late. Grace assumed they went to Asheville to a movie, dinner, or the theater.

Ellie's recent visits to the farmhouse started casually enough when Brenda and Ellie, in good neighborly tradition, visited Bob after he came home from the hospital. They brought a ham and noodle casserole and a cherry pie. Brenda phoned now and then to ask Grace how Bob was, but Ellie strolled down Cove Road and dropped in one day just before dinner. Grace was in the kitchen with Hannah. Amelia was out somewhere.

"Don't let me interfere with whatever you're doing," Ellie said to Grace. "I just stopped by to see how the patient is doing."

A few minutes later, Grace and Hannah heard Bob's laughter from the living room. Grace looked at Hannah, wiped her hands on her apron, and walked into the living room. "What's so funny?" she asked.

"Just a silly old joke I told Bob." Ellie rose. "Well, I must go now. Brenda sends her love, Grace."

Grace didn't give Ellie's visit another thought until Ellie again arrived several days later, just before dinner. This time she brought a banana cream pie.

"I'll just poke my head in the living room and say hello to Bob." Ellie set the pie on the kitchen counter.

It was not long before peals of laughter issued from the living room.

Another joke? Why don't Bob and I ever laugh like that? Grace wondered. Later, she questioned Bob. "What do you and Ellie find so funny?"

He laughed. "Ellie knows more jokes than all the guys I ever knew put together."

"What kind of jokes?"

He shrugged. "I guess you could call them bawdy jokes."

"Bawdy? Does that mean dirty jokes?"

Bob nodded. "You could call them that. You'd hate them," he hastened to add.

"I guess I would," she replied, but it bothered her. Bob's enjoying dirty jokes with another woman was, in her mind, tantamount to disloyalty. "Why doesn't she take her jokes somewhere else?"

"Oh, come on, honey, they're just silly little jokes."

"Not so silly, maybe. Ellie always seems to arrive just before dinner, when I'm busy in the kitchen."

"You could ask her for dinner."

Grace glared at him. "I don't want to ask her for dinner. I want her to stop coming here with her stupid jokes."

"Grace, honey. What's this about? Neither Ellie nor her jokes mean a darn thing to me."

Grace stiffened. "Are you sure?"

He reached for Grace, took her hand. "Will you stop worrying? Yes, I'm sure. Ellie's just lonely on evenings when Brenda has dinner at Molly's place, and she wanders on down."

"She never wandered down before you were here," Grace said.

"You're worrying needlessly," Bob said. "Making a mountain out of a molehill."

Grace looked at him. She loved him. He was the only man for her, and she didn't want to lose him. But Bob wouldn't recognize a pass if Ellie made one. Some men could be blind to things like that and would never admit that a woman's attention flattered their egos. And some women could be ever so subtle, ever so clever in disguising their true intentions. Suddenly, the prospect of Bob moving back to his apartment in Loring Valley and Ellie visiting him there with her bawdy jokes made his staying on at the farmhouse infinitely more appealing.

Later that evening, Grace wrote in her journal:

Dear Journal:
If it's not one thing it's another. I no sooner work out my stuff about Tyler and Amelia and Hannah and Lucy than I'm confronted with an issue made to order to upset me. What's with Ellie, anyway? We've all been at functions together. I've never heard her telling any kind of joke. She's rather quiet in a crowd. I've never seen her flirt with Bob, or Max, or anyone. Maybe, as Bob says, I'm being ridiculous. My own reaction bothers me nearly as much as her coming to visit Bob with her jokes. After all this time with Bob, how can I be so insecure, such a ninny? Maybe I'll talk to Brenda, see what she thinks.

Grace slipped the journal into her top dresser drawer, behind her socks and underwear.

Ellie did not visit the next day, or the next, or the next, and Grace put the woman and her jokes out of her mind. It was Hannah who drew her attention back to Ellie.

"What is it about that Ellie Lerner that gives me the willies?" Hannah remarked to Grace one evening as she leaned against the open door to Grace's bedroom. Having just showered, her hair hung in damp clumps about her face and neck. She dried it, rubbing briskly with a towel, as she spoke.

"Come in and sit down," Grace said.

Hannah shut the bedroom door, crossed the room, and sat on the edge of Grace's big bed.

"Let's discuss this Ellie thing," Hannah said.

Grace's mind snapped into alert mode. "What about her?"

"She's an odd duck, don't you think? She's obviously interested in visiting Bob, not us. She tells him the silliest jokes, kind of off-color but not filthy, and he thinks they're funny."

"You've heard her jokes?" Grace asked.

"Sure. I listened outside the door. They're not whispering, after all. Bob must be suffering from that whack to his head to think they're funny. And have you noticed how she says good night?"

"No. How does she say it?"

Hannah rolled her eyes. "There are ways to say good night, and there are ways to say good night."

"How does she say it?"

"Gooood-nighht. She'll poke her head into the kitchen and say a quick, snappy good night to us. When she says it to Bob, it's drawn out, lingering."

Grace stiffened. "Seductive?"

"You might say that. Anyway, I just wanted to alert you to keep your eye on whatever's going on. I don't trust that woman. I'd sit in that living room with them whenever she comes over. If she has any untoward intentions toward Bob, you can nip them right in the bud." Silence filled the room before Hannah said, "Why does this remind me of the way Bob responded to Amelia's attentions when you had that birthday party for Tyler years ago?"

"That's when we found out that Amelia and Bob knew one another all those years earlier, when he was stationed in Korea, and Amelia and her husband were there for Red Cross business," Grace said.

"When he walked up the steps to the porch and you introduced them, Amelia looked as if she'd gobble him up," Hannah said.

"I was too preoccupied with everything else to notice that, but then she squired him off for a walk and to see the property while I did all the work at the party. I was fuming. After all, how could I ever compete with the glamorous Amelia? I ran away to Roger and Charles in Branston."

"We hadn't been in Covington long," Hannah reminisced. "I was sure Amelia had ruined it for all of us. I wanted to kill her."

Grace's eyes grew speculative. "Amelia, and now Ellie?" She shook her head. "Back then, with Amelia, I was incredibly insecure. I didn't say anything to Bob or Amelia. It's different now. I talked to Bob downstairs. He isn't the slightest bit interested in Ellie Lerner, he says." She clenched both fists. "But it bothers me. Am I still so insecure, so inadequate?"

"Did it ever occur to you that Bob's the one who's insecure, feels inadequate, and that's why he's receptive to her flattery?"

"What do you mean inadequate? Bob has plenty of self-confidence."

"Maybe not in all things."

Grace rubbed the top of her knuckles as if massaging them. She'd never ever thought of this. Bob was a pillar of strength to her, a safe haven, secure, strong, and very confident. "I don't understand."

Hannah leaned forward, wrapped the towel about her head, and flipped it back. "Darn hair's too long," she said. "You think about it. We blamed Amelia then, and we're blaming Ellie now. Why aren't we angry with Bob? That day of the birthday party for Tyler, Bob could have put Amelia off, reminded her that you were having a party for his grandson. In this case, Bob could simply not laugh at Ellie's jokes, or he could ask one of us to say he's not in. I think he rather enjoys the attention. I'm sure this is his problem as much as it is yours."

"I don't believe that." But something inside nagged at Grace. Was Hannah correct in her evaluation? "What would you do if you were me?"

"I wouldn't let them be alone, for starters. I'd be in that living room every minute she's here."

"Won't that seem peculiar?" Grace nibbled on a nail. Her stomach hurt.

"Who cares? I think if you bring it out in the open, let her know you're on to her, it'll take the wind out of her sails faster than anything else." Hannah raised her eyebrows knowingly.

"I'd have a hard time confronting her about her intentions, but I can sit in the living room with them the next time she's here." Grace rose, her hand on her stomach. "I feel sick." She headed for the bathroom.

The following day at approximately six thirty in the evening, the doorbell rang. Moments later, Hannah arrived in the kitchen. "She's here, Grace. I'll finish up the salad, you go on in the living room."

Grace took a deep breath. "If I go in there it's going to look contrived."

"Forget how it looks; go, and put a stop to this nonsense."

"Don't pressure me, Hannah, please." But Grace removed her apron, ran her hands over her hair, and started for the door. "I'm not at all sure about this."

"Go. Just do it."

Ellie Lerner looked up and smiled when Grace entered the living room. "Oh, Grace, how good to see you. You're always so busy when I stop by."

"How are you, Ellie?"

"Fine. Just fine. Summer's usually the busiest time in the bridal dress business you know, but since last September there's been quite a rash of weddings. It hasn't let up yet."

"That's good," Grace replied.

With his uninjured hand, Bob motioned to Grace, then patted a place on the couch beside him. The gash in his forehead had cooled from red to pink, and the swelling was completely gone. Each day, he experienced less discomfort in his shoulder. In another ten days they would remove the cast from his arm, and he would start physical therapy. Grace knew that the inability to play golf frustrated him, and he had taken to walking the course several times a week while Martin played. Today they had been gone longer than usual, and when he came home, Grace thought that Bob looked drained and had gotten too much sun.

Now, she joined him on the couch. Ellie sat in one of the armchairs nearby.

Ellie wore a skirt and stockings. When she crossed her legs the skirt rose to her knees, displaying shapely calves. As Grace's gaze traveled down to Ellie's fawn-colored sandals, she noticed for the first time Ellie's thickening ankles. She's going to have thick, ugly legs in time, Grace thought with some pleasure.

"Where's Brenda tonight?" Grace asked.

"Over at Molly's. They ask me, of course, but it's family, and I don't feel right intruding."

But it's okay for you to intrude in our lives? Grace smiled. "How thoughtful of you." She hated herself for the nonconfronting blandness of her comment.

The silence in the room was palpable. Bob coughed.

Grace said, "I hear you tell great jokes."

"Oh, not really. They're silly."

"I like a good joke," Grace replied.

Bob cleared his throat. "Tell Grace the one about the two boys who ran away from home."

"Two boys? I can't remember that one," Ellie said. She uncrossed her legs, and the fingers of her hand tapped the arm of her chair.

Emboldened by Ellie's obvious discomfort, Grace said, "If you wrote down your jokes, you'd remember them."

Bob interrupted. "Grace, why don't you tell Ellie about Melissa's latest escapade."

Grace did not respond, so he said, "That child's into everything. She pulled a canister of flour off the kitchen table. It opened, and what they found in the kitchen was a little ghost covered tip to toe with flour and one heck of a mess."

"Kids," Ellie said. She turned to Grace. "How is Laura's baby doing? I heard he had colic. That's so hard on a baby and his mother."

"Andy's doing fine. No more colic. Laura takes him to work every day now."

"It's nice she's able to do that," Ellie said. "When I had my children, no one welcomed babies at work. I stayed home for eight years, until my second son entered kindergarten. It about drove me nuts, cooped up in suburbia all day with kids and coffee klatches."

"I was a stay-at-home mom," Grace said. "I enjoyed it."

There was no levity in the silence that followed. "It's hard for working women today, and so many work. I don't know how they do it," Ellie said.

"Yes, very hard," Grace said.

Ellie glanced at her watch. "Well, I'd best be off." She stood and smoothed her skirt. "Glad you're so much better, Bob. Good-bye, Grace. My best to Amelia and Hannah."

Grace walked her to the door, then returned to the living room.

"What was that all about?" Bob asked.

"Notice that with me present she didn't have a single joke to tell."

"She wouldn't tell a bawdy joke in front of you. She knows you don't like them, and she's got too much respect for you."

"You'd rather I didn't join the two of you, then?" Grace was beginning to fume, and it wasn't Ellie at whom she was angry. "You enjoy her company, don't you? You'd prefer if it were just the two of you, right? Makes you feel like such a big man."

"Nonsense. What's come over you, Grace? I've been cooped up in this house for weeks now."

"Cooped up? Cooped up?" She moved about the room, adjusted a curtain, straightened a picture, fluffed up the pillow on the chair Ellie had occupied. "You're out with Martin several days a week. You have lunch at the club. When are you cooped up?"

"You gals have been terrific, but it's a change to see a fresh face once in a while. Ellie's jokes give me a chuckle, then I tell Martin and have a second chuckle. You're being childish, making something out of nothing."

Grace's hands went out and she bent forward as if in a bow. "Yes, your highness. You're right, and I'm a fool." Grace's eyes flashed their anger. "How come I never noticed that before?"

"I don't want to fight with you, Grace."

"Well, if you're too confined here, you can pack your bags and call Martin to take you back to your own place." The instant the words left her mouth she regretted them. She was playing right into Ellie's hands. If that woman visited Bob at home, if it was Ellie's intention to seduce him, there'd be no barrier to her behavior except Bob, and, well—she thought of her conversation with Hannah and questioned Bob's sense of adequacy—you never knew.

"Ellie Lerner said once that you remind her of her husband. Maybe she's set her sights on you for her next husband," Grace blurted.

He laughed deep and hearty. "Well, I'll be darned. You're jealous, Grace Singleton."

Ready to explode, Grace stared at him. "You're laughing at me, making fun of me."

"No. I'm not." He rose and moved toward her.

Grace backed away. "Don't touch me."

"Why are you making such a big thing of this? The woman has no interest in me, and I certainly have none in her."

Grace's lower lip curled slightly, and she looked at Bob as if to say, *Don't tell me you believe that crap!* "You don't care one bit how I feel."

Shaking her head, her arms extended to push him away, she blinked back tears.

"Grace, honey, you haven't anything to be jealous of. Ellie's a twit, a silly person who gets some kind of perverse kick out of telling off-color jokes."

"And you're just as perverse, laughing at her jokes. You encourage her. Why shouldn't she think you're interested in her?"

He was by her side now, trying to slip his unfettered arm about her. "Listen to me, honey. I love you."

She moved away from him. "Do you?" Grace ran from the room, tears streaming down her cheeks.

Bob found Hannah in the kitchen. "You've got to help me, Hannah. Grace has gone off the deep end. She resents Ellie coming over here, and she's accused me of not loving her and preferring Ellie's company. Ellie's funny, that's all. I haven't the slightest interest in the woman."

Bone tired, Hannah sank into a chair at the table. Today she had supervised workmen in clearing an area in the woods for the Shade Garden. It drained her trying to make herself understood in broken English and Spanish, and she had ended up bending, stooping, even kneeling—very bad for her knees—to demonstrate exactly what she meant. It hurt to get up, to bend her knees, or even to stretch them out now, and Hannah was weary of talking, of people.

"Ellie's coming here may be totally innocent, as well as your enjoying her jokes, but to a woman who is as honest, and open, and real, and loves you as much as Grace does, it's seditious behavior on your part and sheer nerve on Ellie's."

"Seditious?" Bob lowered his chin and took a step back. "Like in attempting to overthrow a government?"

"I mean that in a most personal sense. Can't you see that? In Grace's eyes Ellie Lerner is trying to usurp her place, win your affection. And your laughing and enjoying her jokes simply encourages her."

Bob's good hand went to his head. "Good God. It's absolutely nothing of the kind. I tried to tell Grace that. I have no interest in Ellie."

"Listening to you two laughing, having a good time in that living room, sure indicates otherwise," Hannah said.

"This is the most preposterous thing I ever heard," he said. "I'm totally innocent of Grace's and your accusations."

"I'm incredibly tired, Bob. I must get upstairs, take a shower, and rest." Hannah rose and started for the door, then turned to look at Bob, who was sitting stiffly at the table. "Self-righteousness isn't going to get you anywhere, Bob. I suggest you eat humble pie, apologize, and court Grace the best way you know how."

Up in her room, with the door locked, Grace pulled the journal from her dresser drawer.

Dear Journal:
Why did I listen to Hannah? I went off half-cocked, was hostile to Ellie, and accused Bob of heaven knows what. If I had wanted to push Bob into another woman's arms, I couldn't have done a better job.

She paused a moment, brought the end of the pen to her lips.

How bold of me to just walk in there and plop myself down. I wonder if Ellie will stay away now. So what did it accomplish? Bob's probably so angry with me, he'll call Martin to take him back to his apartment. Ellie will visit him there. Bob will be lonely. What's more conducive to romance than two lonely people? What have I done? Dear God, what have I done? Why did I listen to Hannah?

Someone was knocking, no, pounding, on her door. "Go away," she said.

"I have to talk to you." It was Bob.

"Go away." Perhaps he had come to tell her Martin was on his way to pick him up.

"I'm not going anywhere. Please, open the door." Bob's voice was soft, pleading, definitely not angry.

He hadn't called Martin. Grace resolved not to turn into a sobbing bit of spineless fluff. She was justifiably angry. So where did righteous indignation get anyone? Grace snapped the journal shut and returned it to her drawer. "I'm coming," she said, and turned to her mirror to try, unsuccessfully, to soften the redness of her face and lessen the puffiness around her eyes. She looked old and awful.

Bob stood in the hallway, hand outstretched, presenting her with a single red rose. "I'm sorry, Grace, honey. Truly sorry."

She accepted the flower and brought it to her nose. She recognized the rich, sweet aroma of Hannah's Chrysler Imperial roses. "It smells wonderful. Thank you."

"I asked Hannah. She let me cut it for you."

"It's the best rose of its kind," Grace said.

"Like you, my love, the best. The very best."

"Bob. I'm so sorry. I was rude."

"You were merely implementing a woman's prerogative to protect her turf. I've been insensitive, letting Ellie visit and laughing at her silly jokes. I should have stopped it after her first visit."

"How could you have done that?"

"Not laugh at her jokes, yawn, or get one of you ladies to say I was out for the evening with Martin. Something like that."

Grace felt her hackles rising. She wanted to snap at him, "So why didn't you?" but she refrained. She sat on the side of her bed. "Why do men do that?"

"Do what?"

"Respond to a woman's flattery?"

"Is that how you see it?" He took the rocker by the window. "I didn't realize that's what I was doing."

"Like that time at Tyler's birthday party, going off with Amelia."

He bowed his head. "God, Grace, are you still holding that against me? That was so stupid of me. I felt sorry for Amelia. She'd lost her husband and her kid."

Grace came to him, wanting to sit on his lap, but refrained. She might hurt him by jarring his cast. "I'm sorry, bringing up old stuff like that. I was hurt and jealous." With his coming to her room, his obvious contriteness, and their being able to talk about it, the pain of anger and jealousy had faded, replaced by love and a strong desire for him.

He must have sensed her change of mood, her longing, for he reached up to her with his good arm and grasped her waist. "You drive me nuts, you sexy woman," he whispered. "Damn this cast. I can't wait to get it off and feel like a human being again."

She flirted, looking down at him with eyes that invited passion. "And act like one."

Dear Journal:
Hannah was right after all. I couldn't have gone on fuming the way I was, building up anger. Being there in the living room did make a difference, and that in itself confronted Ellie. She knew. Bet she won't be back. And if Bob needs attention, well, I can give him all the attention in the world.

29

THE LAND BY THE RIVER

"I've come to a decision, Mother." Roger leaned forward over the table. He had invited his mother for lunch at the Sunnyside Cafe in Weaverville, asked her to meet him there at one thirty.

They had ordered, but this was late for Grace and her stomach growled. She felt a bit woozy. She ought to know better by now, and should have eaten something before she left the house. Grace reached into the covered basket of rolls and removed one. When she allowed herself to get hungry like this and edgy, any food would do, even if it spiked her blood sugar the way this white flour roll would do. "What decision?" She gave Roger her full attention.

"I don't want to be in business. I'm not sure what I do want to do, other than get away from everything for a while. Maybe homestead somewhere. There was an ad in the paper." He pulled out a ragged-edged section of the ad page. "Land in South Carolina. 'Off the beaten path,' it says. Water and rich farmland. It's located in a place called Salem."

"I know where Salem is. We went down there to a lake when Miranda and her family visited Hannah. There are beautiful lakes in that area. If I remember right, the land is rolling. You can see bits of mountains, but nothing spectacular like up here."

"What kind of a town is Salem?"

"Let me think. We made a short detour through it. It was gone before you knew it was there."

"The ad says the land is forty-five minutes from Clemson University."

"That doesn't sound too far, does it?" she asked. The waitress brought their Cobb salads and refilled their water glasses. A table with five women near the window emptied. The room grew quieter. Traffic moved silently along Main Street. The sounds of cars stopping at the light at the corner and starting again were muffled by the large windowpanes. It was close to 2:00 P.M. Waitresses began setting tables for dinner.

"I'm surprised you don't want to open a party-planning business. Is it because it hasn't worked out for you and Mike?" The salad, topped with chicken and chopped eggs and tomatoes, tasted great; Grace felt better.

Roger drizzled more salad dressing on his greens. "I'm glad it's over with Mike. It was impulsive and stupid on my part. I'm just sorry if Mike was hurt."

"Mike is hurt, yes, but he'll be fine. He's found a very nice villa, and Amelia's helping him get settled. It's five minutes or less from his studio. It's you I worry about."

"The party-planning business was Charles's dream."

"How wonderful that you helped him make his dream come true. And it's a business Miranda and Paul and their boys like. Now, son, what's your dream, and how can I help you?"

"You can drive down to Salem with me and look at this land."

Grace bit the edge of her lower lip and tried to visualize her calendar. What was she supposed to do this coming week? Didn't she have a dentist appointment? She could always switch her regular Tuesday beauty parlor appointment with Totsy to another day. "I can go with you. Just give me two days' notice, so I can cancel a few appointments."

"We can do it around your schedule," he said. "Give me a call and tell me the best day for you. I'll get directions from the Realtor, and we'll drive down and meet him at the land. I appreciate your going."

"I look forward to the drive with you, Roger."

That was on a Monday. Grace kept her appointment on Tuesday with Totsy and had her hair trimmed. She was wearing it in something of a pageboy. She hadn't consciously chosen the style. All she had done was stop getting perms, and her hair had begun to grow out and fall in this simple manner about her face. Bob liked it, as did Hannah and Amelia, and she did also.

Wednesday, at exactly nine thirty in the morning, Roger picked up Grace, and they headed down the mountain to South Carolina.

It was one of those haze-smothered days with a pale, sad blue sky. Traffic was light on the highway as they drove past Hendersonville and turned off on a road that connected to Highway 25, from where they would pick up scenic Highway 11. It was, in fact, the same route Grace had traveled with Hannah and her family.

"I have to look for the Highway Eleven turnoff," Roger said.

"I'll recognize it. There's a small truck stop–type restaurant on the corner where we make a left turn. You'll be turning across a highway with traffic coming, so you need to be careful. Then we go up a rise and take a left."

Within a half hour, they were driving along on South Carolina's scenic Highway 11.

"We'll pass a place where there's a huge rocking chair sitting up on a rise. Used to be a Realtor's office there, but not anymore," Grace said.

"I'm impressed," Roger said. "You've been here once and you re-member so much about it."

Grace was flattered that he noticed. She might struggle to put a name to a face or to recall something she'd said or done a week ago, but places, scenery, the countryside—all spoke to her with their sym-bols, their colors, and their shapes. Grace could remember every turn in a road, which field had been filled with rolls of hay waiting to be taken to a barn and stored, the color of cows in a pasture, a stand of trees, the dates in the spring when their neighbor's Chinese willow tree flowered each year.

And when she spoke of these things, she made visible to listeners how the world spoke to her. To Grace, trees were not merely green in summertime; they were multihued: chartreuse, mint, celery, the deep rich green of broccoli or collard greens. The shimmer of gray on the backs of leaves revealed by stiff winds were a sure sign of rain, her mother used to say.

Amelia had said she should paint, but Grace had no patience for painting. A brush felt heavy in her hand, and her efforts seemed clumsy. She couldn't translate the light, feathery quality of what she saw onto canvas. Amelia had urged Grace to take up photography.

"You'd like it. There's a system in black-and-white photography called the zone system," Amelia said. "You work toward getting all hues from white to black in the photo. You could do that. You'd see all the details, like the shade cast by a single leaf on the grass."

"I wouldn't have the patience," Grace had said.

Now, as Roger drove along Route 11, she sat back and enjoyed the passing scene: hillsides dappled with sunshine, freshly paved roads offering entry to developments of new homes built high behind thickets of trees. Grace wondered who came to live here, so far from a market, shopping, and doctors. And this very isolation was what her son was seeking.

They drove by Aunt Sue's Country Corner, a conglomeration of small gift shops and a terrific ice-cream shop. Grace noted that Aunt Sue, whoever she was, had added a greenhouse. Another twenty-minute drive brought them to the bridge across Lake Keowee, close to where the dam spilled over from Lake Jocassee. Large homes with docks had been built along the water's edge.

The sign to Salem alerted them that they were close to the turnoff, and they soon turned right onto the road to the Piedmont Forest Nursery. From there the two-lane road rose and fell with the terrain. Periodically, mountains were visible in the distance.

The Alexander Cemetery, a guidepost the Realtor had provided, appeared as they rounded a corner. It sat on a rise to the left. Its monuments and headstones reminded Grace of the Reynolds' Cemetery, where Old Man was buried.

Moments later they turned left onto Easy Street, and about a mile later turned right onto Old Horse Lane, and down a narrow dirt road to the valley, where shrubs and trees nearly blocked out the view of a two-story wooden house. Behind the fence, dogs barked furiously.

An unpaved road veered to the left, then to the right. At the top of the rise, a man leaning against a red pickup waved them on. He wore jeans, a casual shirt without a tie, and an orange and black baseball cap. His face was clean-shaven and friendly.

"Greg Henley," he said, extending his hand, which Roger grasped.

"This really is off the beaten path," Roger said.

Greg lit a cigarette. "It's what you said you wanted. But not completely isolated. There are folks living all up and down Easy Street, and it's only twenty minutes to Walhalla. Markets and so forth are over there." He waved a hand to indicate the land about them. "This land was cleared about four years ago. It's growing back fast. You can pick and choose which trees you want to leave and which you want to take out. Before it was cut, the owners didn't know there was a view of the mountains. You can see how quickly it's recovered."

They stood on the rise beside Greg Henley. The view opened in a wide arc.

"Those mountains over yonder are in North Carolina, same as the ones that butt up to Lake Jocassee," he said.

With no outstanding peaks or unusual shapes, the mountains stretched in an undulating line 180 degrees around. Immediately, Grace thought of a line from a poem by Edna St. Vincent Millay: "These were the things that bounded me." It was gentle land, much easier to build on than most of the land in Madison County.

"Good sites for building," Roger said.

"There sure are. Two sets of folks have bought land. Both of 'em are members of the Sierra Club. Nice folks." Greg pointed out the flagged lots. "That there fellow's got him over four acres, but the land drops off real steep to the river. They'd have to build steps to get down to the water. A lady and her husband from Walhalla bought nearly four acres up on that hill back there." He pointed, then opened his pickup's door and waved them in.

Grace sat squeezed between the men as they drove down to flat acreage and Little River. Once there, they got out and walked around the pickup. A stubby grass covered the earth. Greg kicked at it with his shoe until a chunk came up revealing firm red soil. "Good, rich bottomland," he said. "A man can feed his family pretty darn good from this land. He can drill him a well or use the river, depending."

Greg pulled out a machete from the bed of his pickup and hacked an opening in the screen of weedy brush that concealed the water from view. The river, a branch of a larger Little River, flowed with a soft swish and a whisper. No rapids here, no rushing water, just a sleepy little stream maybe eight feet across to the pasture flanking its other side.

"How much land do you think there is from here to the rise?" Roger asked.

Greg shaded his eyes and studied the area. "Including the bottomland, four to six acres, I reckon."

"I could build on top, have a view, and the benefit of the flatland and river," Roger said.

"You sure could. You'd see part of the mountain range from up there." Greg threw his cigarette stub to the earth and rubbed it out with the sole of his shoe. With relief, Grace watched its smoking tip split apart, the tobacco separate from the paper, and the glow die.

Grace turned from the men and moseyed over to the gap Greg had cut in the bushes. She could see the river clearly. Shoving back branches, Grace got as close as she could. She couldn't see the river bottom, as she could in the many shallow streams and creeks in Covington.

Little River lay several feet down from the edge of the bank. It meandered past bringing to mind songs Grace had always liked: "Old Man River" and "Swanee." She pictured the brush removed along its bank, the river open to sun and air. She wondered if the owners of the land across the river would give permission to cut the weeds and thick growth on his side of the bank. Greg had said that there was a bottom over there, planted in corn or potatoes by a local farmer.

If Roger bought this land, she would urge him to open the view of the river and to have a deck constructed along its bank. Then, if and when she visited him, she could sit down here and listen to birds, and crickets, and other country creatures. She pictured corn growing in the weed-filled field behind her and a scarecrow with a wise, kind face painted on it, like the scarecrow in the Wizard of Oz.

"Come along, Mother." Roger interrupted her musing. "We're going to have a look at the land at the top of the rise, see where I could put a house."

"Put a house? You've decided?" She moved reluctantly away from the riverbank, leaving behind the peace she felt there.

He nodded and focused on the hilltop.

She followed him closely, reaching out once to grasp his shoulder to steady herself on the uneven earth. The top of the rise was flat and offered a good site for a house. Besides a view of mountains, the river would lend itself to view if the brush were cleared.

"I think this might be it, Mother. Land's only six thousand dollars an acre—much less than in North Carolina. It's hotter down here than up in the higher mountains, of course, but with air-conditioning, who cares? It's not nearly as cold as winters are in Covington, and it's far enough away from cities, yet only an hour and a half to Greenville, South Carolina, or Asheville, and just over two hours to Atlanta."

"Fifteen minutes' drive gets you to Lakes Jocassee and Keowee," Greg Henley said. "It's less than an hour to Lake Hartwell on the Georgia border with South Carolina."

Roger stood with his hands on his hips, following the line of hills in the distance. Then he flung both hands in the air as if he were releasing doves at a wedding. "This is nice, very nice, just what I had in mind. Yes, indeed, this will do just fine."

"Aren't you deciding on this a bit too soon? You haven't looked at anything else," Grace said.

"Why look further when this is exactly right?" Roger asked. A sad look crossed his face. "Charles would have loved it here." He turned away.

The pastoral quality, the rolling hills of the countryside through which they drove on the twenty-minute ride to the Realtor's office, pleased Grace and eased her mind from worrying about her son's impetuous decision. The noon traffic in Walhalla seemed heavy but moved steadily on Main Street. Grace counted four antiques shops, a Mexican market, a bank. Fine old buildings that had once been homes were now a funeral parlor and offices of lawyers, Realtors, and doctors.

"Main Street is Route Twenty-eight. That takes you up the mountain to Highland and Cashiers, where a lot of folk from South Georgia and Florida vacation or have summer homes," Greg said. Then he suggested that they have lunch at the Steak House on Main Street before going to his office.

Grace hardly felt like steak and was pleasantly surprised to discover a cafeteria-style restaurant.

"This place is known up and down these parts for its fried chicken," Greg said as they stood in line. "Best I've eaten anywhere."

And the chicken was juicy and delicious, as were the candied carrots and the macaroni and cheese.

After lunch, Greg introduced them to a vice president of the Blue Ridge Bank of Walhalla. Roger set up an account and discussed a loan for 20 percent of the price of the land, which the vice president said would be no problem. Roger would hear from him in a few days.

Greg drove them around Walhalla, a quiet town originally settled by Germans.

"I'm not of German ancestry myself, but let me tell you, we put on one heck of an Octoberfest each year with great eating and dancing. Everyone turns out," Greg said. "The old-timers and the new folks who live in condos on Lake Keowee."

At the realty office, Roger prepared to sign the necessary offer of sale. "The owner surveys the land as it's sold. We have this overview plat of the whole property, but not the lots broken out," Greg said. "The owner figured he'd divide it up to suit the buyers. Nothing under two acres, though."

"As long as there are covenants, and there won't be mobile homes," Roger said.

"There's that, all right, and setbacks, and rules about fences and animals, and the size of the house, nothing under fifteen hundred square feet allowed."

"I could use the name of a reputable builder. I want something simple on one level. No stairs. Three bedrooms."

"If you build out over the hill," Greg said, "you'll have a basement."

"I want enough flat area to build the house and a double garage on one level."

"Don't forget a big covered porch for rocking chairs," Grace agreed.

"Big covered porch and rocking chairs," Roger agreed.

On the trip home, they stopped at Aunt Sue's for ice cream. Along with ice cream, the small shop sold jams, jellies, and gift items. Grace ordered two scoops of peppermint ice cream with chocolate chips. Roger had a double-dip chocolate cone. They ate outside on the long wooden porch.

"I shouldn't have this." Grace contemplated the cup in her hand. "But this one time, I'm going to kick back and enjoy the sugar." She scooped out a spoonful and tasted. "My heaven, it's good."

The dusty parking lot was jammed with cars. Tourists ambled in and out of the small gift shops, many lugging packages. Others sat on the porch, rocking and eating ice cream. A young boy walked a small black poodle on the grass near a creek across the parking area. People left the greenhouse carrying potted plants. A woman sitting at an old upright piano on the porch belted out show tunes. Grace tapped her feet, breathed deeply, and thought, I am really happy, right now, this minute. I am truly happy.

She and Roger had never had a day together like this, without tension or hassle. She was pleased that everything had fallen into place for him. Grace believed that when matters unfolded easily, it was part of a divine plan. The path of least resistance, she called it, because it was meant to be.

"You look completely content, Mother."

"I am. This has been an absolutely grand day. I'm so glad I came along. I like your land—the whole area, in fact. I wish you happiness, my son."

"How do you find happiness, anyway? I've been a restless soul all my life," Roger said. "Charles was my anchor. Now he's gone."

"Don't look for happiness at the end of the road." Grace licked the spoon clean. "Happiness happens along the way, when you're doing things you love. I hope you'll only do those things you truly enjoy."

"I haven't ever really loved any of my careers."

They did not speak for a time. The piano player stopped for a break, and the roar of tires from the highway replaced the music.

"I've always had an interest in the stars. I think I'll see if they have a class in astronomy at Clemson. If they do, I'll take it and get a powerful telescope. Without light pollution, I should have a great view of the sky." Roger wiped his hands. Grace reached over with her bandanna and wiped off a smear of ice cream alongside his mouth. He didn't push her hand away, but smiled instead.

"Orion is my favorite constellation," she said.

"I didn't know you were interested in astronomy."

"Oh, not astronomy, really. Orion is easy to recognize. The three stars of his belt are bright and constant." She would have liked telling him about the theory that the Pyramids of Giza were lined up exactly as the three stars in Orion's belt, but was afraid he would disagree and argue, and the mood of the day would be ruined.

"Once I've got the house up and am settled, you'll come down, and I'll show you Orion up close," Roger said.

"I'd like that." Furrows deepened on her brow. "Roger, are you sure you want to live alone in a strange new place?"

"I have to be alone for a while, Mother. That's what I've learned. It'll be fine, and I will take courses at Clemson University. That'll get me out and meeting people. But don't worry about that now. It'll be well into next year before I'm in a house, and that's fine. We have to have a closing on the land, and I have to find a builder. There's a well to be dug and power hooked up."

"When you move, I'd like to bring Bob down."

"He's welcome." Roger finished his cone. "I like Bob. You ready to go?"

30

CHANGE AT BELLA'S PARK

By August, Andy, now five months old, was a happy, smiling baby, but too heavy for Hannah to tote. The Mexican workmen, with their enthusiasm for children, vied with one another to carry Andy and his stroller to the spot where his grandmother worked. Hannah noticed that even while they worked, the men seemed able to keep an eye on him.

On Saturdays, Lucy Banks helped Hannah weed and prepare the Children's Garden for planting in early June. Her mood, her attitude, everything about Lucy had changed for the better. She had friends at school now, girls and even boys that she met in the Garden Club, and her interest in plants and planting expanded continually. Hannah was delighted.

Max had finally agreed to give up Molly, who moved upstairs to become Laura's assistant. The two women shared an office and worked well together. On the occasions when Hannah went upstairs to speak to Hank about a design, it pleased her to hear them deep in earnest conversation or laughing softly, the way good friends might.

Max fussed and fumed that paperwork was piling up, things were not getting filed, orders were not called in. He interviewed potential assistants and found a reason not to hire any of them: This one was too anxious, another too sloppy-looking, another too well groomed for a job like this, and on and on. Never a practical, reasonable objection.

"You're an intransigent old codger," Hannah said.

"And perverse," he agreed.

"You've interviewed at least a dozen women for this job, and you haven't hired anyone."

"How can I replace Molly? She was so capable and intelligent. I didn't have to tell her when things needed to be done."

"You're the one who decided to expand the historical restorations. We could have kept the park simple, with the Indian Village and the Covington Homesteads," Hannah said.

"A living history museum will be important for Madison County, a contribution to the history of the county."

"And turn Cove Road into a traffic nightmare," she said. "I thought you bought this land to keep out development?"

"I did, but this is bigger than any of us."

Hannah sighed and walked away.

Mary Ann approached her that afternoon. "Hannah, do you think I could do Molly's job?"

Hannah studied the bright young woman. She had always thought Mary Ann was underutilized. "I do, but right now in Max's mind no one can do Molly's job. It'll be tough for whomever he hires. You really interested?"

"I'm bored with being a receptionist. I'm a good organizer. I've organized things for my family, clubs, my church for years. I know what goes on around here better than any stranger would, and I know how Max can be."

"If you think you can tolerate Max for the first few weeks until he gets used to you, I say go for it."

"I thought I'd sit down with Molly first and ask her advice: What do I need to know, say, do, and not do?" Mary Ann said.

"Smart girl," Hannah said. "I'll use my influence."

Andy stirred in his crib, and Mary Ann rose and walked over to him. "He's so precious," she said. "It's so good and so honest having him here at the office. He brightens everyone's day."

"He certainly brightens mine," Hannah said.

31

SIMPLICITIES OF LOVING

Lurina Masterson had never taken her husband's last name, Reynolds. "It's like I always knowed he'd pass before me," she told Grace one day, shortly after Grace's trip to South Carolina. "And I wouldn't let him change his will. That boy, Wayne, he done took good care of that old man for years. He deserves the land up the mountain and the mobile homes." She set down her fork and peered over her glasses at Grace.

"I told Wayne the other day, if he didn't like living in an old house with an old lady, he could bring one of them trailers down here and set it up anywhere he wants on my property. That's when he told me he'd be a-goin' back to live out there in Haywood County in a couple of months. I know he's gotta go, but I sure am gonna miss that boy. He says he's gonna sell the pigs before he goes. I won't let him sell them all. I got to like those big, fat old sows."

Grace had picked up Lurina, and they were having lunch at the new diner in Elk Road Plaza.

"This chili's mighty good," Lurina said. "Just hope it don't give me no heartburn or the runs."

"We'll stop at the drugstore and pick up some antacid for you, just in case," Grace said.

She could see Lurina's eyes taking in the passing scene: people pushing carts from the market to their cars in the parking lot, children hanging on to their mother's skirts or hands, people with parcels strolling along under the covered walkway.

"It's nice to have a place to grab a bite without having to drive a ways," Grace said. Lord, she was beginning to sound like Lurina. Grace smiled over her glass of iced tea. She felt a great tenderness toward the older woman. Had she lived, her own mother would be Lurina's age: eighty-three, or was it eighty-four now?

There had been a time in Grace's life when haste took precedence over forbearance. When she was young, she had moved fast, thought fast, and acted fast—sometimes too fast for her own good. Many of her arguments with Ted in those early years had been a direct result of her irritation at his slow pace in thinking, talking, even walking. Over the years, she had mellowed considerably and grown less impatient. Her friends and Bob never knew how peevish and intolerant she had been.

And now, with Lurina, patience reigned triumphant. Grace had sat quietly before they left for the diner and waited while Lurina, fully clothed, checked to make sure she hadn't forgotten any article of clothing.

"I got my stocking on right, Grace?" she'd asked. Or "Dress looks funny, right here, don't you think, Grace?" Lurina tugged at the material that hung loose across her bosom. "I never goes outta this here house without my brassiere, Grace. Reach round the back of me, girlie, and check that strap, make sure I have the dern thing on."

Grace rose and patted Lurina's back until the old woman announced with pride, "I done remembered it."

What troubled Grace was Lurina's living alone. When Lurina had announced she would move downstairs to Old Man's bedroom, she meant not just herself, but everything. So Wayne hired two men, and they had lugged Old Man's furnishings upstairs and Lurina's down: her parents' huge bed with its mahogany headboard, the wide, heavy dresser, the huge armoire that served as a closet, even the ancient rug, thick with the dust of years. Still, she would be alone.

Grace reasoned that Lurina had lived alone when they had first met. She thought about how Lurina would stand on her porch with a shotgun every time the young Park Service ranger arrived to check on her. Lurina interpreted his coming as an attempt to evict her, though her father had placed the land in trust for the Park Service only after her death. Lurina, with her empty shotgun, let them know she was very much alive.

Old Man had liked the young park ranger and invited him to "set a bit," and in time Lurina's gun remained in the umbrella stand inside the front door.

"What do you think about getting someone to live in the house with you when Wayne leaves?" Grace asked.

"You're a sly one, Grace," Lurina said, "asking me such a question in a public place so's I can't yell at you." She crossed her arms over her chest. "I ain't gonna have no stranger livin' in my house." She wagged a finger at Grace. "And you remember that, girlie."

No one had ever called Grace "girlie" except Lurina. Grace smiled and ducked behind raised hands. "Okay."

They chatted about baby Andy and little Melissa, who, when Grace brought her to visit, tore through Lurina's house like a strong wind whipping off a lake on a fall day. Grace also told Lurina about Roger buying land in South Carolina in a place called Salem.

"Salem's a far piece. We had kin down there. One time, Pa got him out his Ford car, and we drove down the mountain to make a visit. His kin had them a whole mountainside of land and a river and two big pastures and plenty of cows, and sheep, and a big hutch where he kept rabbits. Kept them for the manure, he said." She chuckled. "One time we had to stay on several days with 'em 'cause of a snowstorm down here, which was very rare. We couldn't get us out of their driveway."

"The lakes in that area are beautiful," Grace said.

"Weren't no lakes there then. Jacassee was a valley where folks lived before the government built dams."

Then came a series of questions from Lurina. "Hannah still gonna marry up with Max?"

"Yes. She finally set April as the month."

"Sure took her a long time. You'd a thought Hannah don't want to marry up with Maxwell."

"Hannah had mixed feelings. Remember how you worried about where you'd be buried, and nearly called the whole wedding off? And how you changed your mind about being married in church and got married at home, weeks before the church date?"

Lurina changed the subject. "Amelia still planning to make her another picture book?"

"She isn't sure. She's been busy helping Mike find a place and move."

"And how's your Bob's boy, Russell, and his new wife? We was brides, her and me, more or less the same time. She gonna have more babies?"

"She says not. You know what a handful Melissa is. Tyler's in middle school now, and doing well. He's a good soccer player."

"Watch he don't get hurt."

Lurina got that look in her eyes that Grace knew was the precursor to a tale about a funeral, and she settled back to listen.

"One of them young McCorkle fellows, he done got hisself kicked in the head playing some kind of ball game—soccer, maybe. Died on the spot." She nodded vigorously. "Yessiree. On the spot. Big old funeral. The whole McCorkle clan: old farmers, skinny kids, dowdy-looking spinster ladies, big fat grannies, everyone from that there valley." Lurina pointed out the window to the entrance to McCorkle Creek. "Every dern last one of 'em came, and all the school, it seemed to me. Never seen such a big funeral. His ma took to wailing over the casket and pounding on it till they had to carry her off."

"Where to?"

Lurina shrugged. "Dunno, she was kind of funny in the head anyway, bless her heart. I ain't never seen her again, but I don't go much places. It was kinda sad, though—only fifteen times the bell tolled." Her story done, she reached across the table for the sugar and ladled four teaspoons into her now cold cup of tea.

The diner had emptied. Grace realized they had been sitting and chatting for two hours, but it had been a good catch-up, and she'd even found the funeral story interesting.

Until Ringo, Grace had considered the McCorkles separate from the community of Covington, almost alien. Truth was, their children attended the same schools as Tyler and played on all the teams. The woman next to her in the checkout line at the market might be a McCorkle, as might be the checkout lady herself. A plumber Hannah hired recently to fix a leak in their bathroom turned out to be a McCorkle. A McCorkle had replaced the broken pipe at Bella's Park. What had the McCorkles, or some of them, done to make them objects of mistrust, fear, and scorn in this small community? She was about to ask Lurina when Amelia came in with Mike. Grace and Lurina shoved over toward the walls to make room for them at the booth.

"Well, blessed be, seeing you both," Lurina said. Her eyes gleamed like a child being given candy.

" 'It's good to see you, Lurina," Amelia said.

"Grace was a-tellin' me you got you a new house, Mike."

Mike talked about the new villa, the view, the furniture he and Amelia had selected.

Grace thought he seemed happy, which made her feel better.

A short time later, she and Lurina said their good-byes. Grace drove across the bridge to the old farmhouse and went inside with the old woman so that she could undo Lurina's bra. Lurina slipped into a brightly colored muumuu Grace had brought back for her from Atlanta.

"Sit a bit, Grace—I got something to show you."

Lurina disappeared into her bedroom, then joined Grace in the living room. The box she carried was about the size of a cigar box. When Lurina sat beside Grace on the old sofa and opened the box, the smell of cedar rose, strong and pleasant. Lurina extracted a smaller box, a trifle larger than a ring box. Lying inside of it, on a bed of blue velvet, was a beautifully carved, oval cameo brooch. Grace recognized the intricate carving as a Greek myth. Hades, bearded and powerful with straining muscles, sat astride his rearing steed and grasped the fair Persephone around her waist. Her long hair streamed, her arms flailed, and her mouth stood open as she screamed for help from her mother, Demeter.

"It's the abduction of Persephone. It's exquisitely carved," Grace said.

"Take it out," Lurina said.

Grace cradled it in her palm. "The work is so fine. It's exquisite."

"It's yours," Lurina said.

"Mine?"

"To remember me by. Pa brought it back from the war for me. I never wore it. Too fancy for a country gal like me. It's been a-laying in that there box all these years just waiting to be yours, Grace."

"I can't . . ."

Lurina closed Grace's fingers over the brooch. "You can and you will, girlie." She folded her hands in her lap. "Now, you just set a while and tell me the story about them folks on that brooch."

Grace placed the lovely object back on its velvet bed and studied the intricate delicacy of the raised carving.

"Hades, king of the Underworld, fell madly in love with the beautiful Persephone," Grace explained. "One summer day, he rose from the bowels of the earth and stole her. He carried her off to the Underworld to be his queen. Persephone's mother, Demeter, adored her daughter. Demeter was goddess of the earth. When her daughter vanished, Demeter went to her fellow gods and goddesses and begged for their help. Had they seen or heard anything? Did they know where Persephone was? All the gods and goddesses turned away from her.

"Demeter searched the world, to no avail. Then, one day, one of the gods told her that Hades had abducted Persephone. Demeter demanded that Zeus, the head of the gods and her own brother, force Hades to return her daughter to her. Zeus refused. Bereft and distraught, Demeter cursed the land. Winter did not end. Spring and summer never came. Crops could not be planted. All was chaos. The world starved, and prayed for an end to cold and snow.

"Finally, Zeus forced Hades to return Persephone. But before Persephone left the Underworld, Hades, who loved his wife, offered Persephone a pomegranate, which she ate. By so doing, she committed herself to returning to live with him for half of every year. And that is why, the ancient myth says, we have our seasons."

"So," Lurina said, "when spring comes, Persephone's visiting her ma?"

"Yes."

"The poor girl musta been scared out of her wits, that big man dragging her off like that," Lurina said.

"She must have been."

"And her ma grieving so bad and keeping winter on the land. If she'd never found her daughter, we'd never have no spring."

"That's how the story goes."

"I been wondering all these years if that there brooch had a story and what it was." She patted Grace's arm. "Thanks for telling me."

"You sure you don't want to keep your lovely brooch?" Grace offered her the box.

Lurina shook her head. "I want for you to have it. And that story was the best I ever heard."

Grace decided that for Lurina's Christmas she would find a book of Greek myths with bright, colored pictures depicting each tale, and that would include the myth of Persephone, Hades, and Demeter.

32

THIS TIME OF YEAR:
THIS TIME OF LIFE

To celebrate the Fourth of July, Max, Bob, Mike, the ladies, and Lurina, as well as Russell, Emily, Tyler, and Melissa, drove to the community center field in Barnardsville to see the fireworks. Laura and Hank had been invited to a neighbor's to celebrate the Fourth. Roger was spending the weekend exploring the Salem area.

Mike and Bob spread a blanket on the ground, then Grace and Amelia laid out a feast: chicken and ham and potato salad, fruit, cupcakes, cookies, and iced tea. Everyone was stuffed by the time it grew dark enough for fireworks, and Melissa could barely keep her eyes open.

Standing on their trucks in the adjacent field, the firefighters sent glorious bursts and streams of color hurtling across the sky. Showers of red, blue, and silver exploded above their heads. Everyone clapped, oohed and aahed.

Melissa covered her ears. She could not abide loud sounds. She so reminds me of myself as a child, Grace thought.

Later, with Melissa tucked into bed and Tyler engrossed in a computer game in his room, Bob and Grace said good night to Russell and Emily, and drove to his condo. Bob's cast had finally been removed. His arm was slowly regaining full range of motion and flexibility, but he remained at the farmhouse, and neither the ladies nor Bob had yet suggested a moving date.

As they stood side by side at the balcony railing, a light rain began to fall. They moved inside. "Do you remember the big storm a couple of years ago?" Bob asked.

"How could I forget? Loring Valley was flooded, houses ruined by water and mud."

"I was trapped up here—no electric or phone," he said.

"We were trapped in the farmhouse with water rising up to the porch steps, and I was frantic with worry about you."

"The hill behind this place washed down," Bob said. "Afterward, they dumped boulders along the river. I wonder, with a storm like that one, would it have mattered? Would those boulders have held back the water?"

"Water is powerful. I think it would have washed the boulders up into the yards, maybe even to the villas. You were wise to have a retaining wall built behind this place," Grace said.

"I've never really felt comfortable here since that night," he said.

Grace squirmed, remembering that before buying his condominium in Loring Valley, Bob had asked if he could build a cottage on their land. And after the fire, after his heart attack, she had finally acquiesced to his repeated requests and stayed with Bob when Amelia and Hannah returned to the rebuilt farmhouse last year. She had been miserable. The mountains across the narrow valley had closed her in. Everything Bob said or did had annoyed her. She had felt thoroughly displaced. After several weeks, Bob understood, and bless him, he suggested that he take her home.

There had been a period of estrangement between them, but it passed, and life picked up more or less as it had been before the fire.

"I guess I'll be moving back here soon," Bob said. "Loring Valley's close to Cove Road, but it feels as if we live far apart—you there, me here. Don't get upset. I'm not suggesting you move back. It's just a comment."

"It's a valid thought," Grace said. "What if something happened, and we couldn't get to one another?"

He nodded and said nothing, and soon after, they started back to the farmhouse.

The next day, after Martin picked up Bob for a round of golf, Grace asked Hannah and Amelia to join her in the living room. "I have something I want to discuss with you both."

They settled in their favorite chairs: Hannah by the fireplace, Amelia with her legs up on the couch, and Grace in the wing chair near her. "I've been thinking that Bob and I really have no long-range plans. It's my fault, really. I know he hates living alone. He's never said it, but I think since his heart attack, he's afraid to be alone."

"Can't say I blame him," Amelia said. "Since the car accident when I was burned and Thomas died, I have never been comfortable sleeping alone in a house or apartment."

"The other night, Bob spoke of that storm that flooded Loring Valley and washed down the hill behind his condo. I remembered how frantic with worry I was, and then my not being there when he had his heart attack, and now our car accident. We three have one another. He has no one."

"Are you thinking he should stay on here with us?" Hannah asked.

Grace could not tell by the tone of her question if she were opposed or indifferent to the idea.

"On and off, I've wondered if that would work, but I don't think it would in the long run. He and I need more personal space, yet we need to be living closer," Grace said.

Amelia crossed her legs. "So what are you thinking?"

"Remember how he wanted to buy a piece of our land and build a cottage on it?" Grace looked directly at Hannah. "At the time, we didn't think that would work, but since then, things have happened we didn't anticipate, and you know Bob better. I was wondering how you'd feel, both of you, if he leased—not bought, but leased or rented—a piece of our land and built a small cottage. He'd be closer, more accessible if he needed me or any of us needed him, and yet he wouldn't be living in our house." Grace waited, hoping they wouldn't say no, wondering what she would do if they did.

Amelia spoke first. "I wouldn't mind. He's been terrific. He fixed the bathroom plumbing and put up those shelves I've been wanting in my bedroom. I don't find him the least obtrusive."

Grace turned to Hannah. She had been the most vocal against Bob building a cottage close at hand, before. "Hannah?"

Hannah cleared her throat. "I've been wondering how this thing with you and Bob was going to turn out. It's obvious he doesn't want to leave, but I've had concerns about him living here permanently. He lived with Max for a while and moved back to his condo. Why, I don't know. When I ask Max, he just shrugs. However, as you say, things have changed. For one thing, we're all a bit older."

"So, you wouldn't mind if he built a small place?"

"Not if we could choose the location," Hannah said. "I wouldn't want him building in some spot I've earmarked for a garden, or an orchard, or a berry patch. And the lease idea sounds better to me than selling off a piece of this land."

A great weight lifted from Grace's shoulders. "You have no idea how many sleepless nights I've had worrying over this whole business."

"I can imagine, knowing what a worrywart you are," Hannah said. She stood. "Well, then, it's settled. You tell him."

"Oh, I will. Thank you. Thank you."

"He should build something in the same style as this place," Amelia said. "Not all glass and modern."

"I'll tell him," Grace said.

From the doorway, Hannah said, "Make it part of the lease—restrictions, covenants, whatever. The size of the place, the style of construction, where the road will go in, things like that. Where *will* the road go in?"

Grace shrugged and shook her head. "So much to decide."

"It'll all work out," Amelia said.

Grace invited Bob out for dinner at the Weaverville Milling Company, a rustic restaurant in what had been an old mill off of Reems Creek Road. They chose to sit inside rather than on the back patio, and both ordered trout. Bob ordered wine. Grace requested water. She was trying very hard these days to watch what she ate and to drink lots of water, as her doctor recommended.

"You look like a dog hiding a bone. What you got up your sleeve, Grace?"

Her eyes danced. She squirmed in her seat. "Plenty to tell you. You want to hear it now or after we eat?"

Years ago, at their first meal together at an Italian restaurant in Johnson City in Tennessee, she had been concerned that Bob was an alcoholic, when he drank two glasses of wine at lunch. She smiled now, knowing that he never had more than two or three glasses of any liquor or wine on any occasion.

"So what is it?" Bob asked.

She leaned across the table. "Are you still interested in building a cottage on our land?"

He almost choked on the wine. "What did you say?"

"Amelia and Hannah have agreed to lease you land, if you want, and for you to build a cottage."

She could read the surprise in his face. "Terrific, but why now?"

"They know you better. Amelia appreciated your handiwork, putting up shelves for her."

"Hannah?"

"She's fine with it. She understands the situation."

He sat back. "I hardly know what to say. It's a total surprise. I never imagined . . ."

"You'd like it? Tell me, would you?"

"Of course I would! I've never really cared for my condo. I'll sell it as soon as we make this definite."

"We'd like you to build in the style of the farmhouse, with clapboard siding and a porch. That all right?"

"Sure. The style of the place hardly matters to me." He lifted his glass. "This calls for a celebration. To my cottage." He turned his head slightly and raised his eyebrows. "To our cottage?"

Grace lifted her water glass. "To your cottage close beside us, beside me."

"I can live with that," Bob said.

Dear Journal:

How absolutely wonderful! Bob will be close, but not too close. He'll be happy, and I won't have to worry. We'll have it wired so we can push a buzzer if we need one another.

I wonder if Hannah and Amelia would object if he built close to the road? What if Bob wants to be on the hill? I'll sweet-talk him out of that. He's so thrilled, he'll say yes to anything. This is turning out perfectly.

She paused. Her brow furrowed. Why this sudden sense of anxiety?

Why do I always think something could go wrong? Does something always go wrong? No, but it does often enough, and when you least ex-

pected it—like coming home from the cruise to Lucy's situation, and Laura waiting too long to have a cesarean, and Roger moving to South Carolina alone, and the awful period of jealousy I've gone through recently, and . . .

Stop. Just you stop this, Grace. Every one of those things turned out just fine. This will, too. It'll just take some adjustments, but it'll all work out.

What's really wrong is that I lose five pounds and regain three, and I stay off sugar and reduce my carbohydrates for weeks, and then binge. I absolutely hate myself when I do that.

Grace slammed the journal shut and put it away.

Max sat on the love seat in Hannah's office, a beer in his hand. He laughed. "Except for Cove Road not being our private domain, it'll be like a compound around here pretty soon," he said after Hannah told him about Bob's cottage.

"Last time he asked, Bob wanted to build up on the hillside, but this time, when we suggested a flat area off Cove Road just down a ways from our house, he seemed pleased."

Max nodded. "I can understand that."

"What does that mean, you can understand that?"

"Nothing."

"Oh. Come on, Max, what do you know we don't know?"

Max took several gulps of beer. "Sure we can't talk about something else?"

"No, we cannot. What is it?"

"It's stairs and slopes. Bob moved out of my place because of the stairs. He doesn't want Grace to know, but he's got some kind of a degenerative thing with his knees."

But Bob seemed just fine. A bit stiff when he got up from a chair, but she'd attributed that to his car accident. "Are you sure about this, Max?"

"Of course I'm sure."

"And no one knows about this but you?" Hannah asked.

"Martin does. Bob uses a golf cart now, and Martin takes him for his treatments."

"What kind of treatments?" Hannah asked.

"I guess the accident made matters worse," Max said. "Bob gets some kind of treatment at an outpatient clinic in Asheville, which he hopes will stop the degeneration. It's not cancer, nothing like that. But in time, if they can't arrest it, he could be confined to a wheelchair. Look, Hannah, you've got to promise me you won't tell Grace. Bob will, when he's ready."

Hannah's shoulders slumped. She placed an elbow on the arm of her chair, leaned her chin into her palm, and covered her mouth with her hand.

"He takes medication for the pain and it relieves the stiffness, or he'd never be able to golf or go dancing. It progresses slowly—could be a while before he says anything to Grace," Max said.

Hannah pushed back in her chair and sat up straight. "The golden years are more like brass. They tarnish too easily. I feel terrible about this."

"I do, too," Max said. "Bob's a great guy, and the last thing he wants is to be a burden to Grace."

"What will Grace do when he does tell her, I wonder." She shook her head. "No, I can't even think about that."

"Bob and Martin have checked out several life-care facilities, like Highland Farms over near Black Mountain, and someplace in Hendersonville, and down in Tryon," Max said. "I don't know if you know this, but Ginger met a guy on one of her Scrabble trips, and she's asked Martin for a divorce."

Hannah's hands flew to her head. "At their age, divorce?"

"If we can get married at this age, they can get divorced, I guess," Max replied.

"I'm flabbergasted. I don't know what to say."

"Just don't say anything to Grace about Bob's knees."

"I won't say a word," Hannah replied. "She'd never have a good night's sleep, worrying."

"Let Bob go ahead with his cottage," Max said. "He'll be happy being close to Grace. They say happiness adds years on your life."

He rose to leave, and Hannah also stood. "What's next for any of us?"

Max walked over to her and put his arms around her. She leaned into him, rested her head on his shoulder. "It's going to be all right, Hannah."

She nested against him for a time, and they swayed a little. Max kissed the top of her head, then her forehead. "I've wanted to hold you for a very long time."

Relief swept through her. Weak-kneed, she almost crumbled. "I have, also," she said.

There was a knock on the door, and they drew apart. It was Mary Ann, asking for an appointment with Max.

When she left, Hannah said, "Give her a chance, won't you Max?"

He shrugged. "Why not? At least she's familiar with things and the people around here."

33

THE COTTAGE

There are cottages, and then there are cottages: that was clear from all the books and magazines that Grace and Bob perused as they planned his new home. Some were elegantly appointed, with marble bathrooms and leaded-glass entry doors, stainless-steel kitchens, a Jacuzzi in the bathroom, elaborate fireplace surrounds, and plush carpets. Bob sought simplicity in his 900-square-foot cottage: simple crown molding in the living room, a small gas fireplace, a large tiled shower, and good, sturdy, tightly woven carpeting.

"Put your bedroom facing west," Amelia said. "That's where the winds come from, and it'll be cooler at night."

"For goodness' sake," Hannah said, "don't put your bedroom facing west. That afternoon sun will make the room hot as Hades."

"Hot in summer, warm in winter," Grace said.

Bob threw up his hands. He was in high spirits. "I'll put it smack in the middle of the house, no windows."

They laughed.

Bob had dinner with Russell and Emily one evening. "Whatever you do, do not face your kitchen west," Emily said. "The afternoon sun will blind you when you cook."

"You planning to do much cooking, Dad?" Russell asked.

"Are you kidding?" Bob said. "Grace wants me to get a big freezer for her to fill."

"Grandpa, you going to have a room for me?" Tyler asked.

"Yes, there'll be a room for you, Tyler."

"Room for me, too." Melissa climbed into his lap and hugged him. Tyler rolled his eyes.

Grace never saw anything go up as rapidly as Bob's cottage. Even for a small cottage, a well must be dug, a septic tank and drain field put in, and permits obtained: all things that slowed the start of new construction. Yet Bob's cottage progressed as if touched by an angel. Heavy equipment, plumbers, electricians, drywall people, roofers—even the building inspectors—arrived on schedule. By mid-August, the contractor projected a late-November completion date.

The cottage sat two hundred feet away from the ladies' farmhouse, with a driveway from Cove Road. Because Bob enjoyed morning sunshine and was an early riser, his bedroom faced southeast with low windows that looked out at the once-scorched hillside, covered now with weeds and grasses and boasting young pines determined to establish themselves before their neighbor oaks and poplars grew too high and broad.

The bathroom was large, with extrawide doors and a large shower.

"It's much too big," Grace said.

"Humor me, honey," Bob said. "I've always wanted a shower built for two."

She did not argue with safety bars. Their bathrooms all had safety bars in the showers and tubs, but Bob wanted safety bars for towel racks as well.

The ladies had had their bathroom sinks raised, and when Grace looked at Bob's countertops she thought they looked even lower than normal. "Why so low?" she asked.

"A mistake," he said, "and I didn't want to wait for them to rip these out and put in new ones."

The kitchen, shaded by the wide roof of the front porch, faced west.

"I'm not going to cook much, and if I do, I can time it to avoid whatever sun sneaks in under that porch in the summer," he said.

Bob liked porches as much as Grace did. Life happened before your eyes if you sat quietly on a porch on Cove Road. On the ladies' porch, he had laughed heartily one day while watching José chase and eventually tackle a calf in Max's front yard across the street. Bob had leaned over that railing to wave to Pastor Johnson early one morning, when the good pastor stepped from the rectory in his striped bathrobe to pick up his newspaper. Alma Craine always slowed to say hello when she walked Trixie and Lulu, her new cocker spaniels. Sometimes she led the dogs to the porch, so Bob could pet and admire them. And, perhaps most important, Bob enjoyed seeing the lights of cars pass at night. At the top of the hillside in Loring Valley, there had been no lights to see unless he stood on the balcony and looked down. He knew from experience that looking out at the darkness was depressing, especially when you are older and live alone.

One afternoon, Bob and Roger sat on the ladies' porch and discussed appreciation of property, the state of the real estate market, and the even greater attraction of low interest rates, now that people were seeking a different investment strategy. Bob's condo was on the market and had not sold. Roger's condo would go on the market in November. The two condos were a few yards apart, and if Bob's had not sold by then, they would compete with one another in size, price, and view. The men joked about this, and placed bets as to which would sell first.

Roger shared with Bob his enthusiasm for South Carolina and the land he purchased. "You and Mother will have to come down and visit me once the house is done."

"We'd love to do that," Bob said. "How are things going?"

"Pretty well. I make it down there once or twice a week. I'm considering getting a used Winnebago and just moving down there. They've got the septic in and the well is dug. Construction's started on the house."

They chatted about construction and how it had changed over the years, and new products. Then Roger asked, "You folks have really formed a family unit here, haven't you?"

"You could say that," Bob replied. "I have to thank Grace. We all do. She's the heart of this. When she meets someone she really likes, she loves and nurtures them, and next thing you know, they're included in things, and we all get to know one another."

"What if you don't like someone Mother brings home?"

"We've all got something we could improve on, don't you think? Do you like all your blood kin? Accepting their differences is what matters. You don't have to be bosom buddies with everyone, but you can be tolerant." Bob smiled. "Now take Hannah. She and I haven't much in common. I respect her. I think of her as a distant cousin. She can be a bit brusque, but if you know her loyalty to Grace and you see her with that little grandson of hers, you know there's a darn good woman in there."

Roger nodded. He liked Bob, and wished that he'd had a man like Bob for his father.

As if reading his mind, Bob said, "I think of you as my son-in-law, though your mother and I will probably never get married." He tapped his chest. "In my heart I am married to her, so you're automatically my son-in-law."

Roger and Charles had lived a fairly isolated life, with not many friends, and no family. Miranda and Paul were simply business partners, and they had never socialized. The openness of his mother's life seemed complicated to Roger, and odd. It was a whole new approach to living, and he was afraid to get too deeply involved—afraid, perhaps, that it would not last. For now, however, it was comforting and agreeable to sit with Bob and talk and rock on the porch.

Max commented to Hannah one afternoon as he locked the front door to the offices at Bella's Park, "Bob's walking better, seems to me. Maybe those treatments are working. Probably why he hasn't told Grace. He's hoping for the best possible news."

She crossed her fingers and held them up. "Let's hope."

Hannah had Andy with her that day, and she and Max strolled side by side along Cove Road, pushing his stroller. Their hands touched in the center of the stroller bar. At first, Hannah had been embarrassed to be seen touching in public, but gradually she had stopped wondering if Velma or Alma were watching them from behind their curtains, or what they said or thought.

Anna, and sometimes José, spied on them when the couple sat on Max's porch. Their presence was hardly a secret to Max and Hannah; they could hear the giggles and see their shadows behind those curtains. It was a game they played. Hannah would whip her head around, and they would scamper back from the window. Then the screen door would slam and Anna would appear with a tray of fruit or drinks or sandwiches, her face always polite, no hint of either pleasure or amusement.

"You know," Hannah said one afternoon as they sat eating fruit on his porch. "Remember when we went to hear that singer in Mars Hill, and we talked about putting on some sort of street fair on Cove Road, setting up a stage, doing skits, whatever?"

"Yeah, I remember. Still want to do that?"

"I think it would be a fun thing to do," Hannah said. "Amelia and Mike were talking about it the other day. They'd like to do that skit from—what was that movie?—*Easter Parade,* when Judy Garland and Fred Astaire danced and sang about being a couple of swells."

"I recall the skit. They were dressed like a couple of hobos, right?"

"That's right."

"Why not do it, then? I measured the space inside the lobby and it's too small. So the stage would have to be set up on the road, and everyone living on Cove Road would have to agree."

"I'll talk to Grace and Amelia," Hannah said. "We can get up a letter, or call everyone."

"Let me know. I'll have the workmen set up a stage," Max said. "In fact, we might ask José if he'd like to get that little band he's started together, and give us some fast-stepping music to get everyone in the mood. You work out with the ladies whatever you'd like, and I'll help any way I can."

34

UNA NOCHE GRANDE (A GRAND NIGHT)

August twenty-second, the day of the full moon, dawned clear and hot, and wrapped Covington in a muggy embrace. After the weeks of drought, the plants in everyone's garden drooped, their leaves curled and brown. Only the most hardy of annuals—coxcombs, zinnias, daisies, and cosmos—soaked up the sunshine and thrived in the dry soil. Hardy pink and white Cleome, known as spiderflowers, also flourished in the heat, and grew as tall as Grace. In the fall, Hannah planned to collect their seeds and scatter them on the patches of still-bare hillside behind the house.

Enthusiasm and preparations for the Cove Road party had been under way for weeks. True to his word, Max had a stage erected at the curve in front of the park office, and the street before it was designated for a semicircle of folding chairs. Buffet tables extended from the Lunds' house to Pastor Johnson's vicarage, and it had been decided that José's band of four would play from a smaller stage set up in Alma and Frank Craine's triple-wide driveway. This would leave most of Cove Road clear for tables and chairs and for dancing.

All day yesterday, as part of the festive atmosphere they wished to create, Amelia and Mike, Emily and Russell, with help from Tyler and his friends, sat on old rugs under a tree in Max's front yard and filled brown paper bag luminaries halfway with sand and candles. These would be placed on both sides down the length of Cove Road.

They had spent hours patiently untangling Christmas lights and string-ing them from the fretwork of everyone's porches.

Grace had baked for days: blueberry tarts and sugar-free apple pies, chocolate brownies with and without nuts, and Vienna cakes. The festivities would begin at 6:00 P.M., and Grace expected Bob and Roger, Brenda and Ellie to help transport desserts to the tables set up a bit down the road. Wayne would bring Lurina and a girl from Mars Hill he was now dating, along with the fresh barbecued pork cooked in a pit in Lurina's backyard. Grace had been sad when Wayne and Maureen Greenwood called it quits, but she thought they were like oil and water, and oil and water really do not mix.

The menu, coordinated by Grace and Brenda, included fried chicken and macaroni casserole for those who did not care for pork, sweet potato casserole, fried okra, coleslaw, mashed white potatoes and gravy, creamed corn, creamed peas and onions, green bean casse-role, and Velma's delicious, light-as-a-feather, homemade biscuits. Two days earlier, when Grace went over the menu with Amelia and Hannah, Hannah had looked annoyed. "No one's bringing a salad?"

"I'll help you make one," Amelia said.

"Thanks," Hannah said. "Why don't more people like salad?"

By 5:00 P.M., everyone's cars were parked on their lawns or in their garages. Molly Lund's two adolescent sons, grinning ear to ear, tore from one end of Cove Road to the other on their bicycles. Alma's six-year-old twin granddaughters played tag with Velma's eight-year-old granddaughter. They tolerated two-and-a-half-year-old Melissa and slowed to let her tag them periodically as they dashed around their grandmother's lawn and spilled onto the road, only to be shooed back onto the grass by Pastor Johnson, self-appointed guardian of the children for most of the evening.

At six, just before the children were gathered inside by their fami-lies to be washed and dressed for the grand event, Max flipped the switch, and all the interconnected lights on all the porches on both sides of Cove Road twinkled like a thousand stars.

The children stopped playing. Hands over their mouths, they spun round and round to see the lights on all the houses. "Like Christmas. So beautiful," the twins said at the same time.

Melissa jumped up and down.

Molly's sons ceased ringing the bells on their bicycles and stared, their mouths wide open.

By six thirty, covered platters and bowls of food were carried out and placed on the long buffet table. Cokes and other sodas were jammed into tubs of ice. Pitchers of iced tea and plastic glasses stood on another table.

As the neighbors gathered outside, spontaneous laughter and animated conversations bubbled up, crisscrossed the road, and floated in the balmy evening air. Brenda's mother, Millie, and her husband, Bill, came up from South Carolina. Pastor Johnson, Roger, and Bill sat on lawn chairs in a small circle on the pastor's lawn, engrossed in conversation. Grace, peering from the kitchen window, was pleased to see Roger looking so relaxed and interacting with her friends.

As she stacked a pie on top of a brim-full plastic container of brownies, Grace could see Amelia, Emily, and Mike bending over to light the luminaries. She frowned as Mike, who had reached the edge of the pastor's lawn, crossed to light the luminaries on the other side of the road. He was avoiding encountering Roger, she was certain. When tonight was over, she must find a way to clear the air between them. Their rapid coming together and just as rapid parting had proved an embarrassment, especially to Mike, in this small community.

"I'm glad Roger's moving. I don't care if he is your son," Amelia had said. "Roger's the cruelest, most insensitive man I know. He humiliated Mike. He encouraged and hurt him twice."

What could Grace say? She agreed with Amelia that Roger had been callous in his behavior toward Mike. "Roger's moving soon. Everything will settle down."

"Not soon enough," Amelia had retorted. "And that's not going to change what Mike's been through."

Now, as she watched Roger throw back his head and laugh at something either Bill or the pastor had said, Grace thought, My son, the unforgiven. And she shuddered. Mike and Roger don't have to be friends or even like each other, she thought, but it would be easier on all of us if the two men could tolerate being in the same room. The way it was now, the moment one entered, the other hastily departed. She wished Roger could think of Bob and his family, Lurina and Wayne, Amelia and Hannah, and all her dearest friends as extended family, as she did.

A knock on the door sent her scurrying to pull the last of the pans of brownies and a casserole from the oven. "Door's open. Come on in," she called.

The front door opened and closed, and Grace heard the sound of light laughter. Moments later Bob, Brenda, and Ellie entered the kitchen.

"How marvelous everything looks and smells." Ellie smiled, a trifle self-consciously.

Ellie wore a baggy T-shirt, casual slacks, socks, and sneakers. Their laughter triggered resentment in Grace. She's covering up those fat ankles, Grace thought. Then, because her experience on the cruise ship had changed her over time in many ways, Grace's heart softened, and her annoyance faded.

She smiled at Ellie. "These days, I can't even eat the goodies. I cook for the smells."

"That's incredible self-control," Ellie replied. "If I cooked anything that smelled and tasted as good, I'd eat half of it before I offered it to anyone else."

Brenda hugged Grace. "You're a marvel, you really are. Now, what do you want us to do?"

"Use the pot holders on those brownies. Don't get burned," Grace replied, handing Brenda pot holder mitts.

"Aren't you coming, Grace?" Bob asked.

"You all go ahead. I'll be along in just a minute. I'll stick these few things into the dishwasher."

"We can wait for you," he said.

"No, you go ahead."

"Let me help," Ellie said.

"No. You all go along." She shooed them out, then watched them fall in behind Bob in parade fashion. As they passed, the men sitting on Pastor Johnson's lawn clapped. Molly's sons dashed down their front steps to join the procession. As if on cue, front doors opened. Families carrying platters and trays stepped into line behind the children as Bob led his entourage toward the tables. Grace threw back her head and laughed. To heck with the dishes and pots. She tore off her apron, dashed to the front door, and ran down the porch steps.

Soon the residents of Cove Road were seated in no particular fashion at long tables covered with brightly colored plastic tablecloths.

Bob joined Max, Roger, and Wayne at one end of a table. Grace sat with Velma, Alma, and Hannah at the other end.

"The weather held real good for us, wouldn't you say?" Alma said to no one in particular.

"Sure did," Velma replied.

"It's dry as a bone, and usually when you plan something out-of-doors, sure as sugar sweetens tea, it rains. But not tonight," Alma said with satisfaction, as if she had signed a special arrangement with the rain gods.

"My goodness, but this chicken casserole is good. Was it Grace made it?" Velma asked.

"Emily."

"Grace's recipe, though," Hannah said.

Grace looked up at the sky. "Did you see the moon last night? It came up copper color, and it's doing it again." She pointed to the glow of gold cresting the hill to the east.

"Copper color, you say? I don't reckon I seen it last night," Alma said.

"It was beautiful," Grace said.

From the other end of the table came the sound of laughter. Automatically, Grace glanced about for Ellie. She sat at another table with Brenda, Lurina, and Amelia, and was totally focused on her food. Ellie was more a stranger among them than anyone else. If humor was her way to participate, to make people like her, how could Grace hold that against her?

"No more soda. No, Axel." Molly's voice rose from the next table.

"See whiz, Ma." Axel sulked.

As they ate, the moon, transformed as if by an alchemist's hands from copper to pure and brilliant gold, silently scaled the eastern hills. Light flooded the street.

Suddenly Bob was at Grace's side, his hand on her shoulder. "Look at that moon," he said. "It's too romantic for us to be sitting at opposite ends of the table."

"How about going for a stroll in the moonlight later?"

"You've got a date," he replied and walked away.

At a nearby table, Laura and Hank's chairs were pulled close together. They had gotten a babysitter for Andy. Laura said, "The moon's dressed itself up for our party."

"Indeed it has." Hank kissed her cheek.

Platters of desserts made the rounds of the tables, and when they were done, Max rose and ascended the stage. A drumroll from José's band silenced all talk.

"Ladies and gentlemen, boys and girls. Attention! Please drop your plates and cups into the trash cans provided for your convenience, and come on over and take a seat. The show's about to begin."

A drumroll again. A shuffle of chairs followed, and excited chatter, as everyone cleared their places and moved to the circle of chairs. Wide-eyed and excited, little Melissa and all the young people clustered in the front row.

Dressed as hobos, Mike, slender as Fred Astaire, and Amelia, short and slight as Judy Garland, were first on stage to perform the skit from *Easter Parade*. They danced and sang, " 'We're a couple of swells/we stop at the best hotels.' " Mike's face was smeared with patches of dirt, and Amelia's two front teeth had been blackened. Grace, who had never seen Amelia dance, not even on the cruise ship, delighted in her friend's grace, ease of movement, and confidence. Clapping and cheers filled the air when the skit ended.

Then the three Craine sons and their father, Frank, took the stage in candy-striped shirts, straw hats, and garters, which were on their arms. They began with a barbershop rendition of "Sweet Adeline," did a bit of tap dancing, and sang a medley of a dozen familiar songs including "In the Good Old Summertime," "Down in the Valley," and "In the Sweet Bye and Bye." They, too, were roundly cheered.

Grace was surprised to see Pastor Johnson being helped on stage by Max and led to a chair hastily placed there by Anna. Max handed him a banjo. The pastor flexed his fingers several times. He craned his long neck forward, then bent over the instrument.

"Go at it," Buddy Herrill called.

Others clapped and cheered the pastor on. He raised his head and his gaze wandered past the heads of his friends and neighbors seated below. Then he smiled, and his gnarled fingers touched the strings lightly. He inclined his head. It was a shock to Grace when, in the next instant, Pastor Johnson plucked the notes of a melody with such rapidity and vitality that she thought surely the tune would reach the moon.

An old man usually bent with age and ailments, it was as if Pastor Johnson had been restored to the vigor of youth in those twenty minutes. His fingers flew, his foot tapped. He tossed back his head and grinned as if to say, *Fooled you, eh?* Familiar and unfamiliar tunes rolled off of the banjo, as people hummed along, swayed, and clapped their hands: "Tumbling Tumbleweed," "The Big Rock Candy Mountain," "Sweet Betsy From Pike." After playing several gospel melodies, Pastor Johnson ended with "The Church in the Wildwood."

Then, as suddenly as he had started, the pastor's fingers halted. He slumped slightly, seemed a trifle bewildered, and held the banjo close. A moment of silence followed, and then the applause exploded.

Max joined him on stage. He took the banjo, set it to one side, and helped the pastor to his feet. Pastor Johnson bowed stiffly once, twice, three times. His expression, bright and luminous as the moon, delighted his friends and neighbors, and they rose to their feet, smiling, tears running down some of their faces as they continued to applaud. Pastor Johnson bowed again. Then, flushed and seemingly overwhelmed with emotion, he turned and accepted Max's help to descend from the stage.

José's band started off with "The Mexican Hat Dance," "Tico Tico No Fubrá,"and "La Cucaracha," then slipped into a slower pace with "Besame Mucho" and "Celito Lindo." Couple by couple, people sauntered out into the road to dance: the Craines, the Herrills, Amelia and Mike, Roger and Ellie, Bob and Grace, Molly and her husband, Brenda and her father, Pastor Johnson—who had recovered from the shock of his triumphant performance—and Brenda's mother, who danced a slow fox-trot to everything.

Even Axel, the shyest of the children, jigged. Soon all the children were moving their hips from side to side, hopping around, and doubling over giggling. Tyler lifted Melissa and whirled her about, then placed her shoes on the tips of his and held both her hands. She rolled her head of golden curls and gyrated her shoulders and hips to the rhythms that coursed from José's band. Music wrapped about the dancers and ruffled the air the length of Cove Road.

Grace caught Tyler's eye and blew him a kiss. He looked down at Melissa and grinned.

Then José called, "Let's boogie," and the band launched into "Yes Sir, That's My Baby," followed by "Five Foot Two, Eyes of Blue," and "Boogie Woogie Bugle Boy," and ended with "Scrub Me Mamma with a Boogie Beat."

"Now, that's my kind of music," Max said. He grasped Hannah's hands and pressed her to join him in the street.

She leaned back and shook her head. "I haven't in years."

"Did you ever boogie when you were young?" Bob asked.

"Yes," Hannah replied. "Can't remember a thing about it."

"Go on, Hannah." Bob snapped his fingers; he and Grace were sitting this set out. "The steps, the moves, will all come back in two minutes flat."

Max bent and whispered in Hannah's ear. "Please. I won't let you make a fool of yourself. Trust me."

Reluctantly she rose, and hand and hand, they joined the dancers.

"Listen, now," Max said, "the melody repeats, so will our steps."

It took exactly two minutes before Hannah, following Max's strong lead, relaxed and allowed her body to move to the music. She threw back her head. She laughed and kicked up her heels. She spun and whirled.

Hannah grinned up at him. "Fun."

An hour later, the adults formed a conga line for the last dance.

Taking the cue from their parents and grandparents, all the boys and girls—Tyler with Melissa clasped firmly on his back—held each other's waists and snaked their way from one end of Cove Road to the next.

Later, after the tables and chairs had been folded and transported into the office of Bella's Park, and the trash cans had been carted away, and José and his band had loaded their instruments into the back of an old red pickup and toted them off, after the residents of Cove Road had hugged, said good night, and slipped into their houses, Bob and Grace took a walk in the moonlight.

The moon rode high above the treetops. It glistened on the surface of the stream that meandered across the ladies' property. Moonlight flooded their faces and lit the happiness in their eyes.

Up and down Cove Road, homes were now dark. Like teenagers, they ambled to the site where Bob's new cottage was taking shape. Facing Cove Road, it would be a miniature of the farmhouse, with its covered porch and fake dormers set in its peaked roof.

"The grass is damp," Bob said.

"Good old mountain dew," Grace replied.

"Want to walk on the road?"

She shook her head. "I like the feel of grass, like a carpet. Since the fire, everything's changed with our neighbors. Buddy Herrill uses his power mower and mows all our lawns now."

"Shame Buddy hasn't found a nice girl to settle down with," Bob said.

"Lurina tells me he's got a girl, but she's a McCorkle and her folks aren't keen on the match."

They strolled slowly, seeking to stretch the evening.

"She might be a very nice young woman. They can't all be bad, the McCorkles," Bob said.

"I'm sure you're right," Grace replied. "They can't all be bad."

"Like everything in today's world, Covington has changed."

"Development in Loring Valley's brought so many new people," Grace said.

"They don't bother anyone. Their being here has had advantages, like Elk Road Plaza. It's a heck of a lot more convenient than having to go to Mars Hill to shop for every little thing."

"True." Grace tightened her hold on his arm. "August is almost over. Summer's whizzed by. Soon the leaves will fall. The first freeze will kill the summer flowers. Snow will come, then Christmas, and the year will be over. It goes too fast. Sometimes I wish I could stop time."

"So do I." He squeezed her arm. "Who would have thought, Grace, that at our ages we would have found one another, and in this most out-of-the-way place? Makes you wonder if there's some sort of divine plan."

"Indeed it does." For a moment, Grace considered telling Bob how, on the cruise ship, she had been lifted out of herself and been connected to and with all things, and how in the hospital she had floated out of her body. These occurrences, so real to her, were difficult to put into words, and she could not bear the thought of anyone denigrating what she knew to be real and true. And she was uncertain of her ability to explain such events, fearing Bob would question her or analyze or rationalize her experiences. Grace knew she was not an intellectual; hers was a down-to-earth sort of mind with a touch of the dreamer thrown in. She was not a deep thinker, nor a conceptual thinker. She lived by her heart.

They walked on in silence until they reached the cottage, whose walls were up and whose roof was on. Next would come the interior work of wiring, plumbing, and insulation, then the drywall, paint, and finishing.

"It's going to be nice, living just a walk across the grass," Bob said.

They stepped onto the deck of his unfinished porch. "It'll be great having you nearby." Grace looked down at his legs. "Bob, are you limping?"

"A trifle. I probably banged my knees in that accident. They give me a bit of trouble now and then; it's nothing."

She accepted his explanation. "That moon is magnificent, isn't it?"

"Yes, it is. All in all, it's been a grand night with nice people."

"Covington's been good to us," Grace said. "It's a good place to live. I'm happy here. So are Amelia and Hannah."

Bob unfolded two beach chairs propped against a wall and placed them side by side at the edge of the porch, from where the moon was visible. They sat.

"Yes," he said folding Grace's small hands in his. "You're so right. Covington is one heck of a terrific place to live."

20000

CURRIED CHICKEN SALAD

Compliments to Grace from Ms. Martha, innkeeper, bed-and-breakfast at Ponder Cove in Mars Hill, N.C.

MAKES 4–8 SERVINGS

4 whole boneless chicken breasts
Vegetable or olive oil
2 Granny Smith apples, peeled and cut into small pieces
½ cup currants or raisins
½ cup chopped celery
Miracle Whip or any preferred mayonnaise
3 tablespoons curry powder
Boston or other lettuce
Star fruit, kiwi fruit, or green grapes (one or all of them)
Major Grey's Chutney
Toasted peanuts
Toasted coconut

Slather the chicken breasts with oil and broil for four minutes on each side. If pink, continue to cook. Or boil the chicken breasts, making sure they are cooked through.

Cut the breasts into cubes, place in a bowl, and add apples, celery, and currants or raisins.

Add mayonnaise to taste. Salad can be dry or moist—Ms. Martha prefers hers moist.

Add curry powder.

Place lettuce on plate and place chicken salad on top or in center. Decorate with star fruit or kiwi fruit slices around the plate edge and place a small cluster of grapes on top of the salad.

Offer chutney, peanuts, and coconut in separate serving dishes.

SYLVIA'S NOODLE KUGGLE

Sylvia shared this recipe with Grace when they were young mothers in Dentry, Ohio. It ranks among Grace's top comfort foods and she has learned that she can still enjoy noddle pudding if she eats it in moderation.

> 1-pound bag broad noodles
> ½ of a 4-ounce package of light cream cheese
> 1 pint sour cream
> ¾ cup of sugar
> 5 eggs, separated
> Salt to taste
> 1 tablespoon of vanilla extract
> 2 or 3 small packages of raisins
> (Some people like crushed pineapple rather than raisins,
>   Grace prefers raisins.)
> ½-pound butter
> 1½ cups cornflakes

Preheat oven to 350°F.

Butter an 8-inch or 9-inch X 11-inch casserole dish and set aside.

Boil and drain the noodles according to package instructions.

In a separate bowl, mix all the other ingredients together except the egg whites.

Beat egg whites until stiff and then fold them into above mixture.

TOP CRUST

Melt the butter.

Crush 1½ cups cornflakes and add them to the melted butter. Sprinkle cornflakes-and-butter mixture over the top. Sprinkle cinnamon over all.

Bake for one hour.

ELICE'S APPLE FRITTERS

This recipe came to Grace from an old family friend in Dentry, Ohio. It's not a fat- or sugar-free recipe, but it's delicious.

6 Delicious apples
Lime juice
2 eggs, separated
⅔ cup milk
1 tablespoon lemon juice
1 tablespoon butter, melted
1 cup all-purpose flour, sifted
¼ teaspoon salt
2 tablespoons sugar
Oil for browning
Confectioners' sugar

Core the apples and cut into rings. Soak in water with lime juice to prevent discoloration.

Separate 2 egg yolks from whites and save whites. Beat egg yokes in a small bowl and add milk.

Add lemon juice and melted butter.

Combine the dry items in a bowl and add liquid mixture.

Whip egg whites until stiff and fold them into the batter.

Drain the apple rings and pat them thoroughly dry.

Dunk them in the batter and brown both sides in hot oil.

Drain well, then sprinkle with the confectioners' sugar.

Serve immediately.

DISCUSSION QUESTIONS
FOR *AT HOME IN COVINGTON*

1. Hannah is a pragmatic woman who looks ahead, not back, yet she is dragged into the past by a secret diary. How do you think you would react to such a painful message from the past?

2. As the relationship between Hannah and Amelia deteriorates, on the cruise ship and then at home in Covington, with whom did you most identify or sympathize? Why? What do you think is going on between them?

3. What do you think of Amelia's decision to go to Maine, and to consider moving out of the farmhouse? Is the way she comes to terms with Hannah and the meaning of their lives together in Covington real and natural? Could you identify with it?

4. The moment Tyler tells Grace about the chat room, Grace becomes deeply involved in Lucy's life. Would you have done the same? Do you feel it is appropriate for this novel to address the issue of the dangers of chat rooms?

5. In Laura and Hannah, we have two women who assume how the other feels and thinks. Hannah is unable to tell her daughter how much she loves Andy and longs to be a part of his life. Laura suffers from postpartum depression and cannot express her fears and frustrations. How can two people bridge such a gap? What does it take to give up expectations of what another person ought to be, or say, or do?

6. Did Roger's catharsis in the woods change your feelings about him? In what way? What is the novel trying to say about understanding and forgiveness?